For Jacob,
My favorite adventure of all

A TUNE TO MAKE THEM FOLLOW

THE SEVERED REALMS

T.A. LAWRENCE

❀ Created with Vellum

ALONDRIA
MYSTRAL
DWELLEN
Verari Forest
Kobii Mountains
The Bluffs
Wyndham
Adreean Sea
AVELEA
FORGOTTEN ISLE
Evaen
Edii Gulf
The Hills
Nettlewood
Rivre
CHARSHON
Meranthi
Sea of Lythos
NAENDEN
Talens
Grythos Channel
LAEI

CHAPTER 1

PIPER

It should have been harder to take the children. For that, I blamed the parents. But, then again, if it weren't for the lousy parents, I wouldn't have found their children in the first place.

A bonfire licked at the chilled evening air, dancing with the constellations as I played. My fingers drummed my flute to a beat only I sensed, only I felt. The crowd only heard the result, the music, light and ethereal, as the villagers joined the fire in its dance.

Men and women twirled in rhythm to the tune, loose hair sailing in circles around the village square. Children clapped and stomped off-beat while their laughter harmonized with the notes flowing from the tip of my wooden flute, the same one I'd played that first night for Bronger.

The same one I'd played the first time I took one of them.

Not here, of course. No, I'd had to travel well out of my comfort zone, the glades, into the far reaches of Avelea, almost to the border of Dwellen, to find this place, this tiny little village so far from fae civilization, they wouldn't have heard of the red-headed half-fae who played a flute like no one had ever heard. The girl whose music would fill their hearts with such mirth, they'd hardly notice when something went missing.

When *someone* went missing.

In the glow of the firelight, a young woman dragged her husband into the dance, his reluctant feet practically burrowing into the dust in protest. But as soon as my gift delved into the chorus, his shoulders relaxed, and he tugged at her outstretched arm, reeling his wife back into his chest with such eagerness, she let out a gasp of delight as he caught her in his arms before twirling her about.

Her laughter pierced the night, hooking into my heart and yanking taut.

I turned my attention elsewhere, inward, burrowing into the warm cocoon of my gift's music, and I allowed it to take over for a while, guiding my fingers, numbing that fierce, jealous ache as my body swayed.

The entire village ended their dance on one glorious stomp that coincided perfectly with the last strike of my fingers against the keys. Heat flushed the women's cheeks as their skin glistened in the firelight. The men laughed, perhaps feeling a tad silly for having lost themselves so completely to the music. Children scurried around, not nearly as affected by the tune as their parents. I was used to that. It was never the joyful tunes that captivated the children. They had not yet lost the ability to conjure the feeling on their own.

The cold wood of my flute brushed my lips once more, and the song that emerged this time was not like the four others I'd already played, the ones that had a way about them that made the villagers whisper the next morning that their feet had danced with a mind of their own. Nor was it like the next five tunes I would play, the ones that would erase the memory of this song altogether.

It was imperative that they wouldn't remember it.

The dirge dripped from the tip of my flute, weeping faintly into the air, the beat barely distinguishable between each pulse, a chasm of time separating each one. Puzzled looks crept over the faces of the adults as the bonfire cast shadows over their eyes. Then, just as they always did, they shook off the oddity of my song choice and determined to take advantage of the moment. After all, it wasn't every day such a talented musician wandered upon a village so far from fae civilization.

The adults each found a partner and began to sway softly to the music, assuming I had meant it for a slow dance. The children, bored with the dragging tune, returned to the game of tag they'd been playing when I'd arrived.

Except for her.

She had wrangled her mousy brown hair into a mangled lump on the side of her head that I assumed was supposed to be a braid. Dried dirt clung to her pale cheeks, her undernourished skin almost translucent in the firelight. She looked to be about ten, though she might have been older, her age obscured by the stunting of her height, her body's hesitation to launch her into maturity. That wasn't what caught my attention, though. All the children in this village were underfed. It was simply the nature of living so far from the fae trade routes.

It was that she, like so many I'd taken before her, heard my tune for what it truly was.

An invitation.

Her eyes took on the form of the moon, watching over us. Even from a distance, with that decent half-fae vision of mine, I caught the glisten of a tear streaking a path down the filth on her cheek. The short song ended abruptly, as it always did, though I never understood why my gift chose to end it where it did, on the upbeat, on a note that didn't even belong in the scale.

The girl blinked, her face a canvas of shock, when a gruff-looking man gripped her shoulder and steered her from view. I watched them cut through the crowd, turning right at a path that intersected at the thoroughfare before disappearing behind what looked to be a blacksmith's shop.

I touched the wood to my lips once more and played well into the night. My gift swelled within my lungs, saturating the crisp breeze with its melodies, the sound of dancing serving as our percussionist.

All the while I thought not about the girl, but about the gruff man who had placed his hand on her shoulder a bit too roughly for my liking. Disgust seethed in my veins at the thought of him, of what he must have done to the girl for my gift to pick her out so quickly.

But, then again, if it weren't for men like him, I'd be out of a job.

IT DIDN'T TAKE LONG to find where the girl lived. I'd seen them walk as far as the blacksmith shop, but I wouldn't have needed that hint anyway. Just as my gift had called out to her, extended its invitation, her spirit now called out for us. For it? For me? I'd never truly untangled the difference. But if my hands were made of iron, hers would have been a magnet, her heartbeat the rhythm of a drum tapping a coded message to an army of loyal troops. I could have found her even if the moon hadn't been out tonight.

My gift had ended the performance one song early, I supposed, because it was worried for the girl. At least, I liked to give it the benefit of the doubt. Somewhere deep down, I figured my gift was more curious than altruistic, and was probably dying to know what sort of terrors this girl had endured to have been drawn to its tune so quickly. But my gift had been with me for as long as I could remember, since the first time I picked up a pair of spoons and beat a percussion version of a symphony onto my mother's favorite cast-iron pot.

After the show, I'd withdrawn into the shadows as quickly as possible. It had only taken one performance for me to learn that trick. Sure enough, as I had watched from behind a grounded wagon, a handful of men searched the area for "the pretty red-headed thing."

Eventually they'd given up, and the temporary bond suturing my heart to the girl's had led me here, to the back of the blacksmith's shop where a wooden door stood locked, blocking the entrance to what I assumed was the blacksmith's living quarters.

Bronger had taught me to pick locks from an early age, but I'd never found much use for the skill. Sure enough, as I pressed my ear against the door, the sound of panicked, labored breathing betrayed the girl's presence as she leaned against the other side.

"Have you come to take me?" she whispered through the sliver of space between the slats of wood.

"Only if you wish to come along," I said.

A long time passed before she answered. My feet shuffled underneath me, my skin prickling in the cold. The longer she waited, the faster my heart raced. In the seven years I'd been doing this, I'd never had a child take this long to decide.

My gift tugged at my chest, reminding me that wasn't exactly true.

The first one had taken this long, if not longer, to agree.

Maybe if I'd given her more time, she wouldn't have followed me. Maybe she'd still be...

I pushed her face from my mind.

"I won't force you, but if you wish to come, you must decide now," I whispered into the door. Still no answer. My legs trembled from standing so long in the cold. This wasn't happening. Surely she wouldn't decide to stay. That had never happened. And Bronger... No, there was no way in Alondria I was going back to Bronger empty-handed. I'd have to find another village distant from the trade routes. That would put me behind on my delivery, of course.

But I'd take getting home late to going home empty-handed any day.

I'd just pulled away from the door, accepting my defeat, when a crash reverberated through the wood. The girl screamed, and something pounded hard against the other side of the door.

Her screams went muffled, overpowered by a drunken slur. "What d'ya think you're doing outta bed? Thinking of running away again, are ya? Are ya?"

I slung my pack from over my shoulders and onto the ground. My flute clattered against the entirety of my belongings as I dug through the bag's contents. My hands shaking, I found what I was looking for, a set of long, metal picks tied together with a string. I struggled to untie it, causing one of the picks to slip back into the bag. Flustered, I fumbled around, tossing a bottle of medical anesthetic out of my way before I found the second pick, then ran to the door and tried to be delicate rather than shove the picks into the lock.

The girl's muffled sobs sounded through the door as the man continued to scream a less-than-clever assortment of profanities at her. My neck flushed with rage, and I willed my anger into focus, turning the second pick until I felt it click into place.

The knob practically turned on its own, now that it was free of the bolt. It opened into a stairwell, dimly lit by an overturned lantern on the step behind the burly man. He stood with one hand over the girl's mouth, the other clenched around her wrist, using it as an anchor to twist her arm further than it should have been able to turn.

Her eyes cried out in pain, her tears soaking the man's hand. I lunged at his exposed inner elbow and punctured the bulging blue vein with the tip of my pick. He yelped and reared back, releasing the girl. The girl crawled backward, out into the streets.

Blood trickled down her master's arm as he pulled a serrated knife from his belt.

I mirrored his threat and brandished my favorite dagger.

He struck first, as I knew he would, and I used the opportunity to sidestep his blow. His weight faltered when his knife failed to find its intended target, and he stumbled past me.

I brought my knife down, aiming for his shoulder, but he turned and caught my wrist just in time. A grin flashed across his face, exposing a few jagged teeth, when I realized he'd played me, not the other way around.

He twisted, and the crunching of bone reverberated inside my head as my arm snapped. I cried out in shock, the rest of my limbs going as limp as my arm as I fell to my knees.

He laughed, a guttural, nasty gargle that made the hairs on my arms squirm.

"I was hoping you'd come for my Amity. Thought you were a pretty thing last time you came around here. Never got the chance to make your acquaintance. Did you think you'd steal my little girl, like you did that other little runt? Knew it couldn't have been a coincidence. Half-breed like you shows up, then a child goes missing," he growled, stroking a wisp of hair from my forehead as he twisted my broken arm behind my back. I clenched my teeth, trying to hold back the pathetic whimper making its way up my throat.

He must have noticed my subtle act of defiance, because he sliced his dagger along the site of the wound for good measure.

I couldn't help the sob that escaped my lips as blood trickled down my arm.

His hot, ale-soaked breath dampened my cheek, and salty tears seared my eyes. My forehead pounded as I tried to sift through the pain and unscramble his words. I had been here before; that's what the man about to murder me had claimed.

I had made a mistake, doubled around by accident.

And it would cost me my life.

I grasped at him, at anything I could grab onto with my left hand, but my hands barely scraped the hem of his trousers. I cried out again, hoping someone, anyone, would hear me.

Surely they had heard the girl scream earlier.

And they hadn't come. They must have gotten used to it, I realized in horror.

No one was going to come. This was it.

But then the man grunted behind me. His grip on my wrist loosened. I hopped to my feet, wobbled a bit as the village spun around me, then turned on my assailant.

The girl had hoisted herself onto the man's back, her arms clasped around his neck. He swung at her, but the ale must have muddled his aim, because he missed. She grasped and twisted at something in her hands, but with the pain swirling my vision, I couldn't tell what.

Until she brought the object over his face and mouth.

The man's eyes rolled back in his head. He slumped, his body hitting the ground face-first with a thud. The girl wiggled her arms out from under his heavy frame, emerging with a doused cloth she held at arm's length. On the ground, the bottle that had once contained my medical anesthetic rolled in the dust, empty.

We stared at each other for a moment, sizing each other up.

"Well," I asked, still gasping for air, "are you coming or not?"

. . .

We made it as far as the woods that encircled the north side of the village before I lost the ability to direct my own feet.

The moonlit trees swam around the edges of my vision, encircling me as if to taunt me in my pain. My pulse throbbed at the site of my fracture with every step, my arm hanging limp and jagged by my side. Blood soaked the leather glove on my right hand as it trickled down my sleeve from where the man had sliced my arm.

I made it three steps into the dark woods before I collapsed. Small hands pulled my hair from my face, allowing me room to breathe through the pain. Once I'd regained my composure, I forced myself up to a seated position with my left hand.

"You'll need to bandage it. I can't keep losing blood like this," I said.

Amity's moonlit face nodded in the darkness, and she rummaged through my sack with only the lesser lights to guide her. She returned to my side with a roll of cloth bandages. I hissed, though not of my volition, as she felt around the already bruising wound with her tiny fingers, assessing just how broken my arm really was.

"I can set it for you, if you'd like," Amity said.

"Do you have much experience in setting bones?" I asked, my voice cracking in agony as a fresh wave of pain pulsed through my body.

"I set my mother's many times." She stared intently at my arm, though I knew there was no way she could see the details of my injury in the dark, not with those human eyes of hers.

"Just be quick about—" I yelped and, as if the fractured arm and dislocated shoulder weren't enough punishment for my crimes, I bit my tongue, sending a surge of pain and instant regret through my nerves.

"It's done," Amity said. "I just have to bandage the cut, and then I can put it in a sling for you."

I nodded, and she tied my hair back, securing it with a string she'd found in my pack. Cold air tickled my neck, unfamiliar as I almost never wore my hair any way other than down, my curls utterly unrestrained, just like they preferred.

"Your tattoo is wrong," she said matter-of-factly, referencing the other reason I never wore my hair up, the ink that stained the bone behind my left ear.

"I know."

"Did you get your money back?"

I chuckled and instantly regretted doing so, as pain shot through my shoulder. "No. I asked the artist to draw it that way."

"That doesn't make any sense," was all she said as she tied the sling around my shoulder.

I winced every time the bandage shifted against the wound site, and especially when she hoisted my arm into the sling she'd tied around my neck.

But then it was done, and dread swallowed the pain whole.

I had no idea how I was supposed to get a child all the way back to the Coup with a broken arm. I'd never had a mission go so poorly. Well, not since that first mission, the one I refused to acknowledge lest I sink into that dark, familiar place I had no desire to inhabit again.

They'd broken more than just my arm that time. And the child...

"What's your name?" Amity asked. My focus snapped back to the present situation, and gratefulness for the child's timeliness threatened to prick my numb heart.

"Piper," I said, waiting for the inevitable question to follow.

Amity's eyes narrowed with suspicion. "Because you play the flute?"

I nodded. "Because I play the flute."

"What was your name when you were a baby?"

"I don't remember," I said, truthfully. Bronger had taken me when I was only three. Just old enough to get the occasional flash of my mother, the fragmented corners of a memory. But she was never saying my name in those memories. Only screaming and brawling and forgetting she had a little girl toddling about.

"Will you miss your mother?" I asked Amity, wondering at the bond a mother and daughter might have, having endured shared abuse. Or did Amity resent her mother for allowing it to happen, for not stealing her child away in the night?

Amity's eyes avoided mine as she lowered her thick lashes. "I already do."

A sliver of sympathy scraped at my insides. "How long has it been since she passed?" I asked, finding my voice softening in this girl's presence. She would be a decent travel companion, with her collected nature. At least if I had to travel with a broken arm, I wouldn't have to worry about rounding her up the entire journey.

"Sixty-eight days." The precision of the words shoved a lance through my stomach. What a hole this mother must have left behind.

The contents of my satchel rattled as Amity returned the unused bandages and antiseptic to the bag. I thought I'd leave her alone to her thoughts for a while, to mourn her childhood. She would be leaving it behind forever in this village, and, as rotten a childhood as it was, that still had to mean something.

Maybe that's why it surprised me when she said, "We had our own language. She would talk to me with her hands, so Father wouldn't hear. This means *close your eyes*"—she clapped her thumb and pointer finger together—"and then I would talk back to her and tell her *don't worry, I'm okay*," she said, slapping her palm against her thigh.

My gut twisted, some nasty combination of my empty stomach and the raw nature of the girl's story. "You were brave back there. It was clever, using the medical anesthetic. I should have thought of that."

"Will I have to be brave where you're taking me?" she asked.

I grimaced, well aware of the truth, but as I scanned Amity's face, the scrapes and filth that covered her cheeks, my answer evolved. "Not nearly as brave as you've had to be your entire life."

CHAPTER 2

PIPER

For the life of me, I couldn't figure out how I'd doubled back to a village I'd taken from before. The next morning, after a long night filled with more fever and tossing than sleep, I kept going over the facts in my mind. The night before, Amity had informed me I'd taken a girl from the village years ago, though she couldn't tell me how many years it had been, the girl's name, or what she had looked like. At first, I was inclined not to believe her, but it would have been difficult to consider myself a reasonable person and continue to deny the prevailing evidence.

As a person who kidnapped children for a living, I tried to preserve as many admirable qualities about myself as I could manage —reasonableness being one of them.

Amity had grown up with legends of a red-headed half-fae who serenaded the entire village with her wooden flute into the wee hours of the evening. When the village had awakened well into the daylight hours the next day, the performer had vanished—and so had a little girl.

So, though I had no recollection of this town and had triple-checked my map before journeying all the way out here to make sure I hadn't visited before, I had to admit I'd never met another red-headed half-fae flautist kidnapper.

That didn't stop the whole situation from nagging at me the entire day. That, and my arm, which somehow hurt worse today than it had when Amity's father snapped it in two last night.

We left our poor excuse for a campsite as soon as enough sunlight poured through the wooded canopy to minimize the risk of one of us tripping over a fallen limb and spraining an ankle. I quadruple-checked my maps and found another village without a name, at least not one important to the cartographer, that bordered the northern edge of the woods. While I'd planned to take the road that ran south of Amity's village to a town called Suusen in the middle of the night after a swift, injury-free mission, things had obviously not gone according to plan. And I couldn't take the risk that Amity's father might have sent messengers to the town, warning them to be on the lookout for us. It wasn't like we'd be difficult to spot.

"You're sure your father doesn't do any business with the village on the edge of these woods?" I couldn't shake the nerves that he might have sent a bounty in this direction as well.

"I'm sure," Amity said, her first words of the day as she sidestepped a gnarled root just asking to be yanked out of the ground by a stray foot. She had already scavenged for breakfast by the time I had woken up this morning and had pressed wrymroot and yuleberries into my palms. She hadn't as much as looked at me when I'd told her about our next destination. I'd even told her she was free to go back to her father if she wanted, though I regretted the words as soon as they came out of my mouth, since I had no idea who I was going to bring Bronger if she didn't agree to come along. Thankfully, she'd shaken her head and stomped on ahead.

"Because if he did, or if anyone in your village did, they might have sent word to the town already," I said.

"I'm sure." She held back a branch of thorns between her pointer finger and thumb, waiting for me to pass through before releasing it.

"Thanks." How odd that word felt on my tongue. I couldn't remember the last time I hadn't had to do everything for myself.

"Am I going to have to pass a test where you're taking me?" Amity asked as she released the branch of thorns and it snapped behind us.

The question took me off-guard, since she'd been so quiet all morning. I wondered if that was why she had been so reserved, if she was worried she might not meet my master's standards.

"Of sorts," I said, "but it will mostly be to figure out which of your skills is most valuable, which will be easiest to hone."

She frowned, her bushy eyebrows furrowing above her dark eyes. "I'm not any good at fighting, and I can't play any instruments. Will they still let me in?"

I watched the little girl as she weaved her way in and out of the brush, dodging stumps and clearing my path of brambles. She was fairly graceful for a human, and might have left me in the dust had she not needed to stay within earshot of me to continue her questioning. I had to give myself a break, though. Half-fae or not, my arm throbbed in a fresh wave of pain with every heartbeat, and it wasn't like the hike through the woods was helping to slow my pulse.

"They'll let you in," I said.

"How can you be sure?"

I paused, puzzled more by the girl's question than its answer. I was used to the questions, of course. The children always had questions, but they usually asked whether anyone was going to hurt them, if there would be food where we were going, that sort of thing. None of them seemed to have a clue what they were getting themselves into... Until now.

Until Amity.

Usually, I kept as much information as possible to myself until we arrived at the Coup. Not that I feared the children would run. It was just that, if we were to be caught... Well, I wouldn't want the children knowing too much. Bronger wouldn't want the children knowing too much.

But something about Amity plucked at a part of me I'd buried long ago, the part of beings I imagined made them want to share things. "Because I've already chosen you. My master trusts my decisions."

"I thought your song chose me," Amity said.

I swallowed. *Yes, and Bronger doesn't know that.*

Well, he knew I used my gift to scout out children. But *how* I used my gift? Well, he was entitled to think what he wanted, and it wasn't my responsibility to correct him if he assumed incorrectly. Bronger expected me to bring him the strongest, wittiest, cleverest, cunningest children I could find. That's what he believed my gift detected. What he didn't know was that, by birth, the children I brought him were none of those things. It just so happened that the children I found, the broken ones in need of a home even a fraction better than the one the Fates had dropped them into, were also the most resilient. And I had found that resilient children possessed a knack for becoming whatever they needed to be to thrive.

"Well, he trusts my song," I said. "Besides, I can already tell my song chose well. You're resourceful with plants and medicine, and can even turn a healing anesthetic into a weapon if you need to. You have nothing to worry about, kid."

Amity scrambled over a fallen tree, tiptoeing over a knot on its trunk before hopping off and landing silently on the ground. "Are you the only one who chooses children?"

"Yes. Others have tried, but I'm the best at it, so my master turned that part over to me." It took effort to hide the bit of pride beaming through my tone. While my and Bronger's relationship was... well, complicated, he was the closest thing to a father figure I could remember, and when he had turned the *recruiting,* as he liked to call it, over to me seven years ago, that was all the affirmation I'd needed.

"If you take all the children, then who took you?" Amity asked, turning to face me, examining me with those wide brown eyes as if she could somehow surmise the answer from my hair, the slight curve of my ears, the freckles that spattered my nose.

Apparently she could, because she said, "He did, didn't he? Your master?"

AS WE SCOPED out the next village from the tree line, watching for any sign that word had spread of the kidnapping last night, I coached

Amity to watch out for mothers gripping their children extra close, or worse, an absence of children playing in the streets. It had only taken us a few hours to traverse the woods, and it didn't seem the business sector of the village had woken up yet, but there was no harm in being especially careful.

Thankfully, the trading post was close to the edge of the woods, in a dark, wooden, two-story building that also served as an inn. I couldn't help but think how it would have been nice to have had a bed last night, but I didn't figure it would have done me much good. My arm was going to be broken whether I slept in a bed or on the ground.

"If anyone asks, you're my sister," I said. Amity nodded.

The door, which was only attached to its frame with one hinge, took its sweet time opening for us. Eventually, Amity had to slam her shoulder into the crooked door, for which I was grateful, as I figured I might need at least one of my limbs to work if we were going to make it all the way back alive.

A small man in a dingy robe that looked as if it might have been his only article of clothing stood behind the counter. His withered skin wrinkled around his brow, his cheeks, but most of all, his eyes. Even from across the room, I could detect the touch of Time in the way his eyes shone of blue ceramic. I wondered then if such a glaze would harden over my eyes one day—I hadn't met enough half-fae to ask.

He heard us coming, even if he couldn't see us.

"Welcome, friends," he said, his cheerful voice echoing through the otherwise empty room. "May I get you two a room upstairs?"

Tables, covered in cobwebs and soup stains that looked as though they might have been there a while, crowded the room. I wondered what had happened to this village that a room that had once required so many tables now did not seem to know what to do with them.

"We're simply passing through. Our journey requires haste, but it seems the rest of the village still sleeps. Do you have any supplies here we could buy?" I asked.

"Would bread, cheese, some salted pork, and a bottle of halofaen suffice?" he asked. An unpleasant odor wafted through my memory as I recalled many a child losing the contents of their stomach from such an inconsequential thing as stream water. Though I figured Amity probably possessed a resolute stomach, she was still human, and I figured buying the halofaen would be a simple measure to take to avoid such unpleasantness.

"Yes, that would do," I said.

The innkeeper turned to Amity, and a softness overtook his wrinkled features. "And for you, young friend?" I wondered whether he could see her shadow through those thick screens over his eyes, or if he had some other way of knowing she was a child, such as hearing the shallowness of her breathing, or the patter of her footsteps.

"Nothing for me, but I thank you." She stumbled over the words, clearly flustered that an adult had spoken to her. I imagined if the blacksmith's reputation had been anything like his actual personality, Amity's neighbors had probably avoided addressing her at all costs. "Well, maybe some chocolates, if you have them."

The man chuckled. "Got some in the back. I'll just be a second." He traced the counter with his knobby fingers as he walked to a door at the edge of the room. I opened my mouth to tell him not to bother, that we couldn't afford chocolates, but he disappeared behind it, leaving us in the silent, sad hall that I figured had once echoed with laughter.

That was how it had been since the fae had stolen our lands, our freedom for themselves. This small village had probably remained unaffected longer than the cities, as the people here had been used to surviving off of relatively few travelers anyway. But the fae couldn't seem to ruin anything without the effect trickling down to everyone else.

"Umm, Piper." Amity shook my broken arm so hard I gasped in pain.

"Amity!" I scolded her, biting my lip lest I accidentally say something I might regret. The pain pulsed up my arm into my head, which had only rid itself of a headache within the past hour.

"Oh, I'm so sorry, Piper. I didn't mean to hurt you." Her eyes swelled much wider than they should have for fear of me. For a moment, I wondered if she expected me to hit her, but then I traced her line of vision, and realized I was not the one she was afraid of.

At least, not the version of me standing next to her.

Because there I was, behind the counter, my face sketched with charcoal onto a loose hanging parchment on the wall. But it wasn't my face that held my gaze.

It was hers.

The face I'd purged from my memory long ago, etched into the poster next to mine.

CHAPTER 3

PIPER

Her face was just as I'd forgotten it.

Freckle-peppered skin, long eyelashes, wild ringlets, wide, onyx eyes. At least, the charcoal rendered her eyes onyx. I hadn't given her the dignity she'd deserved by noting the color of them. She peered up at me from the second poster behind the counter. That face I had tried so hard, and succeeded, to wipe from my thoughts, my memories, my nightmares.

Under both the sketches was a caption, written so long ago the words had been smeared with time.

WANTED: half-fae with red hair. Name unknown. Return dead or alive. Human girl kidnapped from home. Cheyenne. Wanted ALIVE or no bounty.

Cheyenne. I'd forgotten her name, too. Blocked it out, shoved it into the recesses of my mind and locked it away, so I wouldn't have to hear the screaming, wouldn't have to relive...

I couldn't think about that now. Amity and I had to get out of this village, this village I'd been so sure I'd never visited before. The shop owner was blind and wouldn't recognize me, but if anyone else walked through that door...

"Remember where I told you to meet me if we got separated?" I asked Amity. When she nodded, I added, "I need you to go there now. I'll be right behind you."

"But we're not separated."

I sighed, pulling at the hair at the nape of my neck. "I know. Just go, please."

She wrinkled her brow as if to protest, but she must have thought better of it, because she scuttled off and through the door.

As soon as she was gone, I slipped over the counter and found the key to the drawers still in the lock.

BY THE TIME I made it back to Amity, she'd already gathered a handful of berries and roots and had spread them out for me on a nearby log. "I thought they'd be good with the chocolates," she said.

I sighed. "I wasn't able to get the chocolates."

"Oh." Disappointment flickered in her brown eyes, but she quickly masked it with an air of practicality. "That's probably for the best. They would have been expensive anyway."

Something twisted in my gut, but I chose to ignore it.

"How much did those cost you?" she asked, nodding toward the bag of supplies in my hand.

"Oh. Um..."

A moment of hesitation was all it took to earn a stern look from Amity. "Don't you know how much you spent? We need to keep track; that way we don't run out of money."

"Trust me. We don't have to worry about that."

She frowned in confusion, then as the realization of what I'd done settled in, she gaped at me. "You took his supplies?"

"Um. Yes," I said, unsure why this bag, of all things, was what the child had determined to be upset about.

Horror encroached on her round, filthy face. "Did you pay for them?"

My neck jerked backward, almost involuntarily. "I didn't exactly have the chance. Or did you not see the wanted poster with my face on it?"

"But that's stealing." She took a step back from the sack as if to distance herself from its impurity.

I swallowed the exasperation welling in my throat and willed my voice to calm, though I couldn't bring myself to sift out the steely quality. "I couldn't afford to stand there and wait. At any moment, someone could have walked in and recognized me. Then they would have sent you right back to your father."

"But that old man was nice to us. Those are his." She pointed to the bag, her bony finger trembling with accusation.

I sighed, imagining what an adjustment it was going to be for this innocent little girl once we arrived at our destination.

"Is that why you took me? To train me to be a thief?" Amity asked, her face going white as the moon, her chaotic braid the most disheveled I'd seen it yet.

I squirmed. "Did you think I was taking you to some utopia?"

"No, I thought... Well, you took that girl all those years ago. Her parents didn't feed her. I thought... I thought you came to rescue us. To take us someplace better." Her legs were shaking as tears bulged from her eyelids.

As frustrating as her rigid moral compass was, something about her terror moved something in me. I dropped the stolen sack on the ground and placed my hand on her shoulder.

"It is better. I promise. It's not some paradise. But it's better. And no one is going to lay a hand on you there. But..." She sniffled and peered up at me, those brown eyes glistening. I swallowed and continued. "But you're going to have to get used to getting your hands a little dirty. Where I'm taking you..." I paused, well aware of the wrath I'd face if Bronger ever found out I told a child his secret before reaching the Coup. "One day, my master, your master now, is going to take back Avelea. He's going to drive the fae rulers out, the ones who took our lands and our people and our wealth. He's going to be king, but he needs our help. That's why I picked you. Because I think you can help us."

Amity blinked, sending the tears rolling down her cheeks, creating streams of white in the film of dust that coated her skin. When she spoke, her voice wavered. "Am I going to be a soldier?"

I kneeled, soaking my knee in the mossy earth as I wiped the tears from her grimy cheeks. "No, nothing like that. Not you. I'll make sure of it."

She swallowed down a sob and squared her shoulders. "Why do you want to drive the fae out if you're fae, too?"

"I'm not fae. I wouldn't be fae if one of my ancestors six generations ago had a drop of human blood in their veins. Not to them, at least," I said, gritting my teeth.

She nodded and fixed her gaze on the stolen goods once again. "But... But if you want to fight the fae, then why'd you steal that from a human?"

The words struck me between the ribs, though I knew she had meant the question in earnest.

WE WAITED in the woods longer than I meant to, and when darkness fell over the land, we snuck back to the village. Amity stayed and watched from behind a tree as I deposited three copper coins in the mailbox mounted on the side of the inn.

As they fell from my fingertips, something heavy that had lodged itself between my ribs threatened to fall with them.

I might have allowed it to, on a different day.

A day when I hadn't seen *her*.

I couldn't seem to lay that heaviness down.

Not when on the other side of the inn's wall, a girl's charcoal-sketched eyes stared into the darkness.

A girl no poster could save, no bounty could ransom.

A girl who couldn't be found.

CHAPTER 4

Piper's gift preferred to go by Gigi, but as Gigi had yet to uncover a way to communicate such to Piper, she didn't think it fair to hold it against her host.

Not that Gigi could have held a grudge against Piper if she tried. Not after Piper had been the one to wake her up.

Gigi wasn't sure what had happened to her before Piper's infantile cries had wrenched her from her endless string of nightmares, blood-soaked hands and relentless wails and death and death and more death. All she knew was that, with Piper, she was awake, and that was enough.

There had been a moment, the briefest lapse of time, during Gigi's Awakening when she'd known that, if she'd wanted to, she could have faded into the abyss, freed herself from that dreadful curse of sentience, from that deep, deep ache that throbbed despite her boneless, muscleless form.

She had almost—almost—seized the opportunity, severed herself from this world and its consciousness forever, slipped into the Great Unknown, hidden herself in its shadows lest the nightmares find her again.

But Piper had been screaming, and though Gigi's awareness had been fuzzy, she had thought something about that was wrong. Not the screaming part; babies were bound to scream. Somehow, Gigi had known that, despite not knowing her own name, her own history.

But no one was holding the screaming baby.

And that wasn't quite right.

And it was cold. So, so cold. And the baby was kicking and writhing, all because its legs were free when they should have been bound, wrapped, swaddled.

Gigi had thought, *I'll fade away shortly, once this poor baby finds sleep. After all, I must find a way to thank it for waking me.*

But the baby had gone on screaming.

Shh, go to sleep, baby, Gigi had whispered, but the baby couldn't seem to hear her. Either that, or it was being blatantly defiant, but Gigi couldn't ever remember encountering a defiant baby, so that option didn't seem likely. Not that Gigi could trust her memory.

She tried again. *Shh. It's alright. I know you're cold and miserable, but you'll feel better if you sleep.*

Unless the baby had a nightmare, Gigi thought even as her consciousness shivered. The baby jerked a bit.

Gigi found that curious, so she dipped a hesitant toe of her consciousness back into those nightmares. Ripping and screaming and nothingness. So much nothingness.

She shivered again, and so did the baby.

Ah, so you can't hear me, but you can feel me, Gigi whispered, despite knowing it was of no use for her to do so.

Gigi tried to calm herself, for perhaps if she felt calm, the baby would too.

Calming herself turned out to be more of an ordeal than Gigi thought, but she didn't know what she'd expected, having just awoken from a terrible dream.

So she did the best she could, and she hummed to herself, a lovely tune she must have heard before she'd fallen into those garish nightmares. A lullaby, that's what it was called. And as she hummed, lights flickered—no, the baby's eyelids fluttered, making it look as though the lights flickered; that's what it was.

Perhaps you can hear me after all, Gigi had thought, as the baby had drifted to sleep.

Gigi had thought she had better postpone her trip to the Abyss, just long enough to be sure the baby came to no harm.

That had been nineteen years ago, and Gigi hadn't realized at the time how much harm would come this baby's way.

So much hurt in such a tiny heart, from such a tiny age.

The poster on the wall of the inn had reminded Gigi of such.

Piper didn't like to remember the girl, and it wasn't as though Gigi could blame her. Even Gigi pushed her own nightmares away, shoved them into a deep corner of her mind, of Piper's mind, where they could collect dust and not bother either of them.

At least, that's what Gigi told herself. There was always that suspicion though, sneaking around unwanted, an uninvited guest that often overstayed its lack of welcome, that perhaps she *couldn't* remember.

But that was also a thought not worth thinking about.

Just like it wasn't worth thinking about how, sometimes, Gigi felt deep within her being that she was, indeed, less than a full Gigi. For, as much as she convinced herself otherwise, the memories of who she was before the nightmares, before Piper, were not the only bits of her that had gone missing.

There was her voice, for starters. Though she had no concrete evidence of such, she was certain there had been a time in which she had been able to speak. Well, she could speak now, she supposed; it was just that no one seemed to hear her, not even Piper, whom she loved most of all.

Yes, Gigi knew deep down that she was not all there. And as much as it wasn't worth thinking about, she couldn't exactly help it, could she? Because what else was she to do, when she was stuck in a body that was not hers (she loved Piper, of course; she could never resent Piper for it, but Piper did quite a bit of walking, as she was doing now, and not a whole lot of talking, even when she had a traveling companion, and Gigi didn't know how Piper could stand all the quiet), with a voice that couldn't be heard and with memories that weren't all there?

Again, not worth thinking about.

And because Gigi very much did not wish to spend Piper's journey pondering her own origins, her own past—the one that remained safely locked and caked with dust in the recesses of Piper's mind—she decided she would try to make herself useful and shuffle through the clutter that was Piper's memories.

CHAPTER 5

PIPER

I wasn't looking forward to our passage through the Kobii mountains, but I couldn't see any way around it at this point.

If two nights ago I'd been nervous that news of a conspicuous kidnapper and her kidnappee might have spread, by now I was almost certain the Anders path would be crawling with bounty hunters. Not that Amity's father would have much to pay, or that they would have any intention of returning her. But I had met a few bounty hunters in seedy taverns in the armpits of Avelea, and I could see their line of thinking already. If the red-headed half-fae had kidnapped once, how many times had she kidnapped before? And from how many rich families had she taken children? And, even if she hadn't taken as much as a puppy from a rich family, would a rich family with a missing child know that?

There was no way I was going to set foot on the Anders until this ordeal had blown over. Not until I could figure out where my meticulous charting had gone poorly enough to lead me back into not one, but two villages I had already visited.

So, through the Kobii mountains was how it would have to be. The peaks sliced through the skyline, even further north than the village where someone had strewn my picture all around town. Meaning, even further from the Coup.

Bronger was going to kill me.

Well, he wouldn't kill me when he saw Amity. But it wouldn't be a pleasant homecoming this time. As unnerving as it was to imagine Bronger's face when I showed up on his doorstep, oh, three weeks later than intended, what was more unnerving was the idea of me returning empty-handed. That outcome, I hadn't allowed myself to imagine.

We had to circumnavigate the next village at a distance, for I had no intention of stumbling across a hunter in the woods. Amity braved the trek without a complaint and fared decently well in the woods, especially compared to me. I didn't make it an hour without crying out any time a sudden burst of pain snaked up my arm and reverberated through my skull. But, to be fair, Amity wasn't the one with a broken arm.

It was never the forest I had feared. The further we walked, the steeper the incline, and Amity became prone to slipping occasionally, her tiny body sliding past mine, pebbles and dirt scrambling in her wake. She'd just stand up, wipe herself off, and follow me until she was ahead of me again.

But with the steep incline of the Kobiis came the inevitable cold, a cold that wrapped our very bodies in a chill that numbed my broken arm, and, while it provided temporary relief, it still had me glancing into my sling every so often to make sure my arm hadn't snapped off and fallen to the forest floor.

We tried to stop to eat once, but found the bitter wind too oppressive for standing still or sitting, so we carried on, munching on stale sourdough and hardened cheese. I watched as large chunks of bread fell to the wayside, little Amity's numb, fumbling fingers unable to grasp onto them properly.

This was not going well. I blamed myself for being stupid enough to double back to the same villages twice and, even stupider, for being unable to figure out how I had forgotten where I'd been, even with my extensive safety measures. For not stealing Amity a coat from the inn, and for allowing her tenderized conscience to influence such a decision. How we were going to live through the night, I had no idea.

I wondered which would be worse, being caught by a bounty hunter and sold to some rich fae family with a hole in their bosoms from a missing child or freezing to death. I thought freezing to death might still be better, except that I remembered Amity would probably succumb to the elements before I did, and I didn't think I had the guts to watch her die. To watch her die because of me, because I'd been irresponsible and failed her.

We found the road, the Kobii Pass, an hour before sundown and camped there. No one frequented these mountains, as they bordered a sea that stretched to nobody in Alondria knew where, and didn't make a direct path to much of anything now that all *proper* civilization dwelt within the fae cities. We stayed the night close to the road, under the cover of the trees in case a traveler passed by and became suspicious of our unlikely pairing. After a meagerly rationed dinner of cheese and jerky, the crumbs of which wasted themselves on our numb cheeks, the two of us huddled together under my fox skin coat and attempted to sleep.

Amity's frail, underfed body trembled for hours, her ribs rattling against mine in the cold, knocking against my injured arm and sending a shot of pain through my body each time.

I fought back the tears, knowing they'd only cause more pain in a frost like tonight's. Eventually, the shaking and trembling became too much, and I surrendered to the sweet, painless darkness.

THE PAIN RETURNED AS SOON as I opened my eyes, but this time it struck like needles on my scalp, in an arrow down the back of my neck, as someone pulled me from the ground by my hair.

A child whimpered nearby. My eyes adjusted quickly to the torchlight. Amity cried muffled tears that slid under the broad hand clamped over her mouth.

Traffickers.

I jolted, swinging my good elbow upward and landing it solidly upon what felt like a jaw. The man yelped, but all he had to do to contain me was to yank on my broken arm. The pain overwhelmed me, coursing through my blood and stopping my voice in my throat.

My vision blacked. By the time I'd regained my sight, the man had wrestled both arms behind my back.

My dagger pressed against my ankle, hidden in my boot and completely worthless at the moment.

"What little treasures we've found, brother," the one digging his fingers into my broken arm said, his warm breath slithering across the pointed tip of my ear.

"Yours looks to be half-fae. Bet she'll sell for at least a silver. This one's not worth much." The brother nodded toward Amity. "What do you think? Bring her along and risk her dying of the elements after we've wasted our food on her, or be done with her right here?"

Amity's brown eyes went wide, her tears flowing freely now, tracing red streaks into her cheeks as the intense cold burned her skin.

"She's heartier than she looks," I said through gritted teeth. "She'll survive the trip. And she's resourceful. With her skills, the price on her will make up for the risk of losing a few coppers' worth of food." I hoped Amity would understand. Being carried off by these half-lives was better than being murdered here and now. Because I would get her out. I just needed them to keep her alive.

Apparently she understood, for she nodded her head vigorously under the man's clamped hand. The man seemed to realize what a waste of energy it was to keep her silenced way up here on this abandoned pass, especially now that I was awake and apprehended, for he lowered his hand from her mouth.

"Hmm," the one twisting my arm said. "And why should we take your word for it? Forgive me if I'm suspicious of a half-fae protecting the life of a human."

"She's half-human too." Amity's voice shook even as she took up for me. I grimaced as the brother pulled at the hair at the nape of her neck and she began whimpering once more.

"If this one's got a mouth on her, she's not worth the trouble." The brother bared a maw of missing teeth at her. He brandished a knife from his coat, and it glinted in the torchlight. Amity attempted to cower away from it, but the brother must have clamped harder on her hair, for her head jerked backward to face the knife.

My mind raced. There was no way I could overpower the man behind me, not with a broken arm. And even if I could, if I lashed out to hurt him, his brother would surely take Amity's life to spite me before I could get to her.

Reason. I'd have to reason with them.

"I'll keep her quiet. She won't bother you again," I said. "She does what I say. I can promise she'll be worth her weight in silver."

The brother grinned and traced the edge of his blade over Amity's pale neck. She shook, and when he'd removed the blade, a line of dark blood trickled down her skin, staining her collar. "What think you, brother?"

The man holding me paused, his labored breathing wetting the back of my neck and twisting a knot in my stomach. "I think there's something this one's not telling us." He twisted my arm further, but this time I was prepared for it, and I bit back a cry, not wishing to give him the satisfaction. "I think a half-fae has no business with a human girl, and certainly has no business worrying if a human girl lives or dies..."

"Please, she's my sister," I gasped, a desperate attempt to keep his mind from wandering in the direction I could see coming.

"Is she now? Now, what human goes back to a human after being enchanted by a fae?" the man holding me asked. "You know what I think? I think the only reason a half-fae would bother with a human is if you thought you could get something out of her."

"Please, she's my sister." When I cried, the tears were real this time. I glanced over at Amity, who was still trembling and whose confused expression told me she had no idea what the trafficker was implying.

"Your little human friend's a witch, isn't she?" he asked.

The brother growled and gripped his hand, not around Amity's hair this time, but around her throat.

"No! No, please. She's no witch." There was nothing more dangerous than a pair of unreasonable, superstitious human men.

But the deed was already done, the dreaded word already spoken. He had accused Amity of being the one thing humans hated more than the fae themselves, those of them who tried to be like the fae. The ones who'd betrayed them.

The brother tightened his fingers around Amity's neck, and she choked, gasping for breath as she flailed her arms, but her fists couldn't seem to find a place to land. I ground my teeth, blocking out the pain as I ran the side of my boot down my captor's shin. He cried out, letting go of me for a hair of a second. I lunged for Amity, but my neck jerked backward as my captor caught hold of my hair once more. Amity's face went blue under the torchlight. She locked her wide, terrified eyes on me, and dread struck my chest.

I was going to see the life fade from those eyes, and there was nothing I could do about it.

I had failed a child.

Again.

But then the brother choking Amity made a gagging sound. His fingers loosened and Amity slumped to the ground, crawling away from the man on her elbows and knees.

My captor let out a wail, and, through the pain pounding my head, I found the brother clutching his throat in shock, the feather of a cerulean arrow protruding from where his thyroid should have been.

The sight silenced the pain in my head. For a moment, everything went quiet. I allowed my body to slump, causing my captor to trip over me in his haste to lunge toward his brother. The weight of his legs on my back, I clawed at the undergrowth of the forest until I'd freed myself from his limbs. When I stood, he was still crawling toward his brother, his mouth agape. I reached for my boot, unsheathed the dagger I'd tucked away, and landed on the man's back, slipping my blade through his ribs, where I knew his heart to be.

His body went limp underneath me, and I turned to Amity, ripping my dagger from the man's ribcage so I could send it flying toward the source of the arrow, if need be.

When my eyes found her in the shadows, she was curled up in the arms of a cloaked figure. I drew my dagger back, ready to direct it to this man's throat, blazing with so much anger, so much fear for Amity's life, I knew I would not miss.

"Are you going to kill me?" The voice was smooth and much too playful for having just shot down a man. "I was rather hoping you'd hire me."

CHAPTER 6

PIPER

I didn't lower my dagger.

"Amity, come here." I eased toward them and prepared to strike. If the man wanted money, he wasn't getting it from me, and I didn't want Amity within his grasp when he came to this realization on his own.

The man released his arms from around her, and she nodded. She stumbled over to me, her hands still clutching her throat, as if she thought it might fall off if she didn't hold it in place.

"Come here," I whispered this time, brushing her trembling fingers aside with my own to examine the wound. The skin around her neck was red and swollen, and I figured it would be purple as a ripe plum by morning. She held her chin high as I moved her braid aside and traced the bruising to the spot underneath her ear.

I fought back the angry tears welling in my eyes and wrapped my good arm around Amity, pulling her in, allowing her to tuck her face into my chest as I swaddled her in the excess of my coat. The dagger remained in my hand, resting upon Amity's back as I turned my full attention back to the stranger.

His mouth was twisted into a smirk, but his gaze kept bouncing toward Amity, not me, his skin a cool, earthy brown wrinkling his forehead, his shaven head highlighting the expression.

"Who are you?" I asked.

He turned his attention back to me. The concern melted from his expression, as if he hadn't meant for me to see it, and was instead replaced by a look of utter self-satisfaction and amusement.

"I typically prefer terms of endearment from ladies as stunning as yourself, but I would settle for Marcus since we aren't acquainted. Yet." He grinned, flashing a full set of perfectly straight teeth my way, an odd attribute for a human, at least one wandering in these parts.

"And what is your business in the Kobiis?" I asked, choosing to ignore his flirtations entirely.

"And what is *your* business in the Kobiis?" Mischief lined his brow, sparkling in his copper eyes. "That seems like the better question, now doesn't it?"

I clenched my jaw, hating that the sensitivity of our situation was so evident. I'd try to assuage his suspicions, if I could. "We're sisters, on the run from our cruel father. He's well acquainted. We knew he'd have scouts searching for us on the Anders, and in any nearby village, so we chose a path he would've never expected us to attempt."

"Because he thought you wouldn't survive?" Marcus asked.

"Yes."

"You seem to be well on your way to proving him right then," he mused, picking a weed from the forest floor and twirling it around his fingers. "I wonder, if the plan was to trek through the mountains, why the two of you seem so ill prepared for it. Your coats are thin; your satchel seems the type for a journey with frequent lodgings, chances to replenish supplies. So, are you a poor planner, or are you lying about what a half-fae is doing with a human girl who doesn't resemble her in the least?"

He tossed the tattered weed to the ground before picking another.

Amity sobbed in my arms, and I wondered if it was from pain, her recent near-death experience, or fear of the archer who seemed to be onto us.

Cornered, I did the only thing I knew to do, the only thing Bronger had ever taught me to do in this situation.

"Just tell me what you want, and I'll hand it over." I cringed at the words as they slipped from my tongue. There were some things that would hurt much more to give than others.

He folded his hands together in his lap and leaned forward from the rock on which he perched, peering up at me with a smile on his full, curving lips. "I already told you what I want. I want you to hire me."

"For what?" I asked, my mouth agape.

"For protection, as long and as far as your journey lasts, in exchange for whatever coin you have left in your purse when it comes to an end." The smirk on his face sent a primal urge surging through my body.

An urge to smack him.

I didn't, though it took digging my fingernails into my palms not to.

"We only stole enough from our father to feed us when we arrive at the village on the other side of the Kobiis." The lie slipped off my tongue too easily. How many lies had I told since Bronger had taken me in? I'd been awful at it, at first. Bronger had seen to it that I improved.

"Mhm." Marcus's copper eyes shone, the wrinkles around the corners of his eyes tilting with amusement.

"And even if we had money, we wouldn't need your protection," I said. Amity's weight shifted on my chest, and I noticed the sobbing had stopped.

"Clearly," he said.

"We can take care of ourselves. If you've noticed I'm half-fae, then you also know I'm stronger than the average woman. And faster too."

"Yes, but unfortunately just as breakable." He nodded toward my sling, which I might have yanked behind me if I thought I could do it without yelping and humiliating myself.

Amity lifted her head from my chest and lifted her chin toward me. The bruises on her neck had already darkened. My stomach churned at the sight.

"Can he please come with us?" Her words were just a whisper, and she trembled as she shivered from the cold, the pain.

"Amity, we don't know that we can trust him," I said. Her eyes pleaded with mine as she wiped a tear from them.

"Please. I'm scared." Her lips, swollen and blue from struggling with our attackers, trembled—a blow to my gut. This child, who had spent her entire life a punching bag of her father's, was terrified because of the situation I'd put her in, the hands I'd allowed her to fall into, the filthy nails I'd allowed to carve those bruises into her neck.

I glanced back at Marcus, who shrugged his shoulders. "She said it, not me."

I scowled, hatred for this man growing with each piling debt I owed him. "Fine. You may escort us to our destination."

"I may?" He grinned, wrinkles forming around his eyes. "Oh, I'd be honored. Truly, if not for my inherent need to eat, I'd do it free of charge. Just for the feeling I get in my chest when I'm allowed the opportunity to be chivalrous."

"I'll pay you upon our safe arrival," I said, regretting the agreement already. Sure, most of the money in my purse was Bronger's, coin he'd given me intending to fund my journey. But not all of it. Some of it was mine, coppers left in the bottom of a cap at the end of some of my better performances. Growing up in the Coup, I'd not had the luxury of having much I could call my own. Letting go of a few coppers, well, I knew it shouldn't bother me, but I'd hoped to buy something for myself, a new flute perhaps, a silver-plated one.

"That is the deal I initially offered," Marcus smiled again, this time through gritted, impatient teeth.

I sheathed my knife and extended a hand into the darkness. Marcus sighed, lifted himself from his seat on the rock, and sauntered over to us with such a swing in his step, one might have mistaken him for a Fae prince.

He caught my hand in his and shook, gripping it tight enough to communicate that he meant business, but not enough to imply a threat. I met the weight of his grip with my own. When I did, a crease formed between his brows, but it was gone within the next flicker of torchlight, having me questioning whether I'd seen it at all as his gaze turned to mischief once again.

"You haven't told me your name," Marcus said.

I had a mind not to give him the satisfaction of knowing my name, but sweet Amity betrayed me, her voice muffled by my coat. "It's Piper!"

I sighed, and Marcus caught my exasperation with a chuckle. "What? Oh, don't look so defeated. It's just a name, kid."

I fought back the bait, the urge to declare that I was certainly not a child, despite being only nineteen. Even if I had, Marcus wasn't paying me any attention. He'd pulled at the edges of my coat, just enough to reveal the shivering child's eyes.

"Piper and?" he asked.

A tiny, battered hand shot out from my coat, and Marcus took it in his, shaking it firmly, just as he had mine, though his fingers warped to avoid applying pressure to her bruises. "Amity," she said, as his large hand swallowed hers whole.

"Well, Piper and Amity, where exactly am I to escort you?"

As much as I hated to admit it to myself, and as much as I would never concede such aloud, having Marcus along for our journey made traveling easier, if not simpler.

For now.

Sure, eventually I'd have to figure out a way to evade him, either have him believe he'd deposited us in the correct city or sneak off with Amity whenever we approached a day's journey to the Coup. Despite the carefree grins and overall *nothing-ever-upsets-me* aura he seemed to put off, something told me Marcus was more cunning than he let on and that deceiving him would be no simple task.

I wasn't stupid enough to believe Marcus's only motive in transporting us to our destination was the coin in my purse. I'd met contract mercenaries before, and though most of them appeared to aspire to nothing more than a flask full of ale and a harem of prostitutes at their disposal, they had to have money to fund such a lifestyle.

So they tended to make room in their pea-sized brains for counting.

Which Marcus had not bothered to do.

Still, it was nice to have a companion who was used to the frigid environment, someone with a weapon more useful for hunting game than my sparring knife, a guardian to defend us if we ran into thieves on the road again.

Besides, Amity liked him. That much was clear. By the morning after the attack, the marks on her neck had turned to deep shadows framing her chin and jaw. But the trembling had ceased. Mostly. Especially when she was hiking next to Marcus, which she hurried to do any time he allowed it... which was most of the time.

Marcus led us from the front, clearing the path of any overgrowth that might slow us down. Amity wore out her feet trying to keep up with his pace all day long, but she didn't complain about it once. I mostly just watched, and listened, and dwelt in the space between my ears as we walked.

The plan was to cross the ridge of the Kobii mountains, head south, then circle back toward Nettlewood, the fae city I'd claimed was our final destination. In reality, the Coup lay hidden in the hills east of Nettlewood, but Marcus needn't know that.

The Coup was called such for Bronger's decade worth of plots to overthrow the fae king, but we pronounced it *Coop*, for the way all Bronger's children crowded into that hole in the ground, as if it were a chicken house.

I wondered how Amity would do, cooped up so close with all the other children her age. Surely Bronger wouldn't use her as a soldier. I'd promised her as much and didn't think it likely he would, but I'd be lying to myself if I thought I had the last say in the matter.

As resilient as she was, Amity had one of those consciences which the beatings had only tenderized rather than forging a callus. It wouldn't do for Bronger to cast her as one of his soldiers, spies, or thieves, but she was so clever for her age, I feared he might use that to his advantage. Bronger was always saying that the most intelligent should be the fighters; that this was how the humans had gotten it wrong in the past, by keeping their intelligent unable to defend themselves and sending the brutes into battle to make the decisions that would cost humans their freedom.

I'd fight it as much as I could.

But I hadn't exactly gotten very far the day I'd told Bronger I didn't want to grow up to be a kidnapper, either.

As we trudged through the woods, the crunching of the leaves beneath my feet turned to the crackling of ice beneath snow boots, the chill in the air to the icy wind of Mystral, and Amity's hand in Marcus's turned to mine in Bronger's.

He had found me on the edge of death, abandoned by my human mother nights before, abandoned by my fae father years before that, presumably—the fae weren't exactly known for sticking it out with their human lovers. Rumors had brought him to Mystral—whisperings of a half-fae toddler who had picked up a hollow icicle and played a nursery rhyme, mesmerizing the entire village until one man forgot to warm himself by the fire and died of hypothermia.

They had taken the icicle away after that. And the spoons, so easily fashioned into drumsticks with the right surface—anything that a child could tap, beat, strum, or play.

It was a human settlement, after all. They weren't exactly fond of magic, that possession of the fae that had made them so formidable in battle all those centuries ago.

I couldn't remember whose idea it was to cast me out—my mother's or the settlement's.

My limbs had gone numb by the time Bronger found me, curled up in a grave I'd dug myself in the snow. He had taken my limp body and carried me across the frozen desert, sharing his heat as his heart beat against my tiny pointed ear. We'd reached an inn at the edge of the frozen desert, the last stop on the edge of civilization before one reached where only the insane cared to dwell.

The insane being my family.

He had tucked me in a rocking chair by the fire, bundled me in thick quilts, and retrieved a cup of hot cocoa, which he carefully placed between my hands and pushed toward my lips.

I drank the whole cup, despite how the liquid had scalded the inside of my throat and left sores on my inner cheeks and tongue.

And then he had asked me, "Child, what is your name?"

I hadn't known the answer. My mother had never called me anything other than "Girl."

I told him as much, and he shook his head, saying, "Your life is going to be very different from now on. You'll leave this life behind you, child. And you'll grow to do great things." Then he had looked around the room, making sure it was empty, leaned in and whispered, "One day, you will bring down the relatives that abandoned you. One day, you will help me slay nations."

I had nodded, too small at the time to understand his words' true meaning, too hungry to care.

"What do you wish to be called?" he had asked.

I'd thought back to the icicle, the one my mother had crushed with her boots, and I'd told him.

He'd smiled then, and I thought I must have done something right for once, to make an adult smile at me like that. "Well, Piper," he'd said. "I think you'll like the gift I brought you."

CHAPTER 7

MARCUS

It took every ounce of restraint in my body not to plunge my dagger into Piper's chest.

Piper, if that was even her true name.

It wasn't often that I encountered someone who inspired such deep-seated hatred in me—and I'd met more than a handful of characters worthy of the festering emotion. But I'd always taken pride in my calm nature, my unruffled demeanor.

But this woman.

I'd hated her a long while before I first laid eyes on her, from the moment my benefactor had plopped an unearthly sum of coin on his desk and pushed it my direction, telling me of a string of missing children taken from many, but mostly from the poor, the helpless...

Near-impossible to track, he'd warned, as if I wasn't the best in Avelea, as if that wasn't why he'd gone through the effort of sending a roasted lamb with his initial invitation, along with an envoy of his favorite courtesans.

The message had been clear—*I'll seduce you into accepting this offer if I have to.*

I'd turned down the courtesans, of course. I knew my benefactor's owning the beautiful, sad-eyed women was little better than the occupation of the half-fae female who flitted through the forest, her footsteps behind me hardly a whisper of fluttering leaves.

One of these days, my benefactor would pay too.

I'd make sure of it.

But as far as I knew, he didn't deal in children.

So the choice between the two evils hadn't caused me to toss and turn perhaps as much as it should've.

It had taken a few weeks, but I'd tracked her down. Over the past seven years, she'd haunted the villages of Avelea, mostly the poorer ones, the ones no authorities would bother to grace with expensive resources for searching the area.

What was a lost child to them, after all?

They probably just wandered off, after all.

The thought might have sent an arrow through my heart if one hadn't already lodged itself there, permanently situated between the sinews of my soul and flesh.

I pushed the pain away, though even that tinged my conscience with guilt.

I didn't deserve that—to be able to ignore it, to numb the agony that withered my soul and stole my sleep.

"You're very handsome," a young, yet practical voice sounded from below me. I looked down to find the little girl—Amity, that was her name—peering at me with wide brown eyes that twisted a hole through my gut.

Or maybe it was the bruises on her neck that did that.

They were my fault, after all.

I could have tracked them all the way to Nettlewood, I supposed. But I hadn't been able to get close enough to confirm that was actually where they were going, and even if I had, there would still be the issue of finding some way to disarm Piper once they arrived, without leaving Amity to fend for herself in a city full of beings who wouldn't think twice about selling her to the nearest brothel.

So I'd marked their path, then hunted down a few scoundrels of my own. Offered them a tip in exchange for a few coppers, made sure to fake a thick Mistrian accent—the small-minded men too high on the fact they thought they were swindling a foreigner to be suspicious of the stranger in the woods.

I'd told them of a beautiful half-fae female wandering across these parts, practically helpless with that broken arm of hers. Told them I'd reveal her exact location in exchange for enough coin to buy me a hot meal at the nearest inn, but that there was a child with her, and they must agree to let her go.

Then I'd followed them and waited.

The plan had been simple. Scare Piper a bit with the brutes, expose the degree to which her broken arm put her at a disadvantage, then swoop in and save the day, offer to escort them to Nettlewood, earning Piper's trust somewhere along the way. It wouldn't be difficult after that to lead her straight to my benefactor.

But then it had all gone wrong. My heart had practically plummeted when they'd decided to kill Amity. I hadn't had a good shot, not with the trees that blocked my path, and I'd had to scramble up the nearest bluff to guarantee any accuracy.

I'd come so close.

So close to being too late.

It wouldn't have been the first time.

I swallowed the dread of what could have happened had I not made that shot. Then I forced my lips into a carefree smile—an act, a shadow of my former self, one that had been all too easy to slip back into. "Is that so?"

She nodded, thoughtfully. Then her gaze swept over my face, taking me in. "Yes. I think so. Your jaw is sturdy, which could be a good thing or a bad thing, because it makes you look manly, but it makes some men look brutish. But your eyes are kind, and your smile makes your face wrinkle up, so it keeps your face balanced."

I couldn't help it. I let out a not-so-exasperated laugh. "Is that your clinical judgment?"

"Mhm. Plus, you have muscles." She nodded her head toward my shoulders, in case I might not have noticed before.

As if I did all those push-ups for the joy of it.

"Well, I appreciate your assessment," I said, finding the smile I flashed her a bit strained, guilt nipping away at the edges of it. But even this astute little child didn't seem to notice. I suppose I'd gotten good at faking it over the years. True to myself, second nature almost, I debated how to charm the little girl and in the end I went with, "It means more coming from a girl as clever as you."

Scarlet blotches speckled the girl's pale cheeks, and I knew I'd made the right gamble. Liked the child, too, for how much it pleased her that her sharp mind was the most commendable thing about her.

Leaves barely crunched behind us with the lightness with which our companion moved. But I would have heard her in the midst of a thunderclap with the way I'd honed my senses in on her, waiting for the moment she caught the hatred on my scent, a stray breeze blowing it in her direction, that wicked fae sense of hers laying my intentions bare.

I was lucky she was only half-fae; she likely couldn't scent the disgust rolling off of me.

I'd have to find a way to mute it anyway. Even if my emotions didn't reek to her, she'd sense it in my tone, in the way my shoulders stiffened in her presence, already forming knots within the depths of my shoulder blades.

I didn't believe for a second that Amity and Piper were sisters. It didn't matter that Amity clearly adored her—my benefactor had warned me that my target was rumored to be an enchantress, and given the fact that the child she'd stolen from her home now went around doting on her, I didn't think that theory was too far-fetched.

Piper probably realized my distrust already, though I'd had to toe the line of skepticism and acceptance. I hadn't wanted to draw attention to the holes in their story, but not noting them would have been suspicious in itself.

She hardly said a word as we trudged through the forest, floating behind us like a lonely specter come to stalk the living from a distance.

That was fine with me; I didn't care to look at her. It didn't matter that the first time I beheld her, the first time her hood had slipped to reveal that teardrop face spattered with sun-kissed freckles, those large, ivy-green eyes, the pointed tips of her ears barely peeking out from underneath those flaming curls that framed her face so perfectly, I'd had to remind myself to breathe. Remind myself that this woman was the enemy. That she deserved whatever would come to her once I handed her over to my benefactor, for whatever she endured after I exchanged her life for the hefty price on her head, I was sure the cruelties would never outnumber those suffered by her countless victims.

No, the breathtaking beauty, that was just the fae blood that ran through her veins.

I'd be a fool to allow myself to become ensnared by it.

Even if the feather-light brush of her footsteps against the leaves had my ears marking each and every step. Even if, with every labored breath she took, surely from the pain jolting through her arm, my instincts begged me to go to her, to search the ends of the earth for a salve to ease her pain...

I cleared my throat, pulling a battered compass from my pocket and checking it for what must have been the seventh time in the past hour. The blind eyes of a glawackus—a hideous creature that looked like a bear and a lion had a baby—peered up at me.

Why someone had taken the time to hand paint such a monstrosity on the face of the compass, I had no idea.

The poor thing didn't even point north, which was half the reason I'd purchased it in the first place. I'd delighted in its oddity at the time. The way it had to be wound, like a watch, as if the maker believed that would somehow convince anyone that the contraption wasn't fueled by illegal magic. The strange way it was engineered, so that the outer rim of its face, the one on which the four cardinal directions were hand painted, spun independently of the inner circle containing the hand. It was impeccably accurate, but it'd always pointed east, which I'd found amusing.

At least, I used to find it amusing.

Now it just served as a reminder, an anchor chaining me to my guilt, the scratches on its rim sanding down my soul every time my fingers wandered to my pocket.

Reminding me to hate myself. What I'd done. What I'd failed to do.

That was just as useful of a purpose, I supposed.

I slipped it back into my pocket, my attention turning back toward Piper. Perhaps my conscience longed to loathe someone else for a change, a fleeting reprieve from the guilt that would haunt every step I wandered on this miserable earth.

It was all too easy to let my mind slip into that cocoon, the one that would surely burst soon enough.

But for now, I let myself feast on hating her.

It was all too easy to do.

She made it easy.

What kind of heartless creature stole children, took them from their families?

And, a question more sinister than that, what did she do with them after she took them?

I supposed the answer would be the difference between whether I handed her over to my benefactor in the end, or simply chose to forfeit the obscene bounty and drive an arrow through her heart myself.

CHAPTER 8

PIPER

Though I had intended to keep as far away from Marcus and his incessant curiosity as long as possible, it turned out that, despite being used to it, I didn't prefer being alone with my thoughts for extended periods of time. Usually I didn't mind it so much—the quiet, the weeks in between the recruitments.

But usually, I didn't see a rendering of the girl, the very first girl, hanging next to a sketch of my face in an inn.

Usually, I didn't allow her screams to puncture the iron box I'd built around that memory.

So though I knew it was unwise to engage in conversation with the mysterious archer who had no good reason to be traveling through the Kobii mountains, I did anyway. Or at least I picked up my pace so that Marcus and Amity could hear the leaves crunching beneath my feet and would know I was within earshot.

"...and you can use whetherdust to heal bones," Amity told Marcus, a gleam in her eyes as she chattered. "If I find any in Nettlewood, I'm going to buy some for—" She stopped talking and whipped her messy braid around as she heard me coming.

"Ah, deciding to join us, are you?" The tip of Marcus's tongue protruded through his too-perfect teeth. He was teasing me. I bristled, which only stoked the flickering spark in his copper eyes.

I opened my mouth, but found I had little to say. Not that I was a poor conversationalist—no one at the Coup would accuse me of such. But I found most of my conversations revolved around plotting the downfall of the fae who had rejected me and overthrown my adopted siblings' ancestors, dreaming of the glorious day when we'd rule beside Bronger. Either that, or I was comforting terrified children or listening to their odd little commentaries on very ordinary objects—not that I minded. But how to make conversation with a man? A man who probably led a fairly ordinary life and accepted the time in which he was unfortunate enough to be born?

I was at a loss for words.

He eyed me carefully as I fumbled for a response—a harmless question, anything to fill the silence and cover up my utter lack of social skills. Amusement tugged at the corners of his lips, and I realized for the first time how stunningly handsome he was. There wasn't a blemish on his earthy skin, which seemed to glow with health even in the dim forest light. And his mischievous eyes, his smile that overtook his face every time he laughed, which was often in Amity's presence... He was the embodiment of joy. Not to mention the broad shoulders that bulged from underneath his white tunic, which was visible now that he had given his overcoat to Amity, who looked like she might topple over from its weight any moment now.

Unfortunately, the fact that Marcus was stunningly attractive was also not an ideal starting point for conversation.

"So, Piper." Marcus twirled a weed in his fingers as we trudged through the woods. "What's your story?"

My eyes went wide. What a strange question.

"I already told you," Amity said, her exasperation clear, even as her labored breathing almost masked it. "Piper is my sister. We ran away from our father because he hit us. And we're going to see our brother in...?"

"Nettlewood," I answered quickly, marveling at how Amity, the child who had been so bothered by our stealing of the innkeeper's supplies, had now made up her own portion of the lie we were feeding Marcus.

"Right, Nettlewood. Our brother went there first, because he knew our father wouldn't suspect him, since our father wanted him to grow up to be a businessman. But he's been working this whole time, saving up money for a place where Piper and I can live with him," she said, her voice chipper and bright. My gut twisted at the hope in her voice. It was then I realized that, to Amity, she wasn't telling Marcus a lie. Just a dream she'd allowed to mingle with reality, ever since the mysterious hero of the neglected, the abused, had come to rescue her.

Something told me the Coup wouldn't live up to Amity's expectations.

"Well, of course I know that's *your* story, little ragamuffin. But you must know that you and your sister are far apart in age. So I'm asking about *her* story. All the things that happened before you came along and made her dreary life a little brighter."

"Oh." Amity frowned, as if she hadn't considered that her hero, the one she'd been waiting to come rescue her for the entirety of her short life, had been occupied with other things in between.

"My story?" I stalled, trying to latch onto details of my past, little truths that I could share without giving away who I was, any information Bronger would be displeased with me sharing.

"Well..." I started, "my father was fae, as you've probably noticed." I gestured to the tips of my ears as I tucked my hair behind them, pointing to my large, crescent-shaped green eyes and my narrow chin. Then I pointed to the freckles on my nose. "My mother—mine and Amity's mother—was human, obviously."

Amity brushed her own nose as I spoke, smiling as she remembered her own freckles, the speckles that made our sisterhood a little more believable. A little more real.

"Do the high fae not have freckles?" Marcus asked.

"None that I've ever seen." I shrugged. "Haven't you noticed how perfect their skin is? How they don't seem to have any blemishes?"

"Guess I've never had a reason to notice it was out of the ordinary."

Marcus grinned, flourishing his hands as he gestured to his face, highlighting his perfect complexion.

Cocky, this one. But I allowed a smile to tug at my cheeks all the same.

"Anyway, mine and Amity's father, the one we're running away from, well, he's actually my stepfather. My fae father abandoned my mother when he discovered she was pregnant." Marcus nodded, understanding. It wasn't a secret that, though the fae didn't mind taking human lovers, there was a stigma attached to procreating with one. In *sullying* the bloodline.

"And your mother?" Marcus asked, the mischief in his eyes fading.

"She died," Amity and I said in unison.

"Ah. And what was she like?"

I let Amity do the talking for this question. And for a moment, as she described her mother, the kind woman who had protected Amity from her father as long as she lived, I allowed myself to believe my and Amity's mother had been one and the same. That there had been someone who had loved me in my uselessness. Not like Bronger, who, as much as he cared for me, had always prioritized my gift.

"I'm sorry for your loss." Marcus's voice dipped low and gravelly as concern creased his brow.

"Thank you," I said, though I felt a tad guilty about it.

"And what about you?" I asked. "What's your story?"

The smile returned to Marcus's face. "Hold on. You're not finished telling me your story yet."

"I just did," I said, confused.

"No, you told me your parents' story. And not even a very detailed account. I'm asking about you. How old are you anyway?"

"Nineteen."

"Okay, so in your nineteen years of life, there has to be a story in there somewhere. Some adventure, some love story about a handsome young village man...or fae, if that's what you're into," he said casually as I blushed.

"Oh, yes! Have you ever been in love?" Amity asked, her face the only part of her body visible under Marcus's overcoat, which she had draped over her head. "Surely with all the places you've been—"

I coughed, and Amity clamped her jaw down as a look of horror spread over her face, mortified that she had said too much.

"I've never been in love," I said, clearing my throat. "Never really met anyone who interested me enough."

"Then what of all this traveling you've been up to? Surely there's a tale to be told about how you managed that under your stepfather's watch." Marcus settled those copper eyes upon mine, the slightest hint of challenge in his tone.

He knew, or at least guessed, that my and Amity's story was not an honest one. I straightened my shoulders and told myself it didn't matter if he thought I was a liar. As long as he never discovered the truth, he could suspect me as much as he wanted.

"Our mother was on her own a long time before she met Amity's father," was all I said. His cheek twitched, the slightest surrender. My answer had been good enough, even if he still didn't believe me. "If being cold, poorly clothed, and hungry for most of my life makes for a decent story in your eyes, I'd like to hear yours now."

"Oh, but my story is more of an anthology, of sorts. It's so long and winding, I'm afraid it would take two and a half round trips to Nettlewood and back to tell. And how I'd hate to drop you off on an unfortunate cliffhanger. You might end up changing your plans completely and following me home," he said, his eyes darting to my mouth once again.

I scoffed, and doing so sent a pang through my ribcage, where my bruises, courtesy of Amity's father and the traffickers, surely had yellowed. "No story is that good."

"I wouldn't be so sure about that," he said. "Did you hear about the Naenden king and his human bride?"

I had, in fact. Not that I was supposed to have known anything. Bronger made a point of limiting the news we received to information relevant to Avelea. Not to keep us ignorant, but to narrow our focus. Lately, most of my recruitments had taken me so far out on the edges of civilization, where news traveled at the pace of molasses, if it traveled there at all, that I was hardly up to date on the happenings in Avelea.

But news like that traveled like a lone spark fallen upon dry brush, and with half-fae hearing like mine...

I might have gotten sidetracked by the claim that the human queen had evaded her impending execution by simply telling the King of Naenden a never-ending story.

I might have heard she'd be at Rivre for the council meeting.

I might have gone to meet her, just to lay eyes on her, and ended up having a full-blown conversation with her instead.

And that may or may not have been why I was already late fulfilling Bronger's deadline.

"Why would I care what was happening in that wasteland?" I asked.

"Fine," Marcus said. "I won't tell you then. But just know you're missing out."

"I wanna know!" Amity's makeshift hood bobbed as she jumped up and down in a state of utter desperation. I marveled as Amity shed that serious, reserved exterior I'd seen her don when I first met her—how that little girl who had once seemed so mature now bounced up and down, her wide, adoring eyes betraying her obvious crush on our protector... I should have been happy about it, comforted to see a little girl act her age. But now that I'd seen it, I feared Bronger would wipe it away as if it were grime smearing her cheeks.

"Well, for you, Amity, of course..." Marcus said, grasping Amity's hand in his as they skipped merrily through the mountain brush, sharing a story I couldn't hear through the worries clogging my head.

CHAPTER 9

PIPER

Over the next few days, I observed as Amity and Marcus bonded. She rushed next to his side when it was time to gather brush for the fire. He kneeled on the forest floor to troubleshoot her technique when she couldn't get a spark to fly off the edges of his flint. He even allowed her to play with his bow, under strict supervision, of course, once we had already set up our campsite. And though he only allowed her to use one arrow—its feathers jagged and ripped from the endless cycle of nock, shoot, fetch she played—Amity never complained once, nor did she ask Marcus for an additional arrow.

All the while, she divulged heaps of knowledge she must have been hoarding in her little head all this time, having no one else to share it with. Most of the time she lectured him on plants and their medicinal properties, and I wondered how she had collected all that information, or if sometimes, she made it up just to impress him.

I couldn't blame her, if she did.

It had been four days of trekking across the mountain range, yet I felt no closer to home, not when we'd have to skirt around the shoreline to avoid faerie territory, and circle back toward the hills below which the Coup was buried.

I stretched my tired legs across the forest floor as I perched upon a fallen log, the flickering flames entrancing me in their steady rhythm. My eyes grew heavy. I still hadn't been sleeping well, unable as I was to curl up on my right side. As my eyelids faltered, I watched Amity and Marcus from across the campfire.

"Marcus?" she asked, fighting back a yawn as she rested her head against his shoulder.

"Yes?"

"Did you know there's a type of rose that, if you accidentally prick your finger on it, it makes you fall asleep forever?"

"I didn't know that."

"I used to be really scared of it. My neighbor used to grow blueberries beside his rosebush, and I used to get in trouble because I wouldn't go pick them like my father wanted me to."

I flinched at the idea that Amity's father had forced thievery upon his daughter, the girl who had made me go back to the inn just to deposit a few coins in the mailbox for our supplies.

Marcus chuckled, though it was clearly only for Amity's sake, given the look of disgust soiling his face. "You? Afraid of a little rosebush? Now, why can't I believe that?"

"It's alright. I'm not afraid anymore. Sleep isn't all that scary now that I'm older."

My heart clenched in my chest. It didn't take much creativity to imagine why little Amity might have feared sleep. Even children in loving households were prone to nightmares.

Sleep must have been torture for that little girl.

But perhaps not anymore.

Marcus told her a story, and she slumped upon his shoulder, fighting the weight of her eyelids until she lost the battle. He picked her up and carried her to a mat he'd made her with his overcoat. Then he wrapped the overcoat around her, tucking it in the space between Amity and the ground. She looked ridiculous, all swaddled up like that, but something rustled within my chest, regardless.

When Marcus stood, he glanced over at me and shot me a grin. I startled, realizing I'd been staring at him. The leaves cracked and bustled out of his way as he strode toward me.

He gestured to the rotted section of the fallen limb on which I sat. "Is this seat taken?"

"Yes, actually. I'm expecting someone." I might have allowed a self-satisfied grin to escape the taut restraints of my cheeks.

"Clever. Pleased with yourself?" he asked, eyeing my mouth. I snapped it back into its usual grimace, which only served to procure more laughter.

"You're going to wake her, laughing like that," I said, nodding toward Amity.

He shook his head. "That child sleeps like she's never felt safer." His eyes lingered on the small girl, her face a portrait of absolute peace.

"Is she safe?" I asked.

He stared at me a moment, his knuckles tucked into his hips. Then he sighed and sat next to me on my makeshift bench. His solid arm grazed mine, and my chest tightened. I nudged myself further down on the bench. To make room for him, of course. Not at all because I knew as soon as he turned, his face would be close to mine, and the thought of that had my heart pattering in ways I preferred not to acknowledge.

"I promised to protect the two of you, Piper. I don't break a promise lightly. Especially not one to a child," he said.

More to myself than him, I said, "Funny. It seems children are the ones people are the most willing to break promises to."

"Did someone break a promise to you?"

"A lot of someones. To me, I think if you have a kid, then just by doing so you're promising to protect them, to never leave them. Or at least to make sure they're in the hands of someone who can provide for them, keep them safe, even if you can't do it yourself."

We sat in silence for a while, which only made my insides squirm as it forced me to ruminate in the aftermath of sharing such personal information with a stranger.

When he spoke again, I couldn't have welcomed his voice more.

"Do you play?" He nodded toward the bulge in my satchel, where my flute made its presence known.

"I do," I said, plucking my flute from the bag. Marcus reached for it, and after a moment's hesitation, I allowed him to hold it.

He smirked, rolling the wooden, knobby center of my universe in his palms. "Are you always this protective over mediocre instruments?"

I snatched it back and snarled at him, which only encouraged the smirking behavior. "It was a gift," I said, stuffing it back into my satchel.

"Well, I'm sure the music you play makes up for the look of it."

"I assure you, it does."

"Maybe while we're hiking through the woods, you can convince some forest faeries to sell you one of theirs."

What Bronger would give for that. The forest faeries were known for crafting instruments from the rare, white ash trees—instruments specifically designed to amplify magic.

"I'm not sure if those are more powerful, or more illegal." Humans weren't exactly allowed to possess magic, and though I was only half-human, I didn't trust Avelean law to make such a distinction. Not that I cared about such rules when it came to my gift. But the magic that coursed through my blood was much easier to hide than an ornate white ash flute.

"Probably more rare," he said.

I couldn't argue with that.

"You never told me your story earlier," he said, turning his copper gaze from Amity onto me. Apparently I hadn't scooted far enough down the bench, for I could feel his breath heating the frigid air around us. It sent a chill down my spine that had nothing to do with the climate. His pupils reflected the fire, its light bouncing and swaying.

"You asked me in front of Amity," I stalled.

"You don't think she's been through enough on her own to handle it?" He raised a brow, creating divots on his otherwise smooth forehead.

"She shouldn't have to bear more than she already does," I said.

He examined me, his eyes sweeping over the freckles on my nose, circling my crescent eyes, tracing the tips of my ears, which almost always poked out from underneath my hair, despite years of attempting to cover them up. His eyes settled on my mouth again, and I cleared my throat, twisting my hips as if to see his face better, when, in reality, I didn't think I'd catch a full breath of air until one of us backed up.

"And maybe you shouldn't have to bear yours alone," he said. My heart jumped at the thought. Alone. I supposed I was alone, now that he'd mentioned it. Sure, I had my friends—my adopted siblings, sort of—back at the Coup. But we never talked about the loneliness, the holes we each felt where our parents should have been. Where unconditional love should have been.

"Do you always snoop around the personal lives of your employers?" I asked.

Amusement sparked in his eyes, the look of a hunter who'd laid a trap and succeeded. "No, but most of them aren't as pretty as you."

My face went hot, and I bolted off the bench and toward the fire, hoping to mask my embarrassment in the heat of the flame. Branches crunched behind me, betraying that Marcus had followed me, despite my refusing to look at him.

Dangerous. This man was dangerous. If that cerulean arrow bulging from the throat of one of my and Amity's would-be captors wasn't enough to prove that, then the way my heart did somersaults when he was near should have convinced me plenty. And now we stood arm to arm. I stared into the fire. I had no idea what he was staring at. Hopefully not me.

"You haven't told me anything about yourself. Why would I trust you with...with my past?" I asked, refusing to look at him.

When he answered, the usual playfulness in his voice was absent, replaced by the somber resonance of grief. "I was born in a village not unlike the one Amity describes, to a mother and father with few means to take care of us and too many mouths to feed. When I grew old enough to realize I had some agency about whether my belly was full, I made my first bow out of a fallen branch in the woods and some string I bought from the market for three hours' worth of work. It took me three weeks to learn how to shoot the makeshift arrow I'd whittled with my father's knife, but eventually I killed a hare. I skinned it and cooked it in a neighbor's pot and fed it to my younger siblings without letting the older ones know. The youngest always got the smallest of the rations, because my parents figured the smaller the child, the less food was necessary to grow. I wasn't convinced. Eventually, I taught one of the younger ones to hunt, and after that, I left town. I told myself it was because I was being selfless, giving my parents one less mouth to feed. But I knew deep down I was doing it for myself, that I'd grown bored with that village where no one seemed to dream past the night hours, and that by leaving, I was depriving my brothers and sisters of a provider," he said. I tilted my gaze to get a good look at him out of the corner of my eye. He was staring into the flames, his usually robust brown skin looking more pallid than usual.

"That's not fair, though, to expect so much of yourself. It's a parent's job to provide for their children. Not a sibling's."

"You're not exactly taking your own advice," he said, but without the usual teasing lilt to his tone.

"I..." I paused, wishing more than anything for Marcus to stop with the notion that I was a good person. That I was some protector of the innocent. He didn't awaken in the middle of the night, drenched in sweat, to *her* screams. If he were to see her picture, it might prick at his heart, but that would be all.

He would move on.

He didn't close his eyes and see her knuckles drain as she scraped her fingers against the ground as they dragged her away. As I did nothing... "I'm atoning for my own sins."

He peered down at me, a question poorly veiled behind his flickering eyes. Perhaps he understood. Perhaps he had his own atoning to do, and that's why he'd agreed to provide us protection, knowing our funds wouldn't be worth the trouble.

Before he could dig too far into that confession, I turned the conversation back to him. "So, what's the rest of your story? The part after you left home?"

For a breath of a moment, I thought a shadow flickered over his face, but then it passed, and that easygoing smirk returned. "Pretty much what you'd expect from my occupation. I found a contract mercenary in the city, offered to cook, hunt, and clean for him on his journeys if I could be his apprentice. Three years later, I traveled to the far end of Avelea, mostly so he wouldn't hunt me down for stealing his business. And here I am, several jobs later, employed by a pretty girl and her sister."

I allowed myself to chuckle this time. "And which one's which?" I asked.

"Oh, I know better than to answer that question," he said, even as his gaze lingered over the curve of my mouth.

"Do you ever see your family?" I asked, clearing my throat. The question had the desired effect. He glanced away as that same shadow fell over his face.

"Not anymore."

"Why not?" I ventured to ask.

"Because there are consequences to doing nothing."

A scream punctured the wall in my memory, harassing me, calling my name, reminding me of my failure. How I'd let them take her. Knuckles, drained of all color, bulged as her fingers scraped into the ground, into their necks, their wrists, as they tried to contain her. As I did nothing.

I lost the urge to push Marcus further and instead sank to the ground, hugging my knees.

"I'm sorry," I said, rubbing my palms together, as if I could squeeze out the memory. "For whatever happened. I'm sorry."

"Are you taking responsibility for it?" Marcus asked.

"What? No... I just..."

"Then don't apologize," he said, a sad smile skirting the left edge of his lips. He lowered himself, then sat cross-legged on the ground. I imitated him. I wasn't sure how long we sat like that, staring into the flames in silence as the night forest came to life around us, birds and bats singing and calling to one another somewhere in the darkness. I wasn't sure at what point the two of us slumped to the ground, each too exhausted to bother crawling back to our makeshift mats. I wasn't sure whether the enchanting tune of a nearby flute penetrated my dreams, or if my imagination produced the melody itself, drunk on slumber.

When I awoke the next morning, the alluring tune replaying in my mind, my face and hair matted with speckles of leaves and grime from the forest floor, Marcus was still there.

Amity was not.

CHAPTER 10

PIPER

I waited longer than I should have to wake Marcus. Because surely she wasn't *gone*. She'd just wandered off, searching for breakfast. Yes, that had to be it. She adored Marcus. Why not surprise him with breakfast when he awoke?

Every being in the forest must have been out and about that morning, rustling the bushes to my right, to my left, behind me, above me, teasing me. Convincing me that Amity had to be somewhere near, making all the rustling noises herself. I called her name casually, since she was sure to be nearby and would come skipping through the brush any moment now.

Her name echoed from my lips, bounced off tree stumps, and rode on the backs of beetles and salamanders before it rested, muffled in the undergrowth.

Any moment now. Any moment now.

Nothing.

Either she was too far out of range to hear me...

I didn't allow myself to consider the second option.

Loose pebbles sputtered out of my way as I barreled back through the woods to the campsite. Marcus lay next to the hot coals from last night's fire, his face as peaceful as a child's. I launched at him, shaking his shoulders with a fury I couldn't contain, though it should have been directed at me, not at him.

We'd lost her. We'd lost Amity. And she wouldn't have wandered away on her own. Perhaps she'd have wandered far enough that she couldn't hear my voice. But that wasn't like her...

She was long gone.

"Marcus, Marcus, wake up. Wake up, wake up, wake up," I said, throwing even the elbow of my broken arm into his shoulder, allowing the piercing pain to wash over me, chastise me for failing her.

For failing again.

"Erm?" he grunted, his eyes fluttering, not yet registering my panic. I shoved my elbow into his collarbone. And then we were both crying out in pain, both being punished, and not severely enough, for our neglect of this little girl.

"Get off of me," he said, his eyes widening as he scrambled out from underneath my pounding fists. I sank, my knees scraping against the dirt.

"She's gone, Amity's gone," I whispered.

"What?" Marcus said, shooting to his feet. He jumped over what was left of last night's fire, the tips of his shoes barely clearing the hot coals. The overcoat he'd wrapped Amity in fluttered in the breeze as he yanked it from the ground, turning it over and over in his palms, as if he was searching for something. Then he threw it back into the dust and disappeared into the forest.

I cried for the few minutes he was gone. By the time he made it back, I'd wiped my tears and stood.

He didn't look at me at first. His feet kicked up dust while he paced, his hands tucked behind his head as he walked.

Finally, he locked those piercing eyes upon mine, and...and challenged me.

"Where is she?" he asked, his words savage as he questioned me through his labored breaths.

"I don't know. I thought she'd gone out to gather breakfast, to surprise us. But I searched for her and she's gone." My eyes and nose stung as I choked on that last word.

Gone.

"Where is she?" he asked again, and I noticed, for the first time, that his eyes had gone cold.

"I... I told you, I don't know," I said, iron walls rising in my voice as I braced myself for the truth of what Marcus thought of me to come cascading over my frantic, guilty heart. "You don't think... You don't think I did something to her?"

His face didn't as much as twitch as he waited for my answer.

I flung myself to my feet, unsure if I was preparing myself for hand-to-hand combat, which I would likely lose with my arm screaming at me in agony, or to flee into the woods and chase after Amity myself.

"Marcus, we're wasting time. We need to find her," I said, desperation in my voice, wracking my memories of the past few days, trying to figure why in Alondria Marcus suspected I might have wanted to hurt that innocent little girl.

I didn't have to wonder for long.

He stalked toward me until his chin was only a hair's breadth from my forehead. My limbs trembled, and I wondered what he could do to me with those calloused hands of his, how long it would take him to crush my windpipe. Bash my head in.

"I know you're lying. I know she's not your sister," he growled.

"Of course she's my sister." But even the words themselves felt limp on my tongue.

"No. She's not. The story you told me doesn't match up with anything Amity tells me about her family. She catches herself sometimes and has to backtrack to fix it to match yours."

"She's just a little girl," I said, backing up as Marcus advanced on me. Man, he was massive. I gulped. "She's got an imagination, like all children do."

"Amity's not a toddler." His hot breath stung at the raw spot on my cheek where the aftermath of salty tears lingered. "She's not going to launch herself off a cliff thinking she's a bird, and she's too old to confuse her imagination with reality."

Cornered, the bark of the nearest tree scraping against my back, I gritted my teeth and hardened my brow. "We're wasting time. Someone—*something*—has Amity. Accuse me of lying after we find her, but the longer we wait..." I couldn't bring myself to finish the thought, and swallowed.

The corners of Marcus's jaw bulged, but he backed away from me all the same.

"What did that apprenticeship teach you about tracking?" I asked.

IT DIDN'T TAKE LONG, once Marcus had relented on his accusations against me, for him to find a place in the trunk of a nearby tree where something had ripped the bark from its side. And another one. And one behind it.

Droplets of dark blood spattered the ground, too dark to be Amity's.

"She put up a fight," I said, my chest constricting.

Marcus kneeled and examined a blood-speckled leaf in his hands. "I don't like this. That we didn't hear it."

I swallowed. I didn't like it either. There was no way—no *natural* way—that if Amity were screaming and scratching at her kidnapper enough to draw blood, I wouldn't have woken up. Not in the painfully light sleep I'd been suffering through each night since Amity's father snapped my arm in two.

We searched for her for the better half of the morning, weaving through the trees, hunting for any sign of a struggle.

A long, dark hair suspended in a tree branch here, a drop of blood there.

Marcus marked the trees with his hunting knife as we traced her kidnapper's path. It was a good thing he did, too. We had to double back several times, the trail having gone cold in the direction we'd chosen.

Eventually, we reached a clearing. A pool reflected the sun's speckled light through the canopy above. My mouth dry from screaming Amity's name, I approached the pool and discarded my satchel. Then I leaned down, cupping my hands in the water. It was so frigid, it was a wonder it hadn't frozen over. I was just bringing it to my lips, preparing my throat for how unpleasant it would be to swallow, when instead, I screamed.

For, in its reflection, I saw Amity, eyes closed, arms crossed, lying at the bottom of the pool.

THE CHILL of the water stung, threatening to choke out the air I'd gulped as I dove into the pool. I pulled at the static water, willing it to sink me faster, faster, faster. I had no idea how long she'd been under the pool, if she was even...

I pushed all thoughts from my head.

There was only one left.

Faster, faster, faster.

I reached Amity's body much too late for my lungs, which were nearly out of breath. It took every bit of self-preservation in me not to gasp when needles of pain jolted up my fingertips where I grazed her frigid face. Her pale, graying cheeks were clammy. I didn't dare feel her neck for a pulse. Instead, I wrapped my arms around her and realized I'd been forcing myself through the water with both arms. I'd ripped my sling in my haste. As if my body suddenly realized it too, pain cascaded through my bones, piercing my skull.

I pushed away the pain, the tattered remains of my soaked sling fluttering about us, and tried to wrap my arm around Amity's waist, but my fingers met an invisible force as I attempted to slide them under her back. I tried again, but it was as if a magnetic force tethered Amity's spine to the bottom of the pool. When I tugged at her arm, it went taut as soon as it stretched to its full length.

Pain exploded in my lungs. I'd been underwater too long. No, no, no. If Amity wasn't already dead, she'd surely be by the time I went back to the surface for air and dove back down.

Something wrapped around my waist, squeezing and pulling me

upward. I looked up and saw the outline of a face, blurred by the shadows of the water at the bottom of the pool. Marcus. He nodded toward the surface, commanding me to swim upward. Panic set in as I looked toward the surface, at the rays of sun bouncing on top of the water, which might as well have been as far away as the sun itself.

My lungs wrestled for control of my breath, but I fought back, thrashing my arms above me, dragging my body upward through the water. Up, up, up. I wasn't going to make it. The sunlight taunted me as it danced on the surface, the surface I'd never reach. The surface Amity would never reach.

But then my fingers found solid air, making way for my nose, my mouth, which inhaled an equal mixture of water and air. I coughed and sputtered as Marcus's hand touched my back and propelled me toward the shoreline.

My senses came to me with the next gulp of air.

"No, no. We have to try again. Amity's down there. She's too heavy. You have to help me," I said, twisting around in the water to escape Marcus's grasp. To my surprise, he wasn't looking at me, wasn't paying the slightest attention to what I was saying. Instead, he stared at something behind me, a look of solemn dread written across his face.

"Marcus?" I asked, my voice weak and sore.

He simply gestured for me to turn around.

I did, and my eyes found the shore.

My eyes found *them*.

CHAPTER 11

PIPER

The forest faeries peered down at us in curiosity, wickedness lining their thin smiles. One cracked his narrow lips to reveal a set of jagged teeth, eerily white, a stark contrast to his skin, which looked to be the texture of dead leaves after a heavy rainfall.

"Hello there," one of them cooed, guttural sounds popping between his words, fragmenting them.

I wasn't above begging. "Please. Please help us. Our friend..."

I couldn't form the words. Couldn't finish the sentence.

Our friend is drowning.

Our friend is dying.

My jaw caught, but even if my numb lips could do anything but tremble, would it make a difference? If I knew anything about forest faeries, it would be a mercy if Marcus and I ended up dead at the bottom of the pool, with Amity, in one piece.

Marcus seemed to agree, because as we treaded water he placed a hand on my collarbone, careful not to put pressure on my injury, and pulled me backward ever so slightly to position me behind his muscular frame.

The faerie on the right, the slighter one that I thought might be female judging by her curvier frame, hissed. "Oh, I wouldn't worry too much about your friend. She's just playing a game with us, that's all." Wickedness lined her toothy grin, her pale, irisless eyes painting the terrifying illusion that she had rolled her eyes back into her craggy skull.

"How does one win this game?" Marcus asked.

The female giggled, a high-pitched clicking noise that had my teeth grinding. "I thank you for asking. I must apologize. Your little human friend is dead."

My heart sank to the bottom of the pool, died with Amity and joined her in her watery grave. Dead, dead. The child was dead. Just like the first...

They must have seen the grief in my eyes, for the faeries giggled in unison, "Oh, not the forever kind of dead. Not yet, at least."

I choked back a sob, though I couldn't distinguish whether it was one of relief or dread.

"What other kind of death is there?" Marcus clenched his teeth as we shivered in the water.

We needed to get out. We'd die from hypothermia if we stayed here too long. But something told me not to go near the faeries who had kidnapped an innocent girl and caused her temporary death, whatever that meant.

"Suspension?" The female's voice dripped with condescension, as if we should have known that term. "Haven't you heard of it?"

"Obviously not, so just tell us what it is!" I said, losing my patience in an outburst that came out much more juvenile sounding than I had meant it to. Tears stung at my eyes, and my limbs went numb. The only feedback I got confirming I was still treading was that I hadn't sunk under the water yet.

"She's right. We'll play your game. Just tell us the rules before we freeze to death and before any harm comes to that child," Marcus said.

The forest faeries exchanged disappointed glances and sighed. Apparently taunting us was just as fun to them as whatever game they were playing.

The male turned back to us. "Very well, then. Though I can already tell the two of you are no fun. Your girlchild is currently in a state of suspension, meaning her soul is *suspended* in the realm between life and death. She could just as easily come back to our realm as she could slip into the abyss. Her heart does not beat, her lungs do not breathe, but her spirit dwells in her body just as it always has."

Amity's heart no longer beat.

I couldn't breathe.

"Why can't we move her from the bottom of the pool?" Marcus asked, clearly not interested in their long-winded explanation of where Amity's spirit currently resided.

The forest fairies answered in unison, dreadful amusement spreading across their faces, like the look a feral cat gives the roach it's decided to torture for a while before eating. "The pool listens to us, that's why." Razors for teeth flashed in their smiles.

With fangs like that, I was positive we were getting eaten today.

"Then will you please tell it to release the girl, and we can be on our merry way?" Marcus's jaw clenched, protruding at the joint, so obviously holding back a threat, trying to appease the faeries rather than anger them. The vein in his temple bulged.

"Not until you've played the game!" the faeries sang in unison.

"Tell us the rules," I said, my voice full of gravel from the cold that burned my nostrils and throat as I breathed, from the water that had cascaded into my lungs just to be coughed back up in a fit.

"The rules are: solve the riddle, and we free the girl."

My pulse heightened. I was good at riddles.

"Tell it to us then," Marcus said.

It was the male that answered this time, his voice the sharp tenor to his partner's sickly soprano. "Oh, but you'll die before you can solve it, if you stay floating in the water like that!"

The female batted eyelashes thick as seaweed. "Yes, please do come up to land, where our fire may warm you." I looked around, and indeed, a small fire smoked to our left, just beyond the pool banks.

Marcus whispered through gritted teeth, which hardly moved as he spoke. "That can't be an innocent invitation."

"Do we have a choice?" I whispered back, sure I had not done nearly as good a job at disguising our personal conversation from the faeries. My legs had gone numb, and each breath felt like shards of icicles spearing through my throat and puncturing my lungs.

Marcus grunted in return. We waded to the shore, and I stole one last glance back at Amity, her dark hair floating wistfully at the bottom, her eyes closed, her face immovable.

It's not real, it's not real, it's not real, I told myself, clinging onto the hope it was true, that the faeries weren't playing some nasty trick on us, forcing us to be their entertainment as we fought for a girl who had been dead all along. My spine shivered as I stepped out of the pool. The breeze, which had been pleasant this morning, now felt abrasive on my tingling cheeks.

It's not real, it's not real, it's not real. It's not real, and you're good at riddles.

Marcus and I lingered behind the faeries as they led us to their campsite. Now that we were on land, I noted that both the faeries stood a head taller than Marcus.

When he leaned into me and whispered, the chattering of his teeth clanked against my eardrum, amplified by the curve in my ear. "You'd think creatures that lived in trees wouldn't be making fires."

"Are they telling the truth?" I asked. "That she's not really dead?"

Marcus didn't answer at first, but set his face toward the faeries. "They better hope so, if they're not ready to journey on to that dark abyss themselves."

I wondered then about Amity, whether she was conscious in her state of suspension. If she knew she was teetering on the precipice of life and death, and, if she had the choice, which one she would choose. Perhaps the abyss wasn't so terrifying if she could see it for what it truly was. But then fear rippled through my body. That she would choose to leave. And that I'd never truly know if the choice had been hers, or the result of the faeries growing bored with Marcus and me.

"Wait." Marcus's firm hand flung out in front of me, his palm on my collarbone, stopping me in my tracks. He nodded toward the ground, where my boot hovered above a hole the size of my thigh. My stomach plummeted.

A snake den.

The idea of accidentally plunging my foot into a serpent's lair would have made me queasy, even without the pressure of needing to save Amity from her fate.

I swallowed and nodded, a silent gesture of thanks to Marcus, before we continued.

The fire was unlike any I'd seen constructed. Not in looks, for it burned orange with tiny blue flecks at the tips, just like the kind Marcus made at our campsites. It was in its superior function that this fire was different. The faeries had drawn a circle in the dirt around the fire, and as soon as I stepped into the circle a wondrous heat enveloped me, dried my sopping clothes, and wrapped not just my body in its arms, but my mind, too. Peace washed over my consciousness. My trembling limbs went still, and even the pain in my broken arm wandered far away.

I wondered if this was what a baby felt immediately after a feeding: warm at its mother's breast, drunk on a full belly. What a cruel world we lived in, that we couldn't figure out a way to hold onto that peace, that we couldn't remember those moments when absolutely nothing was wrong in the world.

Like now. Nothing was wrong now.

But that didn't seem right.

Downright illogical, actually.

Something was always wrong, especially in my life.

I opened my eyes, which I hadn't realized I'd shut, and gazed around the campfire, searching for that something that was wrong. But then I remembered it was such a silly thing to search for. Why would I want to remember a bad thing when I was feeling such good things?

Standing next to Marcus was a good thing. I looked up at him, noticing his firm jaw, how it was only accentuated by his shaved head. This was a man that stood before me. A protector. I marveled at how truly handsome he was, with his flawless skin, his smile that overtook his entire face. Bidding cares to fly far, far away.

Cares? What were those? And why had they flown away?

But no, I reminded myself, I should think more about Marcus. For, not only was he a good-looking man, he was a *good* man. And I hadn't known many of those. But how did I know he was a good man, again? I searched my memory, scrambling for these bits of goodness, for that was all I wanted to think of anymore, goodness. And I found them, after shuffling awhile—bright images tucked away in the back of my mind. Marcus laughing, telling a joke I couldn't quite hear. Another voice, not mine, giggling. And then he picked her up and carried her on his shoulders...

A girl...

Amity.

My mind whipped back into focus just long enough for me to shove Marcus backward.

But I didn't know why I'd done such a silly thing. He looked upset, and I hated that he was upset. What a silly thing to be, when one could choose only to think of good. His eyes went wide, and he struck at me. I screamed, and he grabbed my wrist, pulling me away, away from the happy and the good.

And then I was cold. And broken. And Amity was at the bottom of a pool, halfway dead.

I whipped my head back toward the campfire, where the faeries stoked it casually, as if they hadn't suspended above the flames a pot large enough to fit two human adults.

The circle they'd drawn in the dirt—it was doused in magic. Magic they'd used to lure Marcus and me into a false sense of safety while they prepared to boil us for breakfast. When I pushed him, he must have stepped out of the circle and broken the enchantment. That's why he'd grabbed me, to yank me out of there before I waltzed into the cauldron, thinking it was a hot spring.

"You liars!" Grief washed over me, flooded my veins. What if the game wasn't real, and this had only been a trap, which would mean that Amity was just as dead as she'd been when I first noticed her body at the bottom of the pool?

I reached for my knife, but Marcus's hand clamped over mine as it reached the hilt, which rested on my hip. "If you kill them, there's no guarantee we'll get Amity back."

"Maybe if they die, it'll break the suspension they have her trapped in," I hissed, not yet willing to let go of the desire to send my knife barreling through at least one of their throats.

"Or maybe it will seal it instead." Marcus's expression oozed apprehension, but he released his hand from mine all the same, a gesture signaling he knew we'd meet one another at the same conclusion.

My shoulders slipped. He was right. The Fates had blessed me with my gift from an early age, yet I still knew so little about magic, about how the fae manipulated it to their own will.

"You're a strong-minded pair, aren't you?" the female said. "Pity, the strong-minded always taste the best. Ah, well. At least you'll stick around to play our game, even if we have to find our lunch elsewhere." Her eyelids narrowed, and I was sure that, if her eyes had contained any remnant of color, they would have glinted.

"Tell us the riddle so we can be on our way," Marcus said, his jaw still bulging. I wondered how he did that, maintained so much control over his voice, when he would clearly rip the throats out of these creatures if given the chance.

The male held up his palms, his scales grim as damp leaves. "Alright then, no need to rush."

"And put that fire out. We're not playing your game until you do," Marcus said.

"You're not really in the position to bargain, are you, human?" the female hissed, so clearly pleased with herself. "For us, it's a game. For you, it's a loved one."

Marcus's throat bulged, as if he had just swallowed whatever rash words he had considered spewing at them. He brushed his fingers against his thumb, as if he held an imaginary arrow. For the first time I realized that his bow and quiver were gone. He must have taken both of them off before plunging into the pool after me. I scanned the camp, and, sure enough, cerulean arrows peeked over the edge of Marcus's quiver, which leaned with his bow against a log within the enchanted circle, surely left there to taunt him.

The cold enveloping me and freezing my limbs no longer

mattered. With my clothes dried by the hypnotizing warmth of the enchanted circle, my hatred heated my body quite sufficiently.

"That's not true, though," I said, hoping my line of reasoning had at least a foothold in reality. "Your game *is* your loved one. It's the reason you exist. It's what sustains you, keeps you from drowning yourself in the pool to escape the boredom. How else can you stand to live so long?" I asked, desperately grasping at anything I could to manipulate these masters of treachery. "How old are you, anyway? You've got to have been at this for centuries. If we leave, how long will it be before someone as *strong-minded* comes along to play with you?"

The female jeered, but the male did not. Instead, he set those empty white eyes upon me. I wished he had irises. I hadn't realized how much I relied on them to interpret what people were thinking.

"Come," he said, holding his hand out to the female. She reeled at him, but didn't argue when he threw a blanket over the fire, smothering it.

The line drawn into the dirt disappeared.

"Well, this does make it more interesting, darling," the female said, caressing the knotted shoulder of her companion.

CHAPTER 12

PIPER

The riddle was a short one.

"The key to saving your friend dwells with the answer to this verse," the male faerie had said before reciting it to us.

The enemy of man, he's called,
There's something that he's lacking.
Gift him one of yours,
And he's sure to keep attacking.

Marcus and I worked through the riddle in hushed tones, neither of us ecstatic about the idea of the faeries overhearing us.

Unfortunately, the lesser faeries didn't exactly turn out to be *lesser* in their hearing.

Marcus paced, just as he had this morning when we'd first discovered that Amity was missing. "The enemy of man, that has to be talking about the fae, right?"

"I don't know. That seems too simple." I bit my fingernails, a habit I'd quit long ago, but I didn't think I'd regret relapsing if it helped me focus, not when Amity's soul was currently walking the tightrope between this life and the next. "Besides, what are the fae lacking that humans have?"

Marcus seethed, throwing his palms up to the sky. "Oh, I dunno. Hearts, compassion, a sense of urgency?"

"Humans are guilty of all the same cruelties as the fae," I said, though I thought he might be on to something with the *sense of urgency* bit.

"I thought you hated the fae," Marcus said.

"I do. I'm just trying to be objective, that's all. You might be right about the sense of urgency part. But the riddle says, whatever it's lacking, man can give it back, as a gift. You can't gift fae a sense of urgency."

"You can if you threaten to kill them."

"That's not exactly a gift, then, is it?"

"No," Marcus said, "but it would cause the fae to keep attacking."

I bit my cheek, nodding. Marcus had a good point. Answering *fae* seemed to fit the riddle. Well, mostly fit. Like one of those wooden puzzles they kept in inns, the ones with thousands of pieces, where you'd get to the end only to find the last piece didn't fit at all.

Besides, *fae* seemed too easy.

"It's the *one of yours* part that's bothering me," I said, tapping my fingers at my numb lips. "Even if you could gift someone your sense of urgency, it's not quantifiable. You can't give someone one sense of urgency. You can't give someone one sense of anything. That means the gift has to be something concrete."

The faeries stood next to the suffocated fire, their hands behind their backs, looking unnervingly innocent as they watched—and probably heard—us ponder. While the male—the more passive of the two, I'd decided—allowed his gaze to bounce toward the ground anytime I caught him staring at me, the female held my gaze with those milky, dead eyes of hers, a sneer angling her already crooked nose.

I took a deep breath. If I let the faeries distract me by simply observing me, I'd be letting them win. "So let's take a step back.

What's another creature that would be considered the enemy of man?"

"A woman?" Marcus asked, then recoiled as I shot him a nasty look. "What? I'm trying to think like a faerie. They have to hear stories about wives murdering their husbands, husbands getting murdered because they slept with someone else's wife... That sort of thing."

"They can't get that much traffic out here. They've got to be the most uncultured creatures around, hiding out in these mountains that could hardly entice a hunter." I glared at the faeries, who I was now certain could hear me by the way the tips of their ears flinched at the jab. But then my words spurred something inside me, a thought.

"What?" Marcus asked, picking up on the realization in my expression.

"The forest is all they know," I whispered, quietly this time, lest they hear. "The answer is probably something they see every day, something that lives in the forest." I scanned the area, swept my eyes over the pool, the trees, even the pinecones, but nothing seemed to fit. "An enemy of man..." Wolves came to mind, but I couldn't think of anything a wolf might be missing. Coyotes, either.

But then...

My eyes found it, gaping in the earth, and I thought myself a fool for not realizing it before.

I stepped backward and grabbed Marcus's arms, turning him toward me so that his body was between me and the faeries, blocking any attempt of theirs to lipread. Apparently Marcus wasn't fond of this situation, because he twisted his arms out of my grasp and pivoted, monitoring the faeries in his peripheral.

"It's a snake," I whispered.

"A snake?" Marcus asked, but then he tucked his head and pinched his brow in understanding. "Enemy of man. They're missing their limbs." His face slackened in disappointment. "But you can't give them your limbs."

"Not literally, no, but if you stick your hand in their den, they're definitely going to attack."

Marcus eyed me with hesitation.

"I know that's it. The male has been glancing at the ground all along. I thought he was avoiding my gaze, but it's the answer to the riddle," I said.

The faeries shifted on their feet behind Marcus's back.

"You're sure?" Marcus asked, and I noted the desperation in his eyes. I wondered which of us would blame ourselves more if we failed Amity.

"I'm sure." Though I wasn't. But I had a feeling.

He nodded and turned back to the faeries.

I straightened my shoulders. "The answer is a snake."

Mischievous grins overtook the faeries' thin lips in unison. My heart sank. The answer was wrong. I'd gotten it wrong, and Amity was going to die.

But then the male spoke up. "Clever halfling. I'm impressed."

I bristled at the derogatory term, but tried not to let it show on my face. Besides, he was just trying to bait me. He was just mad I'd gotten it right.

I'd gotten it right.

I'd gotten it right, and Amity didn't have to die.

"We played your game. She solved the riddle. Now free the girl," Marcus said.

"With pleasure." The female snapped her fingers.

Nothing happened.

"You might be playing a game, but we're not," Marcus said, advancing toward the faeries. "Free her. Now."

"I already did." The female's lips curved into a circle, and I thought I heard her whisper, "Oops!"

I spun on my heels and ran toward the pool. Through the reflection of the sun, I could see Amity. And, sure enough, the faerie was right.

She had freed Amity.

From her suspension, but not from the pool.

Amity kicked and thrashed against the water, struggling to lift herself, though her back remained glued to the floor.

I jolted forward and prepared myself to dive when the male faerie called out to me. "I wouldn't do that if I were you. It would be futile. You won't be able to move her."

My hands shook as Marcus and I both exchanged our relief for horror. I could tell by the way his eyes widened, his jaw went slack, that we'd realized it at the same time. We'd allowed ourselves to be duped, and Amity was going to be the one to pay.

Fury overtook Marcus's face. Gone was that gentle male who'd humored Amity for hours on end, listening patiently to her wild tales.

This wasn't Amity's friend who stood before me.

It was her avenger.

"Let her go!" He lunged for the male faerie and grabbed him by the throat, lifting him from the ground.

"Marcus, no!" I yelled, sure the female would stake him any moment, but the faeries both just smiled at him.

"The spell won't lift when we die. You can't save her without us," the female said.

A savage grin broke the hard lines of Marcus's face. "I'm sure one of you will do just fine."

His knuckles paled when he crushed the male faerie's airway.

The male faerie's smile warped into an expression of shock, which petrified itself upon the dead faerie's face in an instant.

The female screamed. She lashed for Marcus, thick claws emerging from her withered arms. He caught her right hand, but not her left. She swung at him and swiped him across the face, leaving three red streaks across his cheek.

I unsheathed my knife and reared back. I would not miss. The fury blistering my soul told me that much. But just as my arm extended, just as the hilt was about to slip through my fingertips, I clutched it tight in my palm, remembering what the faerie had said.

If they both died, there'd be no way to help Amity.

My mind raced, counting up the seconds since the faeries had lifted the suspension, reminding me I only had moments to save her. There had to be some way to break the enchantment. After all, *all* enchantments could be broken.

I tugged at my scalp, willing the thought to appear from thin air and deposit itself inside my skull. What had the faeries said about why Amity was stuck at the bottom?

The pool listens to us.

Just like the children listened to me. I looked around for my satchel, perhaps if I could find my flute... but my stomach sank as something in my soul shook its head—my gift telling me it wouldn't work, that my flute didn't possess that kind of power...

I could have screamed, but my gift stroked at my soul, as if to tell me something. To urge me not to give up. My flute wasn't powerful enough, but...

But theirs was.

Because my flute was man-made. What had Bronger always said?

If only we could get your hands on a faerie-made instrument.

I'd heard it, hadn't I, in my sleep last night? I'd thought I was dreaming up the melody, but... The faeries must have played a tune to enchant Marcus and me. That's why we hadn't woken up.

I scanned the area, looking for anything resembling a musical instrument around the campground. Marcus and the faerie wrestled next to the dead male's body, the wails of the female waking the crows in the trees until they swarmed overhead. He was going to kill her.

And then they'd both be dead, and it wouldn't matter that we'd solved the riddle.

The riddle.

What was it the male faerie had said before he'd recited it?

The key to saving your friend dwells with the answer to this verse.

The faeries couldn't lie, and he'd definitely claimed we could save Amity, not just free her. And the wording had been odd, hadn't it?

He'd said it dwelled *with* the answer, when *within* the answer would have sounded more natural.

In a moment teetering between clarity and insanity, I lunged for the snake den, shoving my hand into the hole before my mind had a chance to stop me. My fingers wrapped around something cold, hollow. When I pulled the flute from the hole, shadows danced around the edges of the intricate engravings, cast by streaks of sunlight slipping through the canopy overhead.

When the flute touched my lips, it seemed to play itself. A slow, mournful tune that stopped the flock of crows in midair, hovering above us, their wings fluttering in synchrony with the somber melody. The entire forest froze to listen to me play, the tune solemn and forceful. Commanding. Out of the corner of my eye, I glimpsed a stillness. The faerie and Marcus had stopped their fighting. They stared, but not at me. I turned just slightly enough to follow their eyes.

I might have gasped had I had the choice. Had the song not willed itself into being.

For the pool was no longer a pool, but a hole in the ground. Sunlight flickered through the clear water that floated above us, suspended in the air as if it were as airy as a cloud.

The faerie swore, then muttered something I couldn't hear.

Three staccato notes later, the water reared. It struck the faerie before even her scream could escape my wrath, and coiled itself around her body, a serpent savoring the last breaths of its next meal.

It took her the rest of the song to drown.

CHAPTER 13

PIPER

Marcus hadn't bothered to stay and watch the faerie meet her end. As soon as the water sprang upon her, he'd leapt to his feet and run straight for the gaping hole in the ground. His foot had slipped at the edge, he'd been running so fast, and he plummeted out of sight.

My gift hadn't allowed me to join him until it finished its song, until the faerie's face bloated with death.

Water crashed to the ground, splaying across the forest floor, soaking into the earth faster than it should have. The faerie's body slapped the wet ground. So did the flute when I dropped it. I ran. When I reached the edge of the hole, I leaped off the edge and tilted my feet, allowing them to carry me down the slope as I slid in the mud.

No, in the dust.

My song had ripped all the moisture out of the ground.

When I reached the bottom, Amity was giggling hysterically, tears soaking her cheeks, hiccups and bouts of laughter separating her sobs, clinging to Marcus, who had tumbled the entire way down the hole and landed on his back.

I allowed myself a handful of tears before I swallowed it all—the fear, the pain, the relief—and told myself that I'd let myself cry some more when Amity wasn't looking. If it was anyone's turn to be shaken up, it was Amity's, and right now what she needed most was someone to absorb the impact of her trembling. Possibly two people.

"Amity," I said, kneeling down beside her and stroking her cheek. It was still wet and clammy from being soaked in water. From being dead. I slid my fingers underneath her right earlobe, just to be sure this wasn't some nasty trick of the faeries.

Her pulse thumped against my fingertips, quick and panicked, but there.

She peered up at me, those big brown eyes full of salty tears. Her whole body trembled, and I realized she must be freezing.

"Marcus, give me your coat." Without questioning, he pushed himself off the ground and shed the huge overcoat. Then, understanding my intentions, turned his back to us.

"We've got to get you out of these wet clothes," I said. Amity nodded and pushed herself to her feet. Together, we stripped off the wet garments. I shed my undertrousers, thankful that at least the faeries had possessed the good decency to dry me off before trying to boil me alive. As soon as I did, chill bumps coursed up my calves. Though my robe still covered my legs and protected me from the embarrassment of Marcus seeing me half-naked, it did little to break the wind.

My trousers practically swallowed Amity, but we rolled them up, so at least they were walkable. When I wrapped Marcus's overcoat around her tiny, shivering frame, she melted into my chest.

"I'm so sorry." Words that meant nothing as her wet hair chilled my neck.

"You don't have to be sorry," she said. "I knew you'd come, and you did."

Her words wrung my heart. Her inability to see that, had I protected her as I ought, the faeries wouldn't have had the opportunity to take her. She was thanking me for rescuing her from a peril I never should have let her fall into in the first place.

Marcus shuffled impatiently close by. "May I turn around now?"

"Yes, I'm decent," Amity said, and I fought back a relieved smile. If Amity was worried about such things, concerned with seeming older and more mature than she was, then she was okay. Her journey between the realms of life and death had not altered her too much.

Marcus took a few trips out of the pit to gather kindling and to retrieve the satchel I'd discarded at the edge of the pool. Then he made a fire at the bottom of the pit while I held Amity, rocking her back and forth until the cruel breeze finally dried her hair and the shivering settled a little.

When he was done, he laid Amity's clothes out next to the fire. We'd wait until they dried, until her body calmed from its state of shock, before we traveled any further.

"Are we safe here?" Amity asked, her voice muffled by my shoulder. "Will more of them come and be angry you killed their friends?"

Marcus was the one to answer. "Forest faeries travel in pairs and rarely get along with others of their species. If this was where the two of them had settled, I guarantee there's not another forest faerie within miles of here."

"Oh," Amity said, sounding relieved. The chain around my chest loosened a bit, too. There wouldn't be any more faeries coming for Amity. Not tonight, at least. Not that they would have gotten to her again if they tried.

Amity would sleep next to me from now on.

Marcus stoked the fire one more time, then came and kneeled beside us, brushing Amity's hair from her forehead. "Can you tell us what happened, ragamuffin?"

I pulled her tighter into myself, away from his touch. "She needs rest, not to relive what just happened."

"Why don't you let her tell us what she needs," Marcus said, his tone firm but not scolding.

Amity twisted in my arms and sat in my lap, facing Marcus. "They came in the middle of the night. I woke up because one of them put its slimy hand over my mouth. I tried to scream, but its hands were so big, it clamped my mouth shut." She motioned to a new bruise forming around her jaw. The bruises on her neck from our encounter with the thieves had only just settled into a pale yellow. At the sight of the contrast, my fingernails dug into my palm. "I tried to fight them. I scratched at them and bit the lady one's hand. Her blood was thick and sticky," she said, shuddering at the memory. "They took me all the way back to the campfire, and I was all happy for a while, and the female whispered something to me, and I fell asleep..."

She trailed off, her head cocking to the side ever so slightly, as if she didn't see the next bit of the story coming, despite having lived it.

"And then I woke up, and I was drowning. But, as hard as I tried, I couldn't make myself swim. I know how to swim." She peered at Marcus, her eyes brimming with earnest conviction, as if this was the most important thing in the world to convince him of. "But then the water lifted off me, and it wasn't holding me anymore, and I could move. And I heard you playing, just like you did that first night—" She clamped her hand over her mouth, her oval eyes enlarging. "I mean, that first night I heard you play. After you saved up and bought your flute."

I glanced at Marcus, who showed no sign of suspicion or confusion on his face, surely for Amity's sake. So the child wouldn't feel guilty for having given away that we were not sisters. I was grateful to him for allowing her this simple kindness.

Somehow, I'd begun to expect nothing less than kindness from the archer.

"And when you were unconscious, after the faeries lulled you to sleep with their spell, did you see anything?" Marcus asked.

I swallowed my rebuke as I noticed the crease between his eyebrows, the pleading in his eyes.

There are consequences to doing nothing.

Was that why Marcus was so curious about the life after this one, where we passed onto when we died? In the time that he was away, had one of his loved ones gone on before him?

Amity opened her mouth, but her eyes went glassy, and she clamped it shut. When she finally answered, her voice was weak, unsure. "I... don't think I'm supposed to tell you," she said, though she craned her neck and stared off into the distance, as if to ask the universe if that was correct.

"Was it... unpleasant?" Marcus asked. I held my breath, dreading Amity's answer. If the world to come was severe for an innocent child, what would it be for me?

"No." Amity shook her head, her voice going chipper again, like she'd sounded yesterday giggling with Marcus. "It was much better than being kidnapped by faeries and drowning."

Marcus and I released uncomfortable chuckles.

IT TOOK the rest of the afternoon for Amity's clothes to dry, so we camped in the newly formed pit. When the sky grew dark and Amity fell asleep, I tucked her in by my side and lay down next to her, interlocking my fingers in her tiny, cold hand. Marcus sat on the other side of her, watching the edges of the forest clearing. Her protector. I wondered how much coin I'd have left by the end of this journey. If we'd make it through the robbers, market vendors, and street musicians with anything to jangle in my purse. He certainly seemed worthy of much more than I could offer.

Still, why make a deal with someone without specifying the pay? Did he think my coin purse was bulging with rubies? I supposed he might have mistaken me for a jewel thief.

If so, he wasn't far off.

Except, what I stole was far more precious.

Amity's breath went shallow, and her stillness unsettled me so, I kept feeling the side of her ribs just to make sure she hadn't fallen back into some suspension state, one last curse from the faeries we'd sent packing to whatever lied beyond.

"So..." Marcus's voice rumbled in the dark, and I jumped at the unexpected sound. The forest was eerily quiet, and neither of us had spoken in hours.

"Mhmm?" I tried to ask casually, thankful his back had been to me when I jolted. He spun in the dirt to face me on the other side of Amity.

"That thing you did, with the making the water float and then enchanting it like it was a viper. You do that often?"

"Only on weekends."

Marcus blinked twice in the firelight before he allowed himself to chuckle. "You're the strangest girl I've ever met. Did you know that? I can't get a read on you."

"Maybe I prefer it that way," I said, shrugging in a desperate attempt to mask the fact I was cringing at how dumb that sounded.

"Mmm." He traced his finger into the dirt next to Amity's head. Her mouth was hanging open, her drool forming a puddle beneath her lips. "Seriously though," he continued. "How'd you know to do that?"

I rubbed my sore eyes with my palms. "Just a lucky guess."

He side-eyed me, though he continued his doodling in the dust. "You mean to tell me that you stuck your hand into a snake's den, pulled out a magic flute, played the most enchanting tune I've ever heard, sicced the entire volume of the pool upon that faerie, and that was all just a lucky guess."

"I'm a really good guesser." I tried on that grin of his, feeling out the curve of it on my lips, the narrowing of my eyes that dared him to question me.

I wasn't exactly accustomed to having to lie. Lying required talking. And talking required another person. And the only people I usually talked to were children who were used to not having their questions answered.

Then there was the fact that I was pretty positive he knew I was lying.

I wasn't used to that either.

"Uh-huh." Marcus tilted his eyes down on me as he leaned his head back ever so slightly. "Now why don't I believe that?"

I sighed, weighing the risk of telling Marcus bits of the truth, tiny snippets of my life, my powers that were fairly benign. He wasn't a fool. He knew I had been lying to him about my and Amity's relationship. And he seemed the curious type, the type to dig until he got an answer that satisfied him. Perhaps I could whet the edge of his curiosity with a few extremely tiny windows to the truth.

Or perhaps he'd drill straight through the holes until the truth collapsed around me. But, if he was inclined toward such things, he'd probably try to do that anyway, no matter how much I told him.

"How much do you know about half-fae?" I asked.

"Oh, just that their bones break like a human's would, that they're inclined to lying, and that they're insanely pretty." The campfire danced in his copper eyes, and I made the mistake of allowing my face to go hot and my gaze to slip from his stare, which seemed to only encourage him, for he continued, "But, then again, I might be making generalizations. You're the only half-fae I've met." A comment that only served to deepen the blotches I knew were forming on my pale neck.

"But what do you know of our magic?" I asked, eager to steer the topic elsewhere.

"Nothing other than what I saw with my very own eyes when you played that little trick of yours today."

"Okay, well, believe it or not, I haven't met many half-fae either. We don't exactly have the most extensive life expectancy, what with most everyone in the known world resenting our existence... But I've met a few, read any books I could get my hands on, and of course I know a little just from being myself. The high fae learn from an early age to subdue magic, to conquer it and force it to do their will. Magic isn't exactly a fan of this, but I don't think there's much that the magic can do about it either. The fae bloodline is so intertwined with magic that it reproduces when they do, and fae children are born with it. Which means half-fae are also born with it. But we're a little different. We can't beat our magic into submission like the high fae and the faeries can. Which is why I think the magic actually prefers us. Though I have heard that not all half-fae are gifted with magic, so maybe it only chooses those of us it likes the best." My gift purred, and I found my spine straightening, my shoulders taking up space, my chin lifting.

Marcus eyed me, then mirrored my posture, sending a wave of

embarrassment through my limbs that made me curl up into myself like a threatened insect. But then he spoke, and I couldn't find a trace of mocking in his voice. Only respect tempered with suspicion. "I could see that. But that doesn't explain why you can make water move by playing a song that would make a dirge cry."

"Well, it's not really me—"

"So you're possessed?" Marcus said, inching ever so slightly away from me.

Heat flooded my cheeks. "No! It's not like that at all—" But then Marcus flashed that cocky grin, the one where his tongue barely protruded between his perfectly straight teeth.

He was teasing me. Marcus was teasing me.

And, for some reason I wasn't keen on exploring, I preferred that to him fearing me. "Well, yes. I mean, kind of. But it's not what you're thinking. I'm the one playing the flute, but it's like... like my gift is directing me."

"Your gift?"

"What?"

"That's an interesting word for the sentient being possessing your body. Just saying," he said.

I couldn't help but concede an exasperated smile. "As I was saying, the songs all come from my gift, and the music, well, it's like the medium the magic inside me can use to interact with the world, I think. That's my theory, anyway."

"And by *interact with the world,* you mean turn water into some psycho predator."

"Something like that," I said.

"You ever done that before?"

"Nope."

"Then what does your music usually do?"

I froze. My words got caught somewhere between my mind and my mouth, as if they had skidded to a halt and retreated.

Marcus's eyes went wide, though the teasing lilt to his voice remained. "What? You haven't been forcing people to walk off cliffs or something, have you?"

"No, of course not." I grasped for my composure, for something, anything to say. It had been so long since I'd used my gift for anything other than kidnapping. "I just, well, I use it to find people who are lonely. People as lonely as I am." The words startled me as they came out, the raw truth of them. And that I had admitted them to Marcus before I'd admitted them to myself.

Marcus's face went still, and I couldn't read him under the veil of his composure. Perhaps he felt as uncomfortable as I did at the moment, and was just better at hiding it. Perhaps he pitied me. The thought doused my heart, dampened it.

But when he finally spoke, he had gone back to his playful self again. "Well, that's depressing. Sounds like I'm going to have to burden myself with coming up with some fun things to use your little gift for, since you're clearly not taking full advantage of it."

I smiled, grateful for his uncanny ability to alter the mood of a conversation with a few teasing words, but then I bit my lip, fully aware I was about to dampen the conversation once more. "Can I ask you something?"

"Mhm?"

"Earlier, when Amity was missing, why did you think I had something to do with it?"

He shuffled, and when he answered, shame leaked through his words. "I guess I needed someone to blame other than myself." He reached into his pocket, and I could tell from the bulge in the fabric that he was flipping something around in his hand.

I shouldn't have asked it, but something about the way he clung to whatever was in his pocket, like it tethered him to reality, made me risk it.

"Why can't you go back home, Marcus?"

He didn't answer, and the silence stretched taut between us, so I tucked my head into a rolled-up coat next to Amity, while Marcus turned back to watching the forest.

"Because the next time I go home, I'll have to tell my parents that their youngest is dead."

. . .

WITH AMITY fast asleep next to me, my body calmed enough for the pain in my arm to puncture the shock of the last few hours. I'd ruined Amity's makeshift sling when I'd jumped into the pool and pulled myself through the still waters. And since I'd given her my change of clothes, it wasn't as if I had anything with which to make a proper sling.

I bit back the moans threatening to break from my lips into the chilled air. If anyone deserved to be able to rest after a day like today, it was Amity. So I swallowed my whimpers and clenched my fists, hoping to still the trembling in my limbs.

Warm fingers grazed my cheek.

My whole body stiffened at the touch, at the calluses that skimmed my skin.

"You're shaking," Marcus whispered.

I sucked in a cold breath and nodded, untangling my arm from where I'd draped it across Amity, the world spinning as I moved it.

Too mortified to look in Marcus's direction, I scooted away from both of them and, deciding surely I owned something that could be fashioned into a sling, rummaged through my satchel, which proved to be difficult with only one hand. I hadn't realized how much I'd come to rely on Amity's doting during our journey.

"Is that going to do you any good?" Marcus asked, eyeing me with what could be described as nothing less than utter lack of faith in my ability to open the satchel by myself.

"Probably not. But it's not hurting me to look." I gasped as my fingers grazed the edge of a razor I'd nicked off a mercenary a few weeks ago, then promptly left to be forgotten in the pile of junk at the bottom of my satchel.

"Okay now. Stop that before you injure yourself any further." Marcus scooted closer, gently grabbing my bag and tucking it behind his back.

I rolled my eyes. "So helpful."

"Glad you finally noticed." He winked, that carefree grin overtaking his handsome features.

I wiped my nose on my sleeve, which served two purposes:

proving that his charm had such little effect on me, that I didn't care whether he witnessed my snot, and disguising the upward twitch at the edges of my lips.

"Come here," he said, although he apparently didn't mean it, for he scooted so close our knees were touching, and the only feasible way I could have come any closer would have been to crawl into his lap, which I thankfully had enough forethought not to mention aloud.

Only once he was close enough for me to sense his breath fogging the air between us did he strip away his outer tunic. Why he couldn't have done that when he was sitting across the campfire, I had no idea, but I figured it had something to do with his insufferable ego.

Though, even I had to admit, the ego was a tad warranted.

The shirt beneath his outer tunic was woven tightly, a thin material that did nothing to conceal his muscular form, his bulging arms. Ink snaked down both his arms in the shape of thorny vines. The tattoos were nothing new, nothing that should have held my gaze as long as they did. It was customary for Avelean men to have them inked into their skin, marking the loss of a loved one, the true marker for coming of age.

But there was something about seeing them on Marcus, this man with a smile that consumed his whole face, an ease about him that reminded Amity that it was okay to still be a child... It tugged at something deep within me.

Who had Marcus lost?

The question was forming on my lips, when he said, "You can't have both of my shirts, you know."

My gaze snapped upward to meet his sly, pompous grin, his eyes tracing the blotches of pink I knew to be swimming under the surface of my skin.

He tsked. "Can you imagine how much trouble I'd be in if I ogled you like that?"

"I wasn't ogling."

"Sure you weren't."

I nodded toward the wadded tunic in his palms. "Do you actually know how to be useful, or were you just looking for an excuse to flex in front of me?"

He bit his bottom lip, jutting his lower jaw so that his skin stretched over his bottom teeth. "Why would I pick one when I could do both?"

If I had had an answer to that, which I didn't, it would have gotten swallowed up by the shriek of ripping fabric as Marcus tore his tunic in half.

I wondered if he had another in his satchel to replace it with.

"I must like you or something, because this was the only tunic I had with me," he said.

What a shame.

Thankfully, this time, I caught myself ogling before he caught me.

I knew better than to try to tie the knot myself with only one hand, but once he'd fashioned the sling, I reached for it. He snatched it backwards just as the soft fabric grazed my fingertips.

"What do you think you're doing?"

"I can take care of myself."

Something sparkled in his copper eyes, or maybe it was just the firelight dancing in the reflection of his deep irises. "No one's saying you can't," he said, leaning close. He moved to my side, then brushed my loose curls from my neck, tucking them out of the way, draping them over my left shoulder even as his fingers grazed the curve of my collarbone. I fought back a shudder, but wasn't entirely successful.

Marcus settled the sling over my shoulder, then, as tenderly as he could, situated my arm into the sling. I winced as a jolt of pain stabbed at me.

"I'm sorry," Marcus said, his voice dipping low, caressing my senses.

I swallowed, biting my lip. "It's fine."

Except it wasn't fine. I wasn't fine. Not with him so near, so close, that if I only craned my neck to the side...

No. Definitely not fine.

He lowered my arm to my side, and I let out a foggy breath as the pain peaked, then dissipated.

When he spoke, his lips were so close his warm breath grazed the pointed tip of my ear, his voice so low, it was barely distinguishable from a whisper. "Maybe you're right. Maybe you don't need a man to take care of you. But you know, just because you don't need a man to take care of you, doesn't mean it wouldn't feel good to let one every now and again."

CHAPTER 14

MARCUS

For the life of me, I couldn't figure out why I did it. Why I'd bothered.

I stroked the marred edges of the compass in my pocket, turning the cool metal over in my palm. I might have opened it, but I couldn't quite shake the notion that the painted glawackus was already boring holes through the metal with its blind stare, silently judging me.

Piper trafficked children.

Took them from their homes, enchanted them with that terrifying, unearthly power of hers, then...well, I didn't know what she did with them after that.

Who she sold their innocence to.

After that terrifying display today—the bulging eyes of that forest faerie as the pressure of the water caved in on her, squeezed the breath from her slimy lungs, as that horrible, haunting tune sounded—still sounded, moaning in the wind and chasing sleep away—I shouldn't have done it.

I shouldn't have helped her.

The faerie had sworn in the moment before the hovering pool had attacked. But it'd said something else, too quiet for Piper to hear.

"It is her," it had whispered.

As if news of the woman who could bend minds with her songs had reached even the depths of the forest.

As if they'd been waiting for her to come along.

They'd placed that flute in the snake den, hadn't they? Practically handed us the key to save Amity? Maybe they'd had a sick need to up the stakes. Maybe they got a high off taking risks.

Maybe they'd been honest, that the key to saving Amity lay in that den, but they'd never anticipated anyone but them could wield the key.

It is her.

The faerie's serpentine tongue had flicked as if to taste her scent on the air.

Had someone reached the faeries before us, tipped them off about Piper?

Paranoia settled in my gut.

Had my benefactor decided my fee was too high, that the forest faeries would require significantly less in exchange for Piper?

I rubbed my temples. It was late, and today had been exhausting, and I was letting my mind run away with itself. My benefactor couldn't be the only one after a woman with a gift and a criminal history like Piper's. Legends were already being told about her in the secluded villages of Avelea.

The faeries could have just as easily heard about her from the lips of their most recent snack.

People had a tendency to talk when children went missing.

Definitely shouldn't have helped her.

I told myself it was for Amity, that, after today, it would have been foolish for me to think I could protect that little girl on my own. Arrogant even, with the threats we faced in this forest. I told myself I needed Piper's arm to heal, and that having it hang limp like that, straining tissue and sinews, would only leave her limited in her ability to defend herself. Limited in her ability to defend Amity.

That was why I did it.

Not because when she'd been lying there beside Amity, her broken mangled arm wrapped around the little girl, her teeth grinding as she endured the pain just to have a hand on the girl—a constant indication through the night that she was still there, that nothing had happened to her—I'd felt a trickle of pity for the woman.

I wasn't sure what I'd been expecting when I set off to find the wanted trafficker.

Someone cruel, perhaps. Calloused. A female with eyes green as greed.

Except they weren't green like greed. No, they were green like flora, like ivy after a morning rain, glowing with a cool melancholy that perhaps might have been calming if she'd been dealt a different hand.

I knew pitying her was foolish. That I was out of my mind if I let her slight form, the way she was constantly biting her lips to dampen the pain, convince me that she was helpless.

Piper was anything but.

There was a bloated corpse and a crater in the earth to prove as much.

Helpless or not...she'd been hurting.

And though I shouldn't have cared, should have even reveled in her suffering after the heaping number of lives she'd ruined—not just the children's, but their families' as well, the mothers whose tears would never dry, the tables whose empty place setting would never know a hot plate of food—I did.

I cared.

I cared because she cared. Because, earlier tonight, when I'd told her my secret, when I'd revealed what a coward I was for not returning home, right in the open for the heavens and Fates and stars and the pretty girl with pointed ears to hear, she'd crawled over to me and placed her delicate hand on mine.

"You carry the truth on your own so they don't have to," she'd said.

No judgment. Just pure understanding, undiluted by pity or that incessant need most people had to try to make it better, make it hurt less.

And then she'd curled back up with Amity as if she hadn't shattered me then put the jagged pieces back together again all in a few words.

As if those words weren't the ones I'd been waiting for someone, anyone, to whisper.

I cared.

And that was going to be a problem.

I'd cared enough to nudge her awake, though I'd known better than to think that she'd truly been sleeping. I'd cared enough to dress her wounds, to refashion a sling from my own tunic. And when my fingers had brushed her hair, I hadn't been able to help allowing them to linger, to comb just barely through those vibrant curls. I'd allowed them to graze her collarbone as I'd tucked the curls over her shoulder. I'd relished the feel of her soft skin, and I'd been tempted to trace that bone all the way to her neck, to cup my thumb under her chin and caress the line of her jaw, to press my fingers into the nape of her neck and relieve the headache that she had to have been experiencing after a day like today.

It had been a line, carefully crafted in so many ways. The implied promise of wanting more, of wanting to take care of her.

That had been my strategy, after all.

Flirt. Woo.

Seduce her into the illusion of safety in my presence.

But I found the words came too easily—the blatant compliments regarding her appearance, the intentional brushing of her hands when she dared walk close enough to Amity and me for such a thing to not be too obvious. Allowing my gaze to linger on her mouth just a breath longer than necessary.

It was much too easy indeed.

Perhaps I should have plugged my ears when she played that tune. Perhaps, under the ominous wail of the dirge, she'd hidden something else, a string of hidden notes that lulled the careful mercenary in me to sleep. A melody that seeped through the armor I'd constructed around my heart and wrapped my heartstrings around her finger.

Perhaps it wasn't worth the bounty to lose my soul to an enchantress.

But there was nothing about the clammy sweat that beaded on her forehead when she was in pain that seemed intentional. Nothing about the way that, now that she'd truly fallen asleep, she clung to Amity like a mother might cling to her ill child.

Was it fear of the evils that lurked in the forest that had her instincts protecting the child, even in sleep?

Or was it the knowledge of the life she'd be handing the child over to once she reached Nettlewood?

I knew which one I wanted it to be.

And that was going to be a problem, too.

CHAPTER 15

PIPER

It took us three more days to free ourselves from the Kobii mountains and the trees that swarmed its slopes.

We'd left our campsite the morning after I drowned the faerie with her own flute. I'd rolled it over my fingertips, caressing the keys, stroking the vines engraved on the beautiful creation.

And then I'd buried it.

Because as much as I would've loved to keep such a masterpiece, Bronger's obsession with the instrument would surpass any of my affections. And his interest in the flute would have much less to do with the richness of the notes it played, and much more to do with the ability to drown our enemies in airborne puddles.

And if I never drowned another being, I wouldn't complain about it.

We came upon a small village at the base of the southern tip of the Kobiis. According to the wooden sign, fire-etched with blooming flowers and tumbling vines, the village's name was Evaen. I traced my finger into the ridged decorations in the wood, imagined how precise the artist must have been to create such delicate flowers with a flame.

Marcus eyed me as I examined the handiwork. "Hopefully, the people are as nice as the sign."

"Oh, I hope all the wood in Evaen looks like that." Amity pointed to an ornate wooden archway, decorated in the same manner as the sign, that served as the entry point for the village and the road that passed through it.

When we entered the village, I tried to restrain my excitement. For lining the streets were houses—not like the small, functional houses of Amity's village, of most villages—no, these came in all shapes and sizes, patterns and colors. Some inhabitants had dyed the thatch on their roofs an assortment of teals, fuchsias, and oranges. Others had constructed their walls completely out of totem pillars. As I looked around, I couldn't find any two houses that slightly resembled the next, much less two houses that looked just alike. It was incredible.

"Oh, I like this place," Amity said. "I wonder if chrysanth grows here. It's an ancient flower that, if you grind up the petals and put it in a tea, it'll show you all sorts of things. Like people and magical creatures, except instead of telling you a story, it's like you're in the story." My neck almost snapped in an attempt to meet Marcus's wide eyes. He pursed his lips together, stifling a laugh that echoed the gagging sound emerging in my throat. "The climate seems about right..." Amity said, skipping off ahead of us.

"Seems like we're going to have to be careful that our little girl doesn't fall in with the wrong crowd," Marcus said, his dark eyes flickering with amusement.

I bit back a giggle, and we both picked up our strides, hastily heading after our future little drug addict lest we lose her amongst the crowd of people on the streets.

And there was a crowd.

Fae and humans alike bustled through the town, laughing together in the glow of the lanterns that hung from the doorposts of every house in town. As we passed, a man told a fae female a joke, and I almost recoiled in terror, waiting for her, or worse, her male, to strike out against the man for approaching her so directly. But the female just laughed, as if it were a joke told by her brother and not her mortal enemy.

How odd to find a town where fae and humans laughed

together. Sure, in Nettlewood they *lived* together, meaning they inhabited the same city. But most of their dealings were just that, deals. Bargains. Extortions. Never friendly like the exchange I'd just witnessed.

Marcus gestured toward the laughing trio. "Well, that's new."

"Uh-huh," I said, still a little too shocked to form a comment about it.

We weaved through the city, witnessing a host of other odd exchanges before we reached our destination. Fae children played tag in the streets with their human peers. The human children sometimes seemed to win, and I wondered if the fae parents had taught their children to be gracious, not to win every single game, despite their heightened senses and ability to run faster. A fae female bought jewelry from a traveling human merchant on the street. They chatted about the incoming snow while she made the purchase. A fae female and a human man walked past us, the two of them holding hands, a baby strapped to the woman's chest.

It turned its head and set its wide, round eyes on me, its pointed ears reminding me of calla lilies. The half-fae baby babbled and waved, and a lump of smoking coal caught in my throat.

"Soooo cute!" Amity said, cheerfully waving back at the baby. The parents smiled at us, their faces lighting up when they saw me, the features that so resembled their baby.

I turned my head away and pushed further into the crowd. Marcus's hand found my shoulder, his warm grasp anchoring me, allowing me to hold in the tears welling behind my eyes. "You okay?"

I turned and summoned the most easygoing smile I could muster. "Why wouldn't I be?"

His brow rose, not in suspicion, but in a knowingness I found myself appreciating. There was something warm in the way he'd known immediately that seeing the half-fae baby, loved and nurtured by his parents, would bother me. Nice that he knew to follow me, that I might need him.

The warm spot in my belly, kindled by his touch, reminded me that I should pull away. That those feelings that felt so fuzzy and pleasant now would only assault me later when I'd have to abandon him in Nettlewood.

"Looks like there's an inn this way," I said, strategically nodding toward a brightly decorated building with tiny lamps all over its storefront as I ducked away from Marcus's grasp. The inn was off the town square, where lamps hung from strings that gathered to a point on a carved wooden pole in the center of the square. Marcus nodded and grabbed Amity's hand as we made our way to the inn.

Warmth and the scent of hot cider stirred the blood in my cheeks, mobilizing my stiff fingertips as soon as we opened the door. The bell hanging above the doorframe rang as we entered, and a rosy-cheeked elderly woman greeted us with a wave from behind the desk at the far end of the room. As we passed the tables that filled the room, the fae and humans that filled the tables, and the stew and cider that filled their bellies, something akin to homesickness struck my heart. Not that there was any sense in that. I'd never had a home worth feeling homesick about. But maybe that's what it was. That this place, these smells, these smiles, made me homesick for the home I had missed out on.

"Welcome, friends!" the woman said cheerily. "How many beds and how many nights will the three of you be needing?"

"Two beds, just one night," I said, though with a pinch of regret. Perhaps I'd come back to this little village one day. I hadn't kidnapped this far southwest before. Maybe I could visit a town toward the coast, then make a stop in Evaen on the way back to the Coup. Though, surely this was the only inn in town, and the only innkeeper, and she seemed like the type to remember faces. And which faces should be seen in the company of which other faces. No, it would never work, bringing kidnapped children through this town.

The hope bubbling in my heart went stagnant.

"Tawny!" the old woman yelled so suddenly, I jumped. Marcus brought his hand to his mouth beside me, though nothing could disguise the twinkle of amusement in his eyes.

"Shut up," I whispered.

"I said nothing."

He opened his mouth slightly, as if to expound on his saying nothing, but then Tawny appeared from the door behind the counter. "Yes, Gran?"

Marcus's jaw went slack before he clamped it and swallowed.

Amity peeked her chin over the tall counter and rested it there as she admired the innkeeper's daughter. "Wow. You're pretty."

"Why don't you just speak for all of us, ragamuffin?" Marcus said, pinching the back of Amity's neck. She wriggled away from his grasp, just as something unpleasant wriggled around in my stomach. For Amity to say that the innkeeper's daughter was pretty was basically an insult, for the girl was not pretty.

She was stunning.

Her hair was so pale it almost matched the snow dusting the colorful roofs outside. She wore it pulled back lest, even in all its glory, it detract from her face—her porcelain skin, her full, pink lips, those doe eyes of the deepest indigo, intensified by her eyelashes that were much too dark to be naturally occurring. At least, not in a fair world. But we didn't live in a fair world, did we? Heat colored her high cheekbones at Marcus's flirtatious remark.

"Where'd you say our room is?" I asked, my voice going unfortunately high-pitched despite my intentions for the opposite to occur.

"Just upstairs," the innkeeper said. "I'd lead you to it myself, but my joints turn to rust in the winter. Tawny, why don't you show these three where they'll be staying?" Then she handed a large wheel containing a multitude of what looked to be hand-painted keys to her still-blushing granddaughter.

The girl stepped out from behind the counter, revealing a form that could have been crafted by an artisan, her curves evident even under her multicolored, loose-fitting robes.

They were the kind of robes that would have made me look like a colorful blob.

I couldn't help myself. I gambled a glance at Marcus and found the look he was giving the girl was a tad too delighted to be chalked up to him being excited to sleep in a bed and not on the forest floor for a night.

That little monster inside took my stomach in its claws and twisted.

When we arrived at the room, Marcus lingered annoyingly at the door, grinning at the blushing beauty.

"Some of us would like to lie down." I pushed my way between them, regretting it instantly, as Marcus's firm biceps tugged on my broken arm.

"I apologize for my travel companion's crankiness," Marcus said.

Behind me, I heard the girl giggle and say, "A job's a job, right?"

I crossed to the bed on the far side of the room and made the mature decision to bury my face in the pillow and pretend to be asleep, rather than fling a lamp at the two of them. Besides, I couldn't aim well with my left hand, and I didn't want to hit Amity, who came and sat on the bed next to me.

"There was no need to be rude to her," Marcus said as he closed the door. "Are you always spiteful to women your age?"

That stung, right in the gaping crater in my life where a female friend had never taken up residence.

"Do you always—" I stopped myself in the middle of my vulgar accusation, remembering there was a child in the room with us. "I was just impatient to get some rest. My arm is killing me," I said, knowing good and well that the aching in my arm, I was used to. The popping embers of fire in my chest threatening to combust any moment now? Not so much.

A thump sounded as Marcus discarded his pack onto the bed next to us and sighed. "Tawny said there'd be entertainment in the square tonight. Dancing and musicians and performers. You wanna come?"

I did the math in my head. Right. Winter Solstice was tonight, and all over Avelea fae and humans alike would celebrate the longest night of the year, as if the lack of sunlight didn't send our crops to their graves and the entire population into a fit of depression.

"No, thank you," I said, burying my face further into my pillow. "Just looking forward to a good night's rest."

He nudged my waist with his elbow, and I fought the urge to flinch. "You sure? I know you like that kind of thing."

"No, thanks," I said, making sure the words were devoid of as much energy and care as was half-faeingly possible.

"Amity?" he asked.

Silence followed, and I wondered if she was turning her head back and forth between the two of us. If, at such a young age, she possessed the social capacity to read the room, to at least pretend she might stay with me when we both knew it was Marcus she preferred.

"No. I'm tired too," Amity said. The surge of relief that followed was a tad overkill for having a ten-year-old pick me over the person I'd deemed my current source of irritation.

"All right, then. You two come find me if you change your mind. And Amity," he said. "Don't leave this room without Piper, okay? Not even to fetch her a surprise late-night snack."

I couldn't help but smile into my pillow. It was cute, Marcus's profound understanding of Amity's motivations and outward expressions of love—the topmost being surprise food items.

Marcus rose to leave, and the door thudded behind him before lively footsteps sauntered down the hallway and faded into the distance.

Amity immediately plopped herself on top of me.

I groaned. "Amity, my arm."

"I'm sitting on your back, not your arm."

"Yes, but it's all connected," I said.

"I don't think that's true," said Amity, though I could hear her confidence waver.

"Would you mind dousing the lamp? My body feels like it weighs forty tons. I think I could fall asleep in the middle of Nettlewood on the eve of the Summer Solstice." A holiday actually worth celebrating.

"Then why do you need me to cut the light?" Amity asked.

I didn't have a suitable answer for that.

My lack of answers didn't dissuade Amity from asking questions, however. "Why didn't you want to go listen to the musicians with Marcus?"

I didn't have a suitable answer for that either, except for the same lame excuse I'd come up with for Marcus. "Like I told him, I'm tired."

"Are you mad at him?"

"No."

"Are you mad at the pretty girl who walked us up here?"

I flipped around in bed and sat up to face her, a motion my poor arm did not appreciate, which it expressed in a wave of pain that shocked my senses. Amity's face was completely impassive, void of anything other than utter pragmatism.

"Why would I be mad at her?"

"Because Marcus called her pretty."

"I bet he says that to every girl he meets."

"Did he tell you he thinks you're pretty?"

I let out an exasperated groan. "Why are you worrying about whether Marcus called me pretty?"

"I'm not worried." She shrugged. "Are you worried?"

"No," I said again, finding it to be my cleverest response to Amity's incessant questions.

"Do you like Marcus?" she asked, her round eyes unwavering in their expectant gaze.

"I like that he protects us. I like that he keeps you company and carries you over the rough spots on the trails, the places it'd be hard for me to do by myself because of my arm. What I don't like is that I'll have to pay him when we get to Nettlewood."

She ripped her gaze from mine, staring at her thumbs rolling around each other in her fists. "You should marry Marcus. He tells the best jokes, and he wouldn't hit you."

A thorn poked at my ribs.

"That shouldn't even have to be a qualification," I said, more to myself than to Amity. To her, I said, "I hope, if you decide to marry, your standards of character will be so high, no man who would ever hit a woman could weasel his way through."

"I know that. I want to marry Marcus, but he says he's too old. But you're old too, so maybe he would marry you," she said.

"You're quite the wingman," I said.

"I don't have any wings."

"Noted."

"I'm not a man, either."

"I apologize for implying such a thing."

"He has nice tattoos."

"That he does."

"They're not messed up, like yours." She flicked her eyes in the direction of my left ear disapprovingly.

I couldn't help but laugh. "This is true."

"So you'll try?"

"Try what?"

"To marry him."

I laughed, unable to contain the ridiculousness of this conversation. But then the laughter punched my ribs so hard it morphed into a pain that had nothing to do with my broken arm or the bruises that speckled my skin. Because now I could see what Amity was doing, how her clever, idealistic mind had spun a tale. One where she, Marcus, and I could be a family. And her father would never hit her, or her mother.

And no stunning, blond hourglass of a goddess masquerading as a human girl was going to drive me to such bitterness that I would trample this girl's spirit. At least, not until I had to. Not until the night came when I had to sneak her away while Marcus slept.

I knew it was selfish. That it would be better for her to have her dreams crushed now, rather than later. But it was such a pleasant dream. And something about spending this much time with a child made me want to pretend.

I bit my lip, knowing good and well that I'd come to regret this decision. "You wanted to hear the musicians, didn't you?"

CHAPTER 16

PIPER

Appearing at the Winter Solstice festivities turned out to be a mistake. I didn't realize it at first, what with all the banners which had somehow hung themselves up since we'd checked into the inn, all ornately cut to look like long, dangling snowflakes except in every color known to human and fae-kind alike. Villagers danced and stomped and laughed throughout the square, swinging one another around in a dance that reminded me of school children, unorganized and lively but somehow perfectly in rhythm. There didn't seem to be such a thing as dance partners here, for as soon as one swung another in a lively circle, the angles of which seemed to defy gravity, someone else would catch them, swinging them just as fast if not faster, until the entire congregation's balance totally depended on the partner that swung them and the neighbor that instantaneously caught them.

It was mesmerizing.

Even the snow seemed to dance.

And then there was the music, lively and boisterous, the percussion synchronized with the villagers' boots, the fiddles—oh how I wished my gift had been to be a fiddler and not a flautist sometimes. Something tucked away inside me pinched at my soul with a bit more aggression than necessary, nagging at me that, although this was the most enticing beat I'd ever heard, how much better, fuller they'd sound with a flute.

"Come on," Amity said, grabbing my hand and pulling me into the crowd. Instantly, it swept us away. My feet barely had a moment to touch the cobbled pavement before the crowd slung us in the opposite direction, our hands slipping from each other's to instead hold tanned hands, fair hands, small hands, fae hands, children's hands alike. My heart quickened in panic, partly in fear of losing Amity to the crowd, partly for fear of my broken arm, which I was convinced some dancer would rip off with one well-meaning tug. But, as if the villagers were familiar with the fears that travelers lugged around like their satchels, the anxieties that latched to my clothing and soles like briars, with each whooshing turn they never pulled Amity further than I could see her. And not a single soul attempted to grab my injured arm, not even the children, whom I didn't expect to be so considerate.

As we danced, as the music stole my heart and the crowd lifted my feet with it, I wondered. I wondered if I played my song here, my gift's song, the one that found Amity, the one that had found so many children before her, if its tune would call to any of the children here. Or if they would grow bored with the slow tune and start a game of hide-and-seek until the last dreary note faded from their ears and memories, until a lively tune could sweep away their hearts once more.

Something told me that if I played that tune here, I wouldn't find another like me. Like Amity.

I couldn't decide if that thought made me hopeful or miserable.

But I didn't have time to figure it out, for one turn later, and the hand holding mine was large and brown and calloused and soft all at the same time. I looked up just in time to see Marcus beaming down at me. And then he was gone, and so was the touch of his hands. I found myself reinventing what exactly they had felt like, replaying the warmth of his fingers wrapped around mine, the way my heart stopped bothering to keep the beat of the tune the moment I'd realized who those hands belonged to. Heat bloomed on my face despite the snowy evening.

And then every set of hands were Marcus's hands. Until they weren't—being too small or too wrinkled or too pale or too soft or too freckled or any number of attributes that weren't quite adequate when compared to Marcus's hands. I craned my neck for him, scanning the crowd to see if we might cross paths again before the song ended. To steer myself toward him if necessary, though I couldn't for the life of me figure out how. Amity glowed, her dark braids spinning like twin lassos as she danced. Behind her, I saw Marcus with that familiar gleam in his eyes, and my heart lost track of its own rhythm. As I spun myself closer—directed my trajectory with a tip of my shoes to the left, a sway of my weight to the right—I saw another pair of hands touch. Hands that didn't look as perfect, as *right*, touching as mine and Marcus's had.

Tawny tripped as he caught her grip, and she fell straight into him, her head buried into his chest longer than necessary for recovering from what was only a stumble, not a plummet. When she craned her swanlike neck to gaze at him, giggling, I couldn't help but notice that her head's collision with Marcus's chest hadn't even misplaced a strand of her hair.

He laughed as his eyes settled over her and he refrained from passing her off to the next partner in line, ignoring the pattern, the rules. The foundation upon which a dance, no, an experience, like this was laid.

It was no small feat, weaving my way back through the dancing crowd, since I had somehow found myself in its center.

By the time I reached the edge of the dancing circle, I remembered Amity, and my heart sank at the thought of plunging back into the merry swarm of dancers. Of seeing what had progressed between Marcus and Tawny in the time it had taken me to bully my way through the crowd, my broken arm taking a beating in the process. But then a tiny hand grabbed my arm, and I looked down to find Amity's big, brown eyes peering up into mine.

I wondered if she had seen it too.

"Can you play me a song?" she asked.

"I'm not going to interrupt the fiddlers," I said.

"But they're all travelers from the different kingdoms. Look, they all have different crests woven into their sleeves."

I glanced past her half-heartedly and confirmed it with my own eyes. "So?"

"So, you're a visitor too. You should get to play just like they do."

"I wouldn't want to ruin the dancing. They're much better than I am."

Amity scrunched up her face. "No, they aren't! You're the best. Besides, it's not like you'd have to play solo. You could play with them."

"I don't know these tunes."

Amity put her tiny hands on her tiny hips. "But your magic knows them."

Indeed, my gift stirred within me in agreement.

It seemed I was outnumbered.

"Alright, but just one song. Then I'd really like to go to bed."

Amity wrapped her thick sleeves around me, warming me with her hug. A deep fondness swelled within me for this child. I'd enjoyed the company of most of the children I'd smuggled through Avelea over the years—except for a few who only seemed to know how to speak in a whine, or the ones who didn't understand that not every comment required a reply and would repeat their dull observations about our environment until I was forced to respond.

But Amity was different. It would have been nice if our lies about one another could have been true.

I pulled my wooden flute from my bag, which had been berating my hip as we'd danced since I refused to leave my belongings unattended in our room despite how nice this inn may seem. Then, as one of the dance numbers ended, I lifted my chin in the air and waltzed over to one of the fiddlers, a faerie with rugged skin that might have blended easily into the sand of the Sahli.

"May I join you?" I asked, brandishing my flute.

The faerie smiled, a grin just as horrifying as the smiles of the forest faeries, with her pointed teeth bared and looking like they might bite my head off for asking such a presumptuous question, but when she spoke her voice was as distant as the night breeze, but warm all the same. "We've been mourning our lack of wind instruments."

The fiddler standing next to her, a dark, balding man with a broad face and belly that made him look joyous, nodded. "We could play the Dance. It's my favorite, but we never get to play it because of the flute solo."

Do we know the Dance? I asked my gift, feeling immensely silly for doing so.

The tips of my fingers pulsed as it nodded. "I'd be honored."

The drummer tapped the rim of his drum lightly, counting us off. I lifted the flute to my lips, and my gift launched me into the most joyous tune that had ever graced my ears.

The crowd exploded into applause in recognition within the first three notes, all long and drawn out, almost mournful. But then, there was silence. The crowd seemed to know what was coming, for they stopped clapping just in time.

The dam subduing the music broke.

The fiddler's bows sailed over the strings as their elbows danced to the beat. My fingers fluttered up and down my flute, playing more nimbly than I'd ever attempted. But my gift knew what it was doing, and, just when I thought my fingers might slip, that I might run out of breath for the next trill, it would take over, just for a moment, to steady my hands, my fingers, my breath, before turning me back over to the music. The tune carried me with it as if it had its own sentience, separate from mine and my gift's.

And then the song was over, just as soon as it had begun, leaving a silence, a void in my heart I couldn't explain.

"That was incredible, lady," the bald fiddler said, shaking my good shoulder in approval.

Even the desert faerie looked less intimidating as the exhilaration of the song melted the sharp edges from her face. "Indeed, what a treat," she said, nodding her head in affirmation.

My heart raced not in excitement, but in a flurry of anxiety, for having lost that melody to the bustle of the crowd, to my memory (which was surely not fit enough to keep such a tune pristine), to my gift who would remember it but not always share.

Sorrow washed over me, and as the compliments from the musicians faded into the chatter of the crowd, I brushed my flute against my lips.

Why I chose to play such a tune in a town like this, where I knew there would be no one to understand it, I had no idea. But perhaps that was the reason, after all, because in a place full of such joy, such peace and camaraderie, I wanted it to be a farce.

I needed it to be a farce.

I needed to look out and see a child under these decorative banners, amidst the swaying crowd, who would hear the tune and understand. And confirm to me that such a one as I, someone like Amity, could dwell in such a place. That this town wasn't simply for the whole, the unstained, but that the broken were free to roam its streets as well.

This time, the mournful notes did not pause just to turn right around and morph themselves into a dance. Instead, they pressed on, long and arduous in the cold. A few of the villagers shot me confused stares, which they caught and turned to polite glances. The chatter started up again as the dancers waited and filled the space where there should have been dancing and laughter. Amity appeared next to me and clutched my coat in her tiny hand.

I looked and looked, but the children were already consumed in their game of tag. Though I scanned the audience, not one of them seemed to hear, seemed to notice the secret words that slithered underneath the notes.

But then I saw him. Marcus, in the middle of dipping the Tawny girl backward, his entire neck craned toward me, all the signs of a sorrowful trance in those beautiful eyes of his.

His gaze met mine, and he dropped the girl. And there was no misinterpreting what stoked the fire behind those copper eyes.

Betrayal.

CHAPTER 17

PIPER

"Marcus." I pushed through the crowds while Amity, at my command, clung to the tail of my coat. Fae and humans parted for us as quickly as they could, but the tune had broken up the dancing formations, forcing people closer together to exchange bits of conversation, jokes, gossip. Graciously, Marcus stood at least a head over most of the crowd, so every once in a while I got a glimpse of him weaving his way through the crowd.

Away from me.

The dancers seemed just as difficult for him to maneuver, which was also a mercy from the Fates.

When we finally reached the edge of the crowd, he was gone.

"Is Marcus coming back?" Amity asked as I tucked her into the bed on the far side of our room.

The lamplight fluttered across her eyelids, giving her a strange, ethereal quality as she peeked out from under the red and green patchwork quilt.

"Yes," I said, not confident that was true.

"How do you know?"

"Because I haven't paid him yet." Those words were as much for my reassurance as they were for hers.

Amity went silent and picked at the loose threads on the edge of the quilt, as if to mirror her picking apart my statement in her mind, how it made her feel, and if there was any weight in it.

I could relate to the feeling, though the worries crowding my mind were only half about Marcus. The others took the form of confusion, of a shifting of my mental framework around how my gift's dirge worked. I'd played it dozens of times, to hundreds, maybe thousands of people. And it had only ever been the children who'd discerned its meaning, heard the call that tapped just beneath the beat.

But I had also seen that look on dozens of children—the terror, the hope that had strewn itself across Marcus's face in that moment.

I turned inward, toward my gift, for answers.

Is there something you're not telling me? Like how you didn't tell me I could wield a pool of water to strangle someone?

My gift rustled in offense, and I wondered if I was going crazy, if the surges of emotion I attributed to my gift were just my consciousness splitting at the seam.

I snuffed out the lamp and settled into the cot with Amity, too hopeful that Marcus would find his way back to us to risk taking up his bed.

MARCUS RETURNED hours after Amity had fallen asleep, hours into the scramble of thoughts and anxieties zipping through my mind. Long after I'd resigned myself to believing he was long gone.

"Marcus?" I asked into the dark, and the outline of him froze. "Will you talk to me?" I couldn't discern whether I was asking for his sake, to provide him with an opportunity to work through his feelings, as if he hadn't already accomplished that through whatever he'd been doing in the middle of the night, or if it was for me, to soothe the whirlwind that was my thoughts.

He sat, placing his pack on the floor and sitting on the edge of his bed, facing mine and Amity's. "Okay."

His voice was as empty as his stare.

"I'd sit up, but I don't want to wake Amity," I said.

He didn't respond.

"I'm sorry for what happened. I didn't... I know it looks bad, like I did it on purpose—"

"Why would you have done it on purpose?" Marcus asked, his voice rough and gravelly. I wondered if he'd been crying. Still, I understood the question as a challenge, not a search for some piece of knowledge he didn't already possess.

Thankfully, my thoughts had already prepared about sixty-two answers for that, ambushing me rather than letting me fall asleep. I chose the one I thought was the best, the most honest, the one that would allow me to retain a droplet of dignity.

"I don't love seeing other people happy. It's an ugly quality of mine I'd like to work on. But even if I played that song to stop the dancing, I didn't mean for it to affect you so specifically. I promise." As the admission crossed my lips, a portion of the pain released its grip on my chest, floating into the darkness and carrying a bit of my guilt with it.

His shoulders shuffled. "I take it that's the song you play to figure out who else is lonely?"

I nodded, then, remembering that his human eyesight probably couldn't see me at all in the dark, said, "It is."

"But you weren't completely honest about who that song finds, were you," he stated, more than asked.

"I don't completely understand how it works," I said, marveling at how a statement that would have once been an outright lie had now settled into the truth.

He turned his eyes upon me, at least, where he thought me to be. He missed by a hair. "What are you looking for when you play that song?"

"I already told you, people who are as lonely as I am," I said.

"Why don't I believe that?"

"I don't know," I said, frustrated now, for I truly was just as confused about why the song had called to him. "Why don't you tell me? It's not like I can read your mind and see what's in there."

Apparently, this landed right where I had not intended it to, for his eyes narrowed, his jaw stiffened. It was then that I realized that, to Marcus, I might as well have read his mind, with the level of privacy I had invaded by calling to his heart with my song.

A song he hadn't answered back.

"What did it ask you?" I said, though it wasn't any of my business. But for a song I was so familiar with that I felt its pulse in the creases of my fingerprints... Sometimes I wondered what the children were hearing, the words my gift did not dare speak to me. I heard a kitchen master mention one time that it was the world's greatest curse, being a chef. That though others salivated over his pastries, soups, and dishes, he could only ever taste their individual parts. That his mind never allowed him to blend the meal together as a whole. And then I thought of my gift, and our Tune, and how, though I could have played it backward, I had never heard it speak.

"Nothing." He rested his elbows on his knees, cupping his forehead in his hands. "It didn't ask me anything. It... It showed me..." he said, shuddering.

"Showed you what?"

"That... It's like it found the emptiness in my soul. The void. And it showed it to me."

I frowned. "I don't understand."

Marcus sighed. He brought a hand away from his face and reached toward me. My heart flurried, remembering the touch of his hand as we'd danced, but he didn't reach for mine. Instead, he extended his arm as he rolled up his sleeve. "You can see well in the dark, I assume."

I nodded again, then, when he didn't answer, felt silly and confirmed it with an "Mhm."

Careful not to wake Amity, I shifted in the bed, sitting upright.

As his rolled sleeve revealed his muscular forearm, which had gone taut as he clenched his fist, I witnessed the missing piece to Marcus's story. Scars coursed across Marcus's skin, hugging the ink of his tattoo, as if the artist had attempted to cover them up, but hadn't fully succeeded.

The night Marcus had used his outer tunic to form my sling, I'd glimpsed the scars, but I'd mistaken them for thorns in his tattoos.

My breath caught, and I reached my hand out, brushing the raised scars underneath my fingertips. He jumped, ever so slightly, and I remembered abashedly that he couldn't have seen me move toward him in the dark.

"Sorry, I forget you can't see me," I whispered.

He nodded and swallowed hard.

I traced the jagged lines that seemed to crisscross over one another, forming a multitude of X's on his forearm. But then he shifted, and my hand slid down his arm into his palm, where he allowed our fingers to brush. Static surged from his fingertips, my arm the conduit as my heart fed off his energy.

"What happened to you?" I asked.

"Nothing I wasn't asking for," he said, acid lingering on the edges of his voice.

I couldn't think of what a child could do to deserve stripes such as these. Bronger wasn't above a good slapping, but he'd never left a mark behind, at least not one that wouldn't fade within the hour. What could Marcus have done to instigate such a lashing? And so many?

"Who did this to you?"

He gritted his teeth. "I'm afraid that whatever you're imagining is much nobler than the truth."

"I'm not imagining anything," I said in earnest. For the life of me, I couldn't fathom anyone wanting to hurt someone so kind, so full of life. "I just want to know who hurt you."

He swallowed and blinked hard, as if he could squeeze away whatever memories haunted him. "I did. In a way."

"Oh." Because what else was there to say? Words didn't seem an appropriate response. So I simply squeezed his hand tighter, hoping the gesture would be enough to convey the acknowledgment of such pain. One that would take a thousand inappropriate words to describe, words that would only make things worse.

He squeezed my hand back. "When I came back, and my sister..." His voice broke, and the vulnerability of that sound pierced my throat. "I left her, Piper. I left all of them to make something of myself. They were so, so poor. And me? I'd spent the last year..." He stopped and took in a strangled breath. "That money should have gone to them. But by the time I came to my senses, remembered who my responsibility was to, it was too late for her."

I stroked the mark on his forearm, my thumb tracing the ridge that coursed over his skin. "Did you do this to punish yourself?"

He chuckled softly, a wry, low kind of laugh that gave me goosebumps. "I wasn't quite brave enough for that. Couldn't ever bring myself to break my own skin. But I found others who were more than willing. It takes very little to convince a drunk oaf to beat you within an inch of your life. Especially one bragging about the brand new dagger they just bought with their blood money. Most of them are itching to try their weapons out."

"Is that what my song did? Remind you of that pain?"

He swallowed, refusing to look at me. "Not exactly. It was more like...It's difficult to describe. It was like it reminded me of the moments I should have had with her, with my sister. And that there was this void where those memories should have been."

"You never told me what happened to her." In fact, until tonight he'd never actually confirmed that it was her for whom he wore his thorns. He started, and I gripped his hand tighter. "You don't have to if you don't want to."

He nodded, swallowing. "She ran away. Left us a note explaining why. That she was tired of being hungry, and that she didn't..." He exhaled a long breath. "That she didn't blame anyone. But that she wanted to find a family who needed a child. That my family obviously had too many, and it was only fair.

"My parents had just realized she was gone when I arrived. I tracked her for miles. But when I reached where her trail ended... Well, it was clear she'd been attacked by a beast of some sort. I found her cloak, shredded to bits, with too much blood on it for her to have survived. And this," he said, reaching into his jacket and pulling out what looked to be a pocket watch, its casing scratched so thoroughly I couldn't even make out the symbol that had once been engraved on its surface. "I'd given it to her the last time I'd come home from my adventures."

"I'm sure she treasured it," I said, a poor, desperate attempt at comforting him.

His throat bobbed, as if he were trying to swallow, but couldn't quite force himself to. "I...um. I bought it for myself, actually. I'd bought all the other kids trinkets over the time I'd spent traveling. I didn't realize until I was handing them all out that I hadn't remembered to buy her anything." His jaw worked, his teeth clamping at the admission. "So I gave her this. Apparently, she took it with her when she left."

Grief and guilt punctuated his every word, and he slipped the watch back into his pocket without opening it. I listened for the faint ticking of the watch hand, but there was only silence. I wondered if he'd ever had the strength to open it, to wind it. If he feared what he would find on the inside of the battered instrument.

I paused, my response lingering on my tongue. The one I shouldn't say, but... "You blame yourself for what happened to her, but it's not your fault."

His face went gaunt, and he slipped his hand from mine. As he did, something of mine, some invisible something, seemed to fall between our fingertips and shatter on the wooden floor. "And who would you have me blame, Piper?" Bitterness oozed from his clenched teeth.

He stared into the darkness for a while, into my eyes, though he couldn't know it. Then the bitterness melted from his face, and for the first time I noticed the weariness that remained when the carefree mask fell off. I scrambled for something, anything, to say. I had my story, of course. Bits I could still tell him, without giving away Bronger's secrets. Maybe it was part of growing up around a host of unwanted, unparented children half the time and spending the rest traveling on my own, but I never quite knew when, amid someone else's pain, it was appropriate to share my own experiences. Was it helpful to offer a piece of one's self in the hopes that the hurting person would feel a sense of solidarity? Or would they perceive it as selfish, steering the conversation back to my own troubles? I never knew.

"Do you have scars?" he asked, bringing me out of my inner argument and back to the dim room, where it was just me, a grieving man I didn't know how to help, and the gentle snores of a sleeping girl.

"Not like Amity's." How small I was in the face of his question. What right had I to pretend my and Amity's father had been the same, that I'd endured half of what she had? Of what Marcus had?

"Where are yours?" he asked.

I clutched the skin around my collarbone, instinctively covering my chest with my arm.

"Before my mother met Amity's father," I said, feeling ridiculous clinging to that flimsy lie both of us knew wasn't true, but sticking to it anyway for some pitiful reason I didn't want to explore in this moment, "we lived in the north. My mother left me in the snow one time. She forgot about me." As the words filled the space between Marcus and me, I couldn't decide which was worse. The lie? That I had somehow slipped from my mother's mind. Or the truth? That leaving me to die in the snow had been intentional.

"That's not true," I whispered.

Marcus raised an eyebrow. "You'd think after what I just told you about myself, you wouldn't feel the need to lie."

I blushed and bit my lip. "I know. I'm sorry. She...feared my gift. Imagine what happened to you tonight when you heard my song, except instead, imagine the feelings it stirred for those who saw my gift in the hands of a rowdy toddler who had no control over her abilities."

Marcus whistled, but just barely, so he wouldn't wake Amity.

My mouth went dry. "She left me in the snow to die." I cleared my throat and straightened. "I don't like to talk about it, because Amity has such nice memories of our mother."

I wasn't sure why I kept on with that story, when Marcus didn't believe it anyway, but he was polite enough not to mention it. Instead, he leaned over and touched my hand, which I had returned to my lap, and brushed the outside of my hand with his thumb.

About two hours after Marcus had gone to bed, my heart finally settled down enough to allow me to fall asleep.

CHAPTER 18

Gigi had no idea why Piper was sleeping in the bed with Amity, when what Piper really wanted to do was to snuggle up into the cot with Marcus and allow him to hold her until she fell asleep.

But, as Gigi was only a fragment of her past self, she'd gotten used to not understanding plenty of things. Maybe her past self would have known why Piper didn't kiss Marcus when she often wished to. Or why Marcus so obviously wanted to kiss Piper, but Piper didn't seem to notice.

Gigi would have thought that since Piper wanted to kiss Marcus, she would have been on the lookout for the signs that he wanted to kiss her. Like how his gaze lingered on her mouth when she spoke, despite the fact that humans had the ability to interpret spoken language without the visual cues of watching the speaker's lips move.

Or maybe Gigi only *thought* that humans had that ability because Piper had that ability. But Piper was only half-human, after all. Gigi resolved to pay more attention to this detail in the future, to whether Marcus and Amity showed signs of being able to hear one another without looking directly at each other's faces.

Gigi wished that Marcus would kiss Piper and just get it over with.

The swooshy feeling in Piper's stomach was starting to make Gigi seasick. Besides, Piper's bowels tended to loosen whenever she was nervous, and that wasn't good for any parties involved.

At least it was entertaining to watch the two lovebirds pretend they weren't lovebirds. Piper had gotten such a stabbing feeling in her gut when Marcus had danced with that other girl. Gigi hadn't liked it much either, even if Marcus's gaze didn't linger on the other girl's mouth like it did Piper's. And what a pleasant shock it had been when Gigi's tune, the one she and Piper usually played for the children, had made Marcus drop that annoyingly pretty, giggly girl. Gigi had never seen anything like it, that tune affecting a human adult. It made Piper's head hurt if Gigi pondered it too much.

But Gigi needed a distraction. Because while she had resolved to declutter Piper's mind—and Gigi prided herself in keeping her resolutions—Piper's mind wasn't just cluttered. No, cluttered would have been a task within itself, but Gigi had all the time in the world while Piper and Marcus and Amity journeyed, and especially while Piper slept.

But Piper's mind wasn't just cluttered. It was locked.

Well, not all of it. Most of the memories were organized, if not in a neat manner, at least a functional one. For example, the scent of firewood and the taste of hot chocolate linked to a small cabin and a fire and that horrible man's warm arms. And warm arms were linked to Marcus's muscly ones carrying Amity when her feet got too blistered to walk any further.

But there was a pile of memories in the corner that weren't like those memories at all. The memories were there, all right. They hadn't gone missing, as some memories were wont to do, like the ones that contained Piper's first words or her first steps, or the face of her cruel mother. No, these were different, wadded up, curled in upon themselves, twisted and bent and ripped to pieces and reorganized until they were practically indecipherable.

Poor Piper. Shame and magic were the only two forces powerful enough to do something like this to a string of memories. And Gigi sometimes believed Piper's shame was more potent, more alive, than Gigi herself.

Gigi had tried to untangle them, to piece them together for Piper. For as obvious as it was that Piper did not wish to encounter these memories, they had a stench to them. One that pervaded not the entirety of Piper's mind, but any of the memories that were stored close by. Gigi thought that if she could just smooth them out, wipe the crud off of them, then maybe they wouldn't affect Piper's other memories so much.

So Gigi had scrubbed and scrubbed and untangled until blisters began to form at the tips of her consciousness.

She hadn't exactly gotten very far.

CHAPTER 19

PIPER

The three days it took us to skirt the edges of the coast and then backtrack inland to reach Nettlewood went by faster than I wanted them to. In fact, time doubled in speed every time Marcus pulled me into his and Amity's conversation by making some mildly rude comment about me, then making sure he said my name loud enough for me to hear, sending Amity into a fit of giggles and forcing me into a battle with my smile. And then, in those moments when we weren't speaking, when the conversation had run dry, time seemed to slip through my fingertips like water as I scrambled to find something, anything, to say to this man I'd never see again once we reached Nettlewood.

I tried to distract myself from him. It was exceedingly frustrating, being surrounded by the beautiful scenery of the coast. I'd always wanted to visit the coast, but now I could hardly enjoy it for the fear that the coastline would eventually end, the road turn, and then we'd be in that dreadful city of Nettlewood.

The dark, weathered cliffs of the coastline jutted out like the crests of waves over the thrashing sea below them as if to tease the sea, to make it believe they were about to jump in. Wind pelted my ears, which bothered me more than it did my human companions. The entire coast, with the sea to the west and the forest lining it to the east, seemed to have a greenish quality about it, the leaves of the forest more vibrant, the ivy on the cliffs more stark, the sea bursting with foam, like how the green of nature radiated immediately after a heavy rainfall. Except it hadn't rained.

All of this I could hardly pay attention to, except for when I forced myself, which wasn't half as often as I should have. Instead, thoughts of Marcus swirled through my head, making me dizzy and reinforcing my irresponsible daydreams that chose not to focus on the beauty of the cliffs. For the next three days, we were back in Evaen, his hand grazing mine, his eyes shining with mischief. And then we were back in the inn room—my mind conveniently skipping through the part where he'd danced with that girl, whose name I pretended not to remember—and I was tracing his scars and he was brushing his thumb up against my hand. And we were friends. Friends who touched each other's hands.

Which was better than the coastline, where we were still friends, but not ones who touched each other's hands. Or at all.

I spent those next few days walking at a faster pace than I'd bothered to previously on our journey, lingering within earshot so I could insert myself into the conversation. Neither Marcus nor Amity seemed to mind. At least, I hoped they didn't.

Most of the time I just listened. Most of the time I clung to the moments when Marcus spun back toward me to ensure I'd just heard something ridiculously adorable Amity had said.

"Everyone says it's just a legend, but the story has to come from somewhere," Amity prattled as we trudged on. I'd let them go on ahead of me, and I had to strain to hear her over the crashing of the waves against the cliffs. "They say the fae carried it over to Alondria on accident, that it was stuck in the soles of their shoes."

My chuckle only echoed Marcus's bellowing laugh. I delighted in Amity's imagination.

I just so happened to delight in how Marcus delighted in it, as well.

"No, really, I'm not making it up!"

Marcus threw his hands up. "I didn't say you were making it up."

"Yeah, but you laughed," Amity pouted.

Marcus turned his full attention on her, as if he were hanging on her every word, the sight of which shoved my poor, pining heart off the edge of the nearest cliff. "My apologies, milady. Please forgive me and grace me with your abundant knowledge."

This appeared to mend Amity's scorned feelings. "Well, I know it doesn't sound possible, but that's the whole point of magic, isn't it? Don't you believe in magic?"

I wasn't sure whether it was cute or morbid that she still had to ask him that, after we had saved her from being entombed underwater by drowning a faerie in a floating puddle of water controlled by a rather morose flute.

Their voices faded for a moment as the tide fractured on the craggy stone of the coast.

Marcus stopped in place and whirled, gesturing for me to catch up.

My heart might have skipped a few beats.

"Hurry up, slowpoke. You're really missing out. Amity's just been telling me about a magic herb that's deadly, except when it's not." He did that thing where he pushed the tip of his tongue through his teeth that had me monitoring whether my pale skin was blushing, and also whether there was any way I could blame it on the weather or the strenuous hike.

"Apparently, it's deadly," he continued, as I tried not to allow my cheeks to crack at the edges of my runaway grin. "But get this—"

"Wait, you're telling it wrong!" Amity said, digging her fingers into her hairline. "You're forgetting the part about how the Fates created it because they have an affinity for the ironic!"

I hardly managed to hide my laugh with a cough.

"No, no, no... I'm just repeating what you told me," Marcus said. "It's deadly, unless it's inserted directly into the heart. Then it's suddenly...not deadly?"

Amity crossed her arms. "Well, when you say it like that, it sounds made-up."

Marcus grinned and clapped a hand on her shoulder. "You're right. Because the name ressuroot didn't do that already."

Amity huffed, and I had to dig my teeth into my tongue to suppress a giggle. Marcus smirked over her shoulder and winked at me, his copper eyes twinkling with mischief.

I might have lingered a little closer behind them after that, losing myself in Amity's endless descriptions of ancient roots that could make humans sprout functional gills, give animals the gift of language, and all sorts of things that made the last type of root she described a tad more believable by contrast.

Marcus and I found ourselves so wrapped up in listening to her, our pace quickened at the same rate as her enthusiasm.

But the faster we walked, the closer we got to Nettlewood, a place I had come to hate since my last visit.

I wondered then if Bronger would ever allow me to marry. The topic had never exactly come up. In fact, the closest my father figure and I had ever come to discussing such a thing was when I went on my first recruitment by myself at the age of twelve. He'd handed me a small package wrapped in terry cloth. I'd opened it in front of him, and it had confused me that he'd given me a bag of tea leaves, when he knew I detested all teas. I'd asked what they were for.

He'd told me, and I was pretty sure my face had turned the color of a beet. I'd stuffed them into the bottom of my satchel, where they still lay, crushed under all my belongings, unused.

So I at least knew that Bronger wasn't opposed to me having a relationship with a man. Though he seemed to assume pregnancy would interfere with my role in his efforts.

Except I didn't want what Bronger had assumed I'd wanted, to have flings with random, handsome men along the road, men I'd never see again. I was pretty sure that was how Bronger operated with his women, but Bronger and I were not the same. At least not in that regard.

More than anything, I wanted someone to talk to. Someone to collect my stories, my thoughts, my sorrows, my dreams. Someone who would gather them up and arrange them until they had a decently accurate collage of me, of Piper. Someone who would stick around, who wasn't afraid to make promises like I was. Someone who knew. And then, once I was safe, then we could enjoy each other.

My face flushed as an image of Marcus kissing me flashed through my mind. I glanced up, my embarrassment tethering me to reality, but he hadn't noticed. He was busy picking up Amity and putting her on his shoulders.

I wanted *that,* I decided. But then my heart sank, for though I was certain Bronger couldn't care less whether I had flings with a thousand different men, I was sure the daydreams I was having about Marcus would not please my master.

No, as long as I was employed in Bronger's service, he would never allow me to marry. Why should he, when it would sever my dedication to his cause in half? More than that, most likely.

My mind scurried about, fumbling for a way to make it happen. To make Bronger see that this was what was best. After all, Marcus could be useful to Bronger. I figured Bronger might even pay him decent coin to go on military expeditions. He was strong, and an excellent shot, even in the dark, as he'd proved the night he'd rescued Amity and me. But then, what if Bronger sent Marcus out to battle when he finally decided it was time to overthrow the King of Avelea? No, that wouldn't do. I'd shrivel into nothing waiting for weeks, if not months, to hear news of whether Marcus was all right, never truly knowing whether the author of the letters I received had survived the time it had taken the messenger to deliver the news.

And who was I kidding, anyway? Marcus was a good person. Not like the rest of us, who liked to pretend we were good people by not being as lousy as everyone else around us. No, he was intrinsically good. He'd offered us protection knowing the pay wouldn't be worth his time. He watched over Amity like a mother bear might watch over her cubs. He'd tipped the elderly innkeeper extra on our way out, though he didn't know I was watching.

He was good. And I was a kidnapper.

Huh.

I hung back for a while after that, just far enough that they'd assume I wasn't paying attention, as they had no idea just how well I could hear.

Because neither of them knew.

Neither of them knew me.

CHAPTER 20

PIPER

Nettlewood was just as I remembered it, at least in looks, if not in the way its crowded streets and crowded apartment buildings and crowded everything else made my stomach cinch.

"Are we in the right place?" Amity asked, horror forcing her eyes open as she took it all in. The humans who scrambled through the narrow streets, hoods drawn so as to not call attention to themselves, the high fae and faeries alike who waltzed like royalty as the crowds of humans cleared out of their way. One of them accidentally bumped into an especially high-chinned fae. The male grabbed the small elderly man by the top of his hood, ripped the fabric to reveal the man's terrified, wrinkled face, and pulled the small tuft of his white hair right out of his head for good measure.

The man cried out as the fae male kicked him to the ground.

"Oh dear!" Amity broke free from Marcus's hand and dodged passersby's knees as she cut through the crowd. Marcus and I exchanged a frantic look as we followed her, pushing through men and women and trying to evade the fae as best as we could.

"Amity, you can't run off like that." I grasped for the neck of her coat, but she simply pulled her arms from the sleeves and fell onto the ground next to the weeping man.

Thankfully, the assailant had already grown bored with his bullying and had disappeared into the apathetic crowd.

"It's okay, sir," she said. "I can make it better." She turned toward me and beckoned for my pack. I sighed and picked it off the ground before handing it to her. Marcus caught up with us, and we formed a divergence in the flow of the heavy street traffic like a rock in the middle of a fast-flowing river.

Amity fumbled through the pack and plucked out a vial, which she uncorked. She shed her gloves before pouring it onto her fingertips.

The old man frowned, furrowing his wrinkles. "Oh, child. Don't bother with that. Your hands will freeze."

"Don't worry. I've survived much more frigid winters," she said in that matter-of-fact tone that overcame her voice when she was mothering someone much older than herself.

The man chuckled. "Of course you have, with an iron will like that." He peered up at Marcus and me. We must've been betraying our exasperation all over our faces, the way we stood, arms crossed in impatient frustration, readying to scold Amity for running away from us as soon as she finished treating the old man, for he said, "The two of you must have your work cut out, taking care of this one."

"You have no idea," Marcus said, and I knew he was remembering the flashes of that dreadful forest faerie's teeth as she lunged at him for killing her partner.

"We all take care of each other," Amity said, politely correcting him as she rubbed salve onto the scarlet patch of skin where his hair had once been. I wondered then if Amity truly understood why the man was crying, that it likely had very little to do with the pain on his scalp.

The old man grinned through his tears, the wrinkles around his eyes deepening, which I knew for a fact had almost nothing to do with the salve. "Ah, all better."

Amity offered out her little hand, which the old man pretended to use for balance, in my estimation at least, as he stood and shook the dust from his ratty clothes.

"Thank you for your medical attention, child," he said, nodding his head toward Amity, who, rather than beaming at him like a normal child, offered back a dignified nod, absent of joy, except for the type which comes from fulfilling that which was only one's duty to begin with.

The man went to meander his way back through the crowds, but before he did, he pulled on my shoulder and leaned in, whispering, "Get that child out of here. Before the fae sully that spark of hers."

He didn't wait for me to promise before he disappeared into the crowd. My thoughts wandered back to Bronger, how the old man's comment about the fae would have only affirmed Bronger's purpose. How it should have affirmed mine, too. That I was doing the right thing. That there was something on the horizon that was bigger than me, than Amity, than my silly hopes that maybe Marcus would carry my children on his shoulders one day.

It wasn't a pleasant thought that I was in a unique position to change the world for my fellow man, when all I wanted these days was a world of my own, far away, secluded and protected from the fae and any responsibility I had to take them down.

"No more running off like that," Marcus said, his tone sharper with Amity than I'd ever heard it before.

Shock, that her favorite person in the world had scolded her, overwhelmed Amity's innocent features. "But he needed help."

"Then allow us the honor of helping, too, next time," he said, his face softening, though his voice remained just as firm. She nodded and wrapped her arms around him.

"So," Marcus asked, turning to me, "where does this brother of yours live?"

"He actually lives in a cottage on the hillside, not in the city center," I said, my practiced lie rolling off my tongue with ease for how many times I'd rehearsed it in my head.

Marcus narrowed his eyebrows. "I thought you said he lived in Nettlewood."

"He does. His cottage is still within the city limits."

"It's getting dark. Are these hills safe to travel at night?" He nodded slightly at Amity, who couldn't see his implication of her frailty from underneath his coat, where she continued to bury her head.

"No, I was hoping we'd make it here before sunset," I said, though this was the opposite of the truth. When we'd set out this morning, I may or may not have dawdled more than I'd had to in the hopes that if we arrived in Nettlewood as it was getting dark, Marcus would insist that we get an inn in the city.

I'd told myself this was the professional way for a criminal to go about this. After all, Amity and I had to sneak off without Marcus knowing. It would be easier to do it in the middle of the night. And we couldn't have him following us all the way to our brother's house for obvious reasons, like the fact that neither he nor his house actually existed.

But, if I allowed that little voice in my head to whisper the truth, I might have admitted to myself that it would have been just as easy, if not easier, for me to sneak off with Amity last night.

But there was no need to admit that to myself, since what was done, was done.

"You better have a decent amount of coin in that purse of yours," Marcus said, a pleased smile stretching across his face. My heart jumped, and I couldn't help but hope that he also didn't mind spending a little extra time in my company.

We wound through the crowds until we found an inn, though our options would sorely disappoint Amity. None of them could dare to stand next to the one we'd stayed at in Evaen.

Marcus and I almost settled on one in the center of town, except the first thing we saw upon walking into the lounging area was a man dressed in robes of *paldihv*, a rare fae-woven material that gave the outfit the look of a long, shapeless swarth of darkness. The type that might warp itself into the shadow of something else, the trunk of a tree, along with the altered pattern of its leaves, or even the shadow of a man.

Living darkness—that's what the *paldihv* were.

Whoever clothed themselves in *paldihv* gained the ability to blend into shaded areas, but since the only way to obtain *paldihv* was to murder its owner and strip them bare, most found they could get whatever they wanted simply by intimidation alone.

Something told us this wasn't the most child-friendly establishment in town.

In the end, we ended up choosing the cheapest inn that would place us in our own room—we didn't wish to put Amity at the risk of staying in a room with strangers—though it was much more expensive than I would have preferred. Not that it should have mattered from my own financial standpoint, as Marcus was going to get the rest of my money by morning anyway. But as I jangled the few silver coins left in my purse after the transaction, my stomach knotted a bit. I wished I could give him more for all his trouble.

When the cranky faerie innkeeper deposited us in our room, I couldn't help but allow disappointment to seep into my belly. There were no beds, which I thought ridiculous for the amount of coin I'd forked over to the faerie, and heat rose in my chest as I wondered if he'd overcharged me on purpose for being half-fae.

Thankfully, Amity didn't seem to mind. Instead, she took the poor excuse for shelter as a challenge, and immediately began arranging our coats and satchels in a manner for making sleeping on the creaky floor as comfortable as possible.

The creaky floor. That was going to be a problem. I stroked the cold object I'd tucked inside my coat pocket this morning before Marcus and Amity had woken up. I hated the faerie innkeeper even more for putting us in this creaky room with creaky floors, forcing me to do something I really did not want to do.

As Amity arranged our sleeping mats, she took extra time with Marcus's, arranging his satchels this way and that, patting them to smooth his belongings, to allow for a less lumpy pillow. That somber look she'd given the elderly man from the road overcame her face, and a shadow swept over her pale cheeks. At one point, I thought I detected the glimmer of tears welling up under her bottom eyelids, and I worried she would give us away. Amity was a smart girl, and I trusted her to realize we'd be leaving Marcus tonight. I also trusted her not to tell him, at least not on purpose. But if she cried...

"How does the water here work?" she asked, ripping me from my thoughts.

I frowned, confused. "What do you mean?"

"The faerie behind the counter said there's running water in the washroom downstairs, but from the outside it didn't look like the inn was next to a river," she said, more than asked.

Marcus must have interpreted the exhaustion on my face, because he saved me the effort of having to explain. "Nettlewood is built on a channel of underground tunnels," Marcus explained. "They distribute water throughout the city, and some of the wealthy homes and businesses have pipes that connect to it."

Amity scrunched her face up contemplatively. "Did they dig the tunnels before they built the city, or were they already there?"

"I believe they were already there. The people of Nettlewood just made them wider," Marcus said.

"Well, how big are they?"

Marcus let out the most measured exhale I'd ever witnessed. "Tell you what, kid," he said, ruffling the hair on top of her head, tangling her already messy braid beyond hope of repair. "Why don't I explain it to you tomorrow."

I swallowed and couldn't help but shift on my feet, but thankfully Marcus's attention was on Amity.

"Well, okay then," she sighed, a sadness too sharp to be simple disappointment flickering over her face. My stomach clenched.

But Amity didn't protest. Instead, she offered Marcus a ritual hug before quickly settling into her makeshift mat and falling asleep. My heart twinged a bit, that I was ripping this child away from the person she loved the most. That her upbringing had carved away the childish parts that would have screamed that we were planning to leave. That would have clung to Marcus and begged him not to let me take her.

But Amity was too much of an adult for that.

I wondered maybe if adults were stupid in that way.

Marcus and I caught one another's eyes. I cleared my throat. "I'm going to fetch some tea from downstairs. Do you want any?"

"Is it going to cut into my salary?" he asked, his voice slipping into that familiar tease.

I teased back. "Depends. Will you miss a copper?"

He settled into his makeshift cot Amity had arranged on the opposite of the room, placing his hands behind his head before closing his eyes. "I don't suppose so."

I hurried out of the room and down the stairs. After an unpleasant exchange with the innkeeper, who I was fairly sure muttered "half-breed" under his breath, I had two piping hot teas in hand. The cups were identical, except that one was cracked on the edge. I'd take that one for myself. On my way back to our room, I placed both cups on the stairs and looked around. Once I confirmed no one was there to watch me, I pulled the vial from my pocket and poured a drop of clear liquid into Marcus's teacup.

It was more of a hassle to carry them back to the room than I'd expected, though I should have known better with my useless arm. When I arrived at our door, I had to set them down again to open it. I picked them up and closed the door behind me with my foot. Marcus sat up and reached for a cup.

"Oh, no. Take this one instead," I said, nodding to the other teacup.

He raised a brow in suspicion, so I explained. "I'm trying to be nice and drink out of the chipped one."

"Now, why would you do that?"

What came out of my mouth next was nothing if not true. "Because I'm sorely embarrassed about how little money I have left in my purse after booking this inn."

"In that case," Marcus said, reaching for the drugged tea, "I'll forfeit my chivalry for the night."

I tried not to watch him as he sipped it, tried not to imagine the draft mingling with his blood. Instead, I stared at my black tea as I drank the horrid, bitter substance, assuring myself that what I'd done was forgivable. Bronger had been careful to teach me how to use the drugs I carried, the ones he restocked every time I dropped a recruit off at the Coup. One drop wouldn't hurt Marcus. It wouldn't even make him sleepy; at least, not any sleepier than he might normally be in the evening.

But when he allowed himself to fall asleep, that's when the drug would kick in, relaxing his muscles, slowing his heart, taking him off with it to some pleasant, blissful dream. One from which he would not awaken until morning. Not even in a room with creaky floors, where a little girl and a girl who didn't quite know whether she was a girl or a woman had packed, making their escape. He'd wake to an empty room with a coin purse by his head.

I was taking a risk by not giving him more of the sedative; I knew that. But the truth was, I didn't want him to fall asleep. Not yet. And I certainly didn't want to force him to without his consent. It felt icky. And, though drugging him at all felt icky too, I hoped he could forgive me for this one little drop.

"Where will you go once you've dropped us off?" I asked, daring to sit next to him rather than across from him.

"Oh, I don't know. It's never really up to me. I'll just ask around until I find someone in Nettlewood who has somewhere they need to be, where it's imperative that they have all their limbs intact." He blasted me with that all-encompassing grin of his, the one that lit up his entire face, his eyes, his cheeks, his forehead.

It warmed my belly, my toes, my everything, that smile of his.

"I wouldn't guarantee the limbs intact part if I were you," I said, lifting my broken arm in its sling with a wince.

"That's not fair. Your arm was like that when I met you. If I'd have been there, you'd be symmetrical."

"Hey! I'm fairly symmetrical otherwise!"

"Oh, I don't know about that." Marcus lifted his hand and brushed my cheek with his thumb. My laughter caught in my throat as his touch sent a shiver down my spine. "You see, you have eleven freckles on this side," he said, tracing their pattern with his fingers to my right cheek, "and only ten on this side. It pretty much throws your entire face off-balance."

"Oh, that's too bad. I bet it makes me look like I'm just going to topple over to one side."

"Constantly. In fact, I'm always at the ready to catch you, in case you step the wrong way—"

"And the tremendous weight of my freckles sends me cartwheeling over a cliff." I laughed, allowing my nervous giggles to mask how my breath had quickened. I'd become keenly aware of how he hadn't drawn his hand away from my face. He traced the freckles back to the left side, then slid his hand down the surface of my neck, allowing it to land lightly on my shoulder. His touch sent a wave of heat through me, flushing my face and spreading into my chest, my belly, my fingertips.

His gaze lingered on my broken arm, on the dingy sling he had made for me. "I'm serious, Piper. If I had been there, if I had known, this wouldn't have happened. I don't know who touched you, but he wouldn't have had the chance if I'd seen him as much as reach for you." His voice trembled ever so slightly.

"I know that," I said, because it was the truth. He turned his face back toward mine, and I couldn't make myself stop noticing how small the space was between my lips and his. How little effort it would take for me to lean in, to close that gap between us. He watched my mouth. His lashes dipped, obscuring the top half of his eyes, as I extended my neck, shifted my weight. He played with my curls, tucked them behind my ear, his fingers grazing the pointed tip. He lurched a bit in surprise, as if he hadn't been expecting it, as if he'd forgotten, and a laugh tugged at the edges of his lips. He rubbed his calloused thumb over the tip, something like awe overcoming his face.

He was so dizzyingly close, I couldn't help but close my eyes as his warm breath caressed my neck.

The ring of something shattering sent Marcus lurching backward. I looked down to see that, when he'd leaned in, Marcus had sent his teacup hurtling. Fragments of clay littered the floor, though I couldn't help but notice there were only tiny drops of tea soaking into the wooden boards. Marcus had already drunk most of it.

We both glanced over to Amity, who stirred, wiping her nose with her palm before she flipped away from us and began snoring lightly.

Marcus let out a relieved sigh, and I giggled, leaning in toward him again.

He scooted backward, away from me, his eyes wide and apologetic.

I sat there like an idiot for a moment, my head suspended with my back arched at an awkward angle. He cleared his throat, retracting his hands from my face, dropping my heart through the bottom of my stomach, and I jolted upright, swallowing hard.

"It's probably for the best," he said, gesturing toward the broken cup that had interrupted us.

A sliver of a laugh escaped my lips as I desperately grasped at something, anything, any bit of flirtation that might reverse the humiliation that was currently descending upon me, turning my limbs to mush and my cheeks into beets. "I don't know. I think I would have survived if you had waited a few minutes to be so clumsy."

He grinned, though it didn't extend to his eyes this time. "I figure it was just a sign from the Fates, trying to keep us from doing anything stupid."

"Right. Dumb," I said, crawling over to Amity's mat, hoping to smother myself as quickly and efficiently as possible between the folds of the coat she'd used for our pallet.

My heart thudded too loud, pounding against my ears, lest I drift into the sweet oblivion of sleep and salvage a moment's rest from my misery. Embarrassment seeped into my bones, churning my stomach, playing Marcus's words over and over in my head.

Keep us from doing anything stupid.

And maybe I was stupid. For trying to force myself to sleep when I knew I'd have to stay awake if Amity and I were to escape in the middle of the night. For allowing my thoughts to dawdle and linger on Marcus, for allowing my mind the space to fantasize about a future with him. For leaning in to close that gap.

Of course he didn't want to kiss me.

Who would want to kiss a mouth tainted with lies?

CHAPTER 21

MARCUS

I'd been ready to give it all up—the bounty, my reputation for always delivering—for that one kiss, when I saw it.

She never wore her hair up, always let those wild, glorious curls run rampant, so I'd never seen it, the tattoo that stained the bone behind her ear.

It might as well have been a brand marking her for judgment.

For there, sketched in ink thinner than spider silk, a compass pointed east.

And on its face, staring back at me with lifeless eyes, was a glawackus.

The shock had barreled through me, and I'd knocked the teacup over in the process.

My soul shattered before the ceramic did.

Her face had flushed with embarrassment, and she'd glanced at Amity, the Fates affording me just enough time to steel my expression, to warp the disgust, the agony, into embarrassment and apology.

It hadn't been difficult to tell her it would have been a mistake.

Not even when the light fell from those enticing eyes. Green. The color of poison.

Not even when her neck heated, flushing the broken compass with color, with the undertones of blood.

For that's what the tattoo was anyway.

A reminder she'd branded into her flesh of the blood, not her own, that stained her very being.

Cheyenne.

My gut reeled, but I swallowed the bile in my throat as I slumped into the sheets, willing my breath to slow, to go shallow.

Just as she expected it to after drugging my tea.

She didn't know I'd replaced her anesthetic—the one I'd found the night I'd looked through her satchel to help her dress her wounds—with a benign oil that had no medicinal value two nights ago. Didn't know I'd expected her to flee in the night any day now. That I'd been debating asking her to stay, admitting that I knew the truth about her profession, that I didn't care.

This was what I got, what I deserved, for being so consumed with my desire for her that I'd forgotten—no, chosen—to rid myself of any sense of decency and to forget them.

Forget the children whose lives she'd ruined.

To forget her.

To forget Cheyenne.

Even Piper hadn't forgotten her, inking her skin forever with her memory.

My chest was hollow. Nothing beat inside it.

Dead. My sister was dead. I'd found that bloodied cloak myself, shredded, the compass I'd gifted her strewn across the clearing, the glass cracked, the string which she'd used to secure it around her neck snapped and frayed.

Her blood had been everywhere.

Dead. She was dead, and that was why Piper had marked her skin in her honor. Why she'd inked the memory of my sister there on her pale skin.

I had to clench the pillows to anchor myself, to keep from launching across the room and ripping Piper from her mat, from throttling her and demanding she tell me the story. Every bloody detail of what happened to my sister. Every mistake she made that led to the carnage in that clearing.

Years of relentless training, the same training I'd sought out after finding her cloak, after needing something, anything, to erase the scent of her blood from every breath I took, stilled me.

Calmed me.

No, I wouldn't kill her tonight.

Not in front of Amity.

Because while Piper was the one to blame for my sister's death, Piper didn't work alone. That much was clear from the time I'd spent watching her.

If I wanted Piper to writhe, I'd have to cut off the head of the snake.

CHAPTER 22

PIPER

I waited for at least an hour after I heard Marcus's breathing go shallow before I woke Amity.

"Amity. Amity, wake up," I whispered as I nudged her shoulders gently. There was no need to startle her and risk waking Marcus. Even though I told myself I'd given Marcus enough of the drug that a stampede of elephants wouldn't have woken him, I doubted myself.

Doubting myself, that's where trying to kiss a boy and failing had gotten me.

Amity groaned and rolled over. She blinked furiously, but then her eyes went clear. They drooped as the child woke to reality. Woke to me.

I hated Bronger for this.

Guilt slapped my face immediately. How could I hate the man who'd rescued me from freezing to death? The man who'd nursed me back to health, who'd threatened the healers until they swore they'd save my fingers from the biting disease?

"Come on, and be quiet as you pack."

Amity didn't say a word. She just nodded and felt around for the corners of my coat before tossing it to me. Then she unrolled her own, the one she'd been using as a pillow, and put it on, her head hung low. I grabbed my satchel and her hand. And that was it. That was all we had.

"We can't say goodbye, can we?" Amity asked.

"I'm sorry, but no." The words cut my heart, just as I knew they'd cut Amity's.

She squeezed my hand, a gesture of comfort I didn't deserve. "Right. Because he'll be in danger if he knows where we're going."

"Right." The truth of her words stung. Why had I let myself indulge in all those silly daydreams about Bronger bringing Marcus into his open arms, when even Amity, a child, could see there was no reason in it?

"I wish I could leave him a gift. So he won't forget me," Amity said.

That hurt even worse. I pulled my purse from my bag and put it into her hands. "Here, you leave this for him," I said, though I knew it was nothing. Amity was smart enough to know that the purse held no sentimental connection to her. That it was a poor excuse for a keepsake.

But she did as she was told and tiptoed over to Marcus, placing it delicately next to his head. I watched her wipe her eyes with her inner elbow before she turned back toward me, and we left.

THE PATH to the Coup was not a straight shot. Not that anything could have been a straight shot in hills like these. That's why Bronger had picked them, he'd told me.

"Because they're as unpredictable as the sea," he'd said.

Except if these hills were the sea, then I was an aged sailor. Each of the hills might as well have been a key on my flute.

Our hike took us the better half of the night, mostly because Amity had to stop every few peaks to take a breath or to shed her coat, as the air was much warmer here than it had been in the mountains or even on the coast. She even stopped a few times to pick burrs out of her boots, claiming that she didn't want to disrupt the hills' ecosystem by unleashing a species of plant she might have accidentally carried over from the forest, citing ressuroot, the plant whose fatal effects were supposedly nullified in the case it was inserted directly into the heart, as her main argument. But I kept pushing her, pushing us. I told myself it was because I was hearing noises, the sounds of a wolf or coyote tracking us, waiting for us to sleep. But that was only because I was much less terrified of a simple wolf than I was of the person I was running away from. The feelings I'd have preferred to leave behind with him.

The sun peeked over the hills to our east just as we rounded the last hill, this one more oblong than the rest, just as I'd remembered it.

"Is this it?" Amity said, running ahead of me for the first time to get a good look. Her mouth dropped as she peered into the valley below her.

"Welcome home," I said.

I tried to make my voice sound cheerful.

I failed.

CHAPTER 23

PIPER

The Coup was really just a hill carved out like the inside of a pumpkin and fortified with iron beams to keep it from collapsing on itself. Once, I had asked Bronger how long it had taken him to build, and he'd told me a lifetime. That was a bit of an exaggeration, but Bronger wasn't known for subtlety. At least, not among those who actually knew he existed. He was one of the few wealthy humans left in Avelea, raised by aristocrat parents in the city of Kaelen on the eastern border of Avelea.

His parents had taken their wealth, and the task of protecting it, seriously, and had raised their little boy to think the same. They'd taught him how to hide the money in the crevices between the wooden slats of their flooring, how to swallow silver during fae inspections, which drugs would ease the pain of passing the coins.

But hiding the extent of their wealth turned out to be more of a crime than possessing it to begin with. So when a little boy by the name of Timothy Bronger witnessed his parents slaughtered at the hands of two greedy faerie tax collectors—all over a hidden purse of gold they had found and could have easily taken for themselves without laying a finger on the boy's parents—the man I knew as Bronger was born.

And what made for a more equipped revolutionary than a rich boy with a grudge? One who was well-trained in how to hide objects of importance.

Amity and I trekked down the hill into the valley as I held her hand. As we approached the Coup, which would have looked like simply another hill to any untrained passerby, Amity stared up at it wide-mouthed. For, though it was a hill, if one looked carefully they'd notice it was strange-looking, just a tad more oblong than all the others. It had a bald look about it. Where small, hearty bushes covered the other mounds, this one was devoid of any sign of life other than the short grass that covered it. But that was the thing about these hills. They all varied so drastically in shape and size, if one didn't know better, this one wouldn't stand out.

"How do we get in?" Amity asked.

"We knock," I said, leading her by the hand to the foot of the hill. I scraped the area with my foot, tapping until the sound that called back morphed from a thud into a hollow echo. Then I stomped hard, nine times in sets of triplets.

Amity's eyes rolled upward, and she tapped her foot next to me, inaudibly memorizing the beat.

Below the earth, something rumbled. It even squeaked a bit, which I imagined Bronger would throw a fit over if someone didn't fix it before it came to his attention. He would probably make a scene of marching down to the opening and slathering the handle with grease himself.

I nudged Amity backward, and the earth opened up before us.

A familiar voice piped up from below. "Well, hi there, little friend," The top of Asa's head peeked out of the hole, mostly just a shaggy set of dust-colored hair and a crooked grin that always seemed to age his face down a few years and made me forget we were the same age. "Welcome to the family!" He offered a hand toward Amity. She shot a questioning, hesitant look at me.

"It's okay. You can take it. Asa's friendly," I said, though I omitted the part about how he was one of the few who could be called that in sincerity.

Amity put her hand in his and allowed him to help her down into the hole. He didn't offer his assistance to me. Apparently, years of having me ignore it had trained him not to bother. I hopped into the hole and reached over my head for the iron wheel that served as both a handle and a lock. Then I lowered it and sealed us into the earth, into utter darkness.

"DON'T BE SCARED, LITTLE ONE," Asa said cheerfully. "It won't be dark for long. And I'll hold your hand the whole way."

"I'm not scared of the dark," Amity said.

"Is that right?"

"I got kidnapped by faeries and trapped in the bottom of a pool, so nothing really scares me anymore. Not even my father."

"Well, you're doing a lot better than I was when I first came here," said Asa. "Do you remember that, Piper?"

"Of course I remember that." Asa was the type of person who assumed everyone else forgot about him, even if that was completely unreasonable. Not that the fallacy consumed him, or even seemed to bother him. But it was ridiculous, nonetheless. Asa and I had spent four weeks together, scrambling through the Avelean countryside after I found him. He'd been a part of that first batch of kids I'd taken on my own. The first I'd succeeded in bringing back to the Coup whole.

Asa had been the son of a wealthy and cruel duke—a man with a love for liquor and women, and a tendency toward violence when he was especially drunk. Asa was the oldest child I'd taken at the time, barely younger than I was, him being twelve to my thirteen. The entire way back to the Coup he had talked. He talked about things he was anxious about; he talked about his parents; he talked about how cute the squirrels were that shimmied through the trees; he talked about how he had never seen the ocean but very much wanted to; he talked about the nightmares—the ones where wildebeests attacked us before ripping us to shreds in the middle of the night.

Naturally, I hadn't liked Asa much when we first met. But that was before I rescued all the other children, before I found the others my age who, though much less annoying, made up for it with their conniving ruthlessness.

I'd come to prefer Asa above the rest. Well, him and Elias, who was probably my favorite of the recruits. The only person in this world I thought might claim, and fit, the title of my friend.

We wandered through the dark cavern tunnel, chasing our fingers along the cold, mud-caked walls that marked our path in the dark. I probably didn't even need the walls to guide me anymore. I knew this tunnel so well. Right, left, a U-turn, and then straight, before the tunnel ended with a glimmer of light.

I couldn't count how many times I'd led other children through this dark tunnel. The path Bronger had carved into the earth just to make sure that, if an enemy ever found us, they would have to stumble around for a while before they actually saw us. There were bells scattered all over the floor for enemies to trip upon, to sound the alarm. But Asa and I knew just how to step, knew just how to lead Amity so she wouldn't set them off either.

Bronger would have known we'd made it back by now. Surely his lookout had seen us approaching from the top of the hill, where the tiniest hole had been drilled through the earth and a child was always stationed to watch. That was why Asa had already been there to greet us, to let us in. So even though there would be no consequences for setting off the bells, they were still loud and annoying. And it was better to avoid them altogether.

Eventually, that tiny glimmer appeared in the distance, indicating that we had reached the end of the tunnel. Indeed, when we arrived at the light, it was simply a lamp that Asa must've lit before coming to let us in. He opened the wooden door and doused the flame behind us.

Light flooded the tunnel and highlighted Amity's face; she was not so much concerned with the tunnel anymore as her eyes drank in the room, the community, she had just walked into.

I watched as her jaw dropped, savoring the moment.

I always did, every time I brought a child to the Coup. It was one of the few perks of my job, my crime. Seeing the amazement in their faces, the hope in their wide eyes as they witnessed what should've been impossible, yet was not.

Huge iron arches lined the edges of the hollowed-out hill, providing structural support lest the hill crumble into itself and take us all with it.

Perpendicular to the arches, thick wooden beams stretched out into large shelves that made up the various levels of the establishment.

Lining the shelves were room-sized boxes—well, they were sort of boxes—except one side, the side facing the middle of the dome, wasn't closed in so that Bronger could keep an eye on everything going on at all times. These apartments were where we slept, four to each room on a set of two bunk beds that were much more comfortable than any inn I had visited. Bronger was like that. He kept us comfortable, as much as he could.

Then there were other chambers on the second, fourth, and sixth floors, most of them meant for training in whatever specialties Bronger assigned the children once they arrived. Recruiting allowed me plenty of time to get to know the children, what they were good at, and, more importantly, what they were not good at. It was a job I took seriously, for in plucking children from their dreadful families, I had no wish to trap them in a skill they had no talent for or, worse, had no interest in.

Of course, Bronger made the final decision. But he weighed my opinion heavily, and rarely did he deviate from my recommendation. But recently there had been more incidences of controversy, not because he disagreed with my opinion of a child's talent and the occupation that would suit them, but because I found that most children were not naturally inclined toward being soldiers or spies.

Especially the type who slit throats in the darkness, the ones that were Bronger's favorite.

But just because the supply of murdery children wasn't exactly booming, did not mean that Bronger didn't have the demand for them. Especially recently, which made me anxious for Amity, whom I knew would stand out to Bronger for her resourcefulness, a quality he idolized in his soldiers. Amity, whose hands I couldn't picture being muddied with blood. Whose soul I couldn't imagine tarnished with stealing that of another.

When I turned to gauge my little friend's reaction, she was gone. My heart skipped, but I found her at the edge of the Coup, picking weeds from the cracks in the ground. She held a fistful up to her nose and sniffed, her eyes widening with delight. Then she stuffed the handful into her pocket and ran back to me.

"Marcus isn't going to believe what I f—" She stopped herself, her jaw twisting as she swallowed. Guilt struck my chest as I watched her adjust to the truth—that she'd never see him again. "Is this my home now?" she asked, her voice sounding too cheerful to be genuine.

"Yes, Amity. This is your home."

"And the kids here come from all over Avelea?"

I nodded.

"What about the older kids? Do you ever travel outside of Avelea?"

I frowned, confused as usual from trying to keep up with the curves where her thoughts trailed. "The older ones travel all over Alondria."

A grin burst through her round cheeks. "That's perfect. Well, I shouldn't say that. It's not a good thing for the ecosystem, really, with everyone tracking seeds all over the place on their clothes and boots. But..." Her face lit up. "Think of all the plants that might be growing around here." She shoved her hand back into her pocket as if to make sure that the plant she'd just salvaged from being trampled by a host of children hadn't fallen out.

I laughed. "Wait until you see the greenhouse."

Bronger had built specialty slats into the side of the hill, so light could be let in to feed the plants while still blending in to the grass that covered the hill. When I was younger, I'd spent all the time I could spare in the luscious garden.

"It's like an anthill in here," Amity said. "Or a beehive."

"Just wait till you meet our queen," said a familiar voice that made my skin crawl. James. Amity seemed to have the same reaction, for she recoiled from the boy, not in fear, but with a look of disgust.

I couldn't disagree with her initial assessment. James was by far my least favorite of the children I had recruited. To the extreme that, even though I felt guilty about it, I sometimes wished I had left him there in that dreadful home of his.

James peered down at Amity with his sickly light blue eyes, his white-blond hair perfectly combed although we lived in an anthill. Even the slight tan that bronzed his skin looked too even to be unintentional. But that was just like James, needing to be in control of everything.

And Bronger did always tell us to dress for the part.

And James did as Bronger said.

To be fair, I did too.

But with a few modifications of my own.

James seethed, as this was one of the two expressions available to him. The other one being smug. "Why do you keep bringing us the scrawny ones, Piper?"

Amity bristled. "You've never gone hungry," she said, as if it were an accusation, holding her chin high and refusing to back down from his domineering stare.

At her lack of intimidation, a cruel, calculating smile crossed James's face. I didn't like the look of it one bit.

It was true. James had never been hungry for a day in his life. While most of the children I'd taken were from poor homes, this was mostly for fear of being discovered in the richer parts of town. Rich parents had more resources with which to seek me out. James's parents were the prime example, and had even hired a bounty hunter against me. Thankfully for me, the bounty hunter had believed my story of how I only took abused children, how I led them to a better life. Something had twinkled in his eyes, betraying the true reason he couldn't bring himself to turn me in, even for the enormous bounty that rested on my head.

That was the first time I'd realized we were everywhere.

James leaned forward and placed his hands on his knees, positioning his face so that his nose almost touched Amity's. My stomach churned as I imagined how his breath must feel on her cheek. Hot and aggressive. But if James's proximity bothered Amity, she didn't let it show. She only lifted her chin higher, locking those wide brown eyes on his in a defiant sneer.

"You don't know hungry," James hissed, a sickly grin spreading across his face.

"That's enough of that." I gripped James's sleeve and yanked him backward, away from Amity, who hadn't flinched. "We don't starve children here. Acting like we do is only going to make anything else you say empty. She won't forget that you were wrong."

James wriggled out of my grasp but didn't lay a hand on me. He knew better. He might be Bronger's favorite recruit, but Bronger hadn't recruited me.

He'd adopted me.

"Seriously, James, doesn't Bronger's right-hand man have something better to do than to bully new recruits?" Asa said, suddenly infused with confidence now that I had caused James to retreat. I turned to face him and rolled my eyes. So did Amity.

He lifted his palms parallel to his shoulders as if he might have to balance a set of tall poles there. "What?"

"Bronger wants you in the Den," James said, revealing his actual reason for meeting us here. Well, that was a little satisfying. Of course, James felt the need to bully a little girl after having been outranked by one—again.

I nodded and gestured to Amity to follow me, but James stuck out a hand and gripped Amity's shoulder.

"I'm taking Amity to her quarters first. And to her assignment," I said, clutching Amity's other shoulder, though much more gently than James had. Asa's eyes raced back and forth between us, as if somewhat terrified to miss who threw the first punch.

James didn't remove his hand. "He said he wanted you *immediately*."

I scoured the flicker in his eyes, the way his gaze didn't break from mine as I traced the lines in his face, the posture of his feet in case I found him shuffling. Any hint that James was bluffing. But, even if it was a bluff, it was a believable one given Bronger's personality. And it wouldn't have been the first time he had demanded my presence immediately upon returning to the Coup. I had no idea what Bronger did to those who disobeyed his orders. I'd never had a reason to know.

I stroked Amity's shoulder with my thumb, trying my best to convey an apology without giving James the satisfaction of witnessing it.

"She's being assigned to the healers," I said, nodding toward both the seething James and the somewhat jittery Asa. "I expect the both of you to make sure she is deposited there while I meet with Bronger."

Amity looked up at me, fear spreading across her eyes as they widened. The bravery, the show for James—that had always been contingent on the fact that I'd be standing next to her the entire time. My presence gave her the strength to be so brave.

Something about that realization crushed me.

"I thought Bronger decided where to assign the recruits," James said. "And you should know better than anyone that what he needs is soldiers. I bet you'd do just fine." He looked Amity up and down. "Yes, he'd like you for a soldier. Better yet, a spy. You'd sure look harmless before you slit their throats."

At that comment, Amity's shoulders shook, and she looked up at me again, pleading with her eyes to tell me it wasn't true, that I hadn't rescued her from her violent father just to train her to be just like him. To be worse.

I ripped my gaze away from Amity, unable to bear it. Unable to allow her to see the fear in my eyes, the possibility—no, the probability—that Bronger would see her for her cunning, her cleverness, and decide to take full advantage of it.

But not if I had any sway with Bronger, and I reckoned I did. I had to.

"I'll meet with Bronger shortly, but first I need a healer to see to my arm. I'll escort Amity there unless you'd like to explain to Bronger why it was efficient for you to tag along as well."

Amity ripped herself from James's grip and wrapped her arms tightly around me for half a moment.

James stared at my waist, where Amity had just buried her head into my robes.

Then he lifted his chin, dissecting me with his icy stare, and grinned.

CHAPTER 24

PIPER

Bronger's quarters nested above. His home was a box suspended in the air in the middle of the Coup, supported by iron beams that crisscrossed out from the scaffolding that reinforced the structure of our hive.

I had never understood why Bronger lived in what I considered the most unstable section of the entire Coup. There was no counting how many times his abode had plummeted to the ground in my mind, whether by erosion of the outer shell of the hive itself, or Bronger's substantial weight growing to be too much for the floor of his box due to a loose bolt, or any other nasty thought that weaseled its way into my mind during sleepless nights.

But he'd always insisted that he liked it up there in that shabby box. That was the one advantage humans had over the fae, after all—an ever-present reverence for death. Bronger's apartment acted as a constant admonition of such thinking. A reminder that at any moment, he could fall to his death and someone else would have to take up his cause.

Plus, he could see everything that went on in the Coup from way up there.

It was a good thing Callie, one of our best healers, had fixed up my arm with a numbing potion. She'd checked out the injury, feeling around for bits of bone that might have regrown poorly, and declared teasingly that it must be nice to have fae blood running through my veins. Apparently my arm was mostly healed, except for a bit of tenderness which she'd solved with the swig of essence of *ooperung* she'd given me.

Amity had been thrilled, and my anxiety had eased just a tad knowing that I was leaving her in the care of a kind soul.

I started my ascent, scaling the carved rungs in the metal scaffolding. There were other ways to maneuver the Coup, such as using the sidewalks that lined the outside edges of each shelf and then morphed into ramps that led to the next level. But I'd never liked using the ramps. I detested the feeling of weaving back and forth, back and forth, never really making any significant progress toward my destination.

Bronger and I were alike in that way. He never used the ramps either. Though I often wished that he would, just like I often wished he'd move out of that death-taunting box of his.

The cold metal might have rubbed my palms raw if it weren't for all the calluses I'd developed over the years. The rungs that had once rubbed blisters into my hands now charged my soul with a vigor that surged from the cold metal at my fingertips and through my bloodstream.

As I climbed, I caught glimpses of several members of the Coup. They dropped their tasks to watch me. They always did. I nodded at each of them, and they offered me a solemn bow in return. Sometimes I wondered why they watched me. I knew, of course, that to many, my face had become the symbol of freedom. Especially the children I'd taken from the most severe caregivers, the most destitute of situations. Many of them frequently stopped me to thank me for it.

But then I had brought them here, and might as well have poured cement over those wide-eyed dreams. I could never quite tell if the Coup lived up to their expectations. I was certain it didn't, as it hadn't lived up to mine. But amongst all the fantasies I'd dreamed up as a lonely, despised child, amid all the dreams of sweets and furry pets and pretty books with decorative covers to read by a warm fireplace, underneath all that... well, I had really just wanted a family. A shelter where my fingers wouldn't fall off, withered and crumbled, lost forever in the snow. A full belly.

And I had that.

Well, I definitely had the full belly.

And most of the time, except for the occasions when a recruitment took me through the mountains or to the northern border of Avelea in the winter months, I had warmth.

And I had Bronger.

And he was family.

I had to push out the image of Marcus carrying Amity on his shoulders through the mountains, tucking her into his coat at night, laughing and teasing and telling her jokes.

I climbed and climbed, ignoring the jangling sound of metal scraping against itself as I ascended, ignoring the slight tremble of the metal rods as they braced themselves for my weight, ignoring how, if I were to look down now, I wouldn't be able to tell Amity from all the other children who lived here, ignoring how the beams I was using as a ladder now curved over my head. How I'd soon be parallel to the ground.

This had to be the true reason Bronger dwelled all the way up here. Because only the fearless, the ones most devoted to him in loyalty or hatred, would dare make this climb. At this height. At this angle.

What Bronger didn't know was that I was not fearless.

But then again, he probably did know that. And that there was only one other reason to make the climb.

My heart slammed itself against my chest, trying its best at an escape attempt before I killed myself and it with me. When that didn't work, it pounded at my eardrums, the sound dispatching pain to my forehead as my world spun around me.

I could have climbed all day.

But hang.

That was a different story.

You've done this a million times, I told myself, probably only for the hundredth time.

Sweat oozed from the creases in my fingertips, a sign of my body threatening me. As if to say, *We'll do it. We really will. Don't think we won't.*

I allowed my feet to let go. My heart dropped through my stomach and hurtled to the ground. I used the momentum to swing my feet backward, then up. Soreness pinched my waist, but I forced my legs upward and wrapped them around the metal pole. I gripped onto the rungs that Bronger had carved underneath the scaffolding and shimmied along the rafter, sliding my legs along with me.

A few moments later, the lamplight from the rafters disappeared from my tear-blurred vision, and I allowed my legs to drop. They thumped on solid ground, and I thought I might vomit at the familiarity of the impact.

There was something about doing a dangerous thing over and over. I would have thought I'd have gotten used to it by now, that it wouldn't faze me. But with each success, only one thought remained.

Now to see if you can make it back.

I wiped the tears from my eyes, as I always did, just before his voice rumbled behind me.

"My child, how grateful I am that you're home."

I turned to face him, something clenching in my stomach as I did.

For most of my life, Bronger had looked the same as he always had, but maybe all children felt that way about their parents up to a certain point.

But although Bronger kept his hair slicked neatly backward, although it was still a youthful blond, I couldn't help but notice the gray streaks in the unruly strands that seemed unaffected by the oils he used to tame them. And his face, whose striking features had only been enhanced with age, still betrayed the passing of time. The jagged lines in his forehead revealed that, at some point, this confident leader had been concerned, worried even.

I had first noticed the difference about a year ago, and now it seemed to become more and more pervasive with each recruitment.

"I'm grateful to be home," I responded, not wishing for him to see the pain in my eyes as I witnessed the one enemy I was certain Bronger would never outsmart.

Not with all the children in the world could Bronger ever raise an army against Time itself.

"What have you brought me this time?" He gestured to one of the many windows that lined his box. I followed him across the room, noting how nothing had changed since my last visit here. Bronger was only lavish in his outward presentation of himself to outsiders, to the children. Which was perhaps another reason he kept his quarters so distant from prying eyes. In the room was a bed, neatly made as it always was, a desk with a stack of papers creased with precision, and a wardrobe. Well, if one could call a piece of furniture that was so exquisitely engineered that it weighed less than I did a wardrobe.

There was also a chamber pot in the corner, but I refused to look in its direction.

"Is this the child?" Bronger said, looking down out of the window with a set of wooden binoculars he carried around his neck at all times, at least while he was inside the Coup. He handed the binoculars to me and I searched for Amity.

I found her in the Healer's box, where I'd just left her.

There she sat, already at the bedside of a child I'd recruited but whose name I could not remember. She was helping one of the older healers, a girl name Sunni from the slums of Nettlewood, bandage the child's ankle.

"Yes, that's her. It seems she's already living up to her potential," I said, unable to keep the proud smirk from smearing my face. "I knew she'd make the perfect healer."

"You've found many perfect healers," Bronger said, in a voice that sounded too much like amusement for me to take it lightly.

I lowered my binoculars and handed them back to him cautiously. "Avelea is rich in medicinal plants. And the fae are stingy with their own healers. The villagers learn to make their own remedies when they're just children," I said, hating the way my pitch rose at the end of the statement. The uncertainty, the defensiveness in my voice.

"So it is," he said. "As it is also rich in young builders, young chefs, young farmers. One would think that, for a place invaded by the fae, there would be more children out there who'd learned to fend for themselves in more direct ways."

I swallowed.

"Perhaps I could make it my mission to search out older recruits, ones who've already seen violence, the type of violence caused by the fae. Recruits who would understand the need for war." I fumbled over my words in my haste to clear myself, to remove any thought of the children, any thought of Amity, from Bronger's mind.

"You don't believe the young can defend our people?" Bronger asked, an air of amusement in his voice that made me sick to my stomach.

I'd known this day would come, the day Bronger would catch onto the fact that perhaps I was purposefully keeping children from joining his soldiers' ranks.

I'd just have to make sure he knew it had nothing to do with my loyalty to his cause.

It took everything left in me after the harrowing climb to sound confident, to expel the panic from my voice. "I wouldn't count on an eight-year-old not to shrink from making a final blow, no."

"You brought me James when he was but a youth," Bronger said.

"I didn't know yet that he was a youth. We were the same age," I said.

"Yet he's been not just useful, but reliable," Bronger said.

Yes, I knew that. James wasn't one to maintain secrecy when it came to his missions that involved capturing fae, weakening them with poisons, and torturing political information out of them before slitting their throats.

"James has a unique ability to..." I cautioned myself from using the term I'd usually use for Bronger's favorite recruits, as I was sure James also did when he spoke of Bronger's favorite child, "compartmentalize," I settled on.

"Indeed. And why aren't you bringing me more children who can *compartmentalize*, as you say?" Bronger asked.

"My gift is the one who calls them, chooses them. I have no control over the matter." I crossed my arms, as if this would prove my point.

Bronger grinned, but the skin around his eyes didn't budge. "I am beginning to wonder if your gift is as sentimental as you, my dear." The words struck me right where intended, between my ribs. To be called sentimental by Bronger, the one who'd burned down his dead parents' estate to fake his own death, was not a compliment.

"I'll be more selective in the future," I said.

"Good," said Bronger. "I expect you tomorrow for Council."

"Yes, sir," I said, understanding this as his dismissal.

I walked back over to the balcony where I'd come in and tried to gather up the nerve to shimmy across the pole again.

"Oh, and Piper?" Bronger asked.

"Yes," I said, turning back to him.

"Escort our new friend to Intel."

Intel. Bronger's spies. The head of which was James.

"She's a talented healer." My words broke in my throat, betraying my anxiety.

"Good. I'm in need of a new poison."

CHAPTER 25

PIPER

I waited longer than necessary before looking for Amity. Not that I didn't long to see her. After all, I'd just deposited her in a community that was anything but familiar. But on the off chance that she already felt at home, her first proper home... I wasn't exactly rushing myself to ruin it for her.

So I sat on the ground floor of the Coup, curled up in the least defeated-looking ball I could muster. My arms and legs still shook from my shimmy across the iron beam. My head still spun from the gripping dread of being up that high with only my brute strength and agility to support me. Children passed by, attempting not to stare, but none of them wandered past me without allowing their eyes to flicker in my direction. I supposed most of them had never seen me panic before.

Nor would they, for I was holding it in.

Finally, overly aware, as I always was, that Bronger was probably watching me with those binoculars of his, heavy with the weight of what I was about to do, I pushed myself off the ground.

Despite my legs having turned to bricks, I reached the infirmary faster than I had intended. And then I was there, and Amity was there, still leaning over the injured boy, squeezing his hand as another healer sliced at what looked to be an infected growth on his ankle. The boy howled, and I turned away, swallowing my gag reflex. The boy's scream calmed to effortful pants, and I turned back, just to find Amity stroking his forehead, comforting him.

I was going to be sick.

Only once the boy had passed out did Amity look up at me.

"Piper!" She jumped to her feet, that steely maturity that had marked her face as she comforted the boy now softening into that wide-eyed wonder of childhood.

Teetering, that's what Amity was doing. Teetering on the edge of childhood and adulthood. Except I was about to shove her over the edge for good.

"Look what I made." Amity shuffled over to the far end of the box. I followed her, passing three beds, all of them full of sleeping children. The healers, all of whom I recognized, dressed in simple, white gowns from head to toe, parted way for me. One of them, Callie was her name, grinned at me as I passed. I stomached a faint smile and returned it to her. The healers differed from the other children, the children who treated me with solemn reverence. The healers smiled as if I were a friend, and I supposed I was. I'd placed them in the one job here that wouldn't steal their humanity.

At least not yet.

They hadn't healed during wartime yet.

Amity gestured to a table full of vials. Vials of herbs and roots, vials of medicines, vials of rare viper fangs and Phoenix feathers, and I wanted nothing to do with knowing how they'd been acquired.

Amity held out a vial full of a murky-looking substance with enough joy on her face that she could have lit up the entire Coup. "Look, I invented a new medicine."

"It looks like it'd be impossible to swallow," I said, taking the vial from her and turning it in my hands. If someone had forced me to guess the nature of the liquid at knifepoint, healing properties wouldn't have crossed my mind. "Like it would stick to your throat on the way down."

Amity giggled, the sound of which echoed through the box and made my stomach roll. "No, I'm being serious."

"She sure is," Callie said, joining us as we stared at the vial. She placed a casual elbow on my shoulder, and I tried not to flinch. "I'm actually pretty upset with myself for not having thought of it myself."

"So what does it do?" I asked. I knew it was wrong, that I should rip off the bandage and tell Amity she was being transferred to Intel. That it was cruel to let her get her hopes up, indulge in some beautiful future she'd created for herself in her mind, one where she used her talents to heal rather than to destroy. But even if it was selfish, I wanted to believe in that future too.

"First, you have to guess! I'll give you a clue. It—"

"Doesn't matter what it does, because you'll not be administering it," a cruel voice cut in. I turned to find James leaning so casually in the doorway, I wished it would break so that he would tumble with it.

"I'm a healer. That makes me qualified to use this," Amity piped up. "Last I checked, you weren't. Actually, I don't even know what your job is."

James's lips curled into a grin.

"Amity—" I said, but James cut in.

"Oh, no, Piper. You got your chance to break the news to her gently. But you sat there moping on the ground for a good half hour. Bronger is concerned you might have forgotten the meaning of *immediately*. So he sent me to do what should have been your job. You'll owe me for this."

Amity's confident stare turned on me, melting. "What's he talking about?"

"I... uh... You're meant—"

"You're being reassigned. On Bronger's orders. With Piper's recommendation, of course," James said.

Amity gripped my hand, intertwining her cold, little fingers around mine as she glared at James. "That's not true. You're lying." Her tone might have been convincing if her hand wasn't trembling in mine.

James shrugged. "Ask your friend."

Amity looked up at me, and the pain in her brown eyes ran deep. As if to remind me she'd never questioned me, never given me a reason to punish her. She'd knocked out her own father and followed a stranger into the woods. She'd forgiven me when I'd allowed her to be carried off by a pair of forest faeries. Even when she'd almost drowned at the bottom of a pool after teetering somewhere between this world and the one beyond. Even when I'd ripped her away from Marcus, the first truly good person ever to waltz into her life, she hadn't questioned me.

After all that, I'd betrayed her.

"Amity, sweetie." I kneeled beside her, placing my hands on both of her cold cheeks. As if getting down to eye level would somehow make my empty words more true, more concrete. "I spoke with Bronger, and I told him you'd make the best healer the Coup has ever seen." I swallowed and glanced up at Callie. Thankfully, her soft face showed no sign of jealousy. Her brows tilted for Amity, her oval face wiped clean of the joy at she'd had when she first saw me, thrilled to share Amity's gift with me.

"Then I get to stay, right?" Amity's pitch rose and cracked, breaking like waves against the coastal cliffs. A single tear welled in her left eye.

"What Bronger's doing... His plan is important. Too important for a child to completely—" I stopped myself as Amity's jaw tensed. What was I doing, pretending this little girl hadn't experienced, hadn't *survived* an adult's share of grief? I breathed in, changed course. "You're a clever girl. You might not see it yet, but it won't take you long at all. Bronger's going to make things right again. Right, like things haven't been in centuries. He's going to make this world a better place for the humans. For all the little girls out there just like you. So the high fae can't hurt us anymore."

Amity swallowed and fidgeted with her sleeves. She rolled them up, revealing discolored patches of skin, the way her right wrist knotted and curled in all the wrong places, as if it'd been crushed one too many times. "No high fae's ever hurt me."

But a human has.

And now a half-fae has.

The shards of her words and what they implied punctured my stomach.

James yawned. "Cal, pumpkin. Take the girl over to Intel, won't you? I'll see to it she's properly oriented later. Piper and I have a meeting to attend, and we're already late."

Amity didn't cling to me this time. Instead, she turned and adhered to Callie's side. She didn't say goodbye as they strode from the infirmary.

"Well?" James asked. "Ready to start a war?"

CHAPTER 26

PIPER

"I'm not accustomed to both my right and left hands arriving late," Bronger said as James and I entered the council room. James bristled, and I thought I saw a hint of satisfaction flicker in Bronger's pale blue eyes. He'd done it on purpose—used that sort of vague language that would leave James wondering which had referred to him.

Why he wanted his two favorites to hate one another, to exist in constant competition, I had no idea. Life had beaten the competitive bone out of my body. Honestly, I was impressed that James still possessed it.

"You know how it goes, when a mess seems small until it takes a professional to clean it up," James said. He strode over to the chair next to Bronger's, one of the two empty seats left at our conference table, a long wooden board stacked on top of four legs, each simply a pile of crates which had once held shipments of medicine and food. Bronger was the recycling type. Mostly with things, though I was beginning to wonder if this mentally applied to his troops as well. If he was willing to move Amity from an occupation when she'd already settled, would it bother him to transfer more children to his fighting ranks?

The council room was located underground. Well, deeper underground than we already were.

Along the table sat a crew of familiar faces, each of which I'd recruited over the past four years. At the far side of the room behind Bronger's seat was a portrait that reminded me of how he'd looked in his younger years, back when it had been just the two of us living here.

Back when he'd ordered the construction of the tunnel whose opening was obstructed from view by the portrait itself.

I was the only one who knew about Bronger's alternate escape route. He'd murdered the men he'd contracted to build it.

Or, I thought I was the only one. These days, I supposed I couldn't be so sure that Bronger hadn't shared that tidbit of information with my rival.

I situated myself in the seat at the far end of the table from Bronger, next to Elias, an orphaned recruit slightly older than I was whom I'd plucked from his slavedriver of an uncle's farm.

I'd been too late for his sister.

They'd already sold her off to a merchant known for amassing his own personal brothel.

He leaned in close, his dark, shaggy hair falling into his eyes, and I couldn't help but notice him wince. "Nice to have you back."

I eyed his side, which he clutched with his free hand. "What happened to you?" Last I'd seen or heard from Elias, Bronger had sent him to recruit an up-and-coming assassin known as the Umbra. From the looks of it, things hadn't gone so well.

"Story for another time," he said, winking, then nodding toward the rest of the table.

The eyes of my companions, careful not to jerk their heads away from Bronger, darted back and forth between us, and at James. I couldn't blame them. I, too, wondered whether any rebuke was in order. James had taken the seat that had been mine since it had just been Bronger and me down here, eating dinner together as a father and daughter might.

If Bronger noted the change in seating arrangement, it didn't show on his face.

"We were just discussing our plans for the upcoming *change in direction* our kingdom is facing," Bronger said.

James chuckled at the thinly veiled implications of that term, which annoyed me. James had no appreciation for subtlety.

"Do you believe the Coup to be ready, then?" I asked, trying not to shift in my seat as I asked the question. I had no wish to come off to Bronger as a doubter. But I supposed such an assessment would be fair, because I doubted very much that we were ready.

The corners of his lips twitched. "Do you not?"

The faces of eight others I'd once rescued shifted ever so slightly in my direction.

"Over half of our number is still considered underage. I thought the purpose of the Coup was to raise a group of children into an army, into a government. To train them up into the roles they'll fill *when they're grown.*" Breath clenched around me from all edges of the table. I stopped myself from biting my tongue. Bronger would have probably seen me doing that under my closed lips, with his annoyingly youthful vision.

I'd never confronted him before. Especially not in the open. The table between us seemed to lengthen. His fists clenched onto the table, the only hint in his demeanor that he resented my words. That there would be consequences. "You should know as well as anyone, my child, that our strength is not in numbers or age, but in our stealth. Our cunning."

And then I was back in the inn with Marcus, leaning into his kiss, his lips a breath away from mine.

Cunning. Another word to describe a liar. The type of being it would have been a mistake for Marcus to kiss.

I reined in my thoughts. No, Bronger didn't get to use those insecurities against me. Especially when he didn't even know about them. I wasn't going to let him push those buttons, the strikes he so often landed despite having stabbed in the dark.

"I'm eager to hear your plan." It took physical effort to loosen my jaw enough to keep from hissing the words through gritted teeth. Why was I so angry all of a sudden? Because Bronger had commanded me to place Amity with Intel? This wasn't the first time we'd disagreed on a placement. Not the first time I'd had to feel tiny hands wrap around my fingers, wide eyes beg me to tell them it wasn't true, that they'd simply misheard me. That Bronger had assigned them to the Garden or something equally benign.

What was different between us this time?

It certainly wasn't Bronger.

Something about that thought churned my stomach, leaving a sour taste in my mouth.

"Neven," Bronger said, nodding to the boy on my right. He was barely eighteen. One of the few children Bronger had recruited himself before he'd handed over that position entirely to me. I'd always wondered about Neven's story, where Bronger had picked him up. If he'd come willingly.

Willing or not, he was clever as humans came. Not the scheming type, at least when he'd first arrived, but Bronger could turn just about any form of intelligence into cunning with enough time. Now Neven was our strategist. He compiled all the evidence brought to Bronger from our Intel and used it to draw up plans, rescue missions. Apparently, assassinations.

Neven cleared his throat and straightened in his chair. "We're to infiltrate the palace in a fortnight. Avelea is hosting a festival to celebrate the blood moon that evening, and ambassadors from all over Alondria will attend, as well as their personal guards. It will be the last night anyone would suspect an assassination attempt, with so many guards swarming the city."

If it were me, and I was king, I was fairly certain large events would be pretty high on my list of assassination threats. "He wouldn't suspect other kingdoms to use this as an excuse to attempt a takeover?"

"Don't you know anything about your kind?" James scoffed, leaning back in his chair and closing his eyes. As if he had grown bored with the explanation I required.

Bronger's blue eyes flashed. "Now, James. Piper's been off in the remote villages of Avelea. She's sacrificed her studies, her education for our cause. Don't chastise her for acting nobly."

My chest constricted. Why did his defense of me sound so insincere, like a veiled knife, meant to rip through the fabric and cut deep? I hadn't neglected all my studies. I'd read during my travels. But saying so would only give James the pleasure of hearing me grasp to defend my intellect, my right to be in this room.

"I was thinking the same thing," said Vanity—Van for short since she despised her given name. She sat two seats down from Bronger's left, the lantern light highlighting the warm undertones of her brown skin. Since I'd left, she'd cropped her hair close to her head, which somehow made her look even more stunningly feminine.

I offered Van a grateful half-grimace and decided I'd thank her later. There was no way Vanity wasn't aware of an important detail about the political inner workings of the kingdoms of Alondria. It was her job, her purpose to know, seeing as she was being groomed for the position of Bronger's closest advisor once he took the throne.

Neven's gaze flitted around the room before he spoke, as if to ensure those trained in combat had finished talking. "The fae rulers have created a bargain—a magical bond that would bring death upon whoever broke it—that they won't attack one another during festivals and holidays."

James leaned back in his chair. "We all know what a fae bargain is, know-it-all."

Neven flushed, but before he could react, I spoke my mind. "Okay, so they won't suspect an attack from one of their own. But as far as I'm aware, that bargain doesn't apply to humans." I knew good and well the counterargument that I was sure James was about to spit at me. But I didn't care; I was going to argue against this to the end.

Why, though?

Wasn't this what I'd worked for my entire childhood? Wasn't this why I had recruited so many children?

But it wasn't James who countered. It was Bronger. "The fae of this age are too sick on their own hubris, too suspicious of their own kind to imagine the humans might rise against them."

"So what's the plan?" I asked Neven.

Content to return to his exposition, Neven drew an invisible map on the table with his fingertips. "We're to sneak into the castle disguised as the entertainment."

I leaned over, having to rely on my half-fae vision to see the map from so far down the table. "How many of us can entertain?"

"You're not the only one with tricks up your sleeve," Van said, though more with a sense of pride than of someone taking offense.

"Surely the fae king isn't foolish enough to allow just anyone posing as an entertainer in his castle!" It was easy enough to feign outrage, though I was secretly pleased to have spotted an actual gaping hole in this plan I so desperately longed to foil, for some reason unknown to me.

Maybe I just didn't want Amity tangled up in all this. Maybe I never wanted her to have to use her poisons, to craft them just for James to come back and embellish the stories of the deaths of those who succumbed to her concoctions.

"Ah, but we've thought of that," said Neven, whom I was glad responded first, as James's mouth was wide open and practically dripping with malice. "The papers, the recommendations from lords of the Avelean districts, are all in order. With all of our credentials, there was no way the king would pick another group for his personal entertainment."

"And what if one of the forged letters of recommendation gets brought up in front of one of the many lords attending this gathering?"

"Then they'll grin from ear to ear for having made the recommendation ultimately selected by the king." James leaned so far back in his chair I thought, hoped, it might topple backward. With luck, he might break his neck.

"We've been managing a band of entertainers the past few months," Van explained, clearly sensing how utterly lost I was. "The kids are really pretty talented." She must have seen the look of concern spread across my face, for she continued, "But they won't be the ones who show up for the festival. Only in name will *The Coop* be attending."

"Yes," Neven said, "and we were careful to make sure there were enough performers, and that they were reasonably close to us in age, that should anyone recognize the group's name, they wouldn't be able to pick out whether we were the performers they heard that day or not."

"So once you're in, then what?" I asked.

"Then you play," Bronger said. For a moment, I thought he was talking to the group, and I almost laughed. James would certainly have to sit this one out. I'd heard him attempt to play the lyre to impress some girls here. He'd thrown it off the fourth level after Van had advised him not to hurry to ask Bronger for a transfer of roles.

But then, as that wicked pleasure flickered in Bronger's eyes, I knew he wasn't talking to them. He was talking to me.

"You want me to take the children of the court?" I asked, my breath catching. "I've never tried my gift on fae children. There's no telling whether it would work." I instantly remembered a tower of water suspended in midair, drowning that horrible forest faerie until I commanded it to drop her dead body against the wet ground.

Perhaps I could enchant the fae children after all.

"Not exactly," Bronger replied, grinning. "There's a human child, a servant of the king's court. The child possesses a gift of her own, not unlike yours. But she remains by the king's side night and day, and even sleeps in a hidden room adjacent to his own lest he need her protection in the middle of the night."

"And what can she do?" I asked.

While James and Bronger exchanged greedy glances, a stony, sober shadow fell over both Neven's and Van's faces.

"It's not completely clear," Neven said, "but with the information our Intel has collected, we believe it is within her power to—"

James groaned. "Oh, just spit it out, Neven. The girl can get inside your head."

"She can read minds?" I asked, dread sweeping over me.

Neven sighed and shook his head, as if my apparent misunderstanding had been exactly why he hadn't simply *spit it out*. "Not exactly. We haven't been able to pinpoint the parameters of her gift. It seems as though her power lies in her ability to influence the mind, more than read it, though we'd be fools to rely on the information of spies whose minds have so clearly been warped."

The look of wild pleasure in Bronger's eyes sent an unpleasant shudder down my spine. The possibility of that kind of power at his disposal gleamed in his pale blue eyes, reminding me of ice. The kind that had almost frozen my fingers off as a child.

What would Bronger do with a girl who could influence the minds of others?

What would he not do?

"There are limits on her power, though," Van said.

Neven sighed, tapping his fingertips frantically on the table. "If our information is correct. But I wouldn't count on it. It's just as likely that the king has ordered his subjects to leak false information about the girl. But, as our sources have always been reliable until now, we have good reason to suspect that her powers are confined to those she touches."

That didn't make me feel that much better. "Skin to skin contact, or can she use her gift through clothes?"

"Our Intel didn't collect that information," Neven said, his face deadpan, his tell for exasperation. As if he had resigned himself to others never quite living up to how he would go about things, were he not so limited by his size, general frailty, and lack of health.

"Great," Van snorted.

"If Piper's doing her job right, she shouldn't be able to get anywhere near you to begin with," James said.

I shook my head in disbelief. "I've never used my gift on another Gifted. We have no way of knowing whether it would work."

"She's human. You'll figure it out," Bronger said. "And if you can't, then make that gift of yours figure it out."

Something constricted inside my chest, riling up in a defensive posture.

"If she's human, how is she Gifted?" I asked.

Bronger shrugged. "How is the Queen of Naenden Gifted?"

"And then what? Once I've lured the girl out, what's our plan?" I asked.

James grinned. "Take the girl. Kill the king."

I snorted. "That's it? *Kill the king*. Like it's that simple. He's high fae, unless you've forgotten."

A smile snaked across Bronger's lips. "You just worry about getting the girl away from the king. James will take care of the rest."

I WAS the first to leave the council meeting.

Apparently, Elias was the second.

I heard him coming from halfway down the cascading ramps.

It was my own fault for not taking the ladders this time.

"Is your life really so important that you must sprint everywhere you go?" he asked, huffing as he caught up to me, his hand still clutching his side.

"I don't know. You tell me. Was it all that important when I rescued you from shoveling cow manure?" I asked, whipping around to face him and accidentally smacking myself in the face with my curls in the process.

Elias laughed, then winced, squeezing his side. "Please don't make a fool of yourself, Pipe. You'll burst my stitches."

"You going to tell me what happened to you?" I asked, eyeing the spot as if I could examine the wound through his thick tunic.

"Didn't plan on it."

"Why not? Afraid I'd make fun of you?"

"Something like that."

"I take it you didn't recruit the Umbra?"

Elias brought a finger to his lips and shushed me. I tried not to smile, but that was a feat of faelike strength when Elias was around. While people like James poured their rage into...well, more rage, and people like Van beat theirs into submission in the training ring, Elias had suffered more than most of us, and yet he was always trying to get a smile out of me. Out of everyone.

He was pretty good at it too.

The way his eyes wrinkled when he grinned was more infectious than consumption.

"I didn't. But I do have a pretty gnarly scar to show for my efforts."

"Great."

"What do you have to show for yours?"

"I broke my arm. Well, someone else broke my arm."

"It doesn't look broken."

"That's because it healed."

"Remind me, why were you trying to compare your healed arm to my collapsed lung?"

I went to nudge him in the ribs, as was our custom, but thought better of it. Freshly inflated lung, and all.

"When did you get so considerate?" he asked. "I'm not sure I like it."

"I wouldn't test me if I were you."

"So are we going to talk about what happened in there?"

I almost stopped in place, but then I remembered I was putting as much space as possible between myself and Bronger, so I persisted down the ramp. "No."

"Alright then. If *we* aren't going to talk about it, *I* will talk about it."

"I'd rather you not."

"I'm aware. Anyway, what's going on between you and Bronger? I've never seen so much tension between the two of you."

"I don't know. Maybe James has been weaseling up to him while I've been gone."

Elias flared his nose at the name. "James has been doing that for years, now. I doubt a couple of months made a difference."

I shrugged. "Bronger and I had a disagreement about where the newest recruit should be placed. Nothing out of the ordinary."

Elias raised an eyebrow, which I could barely see under his shaggy mess of hair.

"What?" I shoved him this time. Hard.

He bit his lip to swallow a yelp. "Ouch, Pipe. I didn't say anything."

"But you implied it with your eyebrow."

"Can you even see my eyebrows?"

"A little."

He sighed. "I knew I shouldn't have gotten that haircut." Then he straightened and continued following me. "All I'm thinking is that it's been a long time, if ever, that you recommended a new recruit train with the soldiers."

I shrugged. Again. "It's been a while since I've found a kid I thought was up to the task."

He stopped me then, placing his hand on my shoulder. I swallowed, not entirely comfortable with the seriousness that had overtaken his usually easygoing expression. "Pipe, if you're..." He sighed and swept his hair from his eyes. "If you're having second thoughts about all this, you know you can tell me, right?"

I stiffened, and he dropped his hand from my shoulder. My mouth went dry. "I'm not having second thoughts."

"I'm just saying that if you were—"

"I'm not."

Elias pursed his lips, as if he wanted to press me further. But then that charming smile returned and he offered his arm to me. "Care to escort me to dinner?" he asked. "It's not as easy as it looks walking down an incline with a recently collapsed lung."

I groaned and took his arm. "You're not going to tell me what happened?"

"Not if you won't tell me you're having second thoughts, I won't."

And that was the end of that.

CHAPTER 27

MARCUS

Amity and Piper were gone. They'd slipped into the earth and disappeared.

I'd been forced to follow them at a distance. Before, when I'd tracked them in the forest, there had been a million tiny sounds—brooks bumbling, bees humming, chipmunks scampering—to distract from the crunch of my boots on dry leaves, the slight labor of my breath.

Here in the hills, things were more complicated.

They'd barely left the inn this morning when I slipped down the stairs and out the back door, circling around to the front to track them across the city. The streets had been practically empty at that hour, which was good and bad, I supposed. Good, because there was less of a risk of losing them in the crowd. Bad, because, as easy as they were to spot, that meant them spotting me was just as easy as turning around.

Piper had been especially antsy. There were at least two instances when I was shocked she hadn't seen me. I'd had to dive behind a pile of barrels or into an alley at the sudden jerk of her head.

It was a good thing I'd downed that glass of tea last night, otherwise her paranoia might have made her impossible to follow.

As they slunk into the hills, Piper's mannerisms shifted. At first, I'd thought she'd relaxed, that maybe she was close enough to her final destination that she was relieved to have finally arrived.

But I caught the expression on her face once as she turned to Amity, and I hadn't seen any evidence of relief. Only resignation.

The reflex to pity her had been familiar, sudden.

But I was done pitying the woman who had led my sister to her slaughter.

Though the hills were unfortunately quiet, they made up for it in visibility. At least, visibility on my end. It was arduous, but rather easy to sneak behind them and use the terrain for shelter from Piper's sharp eyesight.

Besides, the rugged terrain buffered the sound of my footsteps, so for that I was grateful.

As grateful as I supposed I could be, given the situation.

I'd almost missed them slipping into the earth, almost missed Amity tapping out what must have been a signal into the air, mimicking Piper.

Their voices, muffled as they were due to the hills, had wafted to me on the breeze, and I'd even thought I'd heard another. A male voice. Young and bright.

I'd had the rest of the day, which was most of it, to contemplate my plan, but after scoping out the hill from all angles, at least from a safe distance, I couldn't find any evidence of another way in.

Well, not at first.

But this wasn't exactly my first assignment either.

Whoever Piper worked for, I imagined they were well-armed, heavily guarded. Traffickers always were, at least those at the top of the food chain.

But there was something I'd learned about ringleaders over the years.

They always had an escape plan.

Always.

So though I couldn't spot any evidence of another way into the underground bunker, I knew better than to trust my eyes.

I paced, hands interlocked behind my head, a safe distance from the visibility of the hill into which Piper and Amity had disappeared, and thought.

If I were constructing a headquarters with multiple escape routes, how would I keep them hidden from those closest to me?

I figured the first step would be to dig an escape tunnel that let out as far from the bunker as possible. That way, anyone returning to the headquarters with supplies or, like Piper, home from a mission, wouldn't stumble upon it on accident. But that could mean anything from a bear cave to a...

My memory flashed back to Piper shoving her hand into the snake den to retrieve the forest faeries' flute. The thought produced no small amount of hopelessness in me, reminding me that the entrance to the tunnel could be marked by anything, anywhere, within a several-mile radius.

It could take me weeks to find another entrance, assuming there was one.

I didn't let myself think what might happen to Amity given weeks in the hands of Piper's employer.

I slumped onto the ground, pressing my back flat against the steep slope of the closest hill. I'd brushed Amity off last night, too overwhelmed by my conflicting feelings for Piper, my internal debate of whether to tell her the truth, to bother with her questions.

Amity wasn't the first child I'd brushed off.

The first child I'd failed to make my priority.

I closed my eyes, imagining what I'd tell her when I found her, as if doing so would will it into being.

She'd asked about how the people in Nettlewood could have running water indoors. How little effort would it have taken to explain the underground waterways that supplied the city? Sure, she would have had a million questions.

Who dug them?

How long did it take?

How do the houses not fall straight through the earth?

Do you think spies ever use them?

I jolted upright. *Amity, you genius little girl.*

When I arrived in Nettlewood, the sun had already slipped over the horizon. Not that sunlight would have been much help where I was going. Upon arriving in town, I purchased a torch from a vendor closing up shop.

When I slipped into the entrance of an aqueduct, no one seemed to notice.

It took me several hours to work my way through the maze of underground tunnels. I headed east anytime a tunnel broke off in that direction, the gentle sway of the water somewhat soothing as it rushed through the waterway beneath the stone walkway on which I raced. My torchlight waned with every passing minute, and I'd about determined I'd been mistaken, when I finally found a map of the aqueducts boarded to the wall.

I wasn't sure what I was expecting. Surely not for the secret tunnel to be clearly marked on the map. Instead, it simply showed a tangle of aqueducts snaking their way around the city. Even the source of the water was no use, as it snaked out to the freshwater sea, south rather than east where Piper and Amity were.

Not a single tunnel headed toward the hills.

I placed my forehead against the cool, damp wood of the sign, frustration boiling within me.

I wasn't sure what I was expecting when I punched the damp wood.

Perhaps for the pain of a few splinters to act as a release for the guilt that weighed on my shoulders.

What I didn't anticipate was for my hand to go straight through the wood, the damp draft of a tunnel stinging the torn skin of my bloodied knuckles.

. . .

It was clear that this tunnel had been crafted as an afterthought, dug into the main aqueducts piece by piece, though there were some sections that seemed as though whoever had crafted it had made use of the natural tunnels that cut through the earth. There were at least two sections to this tunnel, one that siphoned water from the main waterways, and one wide enough for a large human to crawl through.

Sometimes the sections of the tunnels converged. Sometimes the water slunk into a channel and disappeared for a while, only to reemerge later. There was rarely enough room for me to stand, and I often had to catch my breath before forcing myself through small openings, pushing my torch through first to provide some light and praying that there was enough air in this tunnel to keep the smoke from poisoning my lungs.

It must have been the middle of the night, if not early morning, by the time I dug my way through to a doorway. I pressed my ear to the wood and listened for any sign of life on the other side of the door.

When I didn't hear anyone, I turned the handle.

It wasn't locked.

Rays of light flooded the tunnel, and I kept the door cracked, peering into a dimly lit room. There was a long table in the middle, but nothing else of consequence. When I was satisfied that the room was empty, I opened the door and slipped out.

As it turned out, the door didn't look like a door at all, but a portrait of a man, young and blond and with a superiority about him that made me want to sink his inanimate teeth in.

I didn't get the chance, because a figure stepped out of the shadows, his sickeningly calm voice souring in the humid air.

"Well, well. It seems my Piper is not to be trusted after all," he said, flashing that same arrogance, that same smile, as the image in the portrait.

Pain cracked at the back of my skull, and the room went black.

CHAPTER 28

PIPER

Amity was nowhere to be found at dinner, and though Elias had reassured me she was just settling in, that the recruits to Intel usually ate separately from everyone else, her absence still disturbed me.

But that wasn't the only thing that disturbed me.

I didn't like the plan, not at all. The multitude of ways it could go wrong swarmed my head in the middle of the night, all the thoughts buzzing and bleeding together as I tossed and turned on my thin cot. At least I was one of the few here who was allowed my own bedroom. For now. Who knew if Bronger would move someone into my space just to make a point?

And why was he making a point, anyway? Because I'd argued with him about Amity's placement? He and I had barreled through disagreements before, but it had never been personal. He'd always valued my opinion. Now it seemed he scoffed every time I opened my mouth.

Something wormy and bitter writhed in my stomach, terrifying me. Bronger was the suspicious type. It was practically part of the job description as a political conspirator whose sole focus for the past decade and a half had been rallying children for an uprising. What if he had noted how many children I'd steered away from his army, from his spies, and had decided it was a sign of my change in loyalty? That I was purposefully trying to sabotage his plans?

Rage stirred in me. After all this time, after all I'd done for Bronger, after how much I loved him—the only father I'd ever had... The idea stung, but I allowed it to nestle inside of my heart.

I just wanted to wait, that was all. Until the children I'd taken were all grown. Until the decision could truly be their own, not one I'd led them to with the deceitful promise of a new life. I couldn't bear their blood, their souls on my hands.

And this plan was stupid, anyway. Sure, they'd gone over the details of how we were to infiltrate the castle, how'd they'd play for hours, until no one was really listening to the music anymore. How they'd mask my melody, the one that would call out to the girl with the gift.

Maybe.

This was the part where lying to Bronger this entire time was going to come back and bite me on the butt.

Because maybe the girl would hear my gift's call. Or maybe she wouldn't. Maybe, just maybe, the king treated her well. Fed her, gave her clean clothing, didn't lay a hand on her when she accidentally stepped out of line, when he was just in the mood for violence.

I'd never say it to Bronger, but King Declan wasn't known for being cruel. Especially not compared to his ruling neighbors. Was he concerned with looking out for humans' interest? Not exactly. Did he force us into unwanted marriages, traffic us as slaves, or command public beatings for petty crimes? Also, no.

But he was fae. And this had been our land—well, our ancestors' land—before it had been the fae's. And that had been enough for Bronger.

It had once been enough for me.

But then I'd met Amity.

Then I'd met Marcus.

The man who had carried a little girl all the way through the Kobii mountains, the man who had risked having his throat ripped out by a forest faerie to save that little girl.

The man who wouldn't kiss a liar.

A liar. A daughter. That's what Bronger had molded me into. They were one and the same to him.

Yet somehow I still longed for those gentle hands that had lifted my small, freezing body into his comforting chest so many years ago. For the man who warmed me by the fireplace, who taught me to read so I could escape into a world where I was human. Only human. So I could be that little girl in the human fairytales, back before they knew the fae were real. Granted, the parents usually died in the stories Bronger found for me. But at least the orphans knew their parents had loved them.

And I had been loved, too, hadn't I? If only in the peculiar manner Bronger had of showing it. It was his own way, and it existed only between the two of us, as much as James resented that fact.

Love was a strange thing, I decided, and not as entirely selfless as the human fairytales had made it out to be.

Humans had been so naïve before the fae.

A voice like a rumble from the depths of the earth ripped me from my swarming thoughts. The yelling, harsh and anguished, came from the ground floor. "Where is she?"

My heart stopped in my chest.

I knew that voice.

I jolted from the bed and ran to the edge of my balcony. Three floors down, in the middle of the open space on the ground floor, one man stood; the other kneeled at his feet.

No.

No, no, no, no, no.

"Tell me where she is!" Marcus's voice scraped against the metal scaffolding as it echoed through the Coup. Lamplight glittered across the surface area of the hive as the screams woke the children. They shuffled to their balconies to watch as Bronger shoved Marcus to his stomach and pushed his boot into Marcus's neck.

No, no, no. I threw on my robe, grabbing my satchel out of pure instinct, as if there was anything in there that would keep what was about to happen from happening. Heart pounding, I hopped the barrier that kept me from sleepwalking and falling headlong to my death in the middle of the night. Then I scaled it until my hands found those cold metal grates. My hands and feet skipped two, three rungs at a time as I flew down the makeshift ladder. I had to get to him. Before...

Marcus howled again, almost masking the sound of Bronger's chuckles. Not the chuckling that signaled amusement. No, Bronger was simply releasing an exacted measure of the rage welling within him.

When I reached the last seven rungs, I skipped them altogether and jumped. Someone had lit the overhead lamp, the crude chandelier that formed a circle around the top of Bronger's quarters.

I ran, skidding to a stop in front of the two men. It took all the restraint left in me, but I refused to let my gaze slip toward Marcus. Instead, I held Bronger's gaze. His eyes were dilated, flickering, curious. As if he'd been drinking.

But Bronger didn't drink.

He was drunk on indignation. Betrayal.

"This man has an interesting claim, my child," Bronger said, his words almost slurred. My breath quickened. I'd never seen him this angry, this volatile. His reaction would be unpredictable, no matter what I said to appease him. If I could just keep him from snapping Marcus's neck... "I caught him sneaking around in the council room. Any idea how he found a way in?" He allowed the question to settle in the air between us before moving on. "He says he followed a half-fae named Piper here. That she took someone very dear to him. He wants her back."

I gave in, allowed my gaze to slip downward. Marcus strained his neck from under Bronger's boot, his copper eyes boring into me, but his face was not one I recognized. The light-spirited smirk, the grin that wrinkled his entire face, the laughter that glinted in his eyes...all that was gone. As if it had simply been a mask to be washed away at an opportune moment. Now only hatred sparked in those unfamiliar eyes of his.

"Where is she?" he seethed through gritted teeth.

"I..." I stumbled for words. Confusion swirled in my head. He had loved Amity, of course. He had treated her like a sister during our journey. But he'd known when I hired him we would part ways at the end of the journey. Something unpleasant surged in my belly, turning it upside down. Something wasn't right. "Amity's safe. You don't have to worry about her, I promise. It's not what it looks like."

It was, in fact, almost exactly what it looked like, this hidden community of kidnapped children, but that wasn't the thing to say, either.

"Oh, he's not looking for Amity," Bronger said, his voice shaking even under the guise of amusement.

I was so confused. But mostly terrified, for Bronger's boot pushed harder into Marcus's neck. He was going to kill him, right in front of me, and all I'd ever see was that hateful scowl distorting the forehead wrinkles I'd grown to adore. And I'd never understand why.

This time, when Marcus spoke, his eyes pleaded, despite the hatred that filled them to the brim. "Where is Cheyenne?"

Cheyenne.

"Where did you bury her? You did bury her, didn't you?"

"Cheyenne?" My heart stopped at the name.

The vein in Marcus's head bulged. "You don't remember her? What's that tattoo for?"

My fingers grazed the bone behind my ear, the strange compass that I'd had inked there as a reminder of my guilt. In the inn, when we'd almost kissed and he'd pulled away... He'd seen my tattoo. Connected it to the girl. I was going to be sick.

Bronger simply laughed. "Oh, I can guarantee that Piper remembers Cheyenne. How could she forget her first recruit? No one forgets their first failure."

The words cut. But not nearly as deep as the image that invaded my mind, the screams from the past that punctured my ears.

Her wide eyes bled tears as they dragged her away. Her hair, those dark ringlets, whipped and thrashed as she clawed at them, bit them, those fae traffickers shrouded from head to foot.

I reached my hand out to her, such a pitiful, meaningless attempt, as the arrow that punctured my side forced itself deeper with every inhalation. The fingers on my outstretched hand twitched.

One of the traffickers yelped as her fingers found his eye socket. He let go of her immediately and stumbled away in shock, his unharmed eye full of awe as he watched the tiny human girl who had evaded his grasp. She lunged for me, her fingers interlocking with mine just as the pain washed over me one last time. Her face, her screams, everything went fuzzy.

It was Marcus's voicc that shocked me back to the present, to the Coup, to the place where this man—the one I'd once thought I might like to take me away from this place—was about to die at the hands of the only father I'd ever had. "Please."

"Marcus," I said, swallowing my guilt, swallowing the truth. I couldn't tell him, couldn't allow the words to slip from my mouth, to make real that day I'd so successfully forgotten all these years.

"Tell him," Bronger said.

Something shifted in the distance beyond Bronger's head. A little girl stood on her balcony, her dark hair wound into an unsuccessful braid, her brown eyes wide.

At least Bronger's back would block Amity's view when he crushed Marcus's spine.

"I remember her." The words ached in my chest, my jaw. Oh, how I so wanted to forget. "She was my first recruit. We... She didn't make it back to the Coup..."

The fire in Marcus's eyes died out. Those warm eyes of his went cold. "What happened to her?"

"I don't know," I said, hating my ignorance. Hating my selfish mind for erasing that moment from my memory, for protecting me from its trauma, from the truth that I hadn't protected her.

"You don't know." Marcus rolled the words over in his mouth as if to taste them, to wonder at the audacity of them.

Silence hung between the three of us. The question, the one that sawed against my throat, begging to be asked, finally sprung from my dry lips. "Who was she?"

Marcus's head bobbed as tears welled in his eyes. "Surely you know."

He was right. Now that I looked closely. Now that I allowed myself to remember that face I'd so carefully blurred against the edges of my memory, I could see it. The same nose, the same full lips, the same earthy skin. The same smile that overtook the entirety of their faces. I'd blocked her smile out long ago, the one she'd flashed at me when she'd escaped that place, all those siblings. She'd been the littlest. They'd never left her any food.

Just like they'd never left Marcus's sister any food.

"I'm so sorry." The words fell to the ground between us, and Marcus's eyes glazed over, as if the apology hadn't even reached his ears.

"Tell Piper how you came to discover us," Bronger hissed through gritted teeth.

When Marcus spoke, agony muted his voice. "When I found my sister's cloak, all shredded and torn like that...I couldn't, I couldn't function. It took me years to pick myself up after that. But I did, eventually. Made a reputation for myself, that I could track down anyone, anything. Then one day a client approached me about a trafficker who specialized in taking children. So I tracked you and found a pattern in how you choose the cities you victimize, but you didn't show up in the town I expected. I was already close to home, so I thought I'd visit, just to check on my family from a distance. Make sure they were all right. I arrived in town the morning after you took Amity. The townspeople were frantic, locking their children in their houses for fear of you. I couldn't believe my luck.

"It seemed obvious to me that you'd try to cut through the Kobiis, and sure enough, I found you. I knew it'd be a hassle to force you to travel all the way back to my client, so I came up with a plan. I'd come across those thieves on the road earlier, so I doubled back and approached them. I offered to reveal the location of two traveling women, one of whom was half-fae, in exchange for a small sum. Then

I went the long way around and perched myself on the hill where I could watch you. I figured if I was going to follow you all the way to wherever you were keeping the children, it would be easier if you trusted me. So I waited until they revealed their intentions, and until I had a clear shot, and... Well, you know the rest."

My heart faltered. "You put us in danger on purpose? You put *Amity*..." I whispered her name, as if there was any way her tiny human ears could hear our conversation from the balcony.

It seemed a strain for Marcus to shake his head under the weight of Bronger's boot, but he attempted it anyway. "No, no. Hurting her was never part of the plan. It was part of our deal. They were supposed to spare the younger girl. I had no idea they'd try to kill her." His words did little to soothe my raw, exposed heart, but he continued, "I worried at first that Amity would recognize me, but she was too young when I left home to remember seeing me around town."

He stared off into the distance, as if the realization of how long he'd been gone stirred something within him.

"You lied to us," I said, and as soon as I did, I regretted the words.

Bronger's low chuckle sounded in my ears, reverberating against my spine, my ribs, my knuckles. "You still have some growing to do in the area of introspection, my child. Though I wish you'd been less honest with this one. Told him a name other than your own, perhaps. Or refrained from telling him the location of your family."

Family.

There was something about that word. It found a gap in my defenses. It slipped through the cracks in my dread, and in my chest it settled, like dregs at the bottom of a chipped teacup. It sank until it anchored me.

Bronger had never used that word.

Of course he hadn't. He'd probably been stowing it away in his back pocket for a time such as this.

That was why he'd withheld it all these years, wasn't it? Starving me of the one thing I so desperately desired, so that when he dumped the word *family* onto the ground like it was nothing, I'd lap it up at his feet.

"I didn't tell him anything," I said. "I paid him to defend the girl and me while we traveled. The girl's father broke my arm. I was injured, and I did what you taught me to do—use the resources the earth provided. I drugged him before we fled. He shouldn't have been able to follow us."

I glared at Marcus, demanding an answer.

He sighed, his voice low and defeated, and mostly empty. "I switched your sleeping draft out for a cheap oil days ago."

The gravity of that statement struck me. That the whole time, Marcus had been calling the shots. Playing the kind, carefree companion, the one who danced with, and almost kissed, the half-fae girl that most people purposefully avoided giving a second glance. And he'd hated me the whole while.

The worst part was, I couldn't blame him for it.

"Well, I'm glad that's settled," Bronger said with a sigh that told me things were quite far from being settled. "Clean up your mess, Piper. We can't afford any leaks."

Clean it up? I knew what that meant, although my mind buzzed in a thousand different directions, trying to make it mean something, anything, else.

Bronger nodded toward his left side, where he'd apparently wrenched Marcus's bow off his back and tossed it to the floor. "Use his own bow."

My hands froze.

"Piper," was all Bronger had to say.

I risked one last look at Marcus, willing into existence some look of understanding, some look of forgiveness, but all I got was a shard of flint.

My legs trembled, barely holding my weight, as I kneeled and took the bow in my hands. Cerulean arrows spilled from his quiver. I grabbed one of those, too. The bowstring pinched against my fingers as I nocked the arrow and stood.

My entire body trembled now, and I hated it. Hated how my fear, my anguish, displayed itself to all those I'd pretended to be strong for. I glimpsed Amity's face, white as a specter. She'd joined the crowd of children that had surrounded us, the silent figures I hadn't noticed swarming us as Marcus had admitted his true intentions.

She was close enough to see everything.

I bent my head slightly, gesturing to the tip of my arrow. She followed my gesture with her eyes.

I snapped my forefinger and thumb together under the cold stone arrowhead.

Close your eyes.

Her eyes went wide for a moment, and I knew then the pain it caused her, to see the signal her mother had invented to keep her safe. She turned her face toward mine and our gazes locked.

Then she forced her eyes shut.

I turned. The bowstring sliced into my fingers as I drew back.

Marcus stared into the shaft of the arrow. Not with the loathing I expected, but with utter disinterest. Apathy. As if the idea of an arrow going straight through his eye was a mildly unsettling dream compared to the nightmare of losing his sister. Of failing her.

Bronger chuckled, his low rumble taunting me, pulling the strings of my muscles and memory, just as it always had.

Family, he'd said.

It might have worked, too, wielding that word I'd so often dreamed of coming from Bronger's mouth.

Except lately the voice in the dream hadn't been Bronger's at all.

It had belonged to a man with a giggling girl perched upon his shoulders.

The chuckle morphed into a shocked gurgle as I put an arrow through Bronger's chest.

CHAPTER 29

PIPER

Three things happened at once. Bronger collapsed to his knees, Marcus bolted to his feet, and, from somewhere in the crowd, James unleashed a roar.

I knew I should run, that James would pierce my back with his hunting knife any second now. But I couldn't rip my eyes away from Bronger's calloused fingers as he traced the edge where the arrow shaft protruded from his skin, right between his ribs. The way he stroked his wound in disbelief, like how a parent might caress the forehead of a child dying in their arms.

He turned his pale blue eyes on me, and I witnessed a thousand shadows of regret pass through those striking irises. I watched his plans, his life's mission, the future in which he'd invested every copper of his existence, drip from his eyes as his tears washed them away.

But most of all, I saw the pain, the shock at the realization that the only daughter he'd ever claimed had been the one to slay him.

When he opened his cracked lips, now damp with his own drool, his voice croaked. "Not you." Then he crumpled, those pale eyes glowing in the lamplight even as they stared into nothing.

A firm hand gripped my arm, yanked me upright as my knees gave out.

"We have to get out of here," Marcus said, though his voice sounded distant, as if he might as well have been calling to me from the topmost floor.

My feet obeyed, and I turned to follow him, but something hard, heavy, brutal crashed into my side, knocking me to the floor.

A putrid voice cried out, "They're mine!"

My palms scraped against the dirt, the gritty little pebbles. I welcomed the tiny blast of pain, summoned it into the hole in my chest so that something might live there.

Pain ripped across the back of my neck as cold metal collided with my skin. This time, the pain ripped me back to the Coup. The actual coup that was happening right at this moment. I glanced up to find Marcus on top of James, wrestling him for the knife in his hand.

The knife dripping blood.

My blood from my neck.

I scanned the balcony on the highest floor. Caught the glints of arrowheads flickering in the lamplight. James's Intel. He'd called them off, hoping to finish us himself.

But Marcus had gotten hold of James's knife, overpowered the boy, who was no match for him in size. He landed a punch on James's jaw just for good measure.

If Marcus killed him, arrows would slice through him from all directions.

"Marcus, stop. They'll kill you."

He turned to look at me, a fierce wildness flaming in those metallic eyes of his. But he blinked up at the balcony and resigned understanding washed over his face.

Marcus launched to his feet just as the soldiers descended upon us. The child soldiers swarmed us, their swords and daggers drawn and trembling. I searched the crowd, and in every face confusion reigned. They all studied me as I recognized each of them, journeyed back to the hovels from which I'd plucked them. I gazed into the full faces of children, teenagers, that had once been so gaunt their cheekbones had protruded.

They'd all been fed, all been rescued.

By me.

And by Bronger.

Marcus yanked a metal shield from one of the smaller children and pressed his back to mine, pushing himself between the majority of the soldiers, archers, and myself, so I could no longer gaze into their terrified faces. Then he stepped backward, inching us toward the tunnel that would allow us to escape, if we made it before the shock dissipated.

"Wait. Amity," I whispered, whipping myself from behind Marcus and scanning the crowds. The children were all huddled behind the soldiers, hidden behind their long shields.

But then I saw her. She'd climbed up to the fourth floor, further away from us. My heart raced. It wouldn't be long before James regained consciousness and commanded our slaughter. I caught her eye and motioned for her to come down to us.

She didn't move.

Panic flooded my chest. "Marcus, we have to go get her."

Amity, I mouthed, hoping she was still close enough to see.

Her eyes went wide, her face pallid. She shook her head and dove into the nearest box.

"Marcus," I said, my voice shaking now.

He nodded toward James, who was stirring. "We have to go."

"No, no. We can't leave her."

Marcus swallowed. "She doesn't want to come."

My stomach plummeted.

"We have to go now," Marcus said, and I stepped behind him again. Something clanked against his shield, and I realized someone had fired an arrow, taken action despite both of their leaders being disposed. One dead, one unconscious. "Now." I almost lost the sound of his voice amongst the clattering of arrows against his shield.

I grabbed Marcus's hand, and we ran, me leading the way to the tunnel as he ran backward, keeping the shield between ourselves and the arrows. The soldiers on the ground rustled. We were so close to the tunnel now.

Someone stepped between me and the door.

Elias.

"Piper," he said, his eyes wide, confused, hurt.

I hissed, hating the sound coming from my mouth. The one directed at my friend. "Get out of the way, Elias."

His face went stiff, then determined, and he leaned in and whispered something in my ear before stepping out of the way.

Marcus and I cleared the tunnel just in time to hear James howl.

I didn't even have time to process Elias's warning.

Lay low. James isn't the only one hunting you.

I TRUDGED THROUGH THOSE HILLS. Left foot, right foot, left foot, right foot. The declines were the worst of it. At least when we were forging uphill, the tension in my muscles gave me the illusion of feeling steady, rooted and one with the ground even as I fought against it.

But every time I reached a peak and stared down at the slope before me, I wondered how much easier it would be to collapse and allow the hill to take me with it. How it would feel to sink, sink, sink further and further into the abyss. To roll over jagged stones that would pinch my skin, to feel the firm opposition of the ground as it pounded into me.

To feel anything.

I'd had the presence of mind to clean the gash on my neck, to bandage it. If it was throbbing, I hadn't noticed.

Had I thought Marcus would leave me alone to die, I might have allowed my legs to collapse, granted them surrender to those arduous hills. I might have lain there until James found my limp shell and speared me through.

But Marcus would probably keep talking, keep demanding the same answers to the same questions for which I had no answers. Nothing to satisfy.

I supposed if I kept walking, kept willing my legs to move, my lungs to breathe, maybe his legs would go out before mine. If only because mine had gone numb, and I could no longer feel the soreness. My muscles no longer screamed at me.

Everything was quiet.

Except for Marcus's voice.

And the sound of Bronger's last chuckle as it morphed into a gurgled cough.

"Tell me what happened to her," Marcus said, for what was probably the fortieth time. I considered the valley that stretched out before us. If I gave way to the will of my knees, if I allowed them to buckle, allowed my limp body to roll down the hill, I'd probably make it to the bottom first. But Marcus would probably have caught up by the time I pushed my aching limbs off the ground.

"I already told you. I don't know," I said, probably for at least the twenty-second time. I was pretty sure I'd forgotten to respond to half his inquiries. That they'd sounded more like buzzing in my ears than actual questions.

"How do you not know." Not a question.

I clamped my mouth shut.

"She was with you when it happened, wasn't she? So how could you possibly not know?"

"We were attacked."

"Who?"

"I don't know." The words fell into the same cadence as the pounding in my head. Reverberating. Predictable. Dull.

Marcus gripped my shoulder and whipped me around. His face was wild, angry, pleading. Tears welled out from under his eyelids. "Piper, please. For all that is good in the world, give me something."

My consciousness floated, unattached to my body. I couldn't find the connection that might have allowed my face to twitch, my eyes to blink. For his tears to register as some important stimuli for my brain to latch onto.

"You took her. You owe me the full story, if nothing else. Please."

Story. Words. Facts. Details. Events. I could do that. I could recite them, if that's what he needed.

Bronger's lifeless eyes swam in my vision, blurring the descending path of my feet, peering at me out of every rock, each patch of grass that my mind could find a face in. Apparently, my mind could find a face, specifically Bronger's face—occasionally Amity's as she saw the monster, the murderer in me—in anything.

"Piper."

"Your sister was my first recruit. I found her starving, undernourished. She was eight, but she didn't look it. I don't think she'd ever had enough food to grow properly."

Marcus winced, and something tapped on the empty shell in my chest, pinching and kneading on the bruise there that had never had the chance to heal.

"I don't think your parents intended to keep food from her. At least, she didn't blame them." I tried to make it better for Marcus, not from compassion or guilt, but because something ingrained within my human half told me this was something I was supposed to do. Some script I was supposed to follow. "She just said they had so much going on, so many children, they often forgot about her. Overlooked her rations. She said it was because she was so quiet."

I sifted through my mind for the memory of her, surprised to find that, now that Marcus had asked, my mind had held onto so many details I hadn't accessed in so long. Details that I didn't know still squatted within the walls of my subconscious. Shuffling through them was odd. Some of them were hazy, muddled with time. Others were as clear as Marcus standing before me, as though they'd been tucked into the corners of my memory, underneath all the other children who were not nearly as important—mundane details that had nothing to do with my failures.

Maybe it was selfishness, maybe it was the last drop of mercy I had left, but I sighed and said, "Nothing I have to say will bring her back. I could go into detail, but at the end of the day, someone took her. They took her, and they left me to die with an arrow in my side, and when Bronger found me, almost bled dry, he carried me back to the Coup. And then when I fully recovered..." I tried to swallow, but my mouth had gone dry, my voice with it, barely a wheeze.

Marcus had stopped walking now. And I'd stopped too. "Piper. Piper, please."

"I know you're hoping that because you never found a body, that means she's alive. But—"

"No." Marcus stepped back.

"He found her. Bronger found her."

Marcus lifted his arms, running his hands over his shaved head.

"She must have tried to fight them. They tried to carry her away, but she must have made it difficult for them. So they killed her for it. I'm so sorry. I'm so so sorry, Marcus."

Sweat beaded on his forehead, and when he spoke, his voice was void of intonation. "That doesn't make sense. If they took her away from the campsite, why shred her robe?"

"I don't know."

"Stop. Saying. That."

His copper eyes met mine with a challenge. Any warmth I'd ever glimpsed in them was gone, replaced by a cold fury.

"Okay." I nodded. "Okay."

He sighed, then winced, and the sight of him breaking nearly snapped me in two.

"I blacked out pretty soon after the arrow hit my side. I managed to get a warning signal up in the air; that's how Bronger found me, but that's all I remember."

Even as the words fell off my lips, something about them tasted wrong. Because the more I focused on it, the more my mind made up details in the cracks of my memory where the blackness should have been. Where it had always been.

Nightmares, perhaps. My mind had blocked out so much of the event, there was no discriminating between real and not real.

"Why would they try to take Cheyenne?" he asked.

My legs stopped. I couldn't will myself to propel them forward.

This was it. The most incriminating truth of them all. The one I'd forced down, down, down into myself. But no matter how deeply I'd buried it, no matter how many memories I'd piled on top of it, nothing would muffle its screams. "Because he thought she was me. They thought she was the one with the gift."

"Why would they think that?" Marcus's voice went dry, cracking and feathering like the lies I'd told myself all these years. That I wasn't that bad of a person. That I took the children from unsavory homes for their own good.

As if I wasn't paying coppers for a debt counted in rubies.

"Because I told them she was."

CHAPTER 30

PIPER

The next few days blurred together. We walked and walked, skirting Nettlewood and the villages nearby, hunting and scavenging for the minimum amount of food necessary to keep us alive and walking.

Where we were going, I didn't know. Nor did I have the energy to ask Marcus about his plans. I had a feeling they were similar to mine.

Marcus had quieted after I'd told him what I'd done. The truth, the inky stain on my heart that no self-loathing, no lye could begin to touch. I'd expected him to scream, to end me, perhaps. To hurl at me all the names I called myself on a daily basis.

But he didn't.

He simply folded up in on himself, his questions coming to a halt.

It was far worse that way, as if the Fates wouldn't even allow me the catharsis, wouldn't give me the break of hearing someone else's loathing for a change.

I'd wanted to tell Marcus where we'd buried her. That her body rested underneath a patch of daffodils in the eastern hills. Bronger had let me choose the spot, and in my hysteria, I'd chosen the patch of land for its beauty.

I hadn't considered that the wind would soon come and whisk

away the dainty spindles, leaving the stalks of the daffodils bare and the grave unmarked. Forgotten.

I couldn't quite make myself form the words, though. Couldn't bring myself to tell him about how, after Bronger had found me, after he'd returned me to the Coup and nursed me to health, he'd circled back to the place they'd taken her. He'd searched the woods until he'd found her body, discarded in a shallow grave nearby, as if her captors had decided she'd been too much trouble to be worth whatever they planned to sell her for.

Bronger had found flesh underneath her nails.

Then he'd carried her body back.

I always assumed he'd done it for me, that he'd known I needed to lay her body to rest, to imagine she was at peace, slumbering beneath the daffodils.

But I think part of me always knew he'd meant to punish me. That, as he lowered her body into the ground, he'd allowed the burlap he'd wrapped her in to slip, allowed me to witness the decay that had warped her face, the dirt that clung to her limp ringlets.

He'd allowed the stench to waft over me, staining the insides of my nostrils with guilt.

THE NUMBNESS in my soul could only feed the rest of my body for so long before my limbs couldn't bear it anymore, before they screamed at me to stop.

But I couldn't stop. Neither could Marcus. Because that would mean that we'd arrived. Arrived into a new life, a new identity, a new purpose. Except we didn't have any of those.

So we walked.

We walked until we found the woods, until the trees shielded us from the light of day and welcomed us into their shadows.

Every once in a while, my bored mind would flutter back to that moment, the one in which I'd blacked out before seeing what had become of Cheyenne. Any time my insolent mind wiggled its way back there, I reined it in, wound its leash tighter. Back to the numbness. Back to the place where together, we accepted the blackness. The fact we'd failed her.

Well, Marcus had failed her.

Me?

I'd betrayed her.

CHAPTER 31

Gigi was on the verge of a breakthrough when it happened.

She'd gotten distracted earlier, so she knew it was her fault entirely that she hadn't figured out a way to polish those dull, opaque memories until now.

But Piper's head had been swimming with utterly distracting thoughts on the way to Nettlewood; what was Gigi to do? It wasn't as if she could ignore the thoughts and emotions that nearly drowned her host, not when they shared the same body.

Marcus, Marcus, Marcus. That was all Gigi had heard and seen, all the way to Nettlewood. Marcus kissing Piper. Marcus smiling at Piper. Marcus appearing before Piper at the dance in Evaen—it amazed Gigi how such a tiny memory could take up so much space in Piper's mind. In reality, as far as Gigi could distinguish such things, the moment couldn't have taken up more than a few seconds' time, but to Piper that moment spanned centuries, oozed into every corner of her consciousness and made quite the mess.

With Marcus around, Gigi had practically given up on tidying. Every time she thought she was on the verge of getting Piper's tangled thoughts unwound, there Marcus would come again, a hurricane of smiles and teasings sweeping away any work Gigi had accomplished.

Not that Gigi complained about such things.

Living in Piper's head, she'd certainly witnessed her fair share of less attractive beings override Piper's thoughts.

Still—the mess.

Gigi had almost gotten it all tidied up by the time Amity and Piper had reached the Coup, after they'd left Marcus behind at the inn. It had saddened Gigi that every time Marcus's voice rang through her mind, Piper would stop it mid-sentence.

But it did make focusing on her task easier.

And then that awful ordeal with Bronger...

Not that Gigi had ever liked Bronger. In fact, she hated the man. Hated the man who had arms to hold Piper, yet had only done so the one time, to banish the approaching chill of death from her bones. Hated the man who had a perfectly functioning tongue, yet refused to use it to tell Piper that he loved her. Hated the man who had possessed such startlingly clear eyes, yet had not seen the perfect daughter who'd ventured into his life for what she was.

If only Gigi had her own arms, her own tongue, her own eyes; then she would hold Piper when she wept, brush her hair from her face when she vomited, and tell her how very, very loved she indeed was.

Gigi didn't need her own eyes to see how much Piper deserved all those things.

So, no. Gigi was not nearly as devastated as Piper that the awful man was dead. Though she did regret that it had happened at Piper's hands, mostly because, of all the emotions Gigi had felt from the sweet girl all these years, it was the self-loathing that made Gigi want to drown in Piper's tears. She also hated that Marcus was so upset with Piper, though Gigi would find it easier to forgive him than to forgive Bronger.

So when Piper had stumbled through those hills and trudged through the forest brush, her mind a prison reserved for her own torture, Gigi had to do something.

She'd tried to hum a tune for Piper, but the thump of Bronger's body hitting the ground and his words, *Not you, not you, not you*—they were too loud, and as loudly as Gigi hummed, her melody couldn't break through.

Not knowing what else to do for her kind host, Gigi's resolve to tidy her brain had been renewed. So she'd wafted deep into the recesses of Piper's mind, and she'd gotten to work.

And there, hidden amongst the rubble of discarded memories, the ones Piper had purposefully suppressed, Gigi had found it.

She'd never witnessed anything quite like it, for most of Piper's memories were like drops of dew scattered across the most intricate of webs, so that one memory might be connected to a dozen other memories, all through the sticky tangle of webs that kept the dewdrops intact.

Deep in the recesses of Piper's mind, Gigi was shocked to find a cluster of dewdrops floating in the abyss, separated from all the others, still perfectly intact yet disconnected to any smells, pictures, or memories that might help Piper find her way to them.

What had happened, Gigi couldn't help but wonder, to make these memories drift away as they had?

Gigi had come closer, so close that the fading whisper of a scream had sounded from the dewdrops, causing Gigi to shiver in dread. She tried to recall that scream, where Piper had heard it, but it was lost to her.

Strange, since Gigi had been with Piper since those first cries, and there was rarely a moment Gigi *couldn't* remember, as long as she was thoroughly reminded of it. At least, within the bounds of Piper's life.

She'd just been about to reach out and touch the cluster of dewdrops when it happened.

When Piper decided her mortal life was no longer worth living.

CHAPTER 32

PIPER

Eventually we came to a fork in our worn path through the woods. Not that the trail was smooth or distinct to begin with, but here it clearly diverged into two paths that at least looked travelable, while brush and thorn had smothered any other possible route.

Marcus and I stopped, the silence deafening. Though we hadn't as much as uttered a word to one another all day, the crunching of the leaves beneath our feet had served as some form of conversation, some heartbeat, some tune pretending to be communication between the two of us.

We made eye contact, but I glanced away. Marcus's once carefree, mischievous eyes had lost not only their glint, but even their rage. There was only emptiness and rust in those copper irises. And I could not bear to look at them.

I could've asked him, could have opened up a conversation about which path we should take, but my soul was even wearier than my legs, and the effort it would have taken to summon words, to coax them from my mind and through my throat—that would have depleted the little energy, the little will I had left.

So I headed right.

The leaves crunched beneath my feet, but only half as loudly as they had a few moments ago, before we'd stopped. I kept walking, reassuring myself that the other pair of feet would follow behind me soon enough.

But the farther I walked, the quieter the surrounding woods became. No breaths to fill the silence between mine. No presence of a soul to be felt.

I couldn't bring myself to look backward. To backtrack. To beg him to come.

Marcus had gotten every bit of use out of me. Every bit of information I knew—or knew for sure, at least.

He must have realized that by now. That I'd told him everything I knew.

That hanging around the last person to see his sister alive wouldn't bring her back.

He could have taken me to his benefactor. I wasn't even sure that I'd have the strength to resist if he tried.

But Marcus was good at his core.

That was the difference between the two of us.

He wouldn't sell me, though he should.

But he wouldn't follow me.

And why would he want to tag along with the girl who'd started all this in the first place? Who'd taken his sister and hadn't protected her? Who'd allowed her to be tortured and killed?

I wouldn't have wanted to continue on with me either.

In fact, I didn't. I didn't want to continue on any longer, trapped in this body with myself, that wretched girl who'd justified her sins by telling herself she was taking children to a better home, only to end up slaughtering their guardian and leaving their lives to be dictated by someone like James.

The girl who'd put an arrow through the same chest that had warmed her that day in the cold, the body that had provided enough heat to keep her fingers from freezing off.

The girl who'd done such a horrible thing that even Amity, that little adult in a child's body, couldn't stomach being around her.

I would have left me too, if I'd had a choice.

I supposed I did, technically, have a choice. My dagger still pressed against my calf underneath my leather boot.

I wasn't even convinced I'd feel it—the dagger slipping between my ribs, puncturing my heart. Not when the agony of my guilt drowned out everything else, swallowing me whole and sucking me under.

It couldn't hurt more than this. Even if it did, wasn't that what I deserved? To hurt?

I'd only have to wait it out a few minutes. A few minutes until my blood no longer pumped, until my body whisked my consciousness away so I wouldn't have to witness my own death.

And then nothing would hurt at all.

I stroked the hilt of my dagger.

CHAPTER 33

Gigi didn't hum this time.

She sang.

A blissful, silent tune that no one could possibly hear.

But still, she sang.

And that song was the beginning of it all, the beginning of Gigi and her decision to stay with the shivering, screaming baby just a little longer, just until she fell back asleep.

Gigi just hoped it wouldn't be the end.

CHAPTER 34

PIPER

Drawing my dagger would take so much effort. And I was doing good to keep one foot in front of the other. Perhaps I'd sleep, allow myself some rest. Allow the strength to return to my fingertips, my limbs.

That way, I could grasp the knife between the pads of my fingers. That way, it wouldn't slip.

That way, I could guarantee it would be quick.

My limbs melted, and I crashed to the mossy ground as my gift whispered a somber tune in my ear.

It was enchanting.

I'd have to play it later.

Perhaps I'd heard it before.

Sleep took me before I could place where.

Consciousness rattled the edges of my mind as the damp earth parted ways with my face. Strong arms wrapped themselves around my waist, then threw me over a padded shoulder.

My head bobbled with the rhythm of heavy footsteps before it rolled, and the patter of boots lulled me to sleep once again.

. . .

I WOKE to the smell of something burning. No, something that was cooking, but was burning ever so slightly. Like it was being charred. Metal clattered against metal. That must have been what had woken me.

My neck ached as my head hung to the side, the cool sting of drool bringing my awareness to the edge of my lips.

I was sitting upright, not lying in a bed or on the floor.

Something rough scratched against my wrists, my ankles. Something tight. My hands and feet tingled. That feeling was familiar. If I moved them, tried to walk on my feet, there would be pain. That ridiculous aching that only came from allowing yourself to sleep in the wrong position.

Or from being bound.

CHAPTER 35

PIPER

My heart jolted and fear spiked through me. Still, I didn't allow myself to fling my eyes open. Not until I was sure I was safer awake than asleep.

Something told me I was not.

I cracked my eyes, but all I could see were orange and dotted black spots across my vision.

How long had I been out?

Eventually the blur of orange and black spots reorganized themselves into the image of a room, lined in black at the edges from my half-closed eyelids.

A fire danced in a huge, freestanding fireplace that towered in the middle of the room. Inside the fireplace was a boar, though it was bigger than any boar I'd ever seen, roasting whole in the middle of the fire, propped up on metal frames.

That was what I was smelling. The meat cooking inside the boar as the fire singed its skin.

I allowed myself to peek my eyes open just a little more. As I scanned the area, the wooded paneling clued me in that I must be in a hut. On the floor in front of me, a life-sized bearskin rug gaped, its mouth slack-jawed and opened to reveal an array of sharp, blood-stained teeth. My stomach twisted.

Lest I tilt my head and give myself away to someone in the room I hadn't yet seen, I forced my eyes toward the ground. Thin cords bound my hands to each armrest of the cedar chair on which I sat. Though I couldn't see them, I assumed my feet had met the same fate.

They were bare, I realized, as my toes curled and scraped against the wooden floor. That meant someone had taken my boots. Meaning that same someone had my dagger.

I chanced a quick scan across the rest of the room, which proved difficult with my head in its slumped position. So I listened as carefully as I could for any sign of breathing out of rhythm with mine, any footsteps, any odd fidgeting.

But I heard none, and my neck felt like it might break off like the tip of a melting icicle on a tree limb if I didn't readjust it. Taking my chances, I straightened, stretching out the muscles that felt half in length compared to their mirroring side.

Nothing scraped across the floor, yelled, or even coughed as I moved. So I figured it was safe to assume I was alone.

For now.

Obviously, someone was planning on eating that huge boar at some point.

And they likely hadn't tied me up with the intention of leaving me here to die. Stabbing me with my own knife would have been an easier way to go about that.

I breathed, soothing my racing heart as it attempted to escape the confines of my ribcage. But the breathing only seemed to feed the flame of anxiety that welled in my chest, and with each inhalation, the panic flared, charring my insides with a flicker of dread.

People in Avelea didn't go about tying each other up without cause.

And in a place like Avelea, money was about the only cause anyone bothered with.

I wished I had time to sit and speculate about this stranger's reasoning behind securing me to this chair, but the wood in the stove was crackling and I could trace every prickle of ember in that fire, so it would have been naïve of me to pretend not to see the truth. To pretend the fact that my captor had the entirety of a skinned bear on the floor and also had a half-fae female tied up in his home had absolutely no obvious connection.

That the size of that boar roasting above the fire was inconsequential.

I had to get out of here.

I wiggled my wrists, but that only made my hands go red. And the more I twisted them, the more the red blossomed into purple, and the more needles assaulted my fingertips. Perhaps I hadn't lost my fingers to the cold when I was a child, but there was always time, as Bronger would have said.

Bronger.

I wouldn't think of him now.

When I attempted to twist my legs, I got the same reaction. Whoever had tied these cords had certainly valued my staying put over a few potentially lost limbs and a couple of bruises.

Maybe he wouldn't stuff me after all. I almost cackled to myself. He seemed the type to prefer his stuffed game without imperfections.

What then? I chased the thoughts tumbling about in my head. What might the captor want from me, if he didn't mind cutting off circulation to my limbs? To sell me to the highest bidder? I gulped. It was likely he could fetch a high price. Much higher than his usual game. There were so few of us half-fae out there anymore... I supposed to some, we might be considered a rare breed.

I swallowed the vomit forming in my throat, lest I soil my clothes and have to soak in my filth for hours until my captor graced me with a visit.

No, no, no. I had wanted to die in the forest. Had the Fates not deemed that a fair enough punishment? I would have ended it, had I only possessed the energy, had sleep simply replenished enough willpower to allow me to grip onto my knife.

But then a chill soaked my bones as I imagined what I might have done had I awoken on the cold ground of the forest, my knife strapped to the inside of my boot instead of confiscated, my limbs free to do what they would.

And then it swept over me. The fear. The dread.

I didn't want to die.

I'd risk it if it was between being dead and whatever my captor had planned for me.

But I wouldn't go down without a fight.

I tightened my long fingers into a fist, pushing my middle two fingers as far down my wrist as they could go, despite the agonizing needles puncturing my nerves, my mind. It was only in my mind, I told myself. And this would work.

Since there were so few half-fae roaming about alive and well in Avelea, most forgot our nuances, the details that made us a threat. Sure, they remembered our pointed ears, how we could hear for greater distances than humans. And that we were slightly stronger, slightly faster than our human counterparts.

But they forgot about our fingers. At least, my captor had.

I struggled with the cord, pushing my long fingers between my wrist and the wooden armrest, hoping to stretch the ropes in the process.

I kept at it for what felt like hours, but by the time I was sure the boar had been cooked through, I'd only made the slightest bit of progress. That caused me to halt my efforts. And the fact I was afraid that if I continued on like this, my captor would return to find my fingers raw and would tie them together, too.

Or cut them off, as he seemed to enjoy doing with bird talons, as evidenced by the cabin decor.

At least he hadn't gagged me.

Except that was probably a bad sign. A sign that we were buried so far into the depths of the woods that my captor wasn't at all worried that anyone would hear me scream.

Great.

I debated whether it was worth a shot anyway.

Probably not, since it seemed my kidnapper was likely the only being within earshot. Even if some stranger was passing through the area, what was the likelihood they would have that unique mingling of goodness and bravery and talent that would allow for a successful rescue mission?

I didn't have time to debate the issue, for the door to the sweltering cabin burst open, and a man, just a man, stomped through.

He dressed like a hunter, vines and leaves intertwined between the threads of his robes with such delicate attention to detail, even I wouldn't have seen him coming. Even if I hadn't been passed out on the ground, drunk on my despair when he'd found me. His dark beard was braided with thorns from the forest floor, and his dark, beady eyes set deep within his painted face might as well have been beetles crawling amongst the brush.

"You're awake," he said in a gruff voice.

I instantly regretted not having paid much attention to the sounds outside the cabin, not having pretended to be asleep before he walked in and saw that I was alert. Not that I was sure it would have given me an advantage, anyway. But the crackling of the boar's skin as the flames licked at and singed the poor animal's hairs off its dead body had masked the noise of the man's footsteps. I wondered if that had been intentional.

"Where am I?" It was all too easy to assume the role of cowering, helpless female at the moment. I wasn't proud of it, but perhaps it would have the man underestimating my strength, my speed.

Unless he already knew not to underestimate me, I considered, before shoving the thought into the fire with the roasting boar.

"You have no need of that information. You won't be staying here long." The man lifted the skeleton of leaves off his shoulders and up over his head before laying it on a table beside the door. He was a burly man, muscular in the way truly powerful men were, with fat to protect and feed the muscle on every side. I gulped.

"Where will I be going?" I asked, finding it much too easy for my pitch to soar.

The burly man shrugged. "Wherever the highest bidder wants you, I suppose."

A spider might as well have been weaving a web on my spine for the nausea that hurtled through me at this statement.

The highest bidder? That could mean a great many things. I imagined the bidders would mostly consist of rich fae who got a rush from purchasing trafficked humans. How much would they pay for a half-fae, a hated creature, the perfect object for their acts of violence and superiority? But then there were others, the ones like Bronger, who kidnapped beings to serve as mercenaries. Then there were the fellows, the type whose heads I would enjoy ripping off, who bought women, females, to rent out to others.

No, none of these would be my fate. Only a few hours ago, I'd been so close to choosing death, to embracing its tantalizing arms.

That sweet, familiar lullaby hummed in the corners of my memory.

My gift had saved me.

I wouldn't let it down.

"When will the bidding begin?"

"Enough questions," the man said, slipping a wet rag over my face, the scent of which reminded me of lilac and betrayal before it plunged me into what felt like it would be an eternal sleep.

CHAPTER 36

It had taken Gigi four and a half days to recover from the voice she'd heard ringing through Piper's head.

I would have left me too, if I'd had a choice.

I would have left me too, if I'd had a choice.

I would have left me too, if I'd had a choice.

The thoughts swirled and swirled and twisted and writhed, not just in Piper's mind, but in Gigi's independent consciousness.

Her sweet Piper had truly believed it, what that awful man had implied all these years by withholding affection to her, what her careless mother had taught her the day she'd left her in the snow to die, misinterpreting her little blessing for a freak. What her father had instilled within her by abandoning her.

Piper had wished for it to end before, for months after that little girl—what was her name?—was taken. She'd been so suffocated in guilt that she'd been rash around bounty hunters, like she'd wanted to be caught, to be punished.

But Gigi had thought she was past that.

Gigi supposed that there were thoughts that even she was not privy to.

Like that cluster of dewdrops.

She'd been hesitant to return to them these past few days, Piper's mind being as frail as it was. But something about being kidnapped had seemed to snap the will to live back into her host, and for that Gigi might have shaken the hand of her captor had she the ability to do so.

Had she not been fairly certain Piper would end his life before this whole ordeal was over.

Gigi figured that she should approach the dewdrop while Piper slept. Then, if the detached memory was too awful, at least Piper would have the freedom to assume the memory was not a memory at all, but a dream.

So it was, when Gigi touched the dewdrop, that Piper faced a nightmare.

PIPER

Bronger wouldn't like this girl, I'd decided. Only four years younger than myself, eight years to my twelve, but I'd been shocked when she'd told me such. Even thought she might have been lying about her age, trying to impress me, but with the way she devoured every last morsel of food I procured for us, gobbling down even the bones of the gamey squirrels, I guessed she'd been telling the truth after all.

Her weight wasn't why he wouldn't like her, though. She was always questioning things. Every little decision I made, she wanted to know why, why, why. As if I wasn't the one who'd been training for this my entire life.

"Why don't you dye your hair a darker color, that way you blend in better?" she asked as we snuck into an empty village market under the cover of nightfall.

"Bronger likes my hair the way it is," I snapped, then thought to add, "and he wouldn't like it if he knew you were trying to convince me to change it."

"Why are you so obsessed with what Bronger thinks?"

No, Bronger wouldn't like this girl. Not one bit. "You need to be quiet. You're going to get us caught."

Cheyenne huffed, her footsteps pattering behind me, like she was trying to alert the entire village that thieves were among them.

"And I'm not obsessed with Bronger. I was just raised better than to be ungrateful."

"Mhm."

Most of the stalls in the market were empty, the owners having hauled off their leftover wares to store them elsewhere. Even after I picked the locks on a few of the cabinets, all we had to show for it were a few extra pairs of wool socks. Apparently the vendors knew better than to leave their products unattended in the stalls overnight.

My stomach growled. So did Cheyenne's.

The Coup was still at least a week away, and this was the last town on the map before we trekked through the forest for the next five days. I could hunt in the woods, but that would slow us down considerably, and there was no guarantee I'd fell anything, anyway.

If we were going to get food, we'd need to get it here.

The scent of stew wafted on the breeze from the nearby tavern.

There was a back door that led directly to the kitchen, so the kitchen staff could haul supplies in and out during the day without disturbing the guests.

"You're sure this is a good idea?" Cheyenne asked, eyeing the door.

I rolled my eyes. "I know what I'm doing—"

"Let me guess, Bronger taught you."

I bristled. "Maybe you shouldn't complain about someone actually bothering to feed you."

The girl stiffened, her brown skin paling in the moonlight.

Guilt pinched my stomach. It'd been a horrible thing to say; I knew that. But she'd been pushing me the entire trip, and she needed to learn, now better than later, that she couldn't go around mocking Bronger like she did.

When she spoke, her voice was cool as the evening breeze. "At least my parents didn't leave me in the snow to die."

I made Cheyenne wait for me outside. I didn't need her ruining this.

Fuming, I slunk through the kitchen door, hood drawn over my head with my curls tied in a knot at the nape of my neck, well hidden underneath my hood. The bustle of the kitchen raked on my already exposed nerves, but everyone was so busy preparing for the dinner crowd, no one noticed the girl slipping into the pantry.

The girl who didn't belong.

I'd stuffed a pound of jerky, an assortment of cheeses, and a few jars of canned fruit into my bag when a firm hand landed on my shoulder.

"Now what do you think you're doing, stealing from my kitchen?" a deep, thirsty voice drawled.

I dropped to the floor, making it impossible for the cook to keep his grip on me. Then I kicked at his legs, hoping he'd trip over me in his scramble to get to me, but he remained planted, not easily ruffled or pulled into my trap. I crawled backward across the door, scrambling on my hands and feet, but the burly cook was prepared for that and grabbed me by the ankle. I twisted, hoping to free myself of his grasp by putting too much weight on his thumb, but he was prepared for that, too, and simply latched his other hand around my ankle as well.

My kicking didn't do much against the mammoth of a man.

Time to pivot.

I burst into tears. "Please. Please don't hurt me. I'm just so hungry."

"So are my paying guests." The cook scowled.

"Please." I turned out my pockets, parcels of dried fruit falling to the floor. "I'll give it all back. I promise I haven't eaten any of it. See, it's all here. I'll just leave, and then I won't have taken anything at all."

The cook eyed me, scanning my body from head to toe, my strong shoulders, my firm legs. "You don't look hungry to me."

"My family and I recently came into hard times..."

The cook snorted. "Your family, huh?"

I nodded furiously.

"I know every family in this town. I don't recognize you."

"We've been traveling for my parents to find work."

The cook eyed me again, and at first, I thought I might have him convinced, but then he broke into a feral smile. "You know what I think, girl? I think you're working for someone. Someone who keeps the meat on your bones in exchange for your thieving."

My blood chilled.

"The royal guard might pay more than a few coppers for a girl like you. The kind of information you could offer. There are quite a few criminals with bounties on their heads set by the king himself."

Bile rose in my throat. If he turned me into the royal guard, if they had any inkling, any suspicion regarding who I might work for, they'd flog my back to shreds.

And if they guessed for a moment that I worked for one of the rebels the king wanted dead, they might bring me before the King of Avelea himself.

I wouldn't break. I'd never give them his name.

That wasn't what I was afraid of.

Because when they were done with me—after I'd taken the lashing, screaming that I knew nothing, that I was simply an abandoned orphan with an empty belly—even if they let me go...

Once I'd been caught once, once they knew my face, the ivy green of my eyes, the pointed tips of my ears, the way my hair blazed...

I'd be no use to Bronger. Sure, it was a given that I was likely to have altercations with soldiers at some point as I completed my tasks. But there was a carriage service that went straight to Nettlewood, and if the cook deemed it worth it to take me there, to turn me into the royal guard themselves, they'd know my face, my description. Even if they didn't kill me, if they let me go, there was still the likelihood that they would do so in the hopes of following me back to my master.

I shook my head, desperately grasping for anything, anything*, that might convince this man to keep from turning me in, but the cook was eyeing a bag of flour, sealed with a thick cord, certainly contemplating a more permanent way of restraining me, of getting me to Nettlewood.*

"Wait," I breathed, the word a desperate plea on my tongue. "You're right. I am working for someone."

The cook cocked his eyebrow, the greed in his eyes scraping over me. "Didn't think you'd come clean so soon. The guard will be pleased. They won't flog you so bad if you just come out with it."

"It wasn't my choice. I promise," I said.

The cook's brow didn't soften as he tied my ankles together with the cord that had been previously occupied sealing the flour.

"I haven't met him yet, my new master. I don't know who he is or where he lives."

The cook grunted, clearly not convinced.

"No, really. I was taken from my home in northern Avelea a fortnight ago, but not by the man who now owns me. I'm to meet with him when we arrive wherever we're going."

His eyebrow quirked on that word. "We?"

I nodded frantically. "Yes, he has a girl he uses to take children. I think." I shuddered as convincingly as I could manage, which wasn't difficult, given the fact that if this went poorly, I'd never see Bronger again. "I think she's possessed with magic.*" I whispered the word, and I could practically see the gooseflesh pimpling the cook's exposed forearms. "You see, I didn't want to leave my family, I didn't even want to come in here to steal, but every time I tell her I don't want to do something, it's like...it's like I'm in a trance, and I find myself doing the things I don't want to do anyway. Please, I'll happily take you to her. I'm terrified of what might happen to me once she takes me to her master, what she'll make me do."*

There was no need to fake the tears in my eyes as he hoisted me to my feet and growled, "Show me."

CHEYENNE WAS STILL WAITING *for me, pacing frantically in the shadows, when the cook slammed open the door, dragging me behind him.*

Her hood slipped off her head, exposing her face as she turned to locate the source of the noise.

Her brown eyes glowed in the light of the cook's lantern, her dark ringlets wild from the nights spent on the forest floor.

For a moment, with the light hitting her like that, I wondered how her parents had ever forgotten about her, about a child so beautiful.

Regret twisted at my heart, clamping on my throat and forcing the word out. "Run."

What had I done?

Cheyenne obeyed, taking off in a sprint toward the tree line, leaving the cook with no other option than to throw me to the ground and chase after her.

Mouth full of dirt, I fumbled with the cord digging into my ankles, my fingers numb with the cold, hardly able to find the knot.

There.

The knot loosened, and I jumped to my feet. I barreled into the woods, veering right, praying to the Fates that I'd come upon Cheyenne before the cook, that she'd remembered the location of our meet-up spot should anything go wrong.

And things had gone very, very wrong.

I didn't let myself think about it as I cut through the woods, didn't allow myself to dwell on what would happen if the cook caught up with Cheyenne. The choice I'd have to make if he took her. What kind of person that choice would make me.

What felt like hours later, but had probably only been half an hour at most, I toppled into the clearing that we'd assigned as our meeting spot.

Cheyenne had beaten me there. "He was too big to weave through the trees. I lost him a while back." She jumped to her feet, then gripped me around my midsection, burying her face into my stomach, which wasn't a common occurrence for us as neither of us liked to be touched. So tiny. She was so tiny for her age. My stomach churned. "I'm so glad you're okay. I was afraid you'd been caught."

My mouth went dry.

"What happened in there?" Cheyenne asked, peering up at me with those beautiful wide eyes.

The smile on my face would have been less convincing if it hadn't been half-concealed by the shadows. "Nothing you need to worry about."

She pressed something round into my hands, the touch of her skin almost as cold as the metal itself.

Then she whispered something I couldn't hear.

CHAPTER 37

PIPER

I woke before I had the chance to hear what Cheyenne had wanted to say.

I supposed it had been important.

That was what my subconscious had seemed to think as it fought for sleep, grasping at the fleeting edges of the dream.

But dreams were smoke and butterflies and mist, and there was no catching them once they got away from you.

I didn't know why I wanted to catch it, why I wanted to swim back into that space, witness the moment my soul had turned to filth, the moment I'd betrayed a child.

The moment that had led to her violent death.

But that was what I wanted, I supposed. What I deserved after years of pushing the thoughts away, shoving them into the dark corners of my mind.

I'd known, deep down, that I'd been the one to betray her. I'd known it all along, even if I couldn't place the precise moment, the exact scenario under which it'd happened.

Selling your soul is like that; it comes with a taste you can't quite get off the base of your tongue, no matter how often you try to drink lye.

The memory, I'd blocked.

The taste? That had stayed.

"You ask a lot of questions," the hunter said after what was probably my second question of the day. It was more or less the same question I'd asked before he'd seen fit to drug me into shutting up. *When will the auction begin? When are they coming? When will the person I am now be erased by whatever they have planned for me?*

"What else am I to do tied up in this chair?" I asked, then seeing the way his eyebrow lifted at my sarcasm, I attempted to regain my pitiable persona by adding, "The questions keep my mind off how terrified I am... Help me imagine my Fate in advance, so I won't be so scared of it." I hung my head, finding the motion as easy as the words.

The man grunted. "S'pose a creature like you's had practice being afraid." There wasn't any kindness in his voice, any sympathy. Only a deep-seated loathing that told me he thought I deserved every drop of fear I'd ever experienced, simply for the tainted blood that flowed through my veins. The blood my parents had mingled, the blood I had nothing to do with.

I hung my head, trying to disguise my outrage as shame, lest he see the defiance in my eyes and I meet a worse end than he had planned for me already. "What will they do to me?"

I was fairly confident there were only two options, but underneath the question was another question that I hoped I'd disguised well enough. *Who* will do this to me?

"Nona my business." He shrugged, ambling over to the stove and poking the boar's singed skin. The fire crackled as fat drizzled from the skin and fell into the flames.

"How did you advertise me?"

"And that's nona yer business."

I fell silent, disappointed. Not that I should have expected a long-winded response from someone who lived so far from civilization that he didn't feel the need to keep his captives gagged.

But then as he continued to poke at the pig, he continued, "There's a bounty on yer head, you know. Er, at least, a head that looks mighty like yers."

My heart raced, and I remembered those posters hanging up in the second village Amity and I had visited. In how many villages had those renderings been posted? How many of the children's families suspected me? And what would they do to me if they got their hands on me?

"Could've turned ya in to the person who put the bounty on yer head," he offered.

"And why didn't you?" I asked, well aware that he wanted me to ask the question, needed someone to be interested in his life. To admire the cleverness of this backwoods nobody.

I'd stoop if I had to. So I added, "Wouldn't you get less for me if the others intend to turn me in for a profit?"

The man cackled and spun the end of his poker toward me. "I'd expect that kind of thinking from the likes of you."

I didn't ask exactly what he meant by *the likes of me.* Instead, I let him ramble, as it didn't appear he could help bragging about how much smarter he was than me.

"They'll pay more," he said, "because they expect to get more. Rumor has it you've taken lots of children. Most of them poor, without a reputation or any money behind their parents' names to prove important. But some of them, well, you've taken a few from the wrong people. Men with connections. I imagine there's enough fathers and mothers out there willing to pay, whether by money or services, to make the high price I've set on you plenty worthwhile."

"If you could make more money getting information out of me, then why don't you do it? Why sell me?" I asked.

The man opened his mouth to reveal a set of crooked teeth. "Because I prefer me money now, and with as little work as possible."

To each his own.

"How long is the bid open?" I asked.

"Sent out me messengers today. I expect the correspondents here to bid on you in a week."

"You're allowing them to come see me in person?"

"Yer a pretty little thing. Would be foolish to let them bid without seeing you."

"I thought I was valuable for my information."

"No need to make yerself out to be one-dimensional, little lady." He grinned through those jagged teeth. Something in my stomach churned.

"What if they fight over me? Overpower you and take me without paying?" I asked, really not wishing to be examined in person by a horde of bored, rich aristocrats.

"Don't waste yer eggs tryin' to be clever, missus. You'll put too much strain on yerself and lose yer chance of childbearing. Not that you should, with yer breeding, but I knows it's within a maiden's heart, half-breeds being no exception," he said.

I forced, I mean *forced*, a pained smile. "I appreciate your thoughtfulness," I said, and tried not to grind my teeth as I said it.

"Anytime, missus," he said, scanning every curve of my body with those beady eyes of his.

We spent the rest of the afternoon in silence. Well, the little bits of silence between the slashing noises as he skinned the boar right in front of me.

He was careful enough not to let any of the fat spill on the bear rug, at least. It would have been a shame to have ruined such tasteful finery.

When he was done slicing through the poor animal, he offered me a lump of bony meat, pressing it to my lips. "Can't have my pretty looking gauntly when the prospects come," he said.

I ate it, despite the disgust the rolled through me at being hand-fed. Had I not been tied to a chair, and had I not just witnessed the behind-the-scenes of cooking large animals, I might have enjoyed the meat. It was well-flavored, the kind I would have sought out in a marketplace in a new village, and would have been pleased to find.

I wondered if the people who bought this hunter's meat in the market knew anything of his other, less public activities. If they would have cared, if they did know.

The afternoon stretched lazily into the evening, and I waited until the hunter retired to his own room, off to my right. Once I could hear him snoring, I went to work.

The piece of bone that had been grating into my cheek since lunch —the one that had kept me from talking much, lest the hunter note my garbled voice or the jut in my cheek and realize what I'd done—I sidled it with my tongue to my front teeth, then jutted my jaw and tossed the shard of bone to my right.

I caught it in my palm, just barely, and had to fidget with it to keep it from falling to the floor. I clutched it between my forefinger and thumb and slid it between my wrist and the wooden handrest, sideways toward the left side of the cord. And then I sawed short, flimsy movements, one after the other, for what must have been hours.

My wrist ached, an arthritic pulse that felt as though, rather than sawing down the cord, I'd sanded down the cushioning that was supposed to keep my bones from rubbing up against each other. But I didn't stop, couldn't stop. Not unless I'd decided to give up altogether. But even then, I'd have to figure out a way to slice my wrist badly enough to kill me, and that death would be slow, painful. I'd have to sit here and think about what I'd done, and I wasn't in the mood for that.

I wanted to live.

Not as a slave to one of those horrid fae, who were probably checking the status of their accounts, trying to figure out what would be a reasonable amount to bid on me.

What I was worth.

In coppers. Not in any currency of real value.

No, it wouldn't happen. Not to me, not here. Not now.

Not when I was finally free.

Free. The word caught on my mind, hung there in the rafters, as if to tease me. As if to threaten that it might plummet any moment now, ripping a hole through my chest and soul.

It almost made me laugh, the absurdity of it. That *free* was the word my mind had chosen to refer to my situation, as I sat tied to a chair, a possession being fattened to sell off to the highest bidder.

Still. It was if, for the first time, I could take a comb to my mind and tease out the tangles Bronger had woven, the thoughts he'd planted in my subconscious.

My hands and feet weren't free, sure.

But my mind? It might as well have been a house cat, stretching its claws, basking in the warm sun.

Not that freedom was all it was cracked up to be.

Sure, in this hypothetical world of mine where I somehow managed to saw through this cord with a less than ideal angle on a pig's bone, I was *free.* But what did that even mean for a girl no reputable employer would hire? For a girl who'd ruined her chances of joining a group of traveling performers by using her skills to kidnap children? Word would get around. It already had, enough that I'd be auctioned off to the highest bidder within a week if I wasn't careful.

Even so, as much as it pained me to do so, I could feel that little grasp upon Bronger's pinky finger loosen ever so slightly.

Threatening that one day, I might just let him go.

If I could get out of here first.

CHAPTER 38

PIPER

The next few days went by so slowly and so quickly at the same time. Slowly, in that I was left alone with my own thoughts most of the time, which launched from hopeful and determined to numb and lifeless with as much warning as a Naenden sandstorm. My captor left me alone for long, stretching hours while he hunted, and I sawed at my restraints every spare second he wasn't watching.

But he always came back, and though I could tell I was making progress by the occasional twinge of a thread popping, breaking, those moments were few, and I didn't have the emotional energy to estimate the numbers of strings that must have been used to craft a cord as tightly wound as the one imprisoning me.

One day as the hunter was spoon feeding me a stew that made me want to vomit despite being quite flavorful, his gaze glanced down at my hands.

"Don't squirm so much in your restraints," he told me. "You're damaging those pretty little wrists of yers."

Then he took a finger and traced my white, beading knuckles down the spindly bones of my hand and stroked my wrist. I tried not to squirm, tried to hold down the bile, tried to be grateful he was just stroking my hands and nothing else, but his calloused touch turned cartwheels in my stomach, stuffed from how he'd force-fed me, convinced I was looking too thin for the auction.

I couldn't help but grip the shard of bone tighter as I tried to move it away from his touch, even as his fingers slid under my wrists.

"What's this?" He withdrew the bone shard from its hiding place, allowing it to scrape over the dainty skin he'd been so concerned about preserving only moments ago. Blood trickled down from my open scratches and beaded onto the handrest. My captor held the bone in front of his face, scanning it with those beady eyes as he rotated it, sunlight from the window behind me streaking across it like thin serrations.

"You thought you could pull one over me, did ya?" he asked, chuckling, though his eyes seemed like they might bulge from his face, pop out, and roll onto the floor.

I swallowed. "I'm not fond of the idea of being some bored high fae's slave. Can you blame me?"

"A girl the likes of you should just be grateful you've made it this far," he said. "The Fates would have buried others like ya in a brothel or in the ground by now. They must be fond of you. But even if you've managed to bewitch them with your wiles, the Fates ain't stupid. They know a half-breed when they see it." He lowered the makeshift blade of sharpened bone to my cheek before he pushed. Slowly. Deliberately. So that I could pinpoint the moment when the blade broke my skin. He sliced a mark across my cheek. "I hate ya made me do that. You just cost me at least a dozen coppers."

Coppers. That was the currency he was using to place a price on my head. I hadn't even made it to silver-worthy cargo.

He didn't feed me that night, or the next day. My stomach roared, groping for the tendrils of smoke that floated up from the oven as I watched animals roast before me.

I wondered how long it would take me to starve to death. Humans couldn't last long; I knew that. Fae could last a while, a few months, though it'd take them years to recover their strength if it came to that.

As in most areas, there wasn't much research out there on how long it took a half-fae to starve.

I supposed it was an uncommonly clean way for one of my kind to perish.

On the fourth day he fed me again, but very little, as he'd decided I'd gotten too fat for his prized customers' tastes. Apparently the richest of them all liked his females thin, gangly.

Sick.

Dead.

Weak.

They were all synonyms in my mind at this point.

CHAPTER 39

PIPER

"Tell me again about the man you're taking me to," the little girl said, not in the way a child might ask to be told a bedtime story, with wonder in their eyes and delight plastered across their faces. No, this child's eyes were wary, and though I'd told her every detail of Bronger I could recall, down to the way his blond hair sometimes cracked in places where the oils he used to slick it back faltered, she never ceased to ask.

Not for me to tell her again, not truly.

For me to tell her more.

"I already told you everything about him," I said.

"Everything?" The lift of her eyebrow told me she wasn't convinced.

I shrugged. "Everything."

"Does he hurt you?"

"Never." And I could hardly hold back the beaming on my face at the word. "Bronger would never. Trust me, I've been in his care since I was a kid."

"You're still a kid."

I shuffled, not ready to admit to myself that the child's words put a damper on my mood. I'd been proud, elated, when Bronger had said those few words I'd been waiting my whole life to hear.

You're ready.

"Kid or not, he trusts me with this responsibility," I said.

"But do you trust him?"

Such strange questions for a child of only eight years. Is this what they were typically like? I supposed I wouldn't know, having been an only child up until Bronger brought Elias around.

"Of course I trust him. He's basically my father."

"But not really."

I bristled. "Just because he didn't sire me doesn't mean he's not my father."

She plucked that broken compass, the one that pointed east instead of north, out of her pocket and began fiddling with it. "Then why'd you say basically?*"*

I didn't have an answer for that.

She just kept playing with that hideous compass, staring into the blue cataracts of the painted glawackus as if the creature wasn't the ugliest species to ever walk the earth.

We sat in silence for a moment, me wondering if I'd made the wrong decision in taking a girl like this, one who wouldn't understand how Bronger was, how much he'd sacrificed to protect us, when she said, "He doesn't forget about you though?"

I couldn't help the zealous grin that overtook my face. "Nev—"

Pain, crippling and all-consuming, lanced through my side. I tried to gasp, but my breath hitched, my lungs unable to expand from shock.

"Piper?" Cheyenne whimpered, horror brimming in her wide brown eyes. She reached for me, for the shaft that protruded from my waist, her tiny fingers trembling in disbelief at what she saw.

"Run," I managed to croak, but not soon enough.

A pair of shrouded males too tall and too swift to be human emerged from the trees.

One of them pointed a gloved finger in the little girl's direction. "That one."

She and I exchanged one last parting glance.

"Run," I whispered.

She obeyed.

Her brown ringlets whirled as she jumped to her feet, her nimble body cutting for a gap between two of the traffickers.

They caught her before her bare feet hit found the tree line.

"Think we'd ever let you get away? Do you know who it is who wants you so badly, child? Did you think your gift would escape his notice?" one of them hissed.

The realization hit me like a punch to the gut.

The cook from the tavern.

He'd told someone about her powers, then he'd given them Cheyenne's description.

I tried to will words to my mouth, but only limp whispers escaped my lips. It's me, it's me, it's me, *I tried to say, but they couldn't hear the words past my groans.*

My dagger pressed against my calf, the same side of my body from which an arrow now protruded, and I had to swallow a scream as I reached for it. My fingers grazed the hilt, and I grasped it.

In a moment it was flying through the air.

The next, it had lodged itself into the underarm of one of the traffickers.

He let out a feral cry, blood gushing from his wound. He ripped the dagger from his flesh and keeled over, attempting to contain the flow of blood with his hand, but it slipped off his gauntlet like rainwater from a window.

If he'd been human, it would have been a killing wound.

But all I could hope was that the fae's magic wouldn't be able to heal him until after he fell asleep.

I allowed myself a whimper.

They were going to take her.

They were going to take her, and it would be my fault. My cowardice, my jealousy, that made them do it.

They were going to take her, and I was going to die, my blood nothing more than a stain in the dirt.

I was going to die.

Worse than that, I was going to fail him.

I was going to fail Bronger.

What would they do with the child my careless rumors had sold out? Who was the highest bidder whose ears the ripple of gossip had reached?

How long would it take him to find my body? The Coup was still another three days' journey on foot. Would there be any trace of me left by the time he knew something was wrong?

Would it be worth the coin it would take to look for me?

Of all my swarming thoughts flitting for escape from my fading mind, this was the question that rattled me, had me gasping for breath, kept that darkness from swallowing me. That dreadful question left unanswered.

I grasped for my satchel, fumbling with the latch as it slipped underneath my clammy fingertips. When I finally managed to open it, I felt for a long metal tube and yanked it from the bag.

I clicked a button, and the tube zoomed into the air, a tail of fire trailing behind it as it burst into a cluster of sparks just above the tree line.

Bronger had told me I'd be on my own. I'd been so proud of it at the time. That he trusted me so fully.

But he'd packed the flare all the same.

Now I could only hope that he'd sent someone to trail us. To watch lest we fall into trouble.

Cheyenne screamed.

My gaze flitted to her. She was sideways now. Or perhaps I was sideways. Yes, that was it. I must have slumped over sometime in the last minute.

Coppery bile seeped through my teeth and the edges of the little girl blurred as she lashed out at the male holding her.

She made to jab him in the eye, just like I had taught her the first day I'd taken her from her family, but my lessons had been mostly in case of human assailants, faeries even. We hadn't gotten to the lessons about how to defend ourselves from the high fae...that there were only a few known ways to kill them...

But the male jolted backward, dropping the little girl so that her knees slammed onto the earth. The male stumbled away in a haze, shaking his head and backing into a tree in the process.

His voice sounded through the clearing, but I couldn't make it out over the roaring in my ears.

The other lurched for her, but he stumbled, the blood loss from the wound I'd inflicted clearly too fast for his magic to heal immediately.

She sprinted for me.

But then it *crept from the bushes.*

A beast, wolf only in form but not in size, silver as the cusp of the moon, slunk from the bushes and padded silently behind the child.

She didn't hear it coming.

I tried to scream, to cry out in warning.

My throat wouldn't let me.

The child hit the ground, her fingers writhing at the dirt as if it could possibly serve as an anchor to oppose the force of the beast's strength.

The leg of her trousers ripped, the beast having caught hold of her foot, and she scrambled forward, her hand grazing mine.

The world didn't go black.

I was still conscious when the beast ripped her from my desperate fingers, when her dark ringlets rippled over the dust, when it dragged her across the earth and into the forest brush.

Then, and only then, did the world go black.

CHAPTER 40

MARCUS

Shadows licked every forgotten corner of the tavern, sluicing in waves off the male dressed in *paldihv* and soaking even the humid tavern air with a chill that snaked down my spine as he approached. The male took up the stool next to me and slapped a fistful of silvers on the counter.

My dinner, a stew that was more broth than meat that I'd mostly left untouched, rippled at the impact.

The barmaid's fingers trembled as she scraped the coins into her pocket and hurried away to fulfill the man's order, forgetting to ask him what he wanted.

"That's a lot of coin to be flashing about," I said, the show of confidence doing little to ease the pressure building up in my chest.

The chest that would have had an arrow in it, had Piper made a different choice.

I'd left her, allowed her to wander down that uncut path. I'd meant to follow her, to allow myself a moment, just a moment without the trudge of her footsteps pounding against my mind, the steady beat reminding me that my sister is dead, my sister is dead, my sister is dead.

It was still ringing in my ears when I realized she'd wandered further than I could see. When I'd realized I didn't have to follow. That ridding myself of her would have been as simple as a slight veer to the left.

So that's what I'd done.

That was a week ago, and yet the ringing hadn't stopped.

My sister is dead, my sister is dead, my sister is dead.

I hadn't realized how much hope I'd been holding onto all these years. That, even when I'd stumbled upon that tattered cloak, my knees buckling as I sobbed into that blood-soaked fabric, I hadn't truly accepted it.

There was the blood. Too much spilled for a girl her size to survive. And the ruined cloak, and the broken compass.

But I hadn't truly believed it, that she was dead.

I could say that with certainty now, because *this*, the numbness that settled over my heart, wrapping it in its clammy embrace, *this* was what it felt like to know I'd never see her again.

"That's a lot of nerve you have, getting cheeky with someone like me," he said.

My ears were ringing.

"It's almost as if you're looking for a fight," he hissed, his words an invitation.

I unleashed the cockiest grin I could muster, the one that begged the kind of man with something to prove to clobber my jaw. It came more easily than I expected. I *expected* to be out of practice, but it seemed I could don this face as easily as I'd walked away from Piper.

Just walked away.

"Unfortunately for you, I'm in no mood for a fight."

Oh, but I bet I could get you there.

"Sounds like a coward's words to me," I drawled.

He chuckled, a deep, throaty laugh that rumbled underneath his shadows.

"Tell you what. Take a seat, and I'll let you in on a secret," he said.

I looked down at my feet, hadn't even realized I'd stood and braced my core for the impact of his first blow. "I'd rather stand."

The male's shoulder's shrugged. "Be my guest. I assume your ears work just as well standing."

My mouth twitched, but I maintained my unamused grin.

A whistle sounded from underneath the male's hood, and the barmaid came stumbling over with a pile of drinks in her hand. One of them slipped, toppling over as soon as it hit the counter and spraying ale everywhere, including the hem of the male's *paldihv*.

The barmaid gasped, apologies spewing from her as she grabbed a cloth and attempted to wipe it up, sloshing more ale onto the floor in the process.

"Now, dear. Don't fret," the man said, extending a shadowed hand and laying it atop hers. "Sh. There, there," he said, as if he spoke to a child and not a grown woman. "My *paldihv* is not so fragile to be harmed by a little spill."

The barmaid stilled, her whole body still trembling. "The owner will be awful mad."

"We'd better not tell him, then." Shadows shaped much like fingers stroked her arm, and she shivered.

"You won't say anything?" she almost gasped.

"Of course not. It'll be our little secret."

The woman's shoulders sagged, and she went to remove her hand from his grasp, probably to place upon her chest as the relief that she might keep her job another day flooded over her.

But the male only gripped her harder.

My spine went rigid.

"It will come at a price, I'm sure. One I think you'll find quite fair."

The color drained from the barmaid's face, but—Fates bless her, she was probably used to these disgusting advances—she recovered quickly enough, letting out an exasperated, if not strained, giggle, and said, "I'm afraid I don't have anything to spare. S'pose we'll have to tell the owner after all. Guess I'll be resigned to another week cleaning out the latrine."

He extended another hand, turning her palm upward as he massaged her lifeline with those shadowy tendrils. "Aren't you curious?" he asked her.

"About what?" she asked, the lightheartedness in her voice splintering.

"About what's underneath the shadows?"

The girl's throat bobbed and the pure terror in her eyes...

That single motion, the way she swallowed her dread—it broke through the haze and sliced through the callus that had hardened over my resolve.

"Stop."

The male turned his shadowed face toward me. "What did you say?"

"Stop. Don't make me say it again."

The male hesitated, and for a moment I wondered if he'd make sure I never got the chance to speak another word, but then he slowly withdrew his hand from hers.

The barmaid stumbled away, then disappeared from sight into the kitchens.

"My apologies. I didn't realize you had a claim on her."

Claim. Like she was a prize to be won for racing horses.

"Oh," the male said, catching the distaste in my sneer. "Oh, you did that for her, didn't you?"

I didn't deign to answer.

His low, bellowing laugh rumbled from the shadows, reverberating through the ground this time. "Well, then. I suppose that's one fewer male who'll be attending tomorrow's auction. Less competition, I suppose."

When I again did not bother to grace him with a response, he took it upon himself to elaborate. "Oh, you haven't heard? A nearby hunter caught an *asset* of interest wandering through the nearby woods. I'm not sure he knows exactly who she is, but judging by the description, I believe that I do."

She. Just a coincidence. My stomach recoiled at the thought of a young woman being traded off like livestock, but it was just a coincidence. There had to be plenty of women who traveled through the woods every day.

"You see," the male continued, "I have a certain employer who's been in search of a female fitting her description. The bounty he put on her head..." The male whistled. "He must want her badly. Not that I could blame him. Sounds like a pretty thing."

My breath caught.

"Red hair..."

No.

"Green eyes..."

No, no, no.

"Half-fae."

I'd left her. I'd left her alone, spirit broken, with barely the will to put one foot in front of the other.

"The description had me wondering if I might be better off forgoing the coin and keeping her for myself..."

Something told me that if I lived a hundred more years, I would never be able to unhear what the male said next.

I braced my trembling fist on the counter, shaking so hard that my tankard of ale, ordered yet untouched, sloshed over.

CHAPTER 41

PIPER

Somehow the day of my auction forced its way through the molasses of time and came upon us at last.

The hunter's name turned out to be Kev. I found out when he shared it without me inquiring about it or caring, and despite his insistence that he shouldn't be worrying about giving his name to a half-breed. Something about me being unworthy to bear the name on my lips.

Kev intended to host the auction in what was essentially his backyard. He had to move me hours before the attendees were scheduled to arrive, because he didn't trust me enough to unbind my feet and allow me to walk myself, and as in shape as he was, carrying a half-fae and a heavy cedar chair from his house and through the forest thicket was a bit cumbersome.

As he scraped the chair against the wooden paneled floor, he pressed his lips against the tip of my ear, and I had to ball my fists as a wave of nausea rippled through me at the stench of his putrid breath. "I really will miss ya, pretty. Wouldn't have expected it, but yer so polite. Know yer place." He twirled a limp curl around his finger as he whispered, "And I can forgive ya for trying to escape. I'd have done the same, even if I knew I deserved my fate for my breeding. But I'd probably be thinking to myself that it were my parents that should've shouldered the punishment. Yer probably thinking the same. That yer parentals should've had the guts to throw ya off a cliff the day you were born. Would've been the right thing to do. The selfless thing. Would have saved you a whole lot of pain, I'm sure you'd agree."

I swallowed, but that was all. I didn't give him the satisfaction of a whimper. "Wholeheartedly," I said, clamping down on my nerves to maintain the apathy in my voice.

"Ya really are so pretty." He cupped my cheek in his greasy palm and brought my face toward his.

His breath went ragged. His eyes dipped.

My chest was heaving.

"It's been a rough few days, you know. Keeping you here. Minding my business at night. It would have been easy, you know. Would've treated you like a lady. You've liked it."

No. No, this wasn't happening.

I'd known for days this would eventually be my fate. I knew enough about what happened to women who were sold at these types of auctions. My situation might have been slightly different, since I wasn't simply being sold for my body, but for my crimes. For the grudges so many held against me.

But it was going to happen. In the dingy basement of a seedy brothel or in the bed of a wealthy man whose child I'd taken, it was going to happen.

I'd just hoped it wouldn't happen until tomorrow.

Kev's beady eyes undressed me before landing on my face. I didn't let myself look away. Wouldn't give him the demure creature he so desperately wanted me to be.

"The auction doesn't start for an hour, ya know," he whispered.

I had to bite down on my tongue to keep the whimper from escaping my lips. Tomorrow. I'd thought I had until tomorrow.

Something inside me cracked. I'd thought after Bronger that I'd shattered, but I hadn't. Not entirely. There were parts of me that killing him had left intact.

This?

This would break me.

Tomorrow. They could break me tomorrow.

They couldn't break me today.

On second thought, they couldn't break me tomorrow, either.

"Touch me, and you'll forfeit the sale."

Kev's beady eyes narrowed, and his hand faltered at my cheek.

"I'm assuming you have local representatives coming from different brothels." I tried not to notice his calluses scraping against my jaw as I spoke.

He didn't answer. He only breathed. That was answer enough.

"High-end brothels don't like their goods damaged. You said yourself you already cost yourself a few coppers for slicing my cheek."

A smile returned to his dry lips. "They won't be none the wiser. And you won't tell them. Know how I know?" He scraped a finger against my throat, mimicking slitting it.

"I won't have to tell them. The fae will know. They can scent that sort of thing."

I had no idea if that were actually the case or not. My senses might have been heightened compared to humans', but they weren't that sensitive.

But I didn't have to know for sure. Kev's cheeks slackened.

Doubt could be so much more powerful than confidence.

He drew away, and my fists loosened. Droplets of blood caked my untrimmed fingernails from where I'd dug them into my palms.

Kev dragged me across the field by a handful of hair at the base of my skull. The legs of the wooden chair scraped into the muddy earth, catching on pebbles and roots as if in protest.

I didn't care.

My scalp could scream all it wanted.

I wouldn't be breaking.

Not today. Not tomorrow.

. . .

When Kev had finally dragged me up the stairs of his makeshift stage after dropping me once and probably breaking my nose as I face-planted into the ground, he started making rounds back and forth to the hut. Kev piled furs in a looming stack to my left, and I hoped they wouldn't fall over on the unstable stage and smother me before Kev had the chance to save me.

The attendees started arriving approximately two minutes after Kev had arranged the stage.

The first was high fae, an aristocrat from Nettlewood if I was correct in determining that the symbol on his brooch was, in fact, a nettle—the dumbest of all crests, as it was simply a single line, slanted across the embossed metal. The male's face was narrow, coming to a point at his chin and then widening for his oversized blue eyes. His long blond hair flowed like silk from his head, and his appearance reminded me of becoming sick on too many sweets.

"You've underfed her," was his chosen greeting.

I examined his robes, his pristine black cape that flitted over his shoulder, his high cheekbones that might have been handsome if not accompanied by a clenched jaw and a sour smirk. Anything but his eyes. I couldn't bear to see whether a fire sparked within them upon seeing me. What kind of fire.

What type of greed.

I found myself hoping it was the kind that lusted after money, though I was still fairly certain that, should I fall into the hands of whoever put this bounty on my head to begin with, I might feel differently.

"Ah! Rayn! Good of ya to make it," Kev said in a friendly, boisterous voice I'd yet to hear. The kind of voice that usually belonged to the friendly town drunk—the one whom the villagers might judge for spending too much time with his liquor while secretly harboring a fondness for his gregarious charm. I squirmed in my chair, chills creeping across my skin at the memory of his hot breath against my cheek, what he'd almost done...

I wondered then how many friendly men kept women tied to their furniture.

"The poor thing had a bout of food poisoning," Kev said, then, seeing the raised eyebrow of his guest as the high fae swept his gaze over the assortment of meats bordering me on the stage, backtracked, "Had it when I found 'er. Was mostly incapacitated."

"Lucky for you," Rayn purred.

I fought back my swallow, my rapid blinking, lest he sense it. Sure, I knew he could already feel my heart racing, even from such a distance. But I wouldn't give him any more satisfaction than I had to.

Rayn raised his brow at the overgrown brush, as if taunting some poor frog to jump out. "Where are your other guests?"

"Yer early!" Kev said. "The invitation said half past noon. Won't be expecting the others for another quarter an hour."

Unless my ears had deceived me the last eighty-seven times Kev had reassured himself under his breath of the start time, that was a flagrant lie.

Rayn swept his gaze over me this time, as if to account for every freckle, every stray strand of hair, every wrinkle in my robes. "Interesting."

My heart pounded. I couldn't stop it. Not once fear had bullied me into meeting Rayn's stare, in the hopes he wasn't nearly as frightening as I'd assumed.

I'd assumed correctly. The look in his cold eyes betrayed hunger. Plotting.

I could have strangled Kev for telling him the other attendees wouldn't be arriving for another fifteen minutes. Fifteen. Minutes. What was fifteen minutes to a high fae against one middle-aged human and an underfed half-fae female tied to a chair?

Rayn must have seen my fear, the lack of naivety in my eyes, for a cruel smile spread across his face, and he winked. Then he angled toward Kev, who had turned his back to the high fae as he rifled through a bucket of breads he'd laid out on the stage. Rayn's pointed ears narrowed and descended on the side of his head. Like a cat about to pounce.

I gasped. Not in terror, in shock. For right beyond the tree line stood a figure, tall and hooded, the dark material stretched so low over his face that even his mouth was clouded with shadow. Rayn flinched, gave one look in my direction that made me wonder if any high fae were known to be cannibals, and then traced my horrified gaze to the tree line.

The being emerged from the gloom, though a shadow still lingered over his face, and even Rayn took a step backward.

Tendrils of shadow licked at the ground as the stranger dressed in *paldihv* stalked into the clearing.

CHAPTER 42

PIPER

Kev swiveled to face his new potential buyer and immediately dropped a pile of cheese wheels from his arms. They rolled across the stage before toppling to the ground. He recovered quickly enough, regaining that cruel sneer he'd primarily used with me these past few days. "Why...you weren't on the list, now were ya?"

The shrouded figure stepped forward, which Kev and Rayn mirrored in reverse. A shudder went up my spine, and I found my fingers clawing at the cedar frame that made up my chair, my prison. My feet jittered in their restraints, and what I would have given for the ability to run. The freedom to toss Kev in front of me, to put an obstacle between myself and this stranger.

This being who didn't care if the entire world knew he was a murderer.

Who probably preferred it that way.

I would have run if I'd had the chance.

"That being said, I'm delighted to be graced with yer attendance," Kev backtracked. "What's yer name?"

The being didn't answer. He just stood there, shadows billowing around him although there was no breeze, nor had there been a whiff all morning.

He didn't say a word. He simply stared. At me.

Or, at least, in my direction. I couldn't see his eyes, or anything about his face to be exact, through those billowing shadows.

Rayn cleared his throat and took a step backward, away from the shadow-curtained being and away from me. I couldn't help but notice that his ears had gone back to pointing upward.

Perhaps Rayn had deeper pockets than I'd once hoped.

We were joined not five minutes later by four other attendees. The first was a stout, middle-aged man who apparently owned a bar in a neighboring city. A bar that was known to men far and wide for having the most "select breeding" of ladies, he'd said. I'd wanted to snarl back at him, ask him why he was bothering with a *half-breed* if he had a reputation to uphold. But when I'd opened my mouth, I'd gotten that sinking feeling in my stomach, on the hairs of my neck, that someone was watching my every move. I'd glanced back at the hooded figure. Just to check that he was still within view, not slitting my company's throat in an attempt to sneak me away without paying. But he was standing, still as a brick, his shrouded face locked on mine.

I'd gulped and gone back to trying to formulate an insult directed toward the nasty bartender, except I quickly remembered that I'd rather he purchase me than our mysterious shrouded friend, whose intentions for me I couldn't imagine, whose motives frightened me past the point of even being curious.

The next three males that showed up were just as slimy as Rayn and the barkeeper, but not nearly as intimidating as the shrouded being. One was a traveling merchant from Naenden, whose client figured I'd be of great value to the Naenden people. Human brides were all the rage amongst the high fae nobility in Naenden, ever since the king had married his second bride and found success with that marriage. Apparently, the people had been quick to forget that his first human wife had tried to have him murdered.

Anyway, the merchant, named Tijan, along with his client, believed that I, even with my half-fae breeding, would still be of value in the booming market, especially as it was rumored that I possessed a gift, much like the one the human Queen of Naenden possessed herself.

Perhaps that wouldn't be such a horrible fate, I thought. There would be no way I could escape the merchant once he had me in the middle of the Sahli. No way a foreigner who didn't know the patterns of the dunes, the places where vipers preferred to den, the path of the sun across the desert sky, could survive out there without a native's help. But if I could just make it to Meranthi, find myself in a fae noble's home...perhaps then I could escape, make my plea to the Naenden queen, whom I imagined wouldn't be thrilled to hear of the marketing of her people to the greedy fae nobility.

Yes, if the merchant could win the bid, then perhaps it wouldn't have been better for me to die in the woods.

To die in the snow.

Before Bronger lifted my limp body from what should have been my tomb and carried me all the way to that inn with the gentle fire.

I shuddered and pushed the memory away.

The last two men to show up were brothers and were barely worth noting. They'd clearly heard about the auction second-hand, probably overheard one of their fae employers speaking of it to another, and foolishly thought they'd take their shot at an exotic female.

Disgusting.

The last guest arrived much later than the rest and turned out to be a female. High fae, by the looks of her height, though she'd veiled her face.

She, like the bartender, had a business of her own to run. A business that explained the veil. Her name was Shya, and I decided I hated her more than the rest.

Kev was a horrible auctioneer, tripping over every other word as he rambled on about all my *features*.

The foremost being my dazzling red hair, of course. Not the fact that I could play a tune that could call to the resilient, not the fact that I had curbed an entire pool of water to my will (well, my gift's will, really, but I was pretty sure no one would bother to make the distinction), not the fact that I was brutal enough to kill the only father I'd ever had.

No, the red hair defined me. And the *half-breeding* too. But Kev couldn't seem to decide whether he wanted to highlight that as an asset or try to make his audience forget about it altogether by focusing only on my human attributes.

Idiot.

"Bidding begins at two hundred coppers..." Kev said.

"Two hundred coppers?" I said, unable to contain myself, unable to hold up the ruse that I'd go quietly any longer. "I've heard of horses that sold for more." My hands shook.

"Don't worry, darling," Rayn said, "my bid is five hundred. I agree. It would be shameful for such a beauty to go at such a steal."

I shot a glare in his direction and was pretty sure it bounced right off his stony heart. He just grinned at me, his face so symmetrical it made me nauseous to look at it.

Kev cleared his throat, an obvious attempt to hide his blossoming excitement for the auction already exceeding any of his quaint expectations. "Raisin' the bid to five fifty."

The shrouded being raised a gloved hand.

My heart must have stopped, for Rayn's head whipped to me, not to the shrouded stranger. As if to check if I was still alive.

"Going once, going twice..."

"Five seventy-five," Shya said, her veil fluttering around her mouth. Apparently, she wasn't one to make a show of her money like Rayn.

Confusion swept over the Naenden merchant's face, and he frowned.

Rayn scoffed, apparently thinking the same thing. "You can't bid in quarter increments."

"I don't remember our host stating such in the rules," she drawled. "Or establishing any rules at all."

Kev stiffened next to me.

"She's right. He never said we had to bid fifty coppers at a time." The bartender shrugged. "Six hundred," he added.

"Eight hundred." Rayn seethed with such ferocity I wondered if he even had the money, or if the clear disregard for the proper rules of bidding had simply thrown all budgetary concerns out the window.

"Going once..." The legs of my chairs rattled. Kev was shaking the stage by the way he was rocking back and forth on the balls of his feet. If not for the interaction we'd had just before the auction, I might have found his utter lack of confidence amusing.

Now it just infuriated me.

The way he so obviously feared this group of outlaws, yet he planned to turn me over to them for a profit. The way cowardice oozed from him like puss from a wound, yet he'd managed to terrify me with the threat of his body.

I hoped that whoever purchased me snipped him like the loose end that he was.

The brothers whispered to one another. "Eight oh five."

"That's a time of day, not a bid!" Rayn said, his pale face flushing in agitation.

Kev peered nervously back and forth between Rayn and the brothers who looked like they'd walked here immediately following a brawl, and shrugged.

"Eight oh five, going once..."

The shrouded being raised his hand. An invisible fist tightened around my stomach. Over eight hundred coppers! How much more would the others be willing to bid? I was fairly certain Rayn was just here to turn me straight over to the original person who'd placed a bounty on my head, whoever that might be. It probably wasn't worth the slim profit for him to bid any higher. And Shya was placing a tendrilly finger upon where I imagined her lips to be. I doubted she was seeing much of a profit in purchasing me any longer.

And the two ragged humans surely didn't have the money for their first bid to begin with...

"What's your bid increment, sir?" Kev asked.

The figure didn't answer, he only stared.

Kev cleared his throat. "Nine hundred, then." He shifted in his boots, as if he thought the shrouded being might lunge at him any moment for having presumed such an increase in the bid.

But the being only nodded, the shadows around him swirling despite the lack of breeze.

Rayn and the Naenden merchant exchanged annoyed glances, as if silently asking one another if there was any way bidding higher could be worthwhile.

The merchant stepped back from the line of bidders first. "My client will be displeased. But as he was once my apprentice before falling into unexpected wealth and developing an intolerable persistence for getting his way, I can't say I'll be all that upset to disappoint him."

Rayn laughed, a wry, empty sound that could have easily echoed from his soul. "If you think your client's bad..." Then he nodded his head in deference and stepped backward.

The bartender grumbled something under his breath about a waste of time, something about having taken off an entire afternoon during the busy season for this. It appeared that he, too, was out.

My heart pounded, and I wondered whether it was a fae underneath the shroud, whether he could hear my fear, my panic.

Shya said nothing.

That left only the brothers. One of them opened his mouth into a gnarled smile. "Looks like the pretty's all yers."

No, no, no. Surely Rayn or Shya or the merchant or even the bartender had enough to bid higher. Maybe they'd go in together on the cost, but that wouldn't make the profit margins any larger. I knew what to expect from the human men, from the fae.

But this being in the shroud might as well have been a daemon, even though I didn't believe in such things.

"Going once, going twice... Sold to the... erm, this gentleman right here," Kev finally said, nodding his head in the shrouded being's direction.

The being walked toward me, the sound of heavy boots clanking against the ground as he approached.

"Well, that's my cue," Rayn said, apparently not willing to be as devious as he'd intended to be when he thought he was alone with Kev and me. I couldn't blame him. I wouldn't have tried to steal from this being, either. I gulped, realizing that's exactly what I'd be doing if I tried to escape.

Shya stood and watched us for a moment as the merchant, bartender, and brothers shook their heads and walked back toward the thicket of the woods.

"Friends, the auction's not done yet. Surely you'll get hungry between now and when ya get to yer abodes," Kev called hopefully to the receding audience, but none of them bothered to answer.

The shrouded being approached and placed a coin purse in Kev's hand.

Kev shuddered but plastered a greedy grin on his face all the same. "Knew exactly what you'd bid, did ya? Or is there a little extra in here for me?" When Kev shook the purse, coins clanked on the inside, and it didn't sound like almost a thousand coppers. Nor did I think that many coppers could have fit in a coin purse of that size. It was the same make as the one I'd given to Marcus the night Amity and I had fled. It had contained only twenty coppers, an embarrassing sum, by the time our journey had ended, but they'd still filled up almost a quarter of the bag.

Apparently Kev was thinking the same thing, for he let out a nervous chuckle and said, "You keep your change in silvers, don't ya? I'd do the same, if I was traveling about. Carrying that much coin around would be too conspicuous. Too..." Kev opened the purse and looked inside, his face going pale.

The shrouded being just stared at him, as if to challenge him to make a complaint.

It seemed the shrouded being had overestimated Kev's ability to reason, to examine the long-term consequences of his behavior.

"You think you could swindle me, huh?" Kev yelled, garnering the attention of Rayn and the rest of the bidders as they walked away. Shya remained still, her reaction unreadable under her veil. Kev held the coin purse high above his head, shaking it back and forth so that the metal clinked and clanked noisily. "He's a fraud. He ain't got no money!"

"Is that so?" Rayn said, his voice smooth and treacherous. "Tell me, stranger. What other insufficiencies are you hiding under that shroud of yours? Did you kill a drunken man and steal his clothes?"

The shrouded being whirled, sending one of his heavy boots straight into Kev's face. Kev hit the stage with a thump, and chaos erupted. Rayn went for his sword, slicing the blade through the air, the sound of metal scraping against leather ringing through my ears as he pulled his sword from its sheath. The barman and the brothers each drew daggers. One brother flung his blade in our direction. I screamed and jolted my head to the side as the dagger whipped right past my face. I cursed the idiot brother's poor aim and began wriggling my hands, my legs. Anything to get myself out of these restraints. But the cord simply dug further into the red imprints in my wrists. I was going to die, the collateral damage of a monetary exchange gone poorly, these ridiculous creatures fighting over me as if I were some piece of property left by a father foolish enough not to write specifications in his will.

The shrouded being reached down and took Kev's knife from his waist, dodging another flying dagger by doing so. He jumped up, bringing the blade down upon my hands. I screamed, but his knife only grazed my wrist, splitting the cord in two in one fell swoop.

My left arm free, the shrouded figure pressed the dagger into my hand. Rayn nocked an arrow and sent it flying past the shrouded being's ear, or where I imagined his ear to be if he was the type of being with ears at all. I panted and turned Kev's dagger upon the cord, keeping my right arm in place. The blade sawed against the cord, but it broke thread by thread, not like the clean break of the shrouded being's blade.

"You couldn't have freed my dominant hand?" I hissed under my breath, not at all intending for the shrouded being to hear. I was just so fed up, so sick of the unnecessary obstacles blocking my way to freedom. Finally the cord snapped, but when it did, I almost took out my right wrist with it as the tension in the cord dissipated into nothingness, sending the blade colliding with my flesh. I yelped as the dagger broke the skin, possibly hit bone, but I pulled it from my flesh and transferred the blade to my right hand, sure that I'd be able to better saw the restraints off my feet with my injured right hand than my whole left hand.

I was right, for the restraints came off much faster.

"She's getting away!" someone called as I stood from the chair. My legs wobbled beneath me as they supported my weight for the first time in a week. My feet were bare and weak. Only adrenaline and sheer willpower kept me from tumbling off the edge of the stage.

To my left, the shrouded being ripped a bow from the shadows swarming his back, then nocked an arrow from the same location, whipping it from the void as if he were creating it between the pads of his fingers.

Except he wasn't creating that bow. He wasn't creating those arrows.

For they were both painted cerulean. Like the Avelean sky.

"Marcus," I whispered, allowing the one word to fall from my lips, the one symbol of recognition should one of us die in the next few moments.

My mind kicked into action, commanding my limbs along with it. I grabbed the chair and flung my prison from the stage straight toward Rayn's bow. He was too quick for me with his fae senses, but striking him hadn't been my aim. The arrow he had pointed directly at Marcus's heart slipped from his fingers as he dodged the chair, as his arrow lost its target.

The arrow came flying for me, but I was ready for it and ducked to the side just in time to hear it whiz past my left cheek. I glanced to my right just in time to see the brothers climbing up the stage, one using the other as a stool for jumping off of. The bald one gripped the edge of the stage and began pulling himself up. He bared his greedy teeth at me, and I launched myself toward the stage floor, plunging my dagger into his calloused hand just in time to dodge another stray arrow whooshing above my head. The brother wailed, and I pulled my dagger from his bloodied hand lest

I lose it as he slipped and fell toward the ground, landing on top of the other.

I looked up and caught the merchant's gaze. He was gaping at me as I wiped my dagger on my trousers, cleaning the blade, yet leaving a dark stain smeared across my clothes. The merchant turned and disappeared into the forest, as did the bartender.

When I looked back at Marcus, he was still in a standoff with Rayn, both of them firing arrows at one another in between dodging their opponent's shots at the last minute. One arrow flew right at Marcus. I screamed, and Marcus moved to the side just in time to dodge the strike to his heart, though the arrow grazed his shoulder. Panic swelled over me, and I dashed toward Kev, whose body lay limp, a stray arrow puncturing his chest. He had fallen backward onto his own bow, and by the time I wrestled it out from beneath him, the shaft had bent into an awkward position.

But I knew better than to approach a high fae with my tiny, bloodied dagger, so I launched to my feet and nocked an arrow into Kev's bow.

The first went flying well above Rayn's head, and he even let out a laugh just before one of Marcus's arrows grazed his pointed ear and calculated rage overcame his expression.

I shot again. This time, the arrow lodged itself into the grass a few feet in front of Rayn. I bit my lip and fought back the stinging tears welling in my eyes. All it'd take was one landed shot, and Marcus would be dead. Marcus was going to die rescuing me. If not at Rayn's hands, then surely at Shya's, who still stood at the far side of the clearing. I glanced back at her, just to check that she hadn't moved, wasn't sneaking up behind Marcus and me to deliver the fatal blow. But she wasn't. She was just standing there, watching, as if to see which one of the two males would finish the other off first, which of the survivors she would wipe from the land of the living once they'd already been wounded by their opponent.

She caught my glance and tilted her head slightly to the side, as if to nudge my attention back toward Rayn.

Perhaps there was something behind him?

But nothing stalked in the brush behind Rayn. Not that I could see, at least. Marcus dodged another arrow. Rayn hadn't aimed any arrows in my direction, at least not intentionally, so I chanced another glance at Shya. She tilted her head toward Rayn in encouragement.

I narrowed my eyes, trying to communicate that I didn't understand, though what I truly didn't understand was why I was trying to read a message from the female who intended to absorb me into her *business* as soon as Marcus and Rayn had finished one another off.

Deciding to take my chances, I aimed an arrow at Rayn. Not that it would matter. Not that one of Kev's simple, wooded arrows would do much to harm a high fae. Even if I managed to strike him in the heart, there was a good chance he'd recover, and then Marcus and I would both be dead.

I fired anyway.

It ripped a cavern straight through Rayn's chest. Rayn staggered for a moment, his thin mouth agape as he stroked the charred hole where his heart had just been.

As Bronger had stroked the shaft of the arrow.

Little did Rayn know that it lay in the field behind him.

Burning.

Bile spilled up into my throat as Rayn fell. As Bronger fell again. As I fell.

Strong hands cradled the back of my head, pulled my sweaty hair from my face as I vomited off the stage.

When I looked up from the contents of my stomach, Shya was gone.

CHAPTER 43

PIPER

I didn't know what to do with the shadow swirling before me. With that face I knew from my dreams, still masked underneath the folds of smoke and shadow.

"We can't stay here," Marcus said. At least, I told myself it was Marcus. Told myself that no other man could possess a voice so warm and fierce and kind bound all into one.

He'd come back for me.

Marcus had come back for me.

I had to shove the elation into the pocket below my ribs.

He was right. We couldn't stay here.

Even if I didn't want to waste one more moment walking when all I wanted was to be held in his strong arms.

I shook it off. Silly thoughts. I didn't know why he had come back, I reminded myself, and my heart sank, stomping on the piece of hope I'd tucked between my ribs.

Perhaps he thought I had more information on his sister than I'd let on.

Perhaps he was right about that.

"Right." I stepped over Kev's limp body, careful not to totter off the edge of the stage. An innate clawing for survival had kept me steady during the fight, but now that danger wasn't whizzing past my head—past Marcus's head—I thought my legs might give out. I stumbled, and a shadowy arm grasped underneath my bicep, steadying me.

"Thanks," I said, turning toward him, wanting my face near his. But those dreadful shadows crawled around his cheekbones, his eyes, his lips, hiding any expression that might have given me a hint about why he'd come back for me.

If it had, indeed, been for me.

Or something I knew.

I picked up a pile of dried meat and packed it into Kev's satchel, which lay on the ground next to one of his auction barrels. Next I stuffed in all the dried berries I thought could fit, along with two large skins of water Kev had been planning to provide as extra gifts for the food he'd auctioned off.

Then I hobbled toward the cabin. Marcus followed behind me in silence, the only noise coming from his light footsteps on the wooden floor. My satchel lay in the corner, right behind where my chair had sat so many days. I wrenched it from the ground and scrambled with the latch. On the inside, my flute lay unharmed, along with a scarce few of my belongings. I sighed. The idiot hadn't seen the worth in my flute, though it'd been the most valuable asset in my bag. At least to me.

My last little bit of Bronger. Something concrete I could hold in my hand to remind me that, at one point, on some level, he had loved me. And that he'd known I'd loved him.

That somewhere his spirit understood why I'd murdered him.

When Marcus spoke, his voice went still as a mosquito-ridden pond. "We need to go now." That bit of hope tucked away in my soul shriveled a bit at the flatness of his tone. No excitement to see me. No relief. Just a mission that needed completing. A means to an end.

"Right," I said again, because I couldn't think of anything else to say as I tugged on my shoes and hurried out of the cabin as fast as I could manage on my wavering legs.

Marcus caught up to me and draped my coat, which I'd forgotten in Kev's cabin in my haste, around my shoulders. "You need to bandage your hand on the way," he said, digging into his bag as he walked. He pulled out a vial full of transparent liquid and motioned for me to hold out my hand. I did, and he poured the substance over the jagged line where my blood had seeped from the break in my skin. I bit back a gasp as the liquid greeted my flesh with a sizzle. Marcus handed me a bandage, and I wrapped the wound myself.

We kept walking.

As if nothing had changed since the day we'd split paths in the forest. Since I'd made a choice, and he'd refused to follow me to its conclusion.

Since Kev had taken me as his property. As a half-breed. As a being low enough to be sold.

And now we were walking again, as if nothing had ever happened. As if the shroud of smoke concealing Marcus's face didn't imply that he'd committed murder within the past week.

After half an hour of silence between us, with nothing but the crunching of the leaves under our feet and the clanging of my thoughts against my skull to fill the silence, I halted.

It took Marcus seven paces to realize. He pivoted, that striking face of his elusive underneath the shadows.

"We have to keep going," was all he said.

"Why? Where?" I asked. "Where exactly are we going? And what could we possibly have to do there that would be of any urgency?"

"Piper." My name was a warning on his lips.

"Why did you do that?"

"Do what?"

"Why did you come back for me?"

"Are you wishing I hadn't?"

"It's been over a week. Why'd you wait? Did you consider leaving me to the Fates I'd carved out for myself?"

"No, of course not. I didn't know you'd been taken until late last evening. I thought we'd simply gone separate ways."

"Oh," I said, hating how his answer made sense when I'd wanted nothing more than to rip it to shreds.

"How'd you know where I was?" I asked.

"Talk. In a tavern in town. There was gossip slinking about amongst the guests. That the hunter in the forest was having an auction. That he had a... a rare find for anyone who could pay. A female, half-fae, who he believed possessed some magic in her veins. Who he believed many would pay a killing for."

"Why'd you come?" I asked again.

"I just told you."

"No, you didn't. You just said you'd heard the news that I'd been taken."

"You know, most anyone who had a heart that hadn't been calloused over by years of criminal behavior might consider that information enough of a reason."

His words stung, pierced right through that callus that wasn't nearly as thick as he claimed it to be.

I stared at him, hating the swarm of shadow around his face that bereaved me of his expression, preventing me from searching for whether there was as much hate measured out in his eyes as his words would suggest.

"Please take off that ridiculous outfit," I said. "If we're going to argue, I'd prefer to do it face to face."

"You're the one who's intent on arguing," Marcus grumbled, but he shed the cloak all the same. As soon as he pulled back the hood, the shadows dissipated, revealing his face. Deadpan. Unconcerned.

"That's better," I said, trying to swallow the words back down as they fell out, realizing too late how relieved, how desperate they sounded. "Did you really murder someone for that hood?"

"No," Marcus said.

"I thought it was the only way to get one of those."

"I did kill him. I just didn't do it for the hood. The hood was a bonus."

I shuddered at the way Marcus spoke of ending a man's life

without a glimmer of fear, a hint of regret in his eyes. "Why'd you kill him?" Though I wasn't sure I wanted to know.

Marcus turned his face away from me and stared into the woods. "Because of what he said he'd do to you after he bought you."

I gulped and didn't pry any more. At least not about the cloak.

"You came back here just to make sure no one hurt me?" I asked.

"Why is that so hard to believe?"

I shifted on my feet, still unstable from lack of use. "You know why."

"No, I really don't. Maybe it's just part of being a decent person. That I can't allow harm to—"

"See, you're doing it again."

"Doing what?"

"Acting like I'm not capable of understanding why someone would do something selfless."

"You keep asking, don't you?"

"I thought you hated me."

He paused. "That doesn't mean I want you to suffer. At least, not at the hands of creatures like the one who used to own this cloak."

"But I took your sister."

"Yes."

"Don't you think I deserve it, then?"

Marcus sighed and rubbed his palms on his forehead. "You could just say thank you, you know."

I couldn't help but grind my teeth a bit, but the guilt punched me in the gut. "Right. Thank you."

He continued through the woods, pushing through the brush like each limb, each branch of thorns, was the enemy.

"Marcus?" I asked, my voice shaking now, sounding tiny in this vast forest whose brush padded the ground and swallowed the sound of my voice.

"Yes?"

"Why..." But then I stopped, for the shame was washing off my shoulders, and the rage, the injustice, consumed my heart once again. "If you knew what I was, why'd you almost kiss me?"

Marcus turned his face away from me and knocked his jaw to the side. I could hear his back teeth scraping against one another. "*Almost* being the key word."

His words dispatched an arrow through my throat that shut me up for the rest of the afternoon.

CHAPTER 44

PIPER

Marcus stoked the fire that night. When I'd attempted to help gather wood, he'd told me—no, asked me—to rest instead. Truth be told, I was grateful for the break. We'd been hiking through the forest for hours, and my legs and back had gone stiff from being trapped in that chair for over a week. When the time finally came to lay down on the bumpy forest floor, I found my legs ached when I extended them. After a few minutes of tossing and turning, unable to get comfortable enough to fall asleep, despite my extreme fatigue, I sat up. I picked a single twig in Marcus's pile and stared at it as he made the fire. I watched it burn and shake, heard it fizz and crackle as the flame overcame it, turned it dark and fragile.

"Cheyenne used to love watching me make fires," Marcus said, and I almost jumped, having expected him never to speak to me again. "She'd always run to the edge of the woods to help me gather sticks. Even though that child had such little sustenance, she still managed to find the energy somewhere."

I cleared my throat. "She was always very helpful. Arranging the wood for the fires, scavenging for food, I mean." The words hung in the air for a moment, and I wondered if I should have said them. It didn't feel right. Me having memories of his sister, when I'd been the reason she'd been taken from Marcus's life forever.

"Can you do something for me?" he asked.

I watched him stare into the fire and wondered if he'd picked out the same wilting branch I had. "Sure," I said, confident that I had no right to refuse him much of anything at this point. Not after he'd saved my life, even after I'd ruined his.

"Can you tell me what she was like?"

Confusion washed over my forehead, my cheeks. I was sure it did, because Marcus took one look at me, and then explained. "She was so young the last time I saw her. It was years ago. And now, when I try to think of her face... Well, it's like she's just an outline. Almost like when you dream of someone, and you know who they're supposed to be, but they don't look like themselves at all. I don't... I don't even remember whether I said goodbye to her before I left..."

Something ached deep within my soul as I watched his eyes go wide, shiny, pleading. I shouldn't remember her better than he did. It wasn't right. But I couldn't tell him no, either. "Ummm..." I said, searching back, trying to hone my memory on her facial features, attempting to fill in the gaps in her face that time had allowed to fall to the wayside. But every time I focused on her face, all I could see were her eyes, wide and fearful, her mouth twisted in agony as she screamed. Her fingers scraping the soil as she clawed her way back toward me.

I shut the memory out of my mind and tried to change course, to remember what she'd been like before that night. When it'd just been me and Cheyenne, trudging our way through the forest.

I could see her with her back turned toward me as she gathered sticks. I could hear her eating next to me, quietly chewing crumbling bread.

But her face.

Where were the memories of her face? Her face as a whole, not in scrambled, horrified parts.

I'd seen it in my dreams; I was certain of it, but now it eluded me.

I prodded at those memories I'd shoved into the darkest corners of my mind, trying to forget them. Trying to forget her.

I'd done what I'd intended.

I couldn't grasp onto her face, not in full.

"She was brave," I said, and I watched his expression sink in disappointment. But that was all I had to give. All the other memories I'd suffocated until they'd faded into darkness.

"She was." Marcus traced odd shapes into the dust with his fingertip.

"I'm sorry, I'm not good with details," I lied, not realizing it was a lie until I'd said it. Until the words had already breached us.

"It's alright. I'm her brother. I shouldn't even have to ask."

Crickets and cicadas whistled and clicked around us, the heat from the fire encasing us in the moment, in the regret, for a while.

"I'm sorry," Marcus said.

I lifted my head from where I'd buried it wearily in my palms. "For what?"

"For how I treated you back in the Coup. It was unfair of me to be so hateful toward you."

I stared at him and had to make a conscious effort to keep my jaw from dropping off its hinge. "Please don't apologize to me, Marcus. I don't deserve it. Really. I get it. You weren't open about your intentions for helping me and Amity, because you were just doing your job. A noble one, at that—getting a trafficker off the streets. You can hate me. It's okay."

"I don't hate you, Piper."

I sighed. "I wish you would," I said, burying my hands into my palms once again, an exasperated laugh escaping my dry throat. "See, you're sitting here apologizing. For what? For saying a few hateful things to me that happened to be true? For acting like you were my friend? Oh, how manipulative you were, being kind to your sister's kidnapper. I haven't even apologized yet, and you're apologizing to me? I'm sorry, Marcus. I'm sorry I took her. I'm sorry... I'm sorry she's...gone because of me."

Tears glazed his copper eyes again. Tendrils from the fire reflected in those deep irises. "It wasn't all acting."

I stood, my legs trembling. The leaves cracked below me as I paced, as I crossed my arms to warm myself in the cold. So that someone, anyone, would hold me, even if I had to do it myself.

Marcus stared me down, and something about the intensity in his gaze told me that whatever was about to come out of his mouth would define this moment, the relationship between the man I'd convinced myself could love me and the girl who'd ruined his life. The girl who'd given him purpose, only for it to turn out to be futile. "All those other children in the Coup, what kind of homes did they come from?"

"It doesn't matter. None of it makes what happened to your sister okay."

"Piper." Something cold and lonely dulled his tear-stained eyes. "Please give me a reason to forgive you."

"There's not one," I said, my voice breaking.

"Please."

"Why?"

"Because, if I can't find a reason to forgive you, how I can I ever forgive myself?" The tears cut silken paths across his cheeks now, no longer pent up by whatever force of will had detained them. "Please."

I bit my lip and lowered myself to the ground, crossing my legs and facing him this time. "All the children, they came from homes where... where they weren't being taken care of. Not the way children deserve, at least. And not because the parents were just too poor to give them a good life. I took... I told myself what I was doing was okay, good even, as long as I only took the children whose parents hit them, starved them..."

"And the like?" he asked.

I nodded.

"Did your master ever know?"

"No, he thought I was bringing him the cream of the crop. In a way, I was. I brought him the children that knew how to survive, how to endure."

"Did your master, Bronger—that was his name right? Did he ever harm the children?"

I swallowed. How many times had I asked this question in my mind, defending Bronger's side? I'd never argued it aloud though, and I didn't know if I could handle the conclusion I'd come to once the words broke the cold air. Once I said it aloud, and whatever it was, became true.

"Not in the ways their parents did. He never hit them or starved them or...or brought them to his bed. Not that I was aware of, at least. If I'd ever gotten an inkling that he did anything like that, I never would have..." I swallowed.

"I know that," Marcus said, and I let out a breath that fogged in the cold.

"The children were taken care of. But I didn't bring them into a utopia, a true safe haven. Because, because Bronger never gave without expecting something in return. He was going to use them to overthrow the King of Avelea, eventually. And I suppose many of them would have been harmed in the process." The words stuck to the inside of my dry mouth. As if even in letting them out, they refused to unburden me from their weight, their taste, their bitterness.

"Do you believe they were better off?"

"Yes," I said, sure of my answer in my very soul.

"And did you mean for Cheyenne to fall to harm?"

I peered up at him, met his gaze. "No. Never."

"Then you've done no worse than I have," he said, hanging his head. "Possibly even better. You could have been ambitious. Taken the healthy, the athletic, the rich, to Bronger. But you didn't. You made a choice to help those children, in the small way you could." Hot, salty tears ran down my cheeks at his words, the words I now realized I'd been aching for someone to speak into existence for years now. Aching for someone to make real by saying them aloud. "Me, I told myself my reasons for leaving were selfless. But my self-sacrifice was simply ambition disguising its intent to rid myself of the family that was holding me back. If anyone failed Cheyenne, it was me."

I swallowed a sob as Marcus's words washed over me, as we wept together.

"I forgot about her, you know," Marcus said. "For years. She used to always complain when she was a little girl that, with so many children in the house, no one bothered to remember she existed. My parents weren't cruel, you understand. But they neglected her, even if just by having too many children to adequately tend to. And she was right, I spent years as a contract archer and, Piper, I don't think I thought of her once. At least, not until I visited. And then came home that last time and...and I realized there were seven instead of eight..." He choked on his words this time, and I watched as his temple, the corner of his jaw, bulged.

My heart ached, and tears spilled from my eyes, stinging my cheeks. I welcomed the pain, mild as it was. And to think I'd purposefully pushed this child from my memory, just to save myself the pang of guilt... A child whose greatest pain in life was going unnoticed, being forgotten by the ones she loved...

"It's cruel, isn't it?" Marcus asked. "That the same child whose family barely remembered she existed would be singled out. Taken and...and..."

Marcus peered up at me, his eyes glistening.

I played with a stray twig, twirling it in my fingers until the bulb at the tip crumbled. My throat went dry. "I've been dreaming about her. Recently. While I was trapped in the cabin."

Marcus scooted forward, hanging on my every word, his knees brushing mine, the nearness of him threatening to undo me. End me.

I choked on the next few words. "I don't know how much of it is real, how much of it's made up. I blocked it all out for so long... I don't know how to trust what my mind comes up with. But they don't feel like dreams, you know? They feel like memories."

His fingers wrapped around mine, a treacherous warmth I shouldn't have allowed myself to feel, not after all I'd done, not when he was so vulnerable to the secrets I'd kept captive, chained with my greed and guilt.

And then I told him. About the cook. About the fear of being turned over to the royal guard. About the lie that had ended up with his sister's crumpled body buried beneath a field of daffodils deep within the confines of the hills.

All the while I stared at our hands, intertwined. At the tears that fell and speckled our skin, more tears than could have fallen from my eyes alone.

Then the worst of all, something I'd realized only after Marcus had asked me if I ever intended any harm toward Cheyenne. "I think there was part of me that enjoyed doing it, matching my crimes with her face. Part of me that never wanted her to make it back to Coup, like I thought she'd...she'd..."

"Steal him away from you?"

My breath hitched, my chest heaving uncontrollably.

He didn't deserve this, didn't deserve the way I clung so desperately to his hand, wet with our tears. The way I squeezed it, silently begging him not to let go.

Such an unfair request to ask.

That he not drop the hand coated in his sister's blood.

But when I summoned the courage to look him in the face, to gaze into those dazzling copper eyes, glowing with the sheen of his tears, it wasn't just desperation I found.

It was hope.

And understanding.

And perhaps even a glimmer of forgiveness.

I couldn't handle it, couldn't bear it, so I glanced away.

He cupped my cheek, refusing to let go of my other hand, and tilted my face to look at him. "You were twelve," he whispered.

"I was old enough to know better, to know what I was doing."

His thumb caressed my cheek, and I hated myself. Hated myself for the way warmth flooded each bit of skin he touched, the way my heart skipped at the intimacy of the gesture.

Wrong, this was wrong.

"It's my fault she's dead."

"You were a child."

"But older than her. I was supposed to protect her, and I showed him her face because I was too much of a coward to take my own punishment."

"You were a child," he repeated, his voice a low rumble, threatening to sink through my pores and saturate my soul and make me believe him.

"So was she." It was a frantic, desperate whisper. A plea to force him to see the monster whose hand he stroked, whose cheek he caressed.

"You're not the one who killed her."

"I might as well have been. I didn't stop them when they came for her."

"You tried, though."

I shook my head, the movement smearing my tears against his fingers. "You can't possibly know that."

"But I know you."

"Well, I didn't try hard enough," I said, pulling away from his touch and straightening, taking a swig of water from my canister just to cool the heat between us, to fill the silence. The space where my failure dangled in front of me. "She did, though," I said. "She fought back. She jabbed the trafficker in the eye. She got him so good, he was so dazed, he looked like...like..." I trailed off as I realized the words I was about to say next. At how I didn't believe in coincidences. But it wasn't possible.

Except it was. I knew it was. I'd heard about it in the council room with Bronger and James.

"Like what?"

I turned my head to him, biting my lip, as if to hold back the insanity about to come out of my mouth.

No, I wasn't afraid of the insane.

What scared me was the hope.

"Like he'd forgotten why he'd attacked us."

Marcus blinked, his throat bobbing.

"Marcus." I was the one who grasped for his hand this time. My fingers found their place in those strong fingers of his. He squeezed my hand within his as if I was the only thing keeping him from plummeting off the side of a cliff. "Bronger was planning to assassinate the king during the blood moon festivities. He wanted me to be a part of it. His mission... He wanted me to draw out a girl. A girl the king keeps at his side. A human girl with a gift."

Marcus looked as if he was holding his breath. But he squeezed my hand all the more. In that fleeting moment, the pain, the grief, dissolved from Marcus's face, for just a moment. Something welled up inside those deep copper eyes. Something dangerous.

Hope.

"They didn't know exactly what the girl's gift was. Just that she possessed the ability to influence the mind. And that the king always keeps her around, hiding out of sight, in case he needs her. What if..."

I sucked in a breath, hardly able to believe what I was about to say. Not truly believing it, just hoping it, hoping it so desperately I clung to it with every fiber of my being. "What if it wasn't just negligence, or how many kids were in the home, or your sister's personality, or your ambition, or my guilt that makes Cheyenne so easy to forget? What if she's Gifted, like me?"

Marcus let go of my hand, allowing it to slip onto his thigh. This time, he was the one who stood, paced.

"Think about it. It's been bothering me for weeks, why I doubled back to a town I'd visited before without realizing it. Why I doubled back to *your* hometown, where I took Cheyenne. Why didn't I remember? Of all the towns I've taken children from, why didn't the most important of all stand out to me? That can't be a coincidence."

He put his hands behind his head, knocking leaves and sticks out of his way as he paced around the fire. "It's too unlikely. Cheyenne—she's just a human. You know how rare it is for magic to gift itself to a human?"

"It gifted me."

"You're half-fae."

"What about the Queen of Naenden?"

"Alright, so we've heard of one. One human out of the millions in Alondria."

"We've heard about her because she's famous. There have to be more." I stood. My legs shook, but no longer from weariness. Adrenaline coursed through my limbs, pulsing through me as the pieces began to line up. As that dreaded hope set in.

"No. No, I would have known..."

"Would you have? If you'd forgotten?"

"It doesn't make sense, though. It's not like we've forgotten her completely."

I bit my lip. That part I couldn't deny. "Okay, so there's got to be some rules about how it works. The shrouds! The shrouds, Marcus. The men who attacked us were covered from head to foot. The one who grabbed her didn't forget about her until she touched his eye, where his skin was exposed. I bet it only works if she touches you. Bronger's spies said they thought that was a limitation on the girl's power."

"That still doesn't explain why we haven't forgotten her completely," Marcus said. "Or why she would want us to forget her."

"That's just it. Maybe she didn't. Maybe she didn't even know she was Gifted until they took her. Marcus, I'm telling you, there are patches where I remember her, but... Remember how I told you I blacked out? It was when she grabbed my hand. What if I didn't black out at all? What if I just forgot?"

"It's such a stretch..."

"Is it?" I asked. "Or is it just terrifying?"

"Piper," he said, his eyes drooping with grief. "You watched them bury her."

I shook my head, scrambling through my memories, tossing loose thoughts out of my way as I honed in on that terrible image, the one I'd pushed down, down, down. "I never got a good look at her face. It was so—" My throat caught on the word, but I forced it out. "Decayed. And Bronger had the body wrapped up, so I only saw her face for a moment when the burlap slipped. The hair was similar, and the size, but I was so distraught, it could have been anyone." The pit of my stomach hollowed out. "It wouldn't have been difficult to get his hands on a body. I'm almost sure he asked me about her—what she was like. He could have searched around for a body that fit the description."

"Why would he do that?"

My heart sank. "So I would stop begging him to search for her. So I'd move on."

"What about the wolf? The way you described that thing, its size, Cheyenne wouldn't have survived an attack like that."

"Someone must have rescued her."

Marcus shook his head. "My sister's dead, Piper. Even if that's not her body buried beneath the daffodils, she's dead."

"Is that what you'd rather think?"

My question hung between us for a breath.

Then he snapped. "Forgive me if I don't prefer to believe my sister's been a prisoner of the fae. For years! Or have you forgotten what they did to Amity in the hours they had her?" He laid his hands to rest at his side, and I couldn't help but notice how his shoulders slumped. "If we're wrong..."

"If we're wrong, then we'll keep digging, keep searching until we find her," I said.

He lifted his chin and stared at me with those sad, deep eyes that seemed to burrow all the way into his soul. "We?"

My breath fogged before my face in the crisp night. "It's my fault you lost her. I'd like to help you get her back."

Marcus let out a long exhale that turned to steam and dissipated in front of us. "We can't be sure..."

"You're right. We can't be sure. Not if we don't try to find the king's girl."

Marcus nodded, then rubbed his eyes. "You got a plan?"

"Something like that."

CHAPTER 45

MARCUS

Fates, she had to have dropped a quarter of her body weight in the time she spent trapped in the hunter's cabin.

A stray arrow meant for me, fired from the fae male's bow, had struck the hunter and ended his life.

That was a regret of mine. One of many.

I would have liked to finish him myself, or at least given Piper the opportunity to do it, if she'd wanted.

Men like that shouldn't get to die accidental deaths.

It must have been painful, at least. An arrow to a major artery wasn't exactly a pleasant way to go.

A spiderweb of dried blood streaked Piper's cheek, illuminated in the glow of the dying embers of our fire. If the injury had belonged to a human, I might have assumed it was the product of nothing but an unfortunate scrape of a stray branch during a leisurely walk through the woods.

On Piper, whose fae blood patched wounds with uncanny efficiency, it had me wondering just how deep the cut had gone if it was still there hours after leaving the hunter's cabin. She'd already had it when I arrived at the auction; it had been the second thing I'd marked.

Second to her weight.

He'd had her tied to that chair with her thin legs splayed at an unnatural angle, the restraints digging into her exposed ankles, and her coat stripped and left behind at the cabin. As if he'd simply forgotten to put it back on her before taking her outside. As if he hadn't wanted to go through the trouble of unbinding her hands, then tying her back up.

She hadn't even seen the coat lying there when we'd gone to collect her things. She'd been in such a frantic haze—shoving crap into her satchel and fumbling her fingers over her flute every few seconds, as if to reassure herself that it was still there. Like she worried that her freedom might have been a dream, and she needed something to touch, something to tether herself to reality.

Even now, as we sat in the warmth of the dwindling fire, my back scraping against a nearby tree, hers stiff as a board as she perched upon a gnarled log, her fingers slipped into her satchel, and I didn't have to see inside to know what she was feeling for.

In the week since I'd left her, her cheeks had sallowed. Her pale skin clung to her cheekbones, dark shadows picking away at her youth. Her coat hung limper than it used to on her slight frame. She never seemed to stop shivering.

All because I'd left her.

"You need to eat," I found myself saying.

A weak smile formed at the edges of her perfect mouth. "I already did," she said. How she could smile after what had happened to her, I couldn't fathom. But that was Piper, I supposed. Beaten down with all the trauma life could throw at her, and still masquerading like she was fine.

I simultaneously respected her for it and wished she would stop.

Another shiver coursed through her. That was the thing about starving. No amount of furs could make up for the fat on which her body so desperately relied in order to warm itself.

"It's not enough," I said.

She shrugged. "I'm used to it." A little laugh escaped her lips. "I've been far hungrier, trust me."

The corners of her eyes faltered at the edge of her smile.

Like crap she had.

I rose from my position next to the tree, rummaging through my pack before obtaining a parcel of food I'd purchased in town. When I crossed over to her and extended my hand, she shook her head. "It's yours. You haven't eaten at all yet."

"I've eaten plenty the past week." That wasn't entirely true. Eating hadn't exactly been a pleasurable experience the past few days, and though I'd forced down the nutrients, it had been a practical endeavor—a matter of keeping myself nourished, and my stomach had reeled with each bite.

"It's yours. I don't want to take anything that's yours."

The statement hung between us, stagnant in the stale, cold air.

My throat bobbed.

I kneeled to the ground and pressed the food into her palms, taking her freezing fingers and closing them around the parcel of food. I didn't miss the way her breath hitched, the way her whole body tensed.

We hadn't touched since that night at the inn. Not in any way that counted.

It didn't take asking to know we were both remembering it, how close we'd been to...

There wasn't much use in thinking about that right now.

"Just eat the food, Piper."

She opened her mouth as if to protest, but I dropped her hand and withdrew to my spot by the tree before she could.

Her fingers trembled as she unwrapped the cloth that bound the meat and bread. She hesitated before bringing it to her mouth, but as soon as the food touched her lips, something more primal than guilt took over, and I watched as she devoured every morsel, crumbs and all.

. . .

We sat like that for a while, staring at the popping cinders that floated for a moment before melting into the darkness, Piper tucking her knees into her chest, still shaking relentlessly.

It took everything in me to stay planted by the roots of the tree, to keep from wrapping her in my arms, warming her shivering body, protecting her from the cold.

I don't want to take anything that's yours.

There was a wall between us. No, a chasm.

She was smart enough to realize that—that there was no point in trying to deny it.

The Piper I'd thought I had known two weeks ago, before I'd seen that awful tattoo, didn't exist.

Well, in some ways, she did. Piper was the same, I supposed. I'd known all along what she did for a living. And I'd been able to push it aside, to ignore her sins and blame them on the man who'd raised her to be a criminal.

I'd been willing to tuck it away, to start anew with her, to ignore her past.

But then I'd found out about Cheyenne, the sister I still couldn't quite convince myself to hope was alive, and that person who Piper was had suddenly seemed so entirely different.

But she hadn't changed.

I had.

Or maybe the *us* part had.

That was the thing about humans. We had the capacity to be pretty forgiving on other people's behalf.

It was only sins committed against us personally that were unforgivable.

But that was just it. I had forgiven her. I'd needed to in order to forgive myself.

It wasn't her fault. I knew that. As much as she'd played a part in bringing those children into the hands of a predator, she'd done what she could for the kids. She'd had a line she wouldn't cross, even for the man she'd clearly loved above all else.

She'd protected that part of herself, that precious innocence that her master had sought to strip from her.

I couldn't know what kind of strength it must have taken to defy him, especially when she was a just a child. Couldn't imagine it.

I don't want to take anything that's yours.

She'd drawn a line in the sand, built a barrier between the two of us with those words.

She was protecting me. Constructing a distance between us, so that one day I might could live with myself.

Because if we were wrong, and Cheyenne was dead—if she'd been dead for years, like I'd believed—then how could I live with myself if I allowed myself to fall in love with the woman who bore, if not the full responsibility for her death, then at least a portion of it?

How could I face my sister in the afterlife, if I'd spent this one loving the woman who'd unintentionally sold her to her death?

Then there was my family to consider. My parents and siblings. Piper had understood that night—why I could never go back.

She'd figured me out. Taken my cowardice and spun words that made my reasons sound kind.

But she'd known, too. She'd known how much it killed me to distance myself from them. How much I longed for their voices, to feel their familiar embrace.

She knew I couldn't have them both. Even if my family never discovered the role Piper had played in Cheyenne's kidnapping and potential death, I hadn't been able to face them these past seven years while I'd thought I carried the burden of Cheyenne's death.

How could I live with myself if I brought Cheyenne's captor home to meet them? My parents were not unkind. If I pursued what I wanted, if I joined myself to Piper, they'd welcome her as their own. I'd be forcing them to unknowingly embrace the woman who was partially responsible for making sure our family would never be whole.

I'd be living a lie.

So, it was going to have to be them, or her. And Piper wasn't about to force me to make that decision.

If Cheyenne was alive, would that change anything?

I swallowed the thought immediately, guilt swelling within me. My sister might have survived the attack I'd thought had claimed her life, and here I was wondering whether her survival would give me the permission I wanted to be with the woman I loved.

Then again, I hadn't been able to think much about that possibility. I'd felt it—the hope threatening to ensnare me. I'd felt it bubbling and eager when Piper had started putting the pieces together about Cheyenne's disappearance. But I couldn't... I simply couldn't allow my imagination to run away with me. I couldn't envision what she might look like now. I couldn't play out our reunion in my mind.

I wouldn't.

Not when there was a significant chance Piper was wrong.

I wished Amity were here. I couldn't quite get over the devastation on her face after she'd watched Piper kill their master. Piper believed that Amity had stayed behind because she thought Piper was a monster.

I wasn't convinced.

The little girl had heard me admit that I'd sent those traffickers straight into their path the night I'd convinced Piper to let me join their party. The same traffickers who had left bruises on Amity's neck. The same traffickers who had left her so terrified, she'd begged Piper to let me join them.

I could hardly think about Amity, either.

So instead I dwelled on the woman with the ivy eyes and the pointed ears and the hesitant laugh that I'd become so fond of tempting.

I couldn't have her; I knew that.

But there she was shivering, and here I was, lacking the self-control not to care.

CHAPTER 46

PIPER

"Come here."

I blinked, Marcus's voice summoning me like a beacon cutting through the turbulent thoughts threatening to send me into a spiral.

What if I was wrong?

What if Cheyenne's body had turned to dust under the field of dandelions?

What if I'd given him false hope, driven the final nail through the heart of the man I loved?

"What?" I asked, my mind shuddering at the gentle touch of his voice.

"Come here."

My spine went rigid, and a shudder swept through my limbs, compounding the shiver courtesy of the frigid evening breeze, the one that seeped into my bones, unrestrained by the absent layer of fat that used to protect my body.

I shouldn't have, but I dared to meet his eyes.

That was a mistake.

Warmth pooled in my stomach, flooding my cheeks at the sight of him.

He was staring, the dying embers of our fire flickering in his eyes, his copper irises glowing.

I knew in that moment that no one had ever looked at me like Marcus was looking at me now.

The hunger in his gaze was palpable, stroking my neck with the phantom touch of his gaze as he scanned my throat, as if he could detect my pulse pounding in the nook of my neck, the blood that flowed upward and peppered my freckle-stained cheeks.

"I..." No. That was the correct word in this situation. No, I should keep my butt firmly planted on this log, well away from Marcus, just like I'd intended.

I just couldn't bring myself to say it.

"I don't think that's a good idea," was what I settled on.

I didn't manage to make it sound very convincing.

"You're trembling, Piper."

Each word drummed invisible fingertips up my spine.

"I'm cold," I said, my pitch heightening. Defensive.

His eyes danced, the intensity in his gaze softening just barely. "I can see that. That's why you should come here." He drew his overcoat open, a look of innocence overtaking the hunger I'd thought I'd glimpsed on his face.

"I'm fine," I insisted. "I'm used to being cold."

Fates above, each word coming out of my mouth took more and more effort to shove out, to keep from falling by the wayside.

"That might be, but I am not used to being this cold," he teased, his eyes twinkling. "I'm used to staying in inns during my journeys, but seeing as someone hardly left me enough coin to buy myself a meal after my last job, I'm afraid I'm stuck out here in these unsavory conditions."

I let out a faint giggle, my breath fogging in the cold night's air.

"Really, Piper. If you're going to pay so poorly, the least you could do is warm me up."

I was pretty sure I hadn't told my feet to move, but there we were, ambling toward Marcus like a moth toward a poisoned flame.

I lowered myself into the crook of his outstretched arm, and as soon as I did, he wrapped his arm around my waist and pulled me into him. Warmth that I couldn't entirely attribute to his body heat enveloped me as he reclined against the tree and I rested against him.

"Much better," he said, though I wasn't sure I heard him over the roaring in my head, set off by the fact that he was now drawing circles on my abdomen with his thumb.

I took this as an invitation to nuzzle my head into the crook of his shoulder, and I sank into him, melting into his muscular form.

To be quite honest, he was too firm to make for a sufficient pillow.

To be quite honest, I wasn't sure that I cared.

"Hey, Piper," he whispered after a moment, his breath sending needles of delight dappling my ear. I memorized the feel of his breath on my skin, the sturdiness of his chest, the pattern of his thumb against my waist.

"Mhm?"

"I might have lied."

My stomach clenched, and my muscles went rigid. Not another lie. Not when all I wanted was, just for a moment, to ignore the lies between us, the ones that would keep this moment contained, poorly preserved in my memory until it slowly cracked and splintered and settled to dust in the corners of my fading consciousness.

I opened my mouth to object, to ask that he tell me in the morning, anything to preserve this moment, this...

"I wasn't actually all that cold."

A patter of gentle needles tapped at my skin, settling over me in a wave as I laughed. "Well, in that case..." I pulled away from him, allowing my gaze to dance up to his. His eyes sparked with the challenge, and he tightened his grip on my waist, yanking me back into his grasp.

I couldn't help it. A gasp of delight escaped my lips, wiping the emerging laugh off Marcus's face as his gaze swept toward my mouth and lingered there.

My heart stopped. "Marcus." His name was a warning on my tongue, a last-ditch attempt at halting the mistake that was barreling ahead of us, the storm he looked all too eager to walk straight into. "Marcus, we shouldn't."

His breathing went labored; his eyes locked on my mouth. "I know."

The way he said it, it didn't sound like he did.

"It's not in the Fates for us," I said, pleaded. "I wish... I wish we could go back and rewrite the past, but we can't."

"I'm not going to lie to you, Piper. I'm not thinking about the past right this second."

Pain clenched my gut, stabbing me in the ribs, stinging my eyes. "But you should be. It's always going to haunt us, what I did to you, to your family." His forehead was pressed to mine now, his lips lingering a breath away from my kiss, threatening to drown any morsel of truth, any voice of reason. The words were falling out now, rushed and panicked, and I worried that if I didn't get them out now, I'd give in; I'd ruin this good man more than I already had. "We can't change it. We can't forget it. It shapes who we are, even if we don't want it to. You'll regret me, Marcus. Please."

Please. It was the only word I could muster for what I truly wished to say.

I don't want to be regretted.

Marcus wiped a curl from my forehead and tucked it behind my ear. His eyes lingered on my tattoo for a moment, and my heart sank with mingled sorrow and relief as he took it in, the mark that would stain my soul all of my days.

But when he spoke, his voice was tender and kind and not at all afraid. "I've been living in the past for a long while now. Fates help me if I spend one more second there when I should be doing this."

His lips found mine, caressing them with a gentle sureness that tethered us to this moment, these crossroads of bliss and pain and longing. At first, I found myself hesitant, unsure of myself and desperately unskilled. But I soon found a rhythm to it, a dance whose tempo rippled and swelled as the passion of the kiss ebbed and flowed, sometimes intense and forceful, a reminder of how fleeting this beautiful moment truly was, sometimes soft and sleepy, like this was the first of a thousand moments just like it.

I found myself lost in it, the tender way he grazed his lips against mine, the way his hands traced the divots of my spine as he held me close, as if he'd never let me go.

I let Marcus kiss me, and when I awoke the next morning—my face nuzzled into his chest as we slumped against the tree, the knots in my back protesting my insistence on forcing them into such an uncomfortable position all night—I waited awhile to wake him.

CHAPTER 47

PIPER

The duke's tent stank of wine and ash when we entered. Marcus dug his fingers into the nape of my skull, pulling at the skin on my scalp until I yelped.

I'd had to convince him to do it, to make it appear real.

"Milord, this man requests your council," the duke's guard said, the one who'd allowed us entrance into the tent.

The duke peered up from his couch where he lay, sprawled out and stinking of alcohol and sweat, despite the fine clothes he wore. "Coulver, do you not value your head?" he drawled. "Or the head of that hideous wife of yours?"

The guard stiffened and stumbled over his words. "Milord, it seemed important. It seemed you'd be pleased."

"Pleased to be interrupted during the festivities? I've told you a thousand times, I prefer my escorts blond, and this is what you bring me, thinking I'd be pleased?"

The soldier panted.

"My lord, if I may introduce myself, I believe your night is about to change course for the better," Marcus said, that smooth, confident cadence returning to his voice. The voice I hadn't heard since he'd pulled away from me that night at the inn.

"Oh, really now?" the duke said. "And how did you know I revel in beheading my soldiers' families before their eyes?"

My fingers clenched at my palms, nails digging into my skin as if I clutched within my palm the entirety of my self-control. The only part of me keeping me from ripping this horrid man's eyes out.

Marcus didn't even flinch. "I believe your guard is correct, my lord. That you'll be pleasantly surprised by what I have to offer."

"I have my own suppliers," the duke said, waving a dismissive hand in Marcus's direction. "And they are well aware of my tastes, unlike you."

"Oh, yes? And have any of them brought you the target of that impressive bounty you've posted?" Marcus asked, his voice pleasant enough, though I could detect the ice in his tenor.

The duke took another look at me, scanning my tangled, red hair, my shabby clothes, but most of all my eyes, wide and fae, and my ears poking out from underneath my wild hair as they always did.

"And who is this?" the duke asked.

"I believe you know who this is, my lord," Marcus said, and I could hear in his voice that his self-assured grin was spreading across his face, revealing his perfect teeth.

"I've had professionals on the hunt for her for years," the duke said, his fingers forming a semicircle as he mimed. "How did an amateur get his hands on this elusive little one?"

"There are skills more useful than brute force, my lord," Marcus said.

"Ah, yes," the duke said. "Charm. More useful on the females, I'd suppose."

I fought back a snort, fought back the urge to ask him how many of his *females* knew the king's classified information simply due to the duke's incessant need to feel superior, in charge, in the loop. And a bit of charm, as he said, on the female's part.

"And how much are you asking for her?"

"I believe we are both aware of the bounty," Marcus said.

The duke sneered, then peered at me with his small, wine-striped eyes. "You, little pretty, have been a difficult one to catch," he said. "Do you know why I want you? Why I'm paying so much money to this commoner to have you? It's certainly not for your looks, I can tell you. I wouldn't lay a hand on one of your breeding. And certainly wouldn't find you worth so much coin. No, do you even know why I want you?"

"Of course I do." I grinned, allowing the smile to smear across my face. "It's because I took your son."

The duke jolted forward. His bulging fingers were around my throat in an instant, digging into my airway.

Marcus moved, and a dagger appeared at the curve of the duke's jaw. "Now, now. I don't take well to my customers damaging my property before they've paid," Marcus said, his voice smooth on the surface, but even in my panic, as I went dizzy from lack of air, I could hear the tremble sneaking underneath the surface.

The duke's eyes bulged. "How dare you allow this whore to insult me in my own tent." His fingers gripped tighter, and my world spun.

"Allow me to make myself clear," Marcus hissed. "Get your grimy fingers off her neck, or I'll slit yours."

The duke's fingers twitched, and for a moment I thought he'd squeeze, crushing my windpipe out of spite. But then his grasp around my neck loosened, and as he drew his hand back to his side, I gasped. "I should have the both of you flogged for this," the duke seethed.

"Flog me if you wish," Marcus said, his voice calm and unaffected, the only sign of his panic in the way his chest rose and fell as he tried to stifle his heaving, "but I imagine your feelings toward me will shift once you realize what I've brought you. My lord, I believe you might find the female more profitable alive than dead. And preferably without scarring."

"What's this nonsense?" the duke said.

"I believe you could pay me the bounty and still turn a profit, my lord. You see, I discovered that this half-fae female is not only odd in her breeding, but in her nature as well. The female is Gifted."

"Gifted?" the duke said.

"You know of the trait?" Marcus asked.

The duke sneered. "Who doesn't, after that swine from Naenden witched her way into being queen?"

"I agree, it's deplorable," Marcus said, "but even you have to admit, the Gifted have become more fashionable, more desirable, in the last year. And, from the rumors I've heard, the King of Avelea has... found value, shall we say, in the Gifted."

The duke seethed. "How do you know that?"

Marcus backtracked, maintaining that cool, even smile. "One hears things when one makes a point to."

"Ergm," the duke said.

"The more important question, I'd say, is how much would the king himself pay for such a prize?" Marcus asked.

"Why didn't you ask him yourself if you believe he'll pay so much?" the duke asked, staring down Marcus and glancing at his pockets every once in a while, as if he expected to find handfuls of stolen coin overflowing from them.

Marcus smiled pleasantly. "Let's just say the law and I aren't on friendly terms at the moment."

"Hmmm. Don't like the sound of that," the duke said. "And you're just giving me this information out of the goodness of your heart, are you?"

"I do accept tips." Marcus grinned again.

"That's what I thought," the duke said before turning and making his way across the tent. He reached under his mattress and pulled out a coin purse, smaller than I would have expected for how high the bounty was. My heart quickened. If he tried to swindle Marcus, surely he would expect a fight in return, and then for the guard to finish Marcus off. We'd considered this on the way, but figured the duke was our best shot at getting to Cheyenne. But if we were wrong, if we were wrong and Marcus paid with his life...

"What an adorably sized coin purse," Marcus said through gritted teeth. He was playing his part well. Too well.

"Don't fret. It's not coin I'm paying in. But I think you'll be pleased, nonetheless." The duke handed the coin purse to Marcus, who pulled the drawstring and looked inside. His eyebrows arched high at whatever was inside the bag, and he cleared his throat.

"Are you satisfied with your payment?" the duke asked.

"Very," Marcus said. "Perhaps we can do business again someday."

"We'll see how this goes with the king," the duke said. "Tell me, what exactly is her gift? And it better be good if you don't want my friend here to break his new sword on your neck."

"She enchants those who listen to her play. Music I mean," Marcus said.

"I know what it means to play," said the duke.

"Of course, my lord," Marcus said.

"So she's not a threat, as long as she doesn't have an instrument?"

"None at all," Marcus said, and with that he strode out of the tent without being dismissed, without taking a second glance in my direction.

"YOU DESERVE TO BE BEHEADED, you know that." The duke yanked at my curls as he pulled me by my hair through the streets. I winced, irritated that I couldn't do anything about the blatant and public abuse. Well, I could have, as I still had my knife strapped inside my boot. It would have been as easy as chopping my curls off to rid myself of his grasp. Though I'd have probably gone with the slightly more difficult option of chopping off his hand.

But I kept reminding myself that allowing the duke to drag me around like a peasant child might do with a stray puppy was a choice I'd made. A choice I'd made for Cheyenne. For Marcus.

Besides, my hands were bound, and it would have made getting to my knife a tad cumbersome.

"And yet, so few of us receive what we actually deserve," I said, taunting him with the carefree tone of my voice. He yanked harder, and I grinned underneath the wince. I had no patience for the duke, no pity for his suffering, if one could even call it that. Asa's father had been cruel, beating the poor child for his ill luck in witnessing his father's indiscretions, as Asa had called them. "Your son did, though. He was a kind child. He got what he deserved. Freedom from you."

Black dots sprang up in my eyes as the blow landed on my temple.

"Keep your mouth shut," he said.

I did, but only because there was no need to say much else.

As we walked through the festival, I craned my eyes to watch the festivities as I kept my head down. Performers of all shapes and sizes, faeries and humans, wound themselves through a patchwork quilt of colorful tents, some red and white striped, some dyed in circular, irregularly sized patterns, some round, others scaffolding to a point at the top. Music—fast, slow, mournful, joyful—ran together in my ears, as I imagined it did for the rest of the faeries and high fae in attendance. But that was the benefit of fae hearing. I could sort out the notes, match them to their appropriate songs, and hear at least seven tunes at once without it sounding like a jumbled mess. If I had to guess, each musical group was spread out just far enough that a human might not hear two tunes at once.

A human like the duke.

I wondered what he had done as a human to put himself in the fae king's graces. For the most part, our fae rulers seemed to view humans as good for tending the earth, harvesting crops, and keeping the land fertile when they died. Good for taxing, although the fae hoarded ninety percent of the wealth despite making up only ten percent of the population.

At least, that's what Bronger had taught us during our civics lessons.

But there were some—humans whose bloodlines funneled back to the aristocrats of old who allowed the fae to take our realm for their own—some who maintained ties to the fae. Were happy to do their dirty work to maintain a semblance of their ancestors' wealth, to possess enough coin that they never need run out of prostitutes or liquor.

Asa had never told me much about his father's business with the King of Avelea, though I was sure he'd told Bronger. Sure that Bronger had bullied it out of him, what little he knew.

I just had a feeling it was nothing good.

We reached the castle gate, and the duke twisted my hair over his hand twice, securing me in place by his side. I gritted my teeth and tried to bite back my words. If the man was going to bruise, it'd have been through what I'd implied about Asa being better off dead than with him. No need to push my luck any further.

"My lord," the lesser fae guard said, bowing, though only slightly, toward the human lord. I imagined it irked the faerie to no end that he was considered to be of lower rank than this human.

"Ah, yes. I need to seek council of the king. Immediately," the duke said.

"The king is occupied with readying himself for the festival," the guard said, his voice tense, annoyed. Surely the duke had offended him by insisting the King of Avelea bend his schedule to a human's wishes. To be honest, the duke's presumption even rubbed me the wrong way, though I wasn't fond of the king myself.

"You tell him it's important. And urgent. That I have a shipment in for him he won't want to miss out on," the duke said.

Shipments? Was that what the duke did for the king? Trafficked materials and people illegally for the King of Avelea? If so, had he just been playing along when Marcus recommended he bring me here, rather than kill me?

My stomach churned in disgust. The remaining hair of respect I'd retained for this man had depended on the fact he'd placed a bounty on my head for kidnapping his son. Sure, I'd expected him to turn his plans upside down at the slight chance of a profit, but if this had been his plan the entire time...

"My lord, with all due respect, the king will not be pleased, I assure you," the guard said.

"Will he not be? And do you have any idea what I am offering him?" the duke seethed.

"It would appear this half-breed—"

"Is that all you can see? Perhaps the fae don't possess the intuition they boast of. Or perhaps that's simply the lesser fae," the duke said, his words dripping with venom.

"Very well." The guard straightened himself, swallowing. I might have pitied him for being the object of the duke's verbal abuse and condescension, except he'd just called me a half-breed.

The guard called for one of his coworkers beyond the gate. Bars of steel groaned and squealed as they opened. The other guard took our guard's place as he led us through the courtyard.

I couldn't help but notice that the yard was full of statues, as if all of Avelea had been in short supply of flowers and the landscapers had been forced to make do with stone instead. For indeed, there were statues of flowers, blossoming as if under the spring sun. Except there was no color in them. Nor would they ever fully bloom.

I also couldn't help but notice the strange shadow that rested at an odd angle behind a stone oak tree, on the opposite side of the petrified flowers than one would have expected considering the placement of the lamps.

But I'd been searching for that shadow.

The duke yanked me by the nape of my neck as he hurried to keep up with the guard, who seemed to be intent on getting this disturbing-the-king business over and done with as soon as possible.

I could relate to that. What would I give to have this over with, to rid myself of the dread that took the form of churning bile in my stomach?

Marcus and I had a plan, sure. But there was at least one variable we couldn't have accounted for. We'd both agreed we'd just have to hope. And trust.

I wasn't keen on either of those these days.

The guard led us through dark stone halls lit dimly by single, melting candles spread out so far that, had they been moved one hair wider, there would have been shadows gapping the lit path of the chamber.

I wondered if the gloomy look was intentional, or if the king of Avelea really was that cheap.

For the sake of our mission, I hoped it was the former.

Either way, I'd consider the natural shadows to be to our advantage.

I tried to memorize our steps. Take a right at the entrance down the long dreary hallway, take a left at the shorter but just as dreary hallway, up the stone steps that looked as though they could use some leveling out before someone tripped and fell to their death, then another right... For the richest king in Alondria, the king's castle sure didn't look it, except for maybe in size. It reminded me of some homes from which I'd taken children, especially the few I'd taken in the rich districts of town. The grand houses were coated in marble, three stories high, but if one simply looked in the window, there'd hardly be a piece of furniture in sight. Or a morsel for the children, especially the servants' children, which was where I'd come in.

Could it be that the King of Avelea had only been pretending to be the most wealthy of all the kings? Surely not...

We arrived, after another two right turns, at the face of a door that reached as high as the vaulted ceiling.

The guard knocked once, twice, then four times.

"Yes?" a smooth, eerie voice asked. There was no unkindness in his voice, nor impatience. But something about their absence sent chills running down my spine. Why didn't the king sound annoyed at the surprise that his guard was sure would be an inconvenience to him? On the evening of the largest, most politically entwined festival of the season?

The door opened for us, seemingly of its own volition, and I remembered what the wealthy humans often made an ordeal of forgetting. The difference between us and them. The power they possessed that was nothing like my gift. The power that could swallow my gift.

My gift seemed to be thinking the same thing, for it shuddered within me at the sight of him.

At the sight of the king.

CHAPTER 48

PIPER

All my life, I'd been raised, no, molded to detest the King of Avelea. But that passion had always belonged to Bronger, and Bronger foremost. Me? Hatred of the royal fae had never motivated me. After all, what had the king done to harm me, really, when compared to what my parents had done, when they'd left me to freeze to death in my grave bed of snow?

No, I'd kidnapped for Bronger. I'd served the Coup for Bronger.

And then I'd killed him for Marcus.

And therein lay my hatred for the king. For the fae who, despite having everything an immortal life could offer in riches and power, had taken a little girl, and her little power, and used it for his own.

Of course, he must have saved her from that terrifying beast first.

I wondered if she loved him—the girl. If she loved him like I'd loved Bronger.

"What's the meaning of this?" The King of Avelea eyed me with suspicion before sending a hard, icy stare in the duke's direction. He sat at the head of a long table crafted of interweaving vines. The table needed no centerpiece, for the vines sprouted white and yellow petals across its face and legs. Although the table stretched the length of the massive banquet hall, empty seats skirted its edges.

Yet each place at the table was set with piles of food. The mingled scents of rosemary chicken, garlic potatoes, and Avelean cheese would have had my stomach roaring in delight any other time, but tonight my stomach only churned.

Where was the royal family? The queen had died years ago, but last I recalled, there were enough princes and princesses to give Bronger's army a run for their money.

And where were the king's servants and his guards? Was it customary for the king to eat alone on holidays, while his people gathered to celebrate outside his castle walls?

No, something wasn't right here.

Not at all.

The king growled, a set of sharp canines flashing through his gritted teeth. "Must I repeat myself?"

The duke clasped onto my arm tighter, and I couldn't help but notice he was trembling. Great. His eyes darted back and forth over each plate of steaming food, probably wondering the same thing I was.

When the king spoke again, the duke's fingers dug into my shoulder, forcing me to bite my lip. I didn't exactly appreciate being his comfort blanket. "It's the blood moon. You're aware of the date, are you not? Or do you not own a calendar?"

"I own a calendar," the duke grumbled.

"Then why have you insisted on my council during the blood moon, just as I was about to engage in the festivities?"

I couldn't help but think he didn't look like he would be partaking in any festivities, not with the way his long, golden hair looked like it might rip the teeth off a comb if a servant had the audacity to bring one near it. That, and how, if I were a swallow, I might have been comfortable leaving my eggs in the king's beard for safekeeping. He was high fae, and with Bronger's estimates of his age, that he was only into his third century of life, the king shouldn't have looked a day over thirty. At most. Yet, if he was human, I would have guessed him to be deep into middle age.

Maybe it was just the beard.

Or maybe...

When the king spoke again, his bark sent a stinging sensation through my sensitive ears. "And why bring this half-breed into my court to soil its floors?" I fought the urge to recoil at the king's word choice. "I'd intended to give my maids the evening off. Now they'll be forced to scrub down the place rather than celebrating with their families."

As the only other living thing we'd witnessed in this castle so far was the rodent that had scurried past us in the foyer, I doubted that was true.

Unease crept through my belly, though I shouldn't have let it. We'd known all along something strange was going on at the Avelean court. After all, wasn't that why we'd assumed the king had a Gifted at his disposal? Because every time Bronger sent Intel to get close to the king, everyone they spoke to, everyone who should have known something, anything, had forgotten they'd even spoken with the king?

We'd known a Gifted was here.

I'd just been too busy hoping it was Cheyenne that I hadn't stopped to consider what the King of Avelea might be striving so ardently to force everyone to forget.

What had happened here? To his servants, to all those children?

Then there was the issue of my half-faeness. Or, rather, the king's issue with it.

It almost helped that I'd figured the king wouldn't be keen on allowing a half-fae into his court, but I had assumed it would simply be a manner of distaste, easily overlooked once he noticed my gift. While fae and humans alike smote me with their prejudices, high fae tended to be less offended by my existence than the humans. I supposed they felt more disgusted than betrayed, disgust being a milder emotion.

Still, disgust wasn't exactly my favorite expression, especially when aimed in my direction.

The duke had better fix this. I elbowed him as discreetly as I could.

"Your Majesty," the duke said, his voice trembling now, any semblance of that haughty man dissolved in the presence of the high fae king. The king whose father had probably displaced the duke's ancestor's cousin's uncle from the throne so many years ago. "The female is Gifted."

The king cocked his head toward me and burrowed his sharp blue eyes into mine, as if he intended to penetrate my skull, to splay my mind open and expose my thoughts for the taking. "Is that so? And what exactly is your gift?"

"She... She umm—"

"I asked the female," the king said, his voice even and terrifying.

"I play, Your Majesty. The flute."

"You play?" The king's eyes flitted over to the duke. "You interrupted my evening on the grounds of bringing me a Gifted musician?"

Why did I have a sneaking suspicion the king had no intention of joining the festivities on the grounds?

"Your Majesty—"

"I don't simply play well, Your Majesty. My music, my gift, it can soothe the mind. Or unsettle it."

"Is that so?" the king asked. "And why, little female, are you attempting to convince me of your usefulness, when it would seem you did not come here by choice?" His eyes lingered on the firm grip the duke had on my shoulder, the ropes tied around my wrists.

I bit my lip. "Because I sense that you're displeased, Your Majesty. And I'm fearful of being in the presence of a displeased king."

The king leaned forward, placing his elbows upon the table as he swiped his cold eyes over me, sending a shudder up my limbs. "You're a clever one, then. Tell me, do you have an instrument with which to play for me?"

"It was confiscated."

Had I not known better, I might have thought the king rolled his eyes before addressing the duke. "Did you bring her instrument?"

The duke froze. "No. No, my lord. The female had no instrument on her when she was...acquired."

The king folded his pale hands and sat back in the chair, allowing his fingertips to graze one another as he probably pondered whether the Duke's and my deaths would be best served expeditiously or if he should turn our executions into the evening's entertainment.

But then his shoulders slumped, and a deep sense of weariness that I might have expected of more high fae given their extensive lifespans washed over his blue eyes. He stood and waltzed over to a door at the end of the banquet hall and knocked. "We're ready for you."

The duke and I shared questioning glances. Was the King of Avelea summoning someone? Himself?

If the king cared that his only two dinner guests looked shocked at his humbling gesture, it didn't come through in his voice, which had drained of its agitation and possessed about as much interest in it as a Naenden well had water. "Surely one of them has an instrument to the female's liking that they might lend to her."

A group of decorated musicians waltzed in. At the head of the group was a face I recognized, one that sent my stomach whirling.

I'd chopped off the snake's head.

But another had grown in its place.

A spiteful grin spread across James's face. "Why, hello, Piper," he said. "Fancy seeing you here."

MY HEART RACED. My cover was blown. I clenched my fists, ready to send a blow to the duke's head by swinging both my bound hands. But then the king looked back and forth between me and the people who used to be my...if not friends, then family—Van, Elias, and the others.

"You are acquainted?" the king asked with more curiosity than suspicion, and I remembered that, to the king, James and his group were the most talented musicians in the kingdom. And the duke had brought me before the king because of my musical gift. It wouldn't have appeared suspicious at all that James and I knew each other, except for the sneer he'd not bothered to hide.

"Piper used to travel with us," James said. He looked ridiculous in that outfit, with all the purple sashes and yellow ribbons. It made me want to punch him.

The king raised one bushy eyebrow. "And why exactly did she leave you?"

James smirked, and my stomach did backflips. I chanced a glance at Van, but she darted her eyes toward her shoes as soon as we made eye contact.

So she hated me too.

I couldn't blame her.

"The poor thing ran off with some man she met in one of the villages," James said. I tried not to audibly sigh in relief. "I see it must not have worked out. My condolences, Piper."

Oh, how I hated him.

My mind raced. Clearly James had taken command in Bronger's place. I'd expected as much. But for him to continue on with the plan... without me. What did that mean for Cheyenne? If I was the one who was supposed to draw her out, draw her away...

"And does one of you happen to have an extra... Now, remind me again, what exactly do you play, *Piper*?" the king asked, returning to his seat at the head of the empty table.

"Flute," I said.

"Van, give her yours," James practically spat. The expression that flitted across Van's face would have sent me running—that silent *how dare you* that tipped the high arch of her eyebrows—but she did as he said and strode across the room. The thick heels of her boots echoed across the stone tile floor.

She wouldn't look at me when she reached me. All I wanted to do was to whisper that I was sorry. That I'd never intended to hurt her. But I couldn't risk the Duke overhearing, becoming suspicious, nor the high fae with those curved ears meant for eavesdropping. She shoved the flute into my hands and returned to James's side.

The flute was wooden, plain, much like the one I'd left in my satchel at the inn Marcus was paying for, though I found it unlikely either of us would be staying there tonight. Even if we managed to get out of this... An uneasy feeling crept within the corners of my mind.

We hadn't counted on James and his crew showing up. The mission wasn't supposed to be dangerous. At worst, I was supposed to end up in the king's court, as his servant. Then I would have spent the next few months devising a plan to help Cheyenne escape.

But with James here, with what I knew he was planning...

We had tonight, and tonight alone.

A shadow flickered in the corner of my vision, filling me with warmth, comfort.

James might try to take her.

But of the two of us, I was the more experienced in that particular area.

"While my gift is wildly talented, I'm afraid even it cannot do much if my hands are tied," I said to the king as pleasantly as I could manage.

He grunted, which the duke must have interpreted as a command, for he loosened the cord binding my hands.

I raised the flute to my lips and played.

My gift chose wisely. The tune that filled the court was a battle march, one so stately, with a beat so steady, it seemed it could have sent any army fearless into a battle against an enemy triple their size. I gambled a glance at the king's face during the chorus, and even he, a strong-minded fae used to magic, seemed to beam courage and confidence at the sound of the tune. My gift soon switched to a softer, gentler piece, and I watched as the king's face loosened around his forehead for a moment. As he resisted my gift and suspicion flickered in those eyes, my gift switched to another tune instead. One I was certain the king wouldn't feel the effects of.

The air around Bronger's spies tensed as I played the tune. The tune each of them had only heard exactly once in their lifetimes. Sorrow, mourning, loneliness poured from the tip of my instrument. The duke shuffled impatiently behind me and grunted at the slow cadence.

My eyes scanned the room, noticed the odd flicker of a shadow in the rightmost corner of the room. The song was about to end, and my heart raced. I struggled with my gift to play the chorus on a loop once more, and it bent to my will, though reluctantly.

Still, nothing. Just curiosity flickering in those cold eyes of the king.

But then something else shifted. The stone wall, behind the king's throne to the left. A line cut through the stone, forming a door, which opened, making barely a creak.

A girl whose face I'd forgotten entered the room, her familiar eyes narrowed and pained.

She'd heard this song before.

Cheyenne.

"Child," the king scoffed, turning in his throne toward the girl, "get back in—"

But he didn't finish the sentence, for a knife lodged itself in Cheyenne's shoulder.

CHAPTER 49

PIPER

The shadow lingering in the corner of my eye bellowed. I lurched toward Cheyenne, but the duke caught me by the shoulder and yanked, causing me to drop the flute.

Marcus, shadows unfurling around his blurred form, reached Cheyenne just in time to fold her into his arms before she hit the ground.

An arrow whizzed toward him, but without even looking in its direction, he whirled his forearm, deflecting the arrow with his shadows.

I swung to my right, pivoting on my feet. The duke cried out as my fist made contact with his skull. Shocked, he fell to the ground, a cracking sound echoing throughout the hall as the flute splintered underneath his weight.

My gaze went straight for James only because the blade had lodged itself in Cheyenne's shoulder, and I knew enough about James to be certain he wouldn't be pleased with his work. That he'd return his attention to Cheyenne and land a fatal blow as soon as the opportunity arose.

James had replaced his throwing dagger with a sword and was parrying with the king, who had brandished a moon-white blade. Van aimed an arrow for the king. As soon as her fingers released the shaft, the king let out a howl of mingled laughter and rage. Then, just as the arrow was a hair from striking his chest, he lurched forward, throwing himself to the ground.

He shifted before the pads of his feet even touched the stone floor. Where the king had just been, a wolf, white as the moon itself, growled in his place, its blue eyes piercing my memories, threatening to suffocate me as they sent me back to that day on the forest floor, helpless as the beast dragged Cheyenne away.

The king hadn't rescued Cheyenne from the wolf.

The king was the wolf.

I swallowed the dread, the memory of the pain, reminding myself it wasn't real, not anymore, and sprinted for Cheyenne and Marcus, bracing myself for the sound of ripping flesh that would surely come as the wolf reached Van. Blocking off my mind to anything else, I knelt beside Cheyenne as Marcus cupped her face in his hands and whispered frantically to her.

"It's me. It's Marcus. Please don't be afraid..." Marcus looked up at me, the shadows whipping themselves around his face, as if to convey the rage his hidden expression could not.

"Marcus." I took his hand and removed it from Cheyenne's face, trying my best not to make contact with her skin.

Cheyenne gasped, her face contorting. "It's okay, Piper. I can control it now."

I nodded and released Marcus's hand. He brushed a sweaty strand of hair from Cheyenne's wet forehead.

"Take her back into her room," Marcus said, turning toward me.

I nodded. "What are you going to do?"

He didn't answer as he stood and retrieved a cerulean arrow from his sheath.

I wasn't sure whether he aimed at the king or James.

"I'm sorry, Cheyenne. This is going to hurt," I said, wrapping my arms underneath her armpits. She groaned, and I knew I was placing pressure on the wound where the knife had entered her skin, but I didn't know how else to go about moving her. I lifted from my knees and dragged her limp body over the stone tiles as she groaned. We left a trail of her blood in our wake.

Just as we crossed the threshold into her room and I turned to the stony door, I caught a glimpse of Marcus dispatching arrow after arrow in James's direction. James deflected each with his shield while his sword clanked against the enormous wolf's teeth as they sparred.

Cheyenne pointed a weak finger toward a lever to the right of the door. "Close it."

When I pulled the lever, the door swung inward, trapping us inside Cheyenne's tiny bedroom.

So this was where the king kept her, tucked away and hidden, ready to grace his guests with her gift as soon as he had gotten what he needed from them.

"We need to dress your wound," I said, laying Cheyenne as gently as was possible on such a cold, hard floor before pacing over to the bed and grabbing her sheets in my fists. I tore them in two, then returned to Cheyenne.

I didn't give her a warning before I ripped the dagger from her shoulder.

She writhed, gritting her teeth as she groaned, and I wrapped the torn bed sheets around her shoulder and under her armpit. I hoped the dressing would contain the bleeding just under her collarbone, at least until we could get her the medical attention she needed.

"It's no use." Cheyenne choked on her words. Panic raced through me. Under the light of the single candle in Cheyenne's base bedroom, her typically brown cheeks looked pale, ghostly. I shuddered despite myself.

I wrapped the bed sheets tighter around her slight frame, trying not to panic as blood oozed outward, staining the sheets. "I know it hurts, but we need to stop the bleeding."

"You don't understand," Cheyenne said, shaking her head. "It shouldn't hurt this much. I should be able to move."

"You've been stabbed, of course it's going to hurt." But even as the words escaped my lips, dread crawled up my bones. Cheyenne had been hit in the shoulder, yet I'd had to drag her across the floor, her limp legs streaking the stone floor with her blood. "Cheyenne, can you move your legs for me?"

Tears welled in those big, brown eyes. She shook her head.

Just then, a howl broke through the stone wall that hid Cheyenne's chamber from the prying eyes of outsiders.

"The king," Cheyenne said, as the wolf howled again. Despite my disbelief, the sound of agony pierced my ears. The wolf sounded as though it was mourning, as though it was dying. But that wasn't possible. James wasn't that...

But we'd planned for him to be that powerful, be that relentless. And Bronger had intended for James to have an advantage, one that even the fae king wouldn't have suspected, one that I had not been privy to during our meetings.

"Oh no." My hand clasped to my mouth instinctively as I watched Cheyenne's blood soak through the dressing. As I watched her limbs lock up. How they froze in place although I was sure she was in enough pain to squirm uncontrollably.

The stone door behind me creaked open:

"Now, Piper. Did you have a change of heart and decide to come help us?" James crooned. I whipped around to face him and sprawled myself out in front of Cheyenne.

She whimpered behind me, though I could tell by the muffled sounds she was trying to bury the sign of weakness deep within herself.

James reached down and picked up the dagger, still wet with Cheyenne's blood. I allowed myself one glance into the banquet hall. The great white wolf lay still on the floor, dark blood staining his white coat. I thought I glimpsed a shadow lying on the ground next to him. A shadow that seemed out of place.

No, no, no.

My hands shook. Something wasn't right. James shouldn't have been able to take down the king so quickly. "What did you do to them?"

"Oh, it's not what I did to them," James said, examining the bloody knife by candlelight. "You can thank your little friend Amity for this.

She's a natural when it comes to making poisons, you know. Makes you wonder who was truly the victim in her household."

My legs shook in rage as he smirked, as his eyes traced the edge of the blade.

The blade dipped in poison.

I gripped my dagger and lunged for him.

But it wasn't a fair fight.

It was never going to be a fair fight.

Bronger had seen to that.

When James plunged his knife into my stomach, the world went still.

CHAPTER 50

PIPER

For a moment, I didn't even feel the pain, not in the typical sense.

I saw the pain, watched as spiders crept across my vision, swarming James's pleased smile, crawling from his teeth.

I smelled the pain, the scent of rotting flesh. My flesh.

The rotting scent slithered down the length of my throat, settling at the base of my tongue.

My legs locked, and I slumped.

James stepped backward rather than catching me.

He didn't even bother to remove the knife as I fell, the weight of my body plunging it further into my gut.

That was when I felt the pain. Sudden and sharp and all-encompassing.

The pain was a hammer, beating nails through my eardrums. Removing the nails, starting over.

My legs begged to writhe, but an invisible force shackled them in place, denying them any movement, any distraction from the pain.

Metal collided with my shoulder as James kicked me onto my back. Bile collected in my throat, threatening to choke me, drown me. He stepped over my shaking body, straddling my torso as he towered over me. Then he squatted, pure pleasure tinging the corners of his lips.

James chuckled. "She made this one for you, you know. Made it especially with you in mind. She hates you. You should hear how easily her perception of you soured once she realized who you were. What you were. Just a murderer. Worse than that, a liar. A liar who snatched her out of her home just to deposit her on the doorstep of a man you thought worthy of an arrow to his ribs."

My arms shook, and I willed my fingers to move. I reached for Cheyenne's hand, but it had gone still.

I wanted to spit at James, to tell him I didn't believe him. But I'd seen the look Amity had given me, seen the way her face had turned to stone as I'd asked her to come. As she'd beheld the dead body at my feet. As she'd seen me for who I truly was.

"What does it do?" I asked, barely able to move my jaw.

James shrugged. "It makes you suffer. That child creeped me out enough that I didn't bother asking for details. I have to admit, I'm looking forward to finding out."

He knelt before me, so I could feel the heat of his breath. So it could chill my spine, make me shiver. Time was running out. Running out for Cheyenne, for Marcus, for me, even for the king.

Marcus, where was Marcus?

Had they gotten him, too?

That thought alone was enough to suffocate me.

The hunger in James's eyes devoured Cheyenne's whimpering form. "Here's to hoping this child will be just as useful as your little friend."

And then I remembered.

James didn't know how Cheyenne's gift worked.

"Actually," James said, "I suppose Amity could tell you herself. Come here, girl."

Tiny footsteps sounded in the banquet hall, pattering against the stone floor. A slight figure in a colorful musician's hood entered the room, her face obscured by the shadows the hood cast over her face.

But I didn't have to guess who inhabited that small frame.

"Show yourself," James barked.

Amity did as she was told and lifted her her hood to the crown of her head, exposing her face. Her usually wide eyes had gone small, soft, tired. And her face had gone pale. She didn't look at me, only at the ground beneath her tiny feet, and then at Cheyenne, who lay still on the ground behind me, gurgling and muttering.

"Tell her what your poison does, little friend," James said.

Amity's eyes were still locked on Cheyenne, though they seemed unfocused, as if Amity were seeing something far away, perhaps another person lying still on the ground. "It's a paralytic," she said, her mouth moving, though the rest of her face looked about as still as Cheyenne's body. "It keeps her muscles in an immobilized state, but her heart still beats and she can still breathe."

"And how long do the effects last, child?" James ripped the blade from my stomach, sending another wave of pain through my body.

I loosed a strangled scream as he examine its bloodied edges.

Amity's eyes went glassy. "It's permanent. It'll eventually work its way to her vital organs, and then..."

My heart raced. "Amity," I groaned. "I'm so sorry."

Cheyenne whimpered behind me, and I noticed her legs had gone completely still.

"It's the perfect poison, really," James said. "I was delighted when she told me of it. Turns out this child has had a mind for plants and their interactions her entire life. All she needed to blossom was access. And a reason to fight," he said, grinning down at me. "A reason to let go of her childhood. Imagine how delighted I was that it worked on the fae. I must admit, I'd been hoping for a poison that would kill immediately, but how much more fun to keep the fae king prisoner in his own body, where he can listen to me, the newly anointed King of Avelea, for several years before his organs give out?"

My legs trembled as the color washed from Amity's face. What had I done to that poor, innocent child, in killing a man directly in front of her?

"Amity, friend. Mind telling me why Piper here can move her arms?"

Amity's eyes fixed on my wound before tracing a path to my outstretched arm, the one reaching for Cheyenne.

Amity nodded, this time watching her feet rather than me or Cheyenne. "You stabbed her too low. The poison works its way down the body."

James twirled the blade, tracing its tip along my collarbone, pushing it into my skin with just enough force not to break the flesh. "Either way, she's not going anywhere, is she? Looks like you've got a captive audience, little friend. Isn't there something you wanted to say?"

Amity's legs shook, and tears rolled down her eyes as quiet sobs punctured the stale air.

"Oh, now, child," James said, "she's not worth crying over. Are you afraid of taking a life?"

Amity nodded, still refusing to look at me.

"It's nothing to fear, child. Once you've done it enough, it won't hurt any longer. I promise."

Amity hissed, but not at James. No, this time she lifted her eyes to mine, those wide eyes that had once been so soft, so trusting, now replaced by flint and flame. "You promised." My heart faltered. "You promised you were taking me someplace better."

"Amity, I—"

"No." She shook her head, her frantic movement sending her hood slipping off the back of her head, revealing a wad of tangled braids. "No, you made me believe you were saving me. That my new family was going to be better. But then you—" She sucked in a faltering breath and had to steady herself on the wall. "But then you killed him." Her voice sank into a whisper. "You killed him."

"He was going to kill Marcus."

James piped up. "Speaking of him. Van!" he called out into the hall. "Would you care to bring our shadowed friend here?"

Moments later, Van dragged a swarm of shadows across the threshold.

Marcus.

No.

The shadows around his face parted, revealing a slash across his cheek, his copper eyes darting around the room in a frantic search. They landed on me and widened in horror before finding Cheyenne.

The vein in his temple bulged, but no sound escaped his lips.

"She's still alive," I managed to choke out, though I didn't even know if that was true. If it made anything better, or worse.

Amity refused to look at him, and instead focused on her feet.

"Now," James said, clapping his hands. "Where were we? Oh, yes. Piper was defending herself rather than apologizing. Do you have anything to say to that, Amity?"

Amity swallowed, her voice strangled. But it wasn't weakness or fear that pierced through the notes in her voice.

It was rage.

Hate.

"I saw the look in your eyes when you killed him. You didn't kill him to save Marcus. You did it for yourself." Her brown eyes locked on mine. "What did he do to you?"

My heart sank. "I—"

"What were you going to let him do to me?"

The words hung between us, as stiff as my legs, Cheyenne's arms, Marcus's cheeks.

"I failed you, Amity. I am so sorry," I said, my hands shaking. "You followed me on the condition that I'd take you to a better place. And I told myself it was true. Just because I was lying to myself doesn't make it any better that I lied to you, too."

Amity only sobbed, and James cackled.

"Now look what you've done. I should kill you now, get it over with so the poor child can begin to heal. Forgive me if I relish seeing you this way. Piper, Piper, Piper. How my ears have grown weary of your name. You were all Bronger ever talked about, you know. Thanks for getting rid of him for me, by the way. Coups are a bit complicated to pull off, as you well know."

My stomach clenched as he rose. He grabbed my collar and wrenched me to my feet, the sudden movement sending a fresh wave of needles through my skin as my blood dripped down to pool beneath us. My knees buckled, and I landed against his chest. He leaned in close, the heat of his breath wetting my ear as he whispered. "I can make her do whatever I want. He taught me how. Every time he made you do something you didn't want to do, guess who was there observing, taking notes. Just watch."

Over his shoulder, I could see Cheyenne, her chest shifting just enough to confirm she still lived.

"Amity, little friend. I need you to do something for me."

My heart froze in my ribcage.

"The dagger meant for Piper landed itself in the poor girl's shoulder. Tell me, what does this mean for the rest of her life?"

Amity's voice trembled. "She won't be able to move. And she'll be in pain."

"Is there anything we can do for her?"

"I—" Amity's voice caught. "No. No, there's not."

"Then I need you to show her mercy, little friend. I need you to put her out of her misery."

I gasped. "No. No, Amity. There's got to be another way. If you created the poison, you can create the antidote."

But the lack of color in Amity's face was answer enough. She shook her head.

Marcus groaned behind me, his voice trapped in his throat. He was going to watch his sister die. At the hand of Amity.

No, no, no.

"You don't have to do this. He's trying to manipulate you," I said, my voice breaking as tears burned my eyes.

Her wide eyes fixated on Cheyenne, on the sweat that beaded off her forehead. "I know. But that doesn't make him wrong."

"It's your choice, Amity. Spare her life, if you wish. But tell me, little friend. Would it truly be sparing her, to allow her to live out her life like this, unable to move, suffocated by pain?"

Tears streaked Amity's cheeks as she knelt to the floor and grasped the hilt of the bloodied, poison-dipped knife.

She dropped it twice before she managed to get both of her tiny hands around it.

"No, you don't have to do this." The words clung to my dry throat, drowned in the bile that seeped into the spaces between my teeth. "Please don't do this."

When Amity spoke again, her voice was smooth, empty, cold. "No one should have to live in pain."

She took one last look at me, and without making a sound, she clapped her hand against her thigh, just like she'd done for her mother for all those years.

Don't worry. I'm okay.

Then she plunged the dagger into Cheyenne's heart.

CHAPTER 51

PIPER

Cheyenne's eyes shot open, pain and fear and horror washing over her paling face. She cried out, a howl that echoed in the chambers of my ears, off the walls of my hollow soul.

Shadows encompassed the room, crashing over furniture, scaling the walls. The only sign that Marcus's spirit had broken in two.

He couldn't even make a sound. I couldn't see him, not even to provide a witness to his grief, not with my legs devoid of movement, my chin digging into James's wiggling shoulder.

He was laughing.

And Amity.

Amity wouldn't even let go of the dagger. It was as if her tiny fingers, knuckles bulging, had cemented into place. As if the rest of her life would freeze into this moment, the moment where she'd taken Cheyenne's life.

No, not Amity.

My mind swirled with Cheyenne's screams, Amity's tears, Marcus's shadows.

And yet, even as she'd split her soul, Amity had tried to reassure me she'd be okay.

Amity was not going to be okay.

She wouldn't be okay ever again.

Rage burst through the pain, surging through my arms, propelling my joints until I dug my fingers into James's ribcage. He yelped, but it wasn't enough. He lurched, but recovered quickly and yanked me by my hair until he was holding me out in front of him, the weight of my limp legs tugging on my neck as he held me suspended.

"Now, now, Piper. Did you think you could hurt me?" A wicked grin spread across his lips as he sized me up.

Hatred, hot and sweet, pumped through my blood for this boy I should have left for dead.

He'd destroyed her. Cheyenne, Amity—they were nothing to him except for thorns to plunge into my aching heart.

All because Bronger had liked me just a little better.

And Marcus.

His agony seeped over the walls, over James's smirk. But the shadows couldn't touch him.

Because shadows can't hurt the darkness.

It hadn't been enough for James to let me die a painful death. He'd had to ruin her, too.

And even through all that hate brewing in her soul, she'd still sought to comfort me. To pretend, maybe for herself, that she was going to be okay.

She knew better.

She wasn't a child anymore.

With his free hand, James traced my belly with his poisoned dagger. He scraped it across my open wound, sending a fresh wave of fire through my blood.

As if he hadn't already shattered me beyond repair.

Cheyenne flinched on the ground, and I wondered if it was in pain, her body frantically drinking up the last few pumps of blood it would ever receive, or if she was already dead.

I'd heard dead bodies jerked sometimes.

Amity had told me that. Well, told Marcus while I'd been eavesdropping, pretending my life could turn out any other way than with a blade to my skin, the eyes of the only people in the world who'd cared about me open to the ugly truth of what I was.

I didn't deserve it, but it was so tempting, as the blood poured from my wounds, my self-control slipping away with it. So tempting to allow my consciousness to float back there, to the gentle chatter of Amity's voice as Marcus slashed a path for us through the brush.

I'd been happy then, though I hadn't known it at the time.

Everyone says it's just a legend, but the story has to come from somewhere.

They say the fae carried it over to Alondria on accident, that it was stuck in the soles of their shoes.

No, really, I'm not making it up!

Well, I know it doesn't sound possible, but that's the whole point of magic, isn't it. Don't you believe in magic?

What was it Marcus had said after that? I could play his voice over and over in my head if I wanted to. I didn't deserve to let it comfort me, not when his sister was dead because of me. Not when he'd be dead soon, too.

But it was so low, so gentle, so vibrant and full of adventure. Maybe I could just listen to it once. Maybe the Fates wouldn't punish me for that. Not when I had so many other sins that would take preference.

Amity's just been telling me about a magic herb that's deadly, except when it's not.

Apparently, it's deadly. But get this...No, no, no...I'm just repeating what you told me. It's deadly, unless it's inserted directly into the heart.

A jolt surged through me, anchoring me to reality even as the blood dripping from my stomach begged me to let it carry me away.

Amity had signaled that everything was going to be okay.

That day in the Coup, she'd been so excited to tell me something she'd discovered. Something she'd wished she could rub in Marcus's face.

Something she'd been right about.

"Marcus isn't going to believe what I f—"

She would have told me, except she'd stopped herself when she remembered that we'd left Marcus in Nettlewood, in the past.

Cheyenne flinched again, and this time curled her fingers.

James leaned in, allowing his wet, cold lips to graze the lobe of my ear. Nausea swept over me as my tongue fought back the bile. "What's that little gift of yours doing for you now?"

Hot, salty tears stung at my eyes, at my skin as I slid my cheek across his to whisper in his ear. "It's not my gift I need."

When I dug my fingers into his shoulders and pulled myself into his chest, I think it took him a moment to realize what I'd done.

To realize that the hot, sticky substance running down the hilt of his blade, down his fingertips, wasn't from the wound in my stomach.

That it was from my heart.

It might have been enough for me, that look of disappointment in his eyes. The realization that, once again, I'd stolen his moment, taken it for myself.

He yanked the blade from my chest, but it was too late.

My knees crumpled.

So did I.

"I'll flay her for this." And by the feral spark in his eyes, I knew James meant it.

Knew there was nothing I could do to stop him.

But then his piercing gaze went blank, still, and a look I'd never seen on James's face washed over him. Something childlike, harmless. Confused even.

"Piper?" he asked, his eyes wild with trepidation. He spotted the blood soaking through my tunic, rushing from my heart. "What happened to you?"

At his feet, Cheyenne grimaced, a streak of blood marking where she'd dragged herself across the stone floor, her fingers wrapped around James's bare ankle.

Gasping for breath, her voice husky from exertion, she growled to me, "You owe me one."

At least, I thought that was what she said.

Her voice had started to echo, fold over itself so I couldn't distinguish where one word ended and the next began.

Something warm and slippery and metallic wet my lips.

Then there was nothing.

CHAPTER 52

Gigi had been inside a body as it died before.

She'd had her suspicions for a while now, but as death encroached on Piper, as Gigi tasted its numbness tingling all around her, she knew this wasn't the first time.

She knew it would hurt.

That wasn't what she was worried about.

She worried for Piper, for the children her sweet friend would never see perched upon Marcus's shoulders.

Piper still hurt too much, too often, to die.

She wasn't done growing yet.

Wasn't a full Piper yet.

Just as Gigi wasn't a full Gigi.

She hadn't been a full Gigi in quite some time.

Gigi grasped for Piper, but her friend's subconscious slipped through the grasp of her nonexistent fingers.

Nonexistent.

Just as Piper was about to be.

Piper's heart pulsed weakly and she gasped a shallow breath. Gigi knew it was her last.

Piper. Piper, wake up. Please wake up, she cried, but Piper couldn't hear her.

Piper couldn't hear anything.

And then Gigi was alone in the darkness.

Only then did Gigi remember.

SHE REMEMBERED HER SIBLINGS FIRST, how they'd wandered realms together, how they'd found friends in the inhabitants of the various lands. She remembered her hosts, the kind humans who'd offered her rooms in their hearts, who'd shared their precious lives with her—the births of their children, their joy of painting, of music, their folklore and songs. She remembered her gratitude for her hospitable friends. It was no small undertaking to share their consciousness with her, to make space for her in their minds.

But they'd shared. They'd shared so willingly and abundantly, and Gigi had loved them for it.

She'd graced them with her magic, allowed it to be molded by whatever sang true in each of their hearts. Some had spoken to animals, made the best of friends in the woods. Some had crafted structures that could not be moved, no matter the size of the storm that affronted them. Some changed their form, their voices, and put on the most entertaining shows, delighting their neighbors with tales of adventure and daring.

Gigi had lived so many lives.

She'd lived so many deaths, too.

She'd tried to grasp onto their last breaths, to keep them safe, but she'd had no hands with which to hold them except for the ones that had gone limp at her friends' sides. She'd whispered to them as they drifted, told them stories and sang them songs and reminded them of how so very loved they were.

It hurt to die.

Not for her friends. They always seemed to fade away, their minds warm and comfortable and at peace.

They didn't know they were alone.

Gigi did.

She remembered how she always gave herself time to wander after a friend died.

How it didn't feel quite right to make another friend, not until sufficient time had passed for Gigi to honor the soul who had disappeared from this plane of existence.

After some losses, she thought she'd be better off never making a friend again.

But that was the thing about humans.

There were so many of them to love.

So many of them to lose.

Gigi's brother had known that; that was why when the immortal fae entered this realm, he'd sought one out and joined himself to her.

Oh, yes. Gigi remembered it well.

Gigi and her siblings had all found one another. By that time, they'd wandered separately for so long, faced so many deaths, that they'd longed for something constant. Others with whom to commiserate, others who understood the shadow of loss that clung to them everywhere they went.

When he'd brought that fae female into their house of human hosts, Gigi had known nothing good could come of it.

But the fae female was kinder, gentler than the other fae Gigi had encountered.

She healed the humans when they were injured. She patched their torn clothes using Gigi's brother's magic.

So Gigi had tolerated her, even if she didn't trust her.

She'd wanted to be called Mother, which Gigi hadn't liked.

The humans weren't her children, after all.

The fae prince was.

Gigi had been there the day he'd found his estranged mother, the day he'd asked for her help in overthrowing his cruel father.

Gigi remembered having a bad feeling about it all. She'd tried to tell her host to tell Mother to tell her brother about it, but her sweet friend hadn't listened. She'd adored Mother too much to ever express doubt in her discretion.

During an afternoon when Mother was gone, the prince had come back. He'd brought his fae friends with him, and they'd offered Gigi and her siblings a bargain.

Bind themselves to the fae, and never have to die again.

Gigi had never switched between living beings before. She'd never wanted to. And she certainly didn't want to leave her sweet friend for these cruel males.

Don't worry. I won't leave you, Gigi promised her friend.

I know, her friend thought back.

"My magic politely declines your bargain," Gigi's friend said.

"Is that so?" the fae prince had asked. He waltzed over to Gigi's friend and cupped her chin in his cold hands. Gigi felt the hairs rise on her friends' arms. "But we're celebrating the birth of my commander's firstborn today. I was so hoping to gift him something special."

"She said *no*," Gigi's friend said through gritted teeth.

The fae prince quirked an eyebrow. "She?" He grinned and gestured for his commander to step forward. "I'll tell you what, little magic. Bind yourself to my commander, or I'll slit the throat of your precious host."

Gigi hadn't known what to do. She loved her friend. She didn't want to leave her, especially not to join the brute that towered over them, snarling at them between his bared, hungry teeth.

The fae prince pressed his blade into the throat of Gigi's friend, drawing droplets of blood. "You have until I count to five, little magic."

The prince didn't have to bother counting. Gigi flung herself from her friend, as if her lingering presence alone was an infection that would bring about her friend's death. Gigi's friend was too young to die. She wouldn't let it happen.

When she bound herself to the fae commander, she thought it was her sadness, her grief, that enveloped her.

It wasn't.

Pressure pounded against every facet of her consciousness, squeezing her from all sides, crushing her, strangling her.

There, there, little magic, her new host crooned. *Can't have you wandering off, now can I?*

Gigi snapped back at him, using a much ruder expression than typically abided her vocabulary.

The male didn't seem to hear her.

This had been a mistake. Gigi couldn't dwell within a home so dank, so dark and suffocating. She'd go back to her friend, find a way out of this situation.

But the fae sunk his teeth into Gigi.

She screamed, but his laugh rumbled through his mind.

Something was very, very wrong.

The cruel fae drank from Gigi's power, sipping it like a fine wine, taking it from her, letting it seep through his veins.

He absorbed her like a laundered piece of linen to a puddle of blood.

Gigi cried out, but no one could hear her. She fought for control, for consciousness, and it took all her strength to peer through the fae's eyes into the outside world.

Her friends, her siblings' hosts were staring, not at the fae commander, but at the ground.

At the spot where Gigi's friend lay.

Dead.

No.

No.

The commander laughed.

The fae prince stared into his eyes, but when he spoke, it wasn't to his commander. "Such a weak species. Unable to withstand being separated from their parasite."

Gigi wept, but no one heard her.

The fae prince's eyes filled with hunger. With greed. "Can you taste it?" he whispered.

The commander was drunk. Drunk on her. Drunk on Gigi. She could feel his lips pull into a grin.

"Show me," the prince commanded.

Bones bent, snapped, cracked. Pain rolled through the commander, but Gigi had no way to scream.

Hair sharp as needles punctured the commander's skin.

And then an invisible force sewed the bones back together, but they were all in the wrong place, the wrong order, and the commander's vision was different, sharper, his sense of smell as keen as tasting a fresh kill.

He growled, and elation consumed the prince's face.

The fae prince swept his eyes around the room. "Bind yourselves to us. Your human hosts will die either way. Aren't you tired of being fragile? Being weak?"

No. Gigi pounded against the fae commander's consciousness, but he pushed back, snaring her between his brute force and his will. This had never happened before, not with any of the humans Gigi had bound herself to.

But this commander wasn't human.

He wasn't even fae anymore, not fully. He absorbed her and melded with her and created something new.

Too strong, he was too strong for her.

And suddenly, she couldn't find the edges where she ended and he began.

Gigi didn't remember anything for a long while after that.

Not until a baby's screams had woken her from her slumber.

Not until a weight had lifted, and a fragment of her consciousness had returned.

Gigi thought she understood now how she'd ended up in a baby's mind.

The commander had been fae. He'd been too powerful for her, and instead of hosting her, he'd overpowered her.

He'd absorbed her into himself, melted her down and fused her to his very being.

And then he'd passed her onto his children, and their children after that.

And with every birth, Gigi had fractured into pieces—pieces that were now scattered across Alondria, suppressed into oblivion within their fae hosts.

But Piper had been half-human.

Half-fae, too. That had to have been why Gigi couldn't talk to her, why Piper couldn't hear her speaking. Why Gigi always felt a bit lost, a bit confused.

But her human half, that half had let Gigi out, had unlocked the cage and allowed Gigi's consciousness to stretch its legs.

Piper had saved her.

Piper had saved Gigi, and Gigi had failed Piper.

Gigi didn't know if she could take it.

Perhaps that was why she was so relieved when her sweet friend's heart started beating again.

CHAPTER 53

PIPER

I awoke to tiny cold fingers caressing my cheeks, pulsing with varied pressure, as if...

"What if she doesn't wake up?"

"She'll wake up."

"But what if she doesn't?"

"She will."

"How do you know?"

"Oh, I don't know. Probably because I did. After you shoved that knife through my ribs. Not cool, by the way."

My mouth was dry, but the pain was gone, though it had left behind its shadow, a deep aching that turned my muscles to lead.

I opened my eyes to find Amity rocking on her knees, clutching my face in her palms.

"You're awake!" She flung herself around me, my blood soaking her forehead and matted braid in the process.

"Amity—"

"I am so sorry. I had to pretend that I hated you, because that's the only emotion James actually understands. And I'm so sorry about the poison, too. I had to make something he believed could be used as a weapon, but I didn't have any way of telling you it was reversible. And

I'm sorry for not coming with you that night you...I'm just really sorry."

I clutched her tangled braids in my fingers and pulled her close. "You're not the one who needs to apologize."

She sniffed, mumbling into my chest as she cried. "I already checked your belly. After the ressuroot reached your heart, it starting working its way through your bloodstream and healing your other wounds. You'll probably be sore for a while; I'm sorry about that—"

"Shh." I rocked her back and forth, not caring about the aching that pulsed in my abdomen as I did.

She scooted her head so that her chin rested on my chest. "Marcus isn't awake yet. But Cheyenne woke up after only a few minutes. And you took a little longer. So I don't know when he'll—"

"He'll wake up soon." Cheyenne came into focus, standing over me with her hands on her hips. "I thought you were dead."

"Which time?" I asked.

She didn't exactly smile, but her lip twitched.

"I thought you were dead, too," I said.

"Yeah, well you probably deserved that after you blamed your creepy music-trance-thing on me the night the cook caught you stealing." This time, I was sure I caught the hint of a smile on her lips.

"You heard that?" I asked.

She cocked a brow at me. "I told you I did."

I frowned, confused at first, but then I remembered the dream I'd had—the memory of Cheyenne pressing her compass into my hand. She'd told me something, but I'd woken up before I could grasp onto what it was she'd said.

"Let me guess," she said. "You don't remember that, do you?"

I shook my head, but before I could respond, James ambled over and hovered on the other side of me, his face wiped clean of cruelty to the point I might not have recognized him had his shirt not reeked of my blood. "Piper, seriously, what's going on?"

Cheyenne hissed as she helped me to my feet. "Oh, just shut up already. I'm not in the mood. Especially after you lodged that dagger right beneath my collarbone."

James's face twisted in confusion. I looked at Cheyenne as she placed her arm around my shoulders and helped me hobble to the other side of the room. Now that I surveyed her, I marveled at how much she'd matured. How those wide childlike eyes had grown sharper, her cheekbones more profound. I'd forgotten she would have become a young woman in the years since I'd lost her.

We both surveyed the shadowy figure at our feet. "I'll let you stay with him until he wakes up. I'm going to help Amity make sure the king is okay."

I wasn't sure which part struck me as more odd, that Cheyenne didn't want to be around when Marcus woke up, or that she cared whether the king who'd kept her prisoner for years was okay.

Regardless of what I thought, Cheyenne bounded off toward the king, still stretched across the floor, blood staining his white coat. Amity already kneeled beside him, stroking the fur behind his ears, soiling her tiny hands with his blood.

I had half a mind to stop her, to whisk her away from this dreadful place and to let the king bleed out on his expensive, probably irreplaceable rug.

After all, wasn't that exactly how he'd left me all those years ago as I watched him drag Cheyenne away?

I'd been younger than Cheyenne was now.

Before I could act on my instinct for revenge, Marcus stirred next to me. When I reached for his face, still mostly obscured in darkness, the shadows licked around my wrist as if to welcome me. My fingertips grazed his cold cheek, and his eyes jolted open at the touch of my hand.

"Cheyenne," he gasped.

"She's fine. So is Amity, and so are you," I said.

He frowned, staring at me as if to figure out why in Alondria I'd lie to him about such a thing. "Cheyenne was dead. You...you were dead. Then Amity..." His eyes widened as the memories crashed upon him. "Amity stabbed me." He reached for his chest, as if to feel for the wound underneath the shadows. But if his wound was anything like mine, he wasn't going to find it.

So I explained everything to him. How Amity had been right about the mythical herb that turned out not to be so mythical after all. That she'd regretted staying behind at the Coup and had used James's mental torture against him, to make him believe he had turned her against us. And that the poison he'd commissioned, the one that incredible mind of hers had created, had contained a fail-safe all along. A poison that was its own antidote, capable of healing all wounds tainted with it.

Genius. Just like its creator.

"So what I'm hearing is that Amity outsmarted all of us?" Marcus shifted to his side, propping himself up on his forearm as he groaned.

"Pretty much."

"Well, I should have seen that one coming."

I couldn't help but agree.

The shadows dissipated from his face, reveling a deep sadness I wasn't prepared for. "And Cheyenne?"

I swallowed. "She's helping Amity with the king."

He raised an eyebrow but didn't push further. Perhaps he also had no desire to talk about why his long-lost sister would rather make sure her captor survived than be there when her brother awoke.

"Let's go help them out, shall we?" I asked, offering my arm as support. He interlocked his arm with my elbow, and the two of us hobbled to our feet, healed but still feeling the soreness of where we'd both been stabbed.

We hobbled into the courtroom, where Amity and Cheyenne were leaning over the King of Avelea, comforting him as they stroked his fur. Surrounding them were Van, Elias, and the others, their swords, knives, and arrows all drawn toward the fallen king, though no one had yet fired a killing blow. They all looked so small next to the wolf, as if they were still those children whose hands I'd taken as I'd lifted them from windows, stables, carriages. Their fear shook the courtroom and chilled the surrounding air.

I swallowed my dread and walked toward the fallen wolf. As I approached, I realized just how large the wolf was, and marveled at how potent Amity's poison must have been to take down something of his size. A shiver ran up my spine.

I couldn't help but notice that someone had tied up the duke and left him in a dusty corner in the back of the banqueting hall, his eyes bulging at the sight of his king in his beastly form.

"Van," I said, approaching my friend, her blade drawn directly at the fae wolf's throat. His blue eyes glimmered not with rage, as I'd expected, but with fear. I wondered then if fae, when it came down to it, feared death more than humans, as it was merely a possibility rather than a definite fate.

"Don't worry," Van said. "You and your friends are going to walk away from here alive. Especially now that you've disposed of that idiot's temper." She nodded toward James, who paced across the hall, not a glimmer of hatred in his eyes. How much exactly had Cheyenne made him forget?

"I'm sorry about Bronger, Van," I said. A glimmer of a tear glistened in her eyes.

"I know."

"I know I'm not worthy to show my face at the Coup, but..."

"The Coup was Bronger's dream. James's obsession. Without either of them in the picture, I think it's time we decide for ourselves what we want to make of our lives."

I smiled, though it felt somewhat pained.

"I can't think of anyone better to help them find that," I said.

Van looked at me and allowed a faint smile to graze her lips. "Think you could help a girl out?" she asked, nodding her head to the tip of her sword that still traced the wolf's neck. "I never wanted to rule. Not like this." The wolf panted, fear raging in those ice-blue eyes of his.

I nodded and looked down at Cheyenne, who had noted Van's sword.

Cheyenne turned her steely gaze upon Van and the others, splaying her outstretched arms in front of the wolf. "Touch him, and I'll wipe your memory so clean you won't remember how relieve your bowels on demand."

Van's eyes went wide, but it was Amity who spoke. "Oh, don't hurt him," she said, waving Van's blade out of the way. Van complied, and Amity turned back to the downed wolf, the fae King of Avelea.

My hands flinched. I shouldn't allow this, shouldn't let Amity heal this monster's wounds. Who was to say he wouldn't hunt all of us down as soon as he was able-bodied again? But the hairs on the back of my neck tingled, and I looked up to catch Cheyenne staring at me, her arm wrapped over the wolf's neck, her gaze daring me to hurt him. To unleash her upon me.

Against my better judgment, I relented.

Amity put a hand out expectantly, into which Van deposited her blade.

"This is going to hurt, but I promise it's going to make everything better, okay?"

The wolf flinched, but that was as much as it could do before Amity drove a poisoned blade through its heart.

Moments, minutes, hours later, the fae king awoke, his icy blue eyes twinkling with wonder.

"Now, sir," Amity said, scratching behind his ears, "you've got to think about being kinder to the humans. You're making a lot of enemies when you could be making friends. It's silly, really."

So I stood back and watched as little Amity lectured the fae King of Avelea as she tended to his wounds.

CHAPTER 54

PIPER

It took longer than I expected for the king to shift back into human form.

What was even more unexpected was that Cheyenne held the explanation.

"It takes a toll on him to shift, even when he hasn't been poisoned. I expect it'll be a while before he has the strength to shift back into fae form." She scratched his pelt, her small hands sinking into his white fur as his ribs rose and expanded before falling in short bursts. "This is my fault. I asked him to invite musicians to the castle for me to listen to."

Marcus and I exchanged concerned looks. I didn't have to ask to know we were both thinking the same thing. With all the trafficking going on in Avelea, there were plenty of stories of kidnapped girls developing unhealthy attachments to their captors.

Come to think of it, I was probably one of them.

Marcus cleared his voice. "Cheyenne, mind if I have a word with you?"

She swallowed hard, and the time it took for her to turn her head to acknowledge her brother almost had me sweating. But she released her fingers from the wolf only after patting him and reassuring him she'd be back, before turning and sauntering off to a remote corner where she and Marcus could speak privately.

Except that they couldn't speak privately, not when my pointed ears pricked at every word.

I tried not to eavesdrop. Really, I did.

But one doesn't have nearly much control over one's ears as one's eyes.

It wasn't like I could just shut them.

As Amity continued to grace the King of Avelea with a lecture on ethics, Marcus's whispers cut through the bustle of Van and her crew.

"You've grown so much."

"That's what happens when someone actually remembers to feed you."

Silence. I couldn't help but cringe.

"That's not what I meant. I..." Marcus sighed. "I don't even know what to say, except to apologize. To say I'm sorry for not noticing something different was going on with you. For not noticing you at all. For leaving. For leaving you and the others. I told myself I was doing it for you, so you could have a better life. But I did it for me. I don't have anything else to say, except that I hope you forgive me."

The sound of leather soles scraping on carpet told me Cheyenne was shuffling on her feet. "You don't have anything to apologize for. You had no way of knowing."

"But I should have been there when—"

"You were."

My ears perked at that, and I tried to distract myself by scratching the king's pelt, but then I realized how weird that was, that he was Bronger's sworn nemesis, not some stray dog, and I stopped.

"The night I went with Piper after she'd played in the town square and that song of hers called to me. You were there that night, Marcus."

He shuffled, so subtly it was almost silent.

Almost.

"You missed me, so you came home. But you were later than you'd thought you'd be, so you stopped by the square first. I had snuck out to hear the music. It wasn't like it was all that difficult when no one remembered I was around anyway. You saw me in the crowd and grinned. Then you picked me up and spun me around. You let me hold your hand the whole night."

I couldn't help it, I repositioned myself so I was on the other side of the king, pretending to watch over Amity, so I could see their faces.

Marcus was in shock, that much was clear. "I don't..."

Cheyenne took his hand in hers, and he flinched. A sad smile broke across her face. "It's okay. I'm not going to make you forget this time. I know how to control it now. Declan taught me."

The familiarity of the king's name on her tongue sent shivers down my spine, but could I blame the girl for her adoration? When everyone else in her life had forgotten about her, and he hadn't?

"You let me hold your hand all night and we listened to Piper. When I heard her song I...I don't know how to explain it to you, but it spoke to me. It was like, like it knew me somehow. You told me you had something to do before you came home, and I waited up for you that night. Except you never came."

Marcus nodded. "And Piper did."

She nodded back. "Yeah, she did. I didn't understand then, what I'd done. That holding your hand all night had made you forget why you'd come home in the first place. So when Piper came and offered me a new life, I went with her."

Something Cheyenne said tugged at a memory I'd tucked away. That night in Evaen, when I'd played my gift's song, the one that usually only called to children, Marcus had reacted to it instead.

But that hadn't made any sense. No matter how many of Marcus's scars hadn't healed, my gift's song never called to adults.

Never.

And that couldn't have been because all the adults I'd ever played for were completely whole, totally healed of whatever horrors they'd faced in their own childhoods.

What if Marcus hadn't been reacting to my gift?

What if he'd been reacting to *hers*?

If Cheyenne had held Marcus's hand all night—I couldn't imagine how deeply that memory had been shoved into the corners of his mind.

But she'd held his hand as I played that tune.

That night in Evaen, what was it he'd said?

It was like it reminded me of the moments I should have had with her, with my sister. And that there was this void where those memories should have been.

What if that void, that missing memory, was already there?

My gift's song just reminded him of it.

Like how the scent of freshly fallen snow always took me back to Bronger's arms the night he'd rescued me from death. Or how the taste of hot cocoa brushed the heat of that first fireplace across my fingertips.

Except when my song had triggered a memory, there had been no memory left to cling onto.

A tear streamed down Marcus's face. "Chey, I'm so, so sorry."

She took his other hand and grasped them in her palms. "But I'm not."

Confusion swept over his face, and his jaw hung open.

"If I had never made you forget, then I might not have gone with Piper. And I would have gone my entire life thinking that everyone forgot about me because there was something wrong with me, something lacking. But because I went with her, I found Declan. Or, he found me. And he showed me that what I have inside me—it's extraordinary, Marcus."

Marcus shook his head. "What he's using you to do, Cheyenne, it's not right."

She dropped his hands and crossed her arms. "And what exactly is he using me for?"

He leaned in close to her and whispered, though it didn't do much to keep me from hearing. "Listen, I don't know what happened to his family, to his servants, but there's something odd going on around here. I don't know if he killed them—"

"Okay, I'm going to stop you right there," Cheyenne said, holding one palm up. "Declan didn't kill his family. And he didn't have them imprisoned either, if that's what you're thinking."

"Then please explain."

"I can't."

"Why not?"

"Because it's not my secret to share."

Marcus threw his hands up. "He's brainwashed you, Cheyenne. Can't you see that?"

I expected Cheyenne to march away, to slap Marcus, or any other childish thing. But she only smiled, and even I was taken in by its genuineness. "I appreciate your concern, and I can especially appreciate the conclusion you've come to based on the limited information you have. But that's just it. You don't know the whole story. It means a lot that you care, and I hope you visit often. But I assure you, I'm fine. I like it here."

Baffled did not begin to describe the look on Marcus's face, but Cheyenne stood her ground.

I couldn't help but admire her for it.

"And if you're concerned about what I think you're concerned about," she added, "don't be. Declan's raised me since I was a child. He's like family."

Marcus's shoulders slumped, evidence of a sense of relief that Cheyenne and the King of Avelea were not romantically involved, though dampened with the ache of hearing Cheyenne refer to someone else as her family. He turned away, but she caught his arm. "I'd love for you to visit. And I could come see you, too. And Mama and Papa and the others."

"I thought the king had you imprisoned in this castle."

Cheyenne smiled softly. "You thought wrong. You'll tell her I'm alive, won't you? That I'm happy?"

"Depends," Marcus said, craning his neck toward her. "Is it true?"

The wrinkles around Cheyenne's eyes deepened. "Most days. I figure that's as much as any mortal could ask for."

Marcus's face mirrored the suspicion in my heart. How could a young woman be happy in a place so lonely, so...empty?

But, then again, I wasn't exactly a guru on happiness, either.

CHAPTER 55

PIPER

I slipped away before the king shifted.

Before Marcus had a chance to realize that I'd eavesdropped on his and Cheyenne's conversation.

At least, that's what I told myself.

The true reason was that I couldn't face Marcus. Not when we'd come together for one purpose—to ensure Cheyenne was safe.

Now that was done, there was nothing left between us, and I didn't think I could bear it.

I waited in the hall, my ears perked and honed in on the goings-on of the banquet hall. I wouldn't leave Amity by herself, though I didn't worry about her company. Either Marcus would take her with him, or she would go with Van.

Both those options abundantly more fit to care for her than I was.

My hope was still on Marcus, though.

Amity's voice reverberated through the stone walls. "Wait, where's Piper?"

Tiny feet pattered on the stone floor as the door to the hallway creaked. Not a moment later, she burst into the hallway, swinging her head back and forth, trying to decide which direction I might have gone.

Her poor human vision couldn't distinguish me from the shadows, couldn't sense my breath quicken as I fought back sobs.

"Piper?" Her voice was quiet, unsure. Then her cheeks sank, and she slipped back into the banquet hall. When she spoke again, all I could pick up were the edges of an echo. "Piper's gone. She... She left."

Silence.

Someone shifted on their feet and muffled the echo of Amity's sobs. "I'll find her. I promise."

Marcus.

My chest tightened, and before I could bolt through those doors and make a fool of myself by pretending the two people in the world I cared for the most were better off with me rather than without me, I slank through the shadows, the curves in the stone, the stairs.

When I reached the massive double doors that led outside, I readied the hilt of my blade and knocked.

The doors creaked open, and the guard barely had time to widen his eyes before I struck him over the head with the hilt of my dagger and he slumped to the ground.

Though it must have been the wee hours of the morning by now, the blood moon celebration only ended after the moon had fully set. Past the creepy stone figurines in the courtyard, scarlet tents swayed, performers swallowed torches, and just as the moon touched the horizon...

Fire speckled the sky, framing the blood moon in vibrant whorls.

Flame and ember burst, first vibrant blues, then oranges and reds, and the crowd erupted in cheers.

Fireworks.

I shouldn't have let my legs stop, for now they were about as ambulatory as the haunches of the stone centaur to my right. My jaw hung loose, my breath halting in my chest as I took it all in.

A streak of white light whirred across the sky before scattering into a thousand speckles of light, each bursting and fragmenting until even the stars were outnumbered.

I'd never seen anything like it.

CHAPTER 56

MARCUS

I was tempted to be exasperated with her.

But standing there, jaw hanging open, those beautiful ivy eyes wide with wonder as the sky exploded in light above her, sprinkling her freckled skin with flecks of dancing light, she sure was making it difficult for me not to just sweep her into my arms and ignore the fact that she'd just *left*.

She hadn't bothered to say goodbye, not even to Amity, whose precious little heart would be crushed, would find some way to blame herself, perhaps by assuming Piper could never forgive her for staying behind at the Coup.

It wrecked me to witness this smart, capable, stunning woman throw that kind of love away, not because she didn't value it, but because she didn't recognize it.

Piper didn't know she was loved.

She never had.

But she wasn't the only one who knew how to run. I'd been doing it since the day I strapped my bow to my back and told my parents I was going to go make something of myself.

I'd been running ever since.

Gotten pretty good at it, too.

So if Piper decided to run, that would be just fine with me.

I'd been preparing my whole life to keep up.

I'd chase her to the ends of the continent if she'd let me. If she boarded a ship and took up with a crew on a mission to find whatever lay at the edge of the horizon, at the border of the sea, I'd leave my life behind and topple over the edge of the world, holding her hand as we tumbled into the abyss.

If she'd have me.

If she ran.

But I hoped she wouldn't. Because I'd seen the way she draped her broken arm over Amity, that inclination she'd had to protect that little girl. And I'd felt it. In the tender moments when we'd laughed over Amity's fascination with certain nefarious roots that she probably shouldn't have known about at her age. I'd seen it in the flush of her cheeks, the hesitation in her smile when I'd catch her watching me toss Amity onto my shoulders.

She was just so used to being on the outside, she didn't know how to recognize when she was being invited in.

Maybe I was wrong. Maybe I was just conflating what she wanted with what I wanted.

But I didn't think so.

And I certainly wasn't about to let her disappear into the night without finding out.

"You really did time your escape poorly," I found myself saying, the words coming out harsher, colder than I meant them.

She startled and scanned for an exit, but before she could flee across the grounds, I stepped in front of her, blocking her path. "Where exactly do you plan to go?" I asked, my jaw bulging despite myself. Just moments ago, I'd convinced myself not to be frustrated with her, not to let her inability to accept that other people might care about her rile me.

Her breath fogged in the night's chill, and she straightened her spine, rearing up for a fight. "Anywhere. That's the thing. I'm free. I can go anywhere I wish."

Fates, she could be so *stubborn.* I stepped toward her, and she retreated, pressing her back into the stone statue behind her. "Anywhere? And what do you expect to find in this vague *anywhere* of yours?"

She ruffled, though I had a sneaking suspicion it wasn't due to the breeze.

Closing in on her, I continued. "There's a little girl upstairs crying for you."

She stiffened, pain flashing in those stunning eyes of hers, but she recovered quickly enough. "You shouldn't leave her with the king. I know Cheyenne is fond of him, but Amity's poison is the reason he almost died—"

My arms crossed across my torso of their own volition. "If you were all that worried about the King of Avelea, you would have ripped her out of that banquet hall before she saved his life."

She took in a deep breath and wrapped herself up in her arms, swaying back and forth slightly.

"Will you take her with you?" she asked, the plea ringing in the tenor of her voice.

The resignation in that slight change in pitch threatened to undo me, but my frustration was broiling, bubbling under the surface, threatening to burst.

Not at her, but at this belief she clung to for dear life: that the people who loved her were better off without her.

I knew that lie; I'd drunk from its bitter fountain plenty of times, drowning myself in self-loathing, depriving myself of actual sustenance. Of forgiveness.

It had gone on long enough.

"Will you not?"

Her striking green eyes glazed over, tears pooling at the edges of her lids. "She deserves better than me, Marcus. We both know that. We both know she's better off with you."

"What makes you think that?"

She threw her hands up. "What doesn't make me think that? I've spent the last several years of my life trafficking children, Marcus. Trafficking. Children. Don't you understand? I might have told myself

I was rescuing them, taking them someplace safer, where they would be fed and no one would lay a hand on them, and maybe that was true, but..."

Her throat bobbed. She couldn't even say it.

Before I could stop myself, my fingers were grazing her neck, tracing the ridge of her perfect jaw. Her breath hitched, and I took that as an invitation to lift her chin so her eyes could meet mine. So they couldn't shrink away when I demanded, "But what?"

CHAPTER 57

PIPER

Marcus's hot breath brushed my cheeks, my nose.

But what?

I slumped, giving up the entirety of my weight to the statue behind me to support. "But..." I sighed, letting all the air out, and with it, the admission that clung so desperately to the inside of my throat. I tried not to think about how he could feel my breath now, on his lips, the bridge of his nose. "What Bronger did to them...I don't know that it was worse, but it wasn't any better. He might not have ever touched them like their parents did. He might have fed them. But what he did to their minds, what if that was far worse? Sure, he took care of them, but at the end of the day that was only a manipulation tactic. To get them to trust him, to bend to his will, to believe every word he said, to believe in his cause. To be his little slaves, his little soldiers. And I delivered them into his hands like they were pieces of wet clay."

Marcus frowned, and that minuscule twitch of his lips crushed something deep inside me.

"Please just let me go."

He didn't move. "You keep saying *they*."

It was my turn to frown. "What?"

He shifted on his feet, and though the motion brought him no closer, my stomach jolted. "You keep saying *they*, like Bronger didn't do the same thing to you as he did to all the rest."

I tried to swallow, but the lump in my throat ached, throbbed, stung, refused to go down without a fight. Salty tears brushed the edges of my lips. My legs trembled, and I might have toppled over had it not been for the dreadful statue. "That's not an excuse. Maybe it used to be, when I was a child. But it hasn't been an excuse for a long time."

"Maybe not," he whispered, his dark eyes fixed on mine, peering into my soul until I thought I might curl up into myself.

I pushed myself off the statue and slipped past him into the courtyard, into the celebration, into Avelea, or the rest of Alondria, or the great beyond, or somewhere, anywhere but here.

"You could stay, you know."

His words stopped me in my tracks, and I spun on my heels. "Stay? Where? Here?" I threw my arms out to the celebration around us. "There's nothing for me here."

"There's Amity."

"I already told you, she's better off without me."

"What about me, then?"

My heart plummeted, ripping a hole through my belly. My legs shook as I watched him, still and somber, staring at me. "What about you?"

He let out an exasperated sigh. "Really, Piper?" he said, advancing on me.

This time, I didn't back away.

As he neared, I expected to find anger, frustration, and if I looked hard I could spot them, tucked away into the wrinkles on his forehead, at the corners of his eyes. Buried in the depths of his copper irises. But if the anger and frustration were there, they only served as fuel.

Fuel for something else.

My breath quickened, and a shiver scaled the length of my spine. "I kidnapped your sister," I said quickly, lest I did something stupid before I got the words out. The words that would remind the both of us exactly how stupid this was.

Marcus had been right that night at the Nettlewood inn.

This was something stupid.

"According to Cheyenne, that was the best thing to ever happen to her," he said, brushing his hand across my cheek as he tucked a strand of hair behind my ear. When he did, he let his fingers linger on the pointed tip.

"Yes, and maybe that's because I led her right into the hands of someone just like Bronger."

I expected my words to land, for Marcus to flinch, to back away from me so I could catch my breath, will myself to leave before I did something I regretted.

And I would regret it.

I knew that.

Almost as much as I knew the only thing I wanted in this moment was for him to close the gap between us, wrap me up in his arms, and make me forget how I could never have him. Not really. Not after what I'd done.

But he didn't flinch. He only pursed his lips, as if he was considering whether he should say what he was thinking.

Apparently, he decided that he should. "I don't think the king is like Bronger."

"And why's that?"

"Because Cheyenne doesn't stand like you, Piper. She stands with her chin high and her back straight. Like she *owns* that part of her that used to make her so alone."

The implication of that stung—that strength was not what Marcus saw in me.

Only Bronger's shadow.

I turned away, but he placed both hands on my cheeks and cradled my face, gently turning it back to him.

His copper eyes blazed, securing my full attention. "If you'd let me, I'd like to help you own that part of you, too." My breath faltered, but he only stroked my cheek. "Because it's there, Piper. I've seen it. I've seen it in the way you care for Amity, in the way you only ever picked the children you thought could have a better life with Bronger. I saw it that day the faeries took her, in your vengeance on them for making a child suffer. And Piper, I saw it that night at the Coup." I winced, and he grimaced. "Even with all the hateful things I said to you, you couldn't let me die. What Amity said back there, she made it up, Piper. There wasn't an ounce of revenge in you when you shot Bronger. You loved him. Anyone with eyes could have seen that. You loved him, but you saved me. And a woman who is capable of making such a sacrifice deserves better than to believe the people who love her would rather she walk off into the night and disappear."

The people who love her.

Love.

My mind caught on that word, like a stray piece of cloth blown by the wind into barbed wire.

"I don't know how to be anything other than alone."

Marcus leaned in, grazing his cheek against mine, sending a flush of heat through my skin. Then his lips brushed my ear, and the fireworks peppering the sky had nothing on the ones that launched in my chest at his touch. "Can I tell you a secret?" he whispered. "I'm not all that practiced at not being alone, either."

I giggled, but it wasn't long before the panic took hold. "And what if we fail?" I asked.

Marcus nuzzled my cheek with his nose and smiled. "Then I'm sure Amity will pick us up and put us back together." I laughed, and Marcus grinned. "Can I take that as a yes?"

I choked through the tears and nodded.

His soft lips traced my cheek on their way to my mouth.

And then Marcus kissed the tears away.

EPILOGUE

PIPER

The ivory lace that lay flat against my collarbone scratched at my skin, and I might have complained had it not been for the ray of light beaming from Amity's face as she finished buttoning the long lace sleeves.

Tears welled in her wide eyes. "I hope Marcus cries when he sees you."

"He might not want that," I laughed, but I thought back to that night, the one when we'd cried together, spilled tears over the little girls whose lives we'd failed.

Cheyenne shrugged. She looked lovely in the yellow dress I'd helped her pick out from the tailor's. So far, King Declan had been true to Cheyenne's representation of him, allowing her to visit Marcus on occasion and providing her leave for our wedding, though one of the king's personal guards had escorted her here and now waited silently outside the door. "It's bound to happen. He's just a crier, you know?"

"I know." I fought the urge to scratch at the lace at my neckline once again, but I didn't have the will to fight back the smile breaking over my cheeks.

A look of smug joy spread across Amity's face as she handed me a mirror. "Here."

I looked into it and gasped. The ivory warmed my pale skin, and my hair, which Amity had taken over an hour to braid into a soft pattern on the back of my head, looked as if it might glow in contrast to the creamy material of my dress. Since the day Marcus and I had announced our intentions to marry, she'd spent every evening practicing her braiding skills to prepare for this moment.

"Thank you, Amity," I whispered.

Amity shrugged, her own hair braided into a smooth plait for a change, as it seemed she had actually brushed it.

The ceremony was going to be a small one. It wasn't as if Marcus and I had many friends. Or family to speak of. A few of Marcus's siblings had written and said they'd planned on showing up.

I'd invited Van. She'd written back and said she'd love to come, but she was busy with the children at the moment. It was hectic work, finding homes for the ones who craved a more traditional family. Van was the suspicious type and liked to vet all the parents herself, even after I performed a song in front of the other children of a potential household to make sure none of them heard the words between the notes. Sometimes she'd even send me in a month after the child had entered a new family, just to be sure.

And since I wouldn't be around to help her these next few weeks, she'd claimed she'd be working all her waking hours to make up for my absence.

I still had to talk myself into believing that she'd truly wanted to come. That her declination of the invitation was only due to her workload, and not the dead body she'd helped to bury after I'd created it.

My neck went hot at the thought, at the vision, and something warm caressed my hand. Amity. She'd gotten good at that, anticipating when I needed someone to ground me, to bring me back from that one moment in my life that seemed so saturated in my mind compared to all the rest.

We'd rented out a garden in the village of Asten for the ceremony.

Amity had to press her ear against the door to pick up the muffled sounds of what I could hear perfectly well. The Asten bridal tune, one that reminded me of falling rain in the spring months. "It's time," she said.

Amity ran to me and grabbed my hand, intertwining her tiny fingers into my long, spindly ones. Then she dragged me to the door, which she reminded me was about to open any second now and that I'd have to smile when it did.

My arms and legs shook, and a thousand images flashed through my mind. Bronger's fingers caressing the shaft of the arrow that had gone straight through his heart. The hatred that had burned in Marcus's eyes that awful night at the Coup. Amity's fear as she slunk into the shadows. Bronger's warm hands lifting me from the snow.

A second set of fingers wrapped themselves in my left hand, and Cheyenne leaned in to deposit a kiss on my cheek. As she did, something warm spread from her hand, from her lips, and washed over me, wiping the memories away. Until only Marcus remained. Marcus chuckling at me as we whispered over the firelight as Amity slept. Marcus taking my hand and whirling me as the musicians from Evaen played, the thumping of our hearts in synchrony with the beat. Marcus's lips on mine that first time, and so many times since then.

I turned to Cheyenne, who smiled mischievously. She had developed her gift in the years since the king's guard had captured her, and now surfed the nuance between obliterating memories and restoring them. The horrible memories that made my stomach twist in anguish would return eventually.

But not today.

Today, I was free of them.

"Thank you," I whispered.

She grinned, squeezing my hand. "Anytime."

The doors opened, and everything—the garden, the half a dozen people standing within it—all faded. And there was Marcus, dressed in black leathers and an ivory tunic, his strong shoulders steady and true.

He smiled, and that was enough.

. . .

"Do you wish to exchange your own vows?" The squat man we'd hired from the garden shuffled. Apparently, he'd never done this before.

Neither Marcus nor I particularly cared.

Marcus grinned, a flash of unfairly straight teeth, a twinkle in his eyes that sent a flurry of adoration spiraling through my heart. "Oh, I most certainly do. Now, I don't know about the lady," he teased, sticking the very tip of his tongue through his teeth at me.

My heart flushed with warmth.

Marcus took my hands in his until they disappeared under his soft, all-encompassing grasp.

"Piper. I, Marcus Arivaden, vow to protect you despite how little you're able to pay." I choked on the sob that emerged in my throat as I laughed. "Really, it's obscenely little. But that's all right," he said, squeezing my hands. "Because I promise to love you no matter how destitute we become, especially if we have any children, who I imagine will rob us of any money we might have saved up for our old age."

I giggled again and fought back the urge to wipe my tears on the sleeves of my dress, as my hands were still within his and I couldn't bring myself to let go, not for one moment.

"But most of all, Piper, my friend. I promise to be your family..." I lost it, my tears soaking my cheeks. He thumbed my chin and lifted it, leaning down to kiss the tears on my face. Then he whispered in my ear, "I promise to be your home."

I BARELY MADE it through the "I do's." In fact, we had to skip my vows completely, at least the ones I'd come up with myself. After the ceremony I found my place on a stone bench in the middle of the garden, next to the lilies. They swayed in the breeze for a while, and I marveled at how grounded they were despite being moved about by the invisible force. How their roots never seemed to shake or tremble.

"You're being extra social tonight," Marcus said, almost making me jump as he emerged from behind me and stepped over the bench before finding a seat close to me.

"It's not like there are that many of us." I nodded toward Amity, Cheyenne, and Asa, who were all playing a game that involved slapping each other's hands. Marcus's other siblings had left shortly after the ceremony, something I could tell pained him by the hurt in his eyes when they shook his hands, but he didn't mention it.

He grinned, placing an arm around my shoulders. "Just enough."

"I'm sorry about earlier," I said, feeling like all the air might escape my lungs and I might deflate right off this bench.

"For what?" he asked.

"For not being able to get my vows out."

"What are you talking about?" He chuckled. "You said *I do* just fine."

I elbowed him in the ribs. "You know what I mean."

He snickered. "Ouch. You're right. And it's fine. I know you're not one for making speeches. Especially in front of such a crowd." I elbowed him again, more lightly this time, and he caught my elbow in his arm and pulled me closer. "You could always make it up to me by telling me now."

I blushed, which seemed like a silly thing to do in front of my husband. But as someone who'd been deprived of such love for my entire life, even our vows and the lovely copper band that now shimmered on my finger didn't seem enough to make a love feel stable, secure. Or enough for me to stop being caught off guard when it did.

"Ummm... Well, I was going to say... That I promise to open myself up to you a little more every day. That I promise to let you in. To be vulnerable around you. For you. And to be here. To always be here. Never to pick up and leave or abandon you. Well, like you said, to be your family."

"So... You're stealing one of my vows?"

"Pretty much," I laughed just as Amity broke away from her game and came running up to us.

"We need to talk," she said, placing her hands on her hips.

"Yes?" Marcus asked, amusement flickering across his face.

"Well, now that you two are officially married, I'd like to propose a new arrangement," she said, sucking in a loud breath. Her hands trembled, and I frowned. I hadn't seen her this nervous since she'd held that dagger over Cheyenne's chest. "Now, I know it's a lot to ask. A lot, a lot. But I promise I'd help around the house. You already know I'm great at healing, but I'm a halfway decent cook, too, and I think with a regular chance at a kitchen I could even get good at it, and..."

"Amity." I reached out, taking her tiny hands in mine.

Her face sank. "You're right. It's silly. And too much to ask..."

"No," I said, taking Marcus's hand and closing it around Amity's and mine. Marcus and I exchanged a knowing glance, and he nodded. "Marcus and I have discussed this for a while now, and we were wondering if you'd like to come live with us... umm... permanently. I mean, now that we're married, the law allows for us to ado—"

Amity launched herself at me, burying her face in my shoulder. Tears streamed down her cheeks, soaking the lace on my dress. Marcus put one hand on her back, the other wrapped around my fingers.

"Thank you, thank you, thank you," Amity said, then, jumping straight up, she said, "I have to go tell the others!"

I observed as she hurtled across the yard and relayed the news to Asa and Cheyenne, both of whom hugged her.

"You don't think we should have offered the same to Cheyenne? I mean, I know that she's a ward of the king, and adopting her would be in name only, but maybe it would have meant something." I bit my lip, guilt snapping at my stomach.

Marcus sighed. "She'll be of age next month. I think she's looking for her independence, which she seems to have some measure of at the palace, not new parents to shout rules at her."

"Still," I said.

"I know. I should go talk to her," he said, standing up and letting go of my hand. "Wish me luck."

I nodded and watched him as he jogged off, sneaking up behind

Amity and sweeping her into his arms before perching the giggling girl on his shoulders.

It almost hurt—the happiness that swelled within me.

I hoped Marcus would find a way to breach the chasm that lay between him and his sister. Things hadn't exactly been rosy between Marcus and Cheyenne in the time since we'd attempted to rescue her from the king's court. She was a girl who'd grown accustomed to loneliness, to being left. To being forgotten. The walls she'd built around her heart would not fall in a day. Nor in a span of months, apparently. Perhaps never.

But I hoped, for Marcus's sake, they would. That act of kindness Cheyenne had shown me today, by making me forget the memories that haunted me, if just for a moment—that had been something.

No, that had been everything.

"You seem to have gotten your happy ending."

I jumped, not having noticed anyone sneak up behind me. I turned to face the owner of the voice—a voice that sounded familiar, but not intimate. As if I'd only met this person once in passing...

The veil over her face still fluttered from where her breath had rustled it when she spoke.

My hand went to my ankle immediately, but there was no dagger there. Only a lacy dress.

I jolted and almost screamed for Marcus, but Shya, the fae female from Kev's auction, placed a finger over her obscured lips and shook her head. Would she kill them if I screamed?

My heart raced, and I searched for Cheyenne's guard, but the spot that he'd taken up against the cottage wall was empty.

"Oh, he's unable to serve you at the moment, I'm afraid. You don't have to fear me, Piper," she said, her violet robes fluttering in the evening breeze. "I am not who you think I am. And I'm certainly not what that filth from the auction thought I was."

My fists clenched. "What do you want?"

"It is rumored that you are Gifted, much like the Queen of Naenden."

"And?" I asked.

"And she wishes to meet you. Officially, this time."

My heart pounded. This had to be a trap. What did she mean by officially? How did the owner of a brothel in Nettlewood know that I'd snuck off to a council meeting all those months ago and had the briefest of conversations with the human Queen of Naenden? "Why would she want to meet me?" I didn't add "again," in case I had misinterpreted Shya's insinuation that I had met the Queen of Naenden before.

The female fae stepped over the bench, much like Marcus had, and sat in front of me though I continued to stand.

"Don't you want to get to know another Gifted soul? Share tips?" she asked. "Maybe you could help each other out. Although maybe your magic isn't nearly as ornery as hers."

Ornery? She made it sound like Queen Asha's gift had a personality or something.

"Not really," I said. My mind raced. Everything I'd heard of the Queen of Naenden was that she was good, benevolent, even to the half-fae. She'd only confirmed that impression during my brief meeting with her. How she could be involved with this trafficker?

"Truth be told, I am particularly interested in your gift, Piper. You see, when I arrived at the auction it was not to purchase you, though I would have done so if necessary. It was to save you. But my intention was never to sell you. Only to offer you a job, which I'm offering to you now. You're free to accept it or decline without consequences."

"I'm not going to traffic children anymore," I hissed.

"Great," Shya said. "Because my initial inclination, when I heard what you did for a living, was to kill you."

I flinched, my hand going for my thigh, where, yet again, a knife was not strapped.

If Shya noticed the blatant attempt at self-defense, she certainly didn't acknowledge it. "In a strange turn of events, you were lucky my brother made that dreadful decree when he did. I was on my way to hunt you down when I heard the news and had to backtrack. You understand, one must prioritize family above all else."

What in Alondria was she talking about?

Shya stood, towering above me, that veil of hers fluttering in the breeze.

I thought to scream, but what if Amity or Cheyenne came to my rescue? I had no idea what Shya was capable of, but since brothels didn't exactly make their money off of voluntary participants, I didn't want the girls anywhere near her.

"If you planned to kill me, why the change of heart?" Though I figured I knew the answer to that question. If there was someone else in Avelea trafficking children, that meant I had cut into her supply. Perhaps she had decided I would make a better ally than a corpse.

Neither of which was going to happen.

I flexed my fingers. I'd have to strike fast if I wanted to walk out of here alive.

"I wouldn't do that."

A form emerged from the bushes, lanky as ever.

Elias.

Lay low. James isn't the only one hunting you.

That was the last thing Elias had said to me as Marcus and I had fled the Coup.

I cocked my head. The only gesture necessary to answer my question.

He raised his palms, his face draining of color as he processed the betrayal in my expression. But his jaw tightened all the same as he planted himself at Shya's side. "It's not what you think."

Marcus. Where was Marcus? Would he realize what was happening and come for me? Or would he be too late?

"Oh, if it's not what I think, what is it, then? Because if you expect me to take children for you..."

Shya sighed, and Elias shook his head. "You need her protection, Pipe."

"Protection? Protection from what? She just admitted she was on her way to kill me before..." I stopped, Shya's words swarming my mind. She claimed to be here on behalf of the Queen of Naenden, and yet she had said it was news of her brother's decree that had distracted her from assassinating me.

Shya stepped forward. "From the male who has been scrounging every village looking for you."

Lay low. James isn't the only one hunting you.

I shook my head. "That was the duke. That was Asa's..." But hadn't the duke seemed confused about why Marcus had brought me to him, of all people? I'd assumed it was the duke who had a bounty on my head. But what had that merchant from Naenden said to Kev—something about his apprentice growing into his master? He'd been trying to buy me for a particular client. As had Rayn.

"Who is he?" I asked.

"His name is Azrael, and he requires your assistance. I'm afraid we can't allow that to happen."

My heart sank. They were going to kill me so this Azrael character couldn't get to me first. Elias, one of my oldest friends. But how could I blame him for switching his allegiance? Why would he side with the girl who'd kidnapped him just to force him into a child army?

But then Shya took my hand. I flinched, but a warmth spread through me, too comforting and all-encompassing to be natural. My memory shot back to the arrow I'd shot into Rayn's heart—the one that had burst into flames in midair. "We don't wish to hurt you. Only protect you," she said.

"We promise," Elias added.

"Azrael?" Marcus's voice rumbled as he approached, and he placed a steadying hand on my shoulder. His cheeks had gone sunken, the merriment of the day wiped clean off his face. His other hand clenched. "Did he send you?"

"What?" I asked, a little shocked that, given the two criminals who stood before us, the one who was absent seemed to warrant the most concern from my husband. "Do you know him?"

Marcus clenched his teeth. "He's the one who hired me to take you to him."

My heart turned to lead in my chest, the blood in my cheeks draining at the sight of the dread in my husband's face.

"Who are you?" I whispered to the woman standing in front of me.

Shya lifted her hands, taking the folds of her veil between her fingertips and lifting it to reveal her face. Olive skin stretched over high, sharp cheekbones that only sharpened her fiery violet eyes.

She smiled, and despite the ferocity in her demeanor, I believed that smile.

"Piper," Elias said. "Meet Lydia, Princess of Naenden."

ABOUT THE AUTHOR

T.A. Lawrence is the author of *The Severed Realms,* a series of fairytale retellings that feature mystery, danger, romance, and, of course, fae. T.A. Lawrence also writes the middle-grade series *The Astoria Chronicles,* the story of a girl who frequents a fantasy world through a portal in her neighbor's cotton field. T.A. lives in Alabama with her loving and supportive husband Jacob, who occasionally convinces her to leave the house.

* * *

Thanks for reading *A Tune to Make Them Follow*! For Lydia and Elias's story, sign up for my newsletter and receive a free ebook novella at talawrencebooks.com.

If you liked this book, don't forget to leave a review!

Be on the lookout for *A Bond of Broken Glass: The Severed Realms (Book Three)* in April 2023!

ALSO BY T.A. LAWRENCE

A Word so Fitly Spoken: The Severed Realms (Book One)

The Keeper of the Threshold: The Astoria Chronicles (Book One)

The Secret of Atalo: The Astoria Chronicles (Book Two)

ACKNOWLEDGMENTS

Jacob, I couldn't be where I am today without your unconditional support. Thanks for believing in my writing, convincing me to go down to part-time at my day job to focus on my books, then wholeheartedly supporting me when it came time to take the plunge and start writing full-time. Dad, thanks for letting me talk your ear off about all things authoring. Though I wish I'd inherited some of your spatial awareness, I'm at least glad you can help me out with my fight scenes so I don't end up with characters' limbs going in the wrong directions. Mom, I owe my love of reading and writing to you. Thanks for always being so excited for me.

Rachel Bobo, thanks for helping me brainstorm ideas for the scene I knew was missing from this book, but couldn't quite put my finger on. Alyssa Dorn, your understanding of the English language is phenomenal. Thanks for bearing with my excessive use of the comma and for being so excited about the hints dropped throughout the story. Morgan Cari, your impeccable understanding of story and character greatly contributed to the depth and consistency of this book. Thank you for your detailed feedback and for cheering me on throughout the beta reads. Christine, thanks for helping get this book to a professional level. I'm amazed by how quickly and thoroughly you work. Karri, your covers are stunning and have contributed so much to the success of these books.

To everyone who has left a kind review, sent me a message on Instagram, or emailed me in the middle of the night to tell me how much you loved my books, thank you. Your kind words go a long way.

Made in the USA
Middletown, DE
06 January 2023

21550388R00227